P9-CQE-183

# THE
# FISH KISSER

**THE GREEN DOOR**
Christopher Lake, SK

Copyright © James Hawkins, 2001

All rights reserved. No part of this publication may be reproduced, stored in a retrieval system, or transmitted in any form or by any means, electronic, mechanical, photocopying, recording, or otherwise (except for brief passages for purposes of review) without the prior permission of Dundurn Press. Permission to photocopy should be requested from the Canadian Copyright Licensing Agency.

Editor: Barry Jowett
Copy-Editor: Natalie Barrington
Design: Bruna Brunelli
Printer: Webcom

**Canadian Cataloguing in Publication Data**

Hawkins, D. James (Derek James), 1947–
   The fish kisser

"A Castle Street Mystery."
ISBN 0-88882-240-5

I. Title.

PS8565.A848F58 2001   C813.'6   C2001-902372-3   PR9199.4.H38F58 2001

1  2  3  4  5     05  04  03  02  01

Canadä

THE CANADA COUNCIL | LE CONSEIL DES ARTS
FOR THE ARTS | DU CANADA
SINCE 1957 | DEPUIS 1957

ONTARIO ARTS COUNCIL
CONSEIL DES ARTS DE L'ONTARIO

We acknowledge the support of the **Canada Council for the Arts** and the **Ontario Arts Council** for our publishing program. We also acknowledge the financial support of the **Government of Canada** through the **Book Publishing Industry Development Program** and **The Association for the Export of Canadian Books**, and the **Government of Ontario** through the **Ontario Book Publishers Tax Credit** program.

Care has been taken to trace the ownership of copyright material used in this book. The author and the publisher welcome any information enabling them to rectify any references or credit in subsequent editions.

*J. Kirk Howard, President*

Printed and bound in Canada.♼
Printed on recycled paper.

| Dundurn Press | Dundurn Press | Dundurn Press |
|---|---|---|
| 8 Market Street | 73 Lime Walk | 2250 Military Road |
| Suite 200 | Headington, Oxford, | Tonawanda NY |
| Toronto, Ontario, Canada | England | U.S.A. 14150 |
| M5E 1M6 | OX3 7AD | |

# THE
# FISH KISSER

## James Hawkins

*James Hawk* (signature)

A Castle Street Mystery

THE DUNDURN GROUP
TORONTO · OXFORD

*Terrorism will be the warfare of the twenty-first century, and cyber-weaponry will form a major armament.*

*This book is dedicated to all victims of terrorism (especially those who succumbed to the New York attack, September 11, 2001), and to all members of the world's security services who have given their lives in pursuit of individuals and organisations who wage this insidious war.*

— *James Hawkins*
*September 12, 2001*

# *chapter one*

The giant ship was evaporating. Twinkling lights from the Calypso Bar, in the aft, were still clearly visible, but the remainder of the vessel was slowly being sucked into the black hole of night. Roger LeClarc strained to see through the mist, telling himself he was dreaming.

"Shit!" He was not.

"Bastards," he screamed after the ship. "You bastards."

With a soft but firm hand the wake of the propeller's wash lifted him above the surrounding sea, offering a tantalizingly clear view of the departing ship. He considered waving, even did briefly, but self-consciously dropped his arm as the swell gently let him down. Was he trying to summon help or simply waving a final goodbye?

"God, the water's cold."

An uncontrollable spate of shivering attacked him—presaging the turmoil headed his way. Gasping frantically, forcing mouthfuls of chilly moist air into his constricted lungs, he retched as the salt-laden ozone stung the back of his throat. "Come back," he yelled. "Come back." But the waves swallowed his voice.

Like the closing shot from an old tearjerker movie, the increasing distance gradually washed the colour from the ship's lights and they faded to grey in the gloom, leaving Roger pondering his chances of being rescued. "Nil," he figured, but then his analytical mind cut in and offered hope. It's the North Sea not the Pacific. Twenty miles to land at most. Plenty of coastal shipping. I'm still alive so I must have some chance. Start swimming ...

Which way?

Home ...

But where is home?

Treading water, he slowly spun, seeking land, lights, life. Finding none, he returned for a last glimpse of the giant passenger ferry, now barely a smudge of radiance in a sea of black, and paddled, half-heartedly, after it.

Céline Dion crooning "My heart will go on" provided an inappropriate reminder of the Titanic to the few unperturbed passengers still clustered in the Calypso Bar, despite the late hour. Few were sufficiently sober, or sufficiently interested, to listen. But Len, the barman, a veteran of a thousand similar crossings, couldn't resist mumbling along with the tune, and three die-hards on capstan chairs at the end of the bar mockingly joined in, then exploded in laughter when he caught on and gave them a nasty look.

"Bloody cops," he breathed, sizing them up with a bad taste in his mouth. Three tall, self-confident men travelling together. Too smart for truck drivers: One grey suit; two blue blazers; hair by Anton or Antoinette; decent cologne—not Price-Right. Not holidaymakers either—too relaxed. Salesmen perhaps? But he shook his head. "Cops—definitely." It was the way they kept constant surveillance, controlled everyone with an inquisitive stare, and sustained a bubble of hostile space around them that kept most at bay during the evening, observing the invisible warning sign: "Dangerous animals—keep back."

"Cops," he breathed again. Not that he cared. His petty pilfering wouldn't attract the attention of a loss prevention officer in a condom factory, let alone a sizeable undercover squad. If he could get rid of them, and the other stragglers whom he knew from bitter experience would keep him up all night, he'd sleep away most of the voyage to Holland.

"Another round, gentlemen?" he inquired as the laughter subsided. Could he push them into admitting they'd had enough?

"Good idea," shouted one, to his chagrin, and they squabbled over whose turn it was to pay.

Thwarted, Len substituted a 1940s Vera Lynn for Céline Dion; The White Cliffs of Dover for Titanic. They'll hate this. They loved it. *"There'll be bluebirds over the white cliffs of Dover,"* they caroused, then exploded in laughter at the dismay on his face.

As Len sullenly pulled the drinks, Vera romanticized about a country which the three London policemen had little knowledge. Shepherds tending sheep and valleys in bloom were not part of their daily landscape. A barren desert of concrete, glass, and steel was nearer the mark; urban chasms of grey flat-fronted buildings, made interesting only by the accidental and unlawful activities of others—at least graffiti and garbage added colour, shape, and dimension.

"Serg, we've got a problem," an out-of-breath, fortyish, fourth member was saying as he joined the group.

His statement, intended for the leader, Detective Sergeant Barry Jones, was pounced on by one of the others, who mumbled into his beer, "You've always got a problem."

A look of warning from the sergeant straightened him up. "Sorry, Sir," he said, pulling himself together with a fixed smile.

"But why not give it a rest. Relax and have a drink. It's your round anyway."

"Sergeant, it's urgent," the newcomer implored, shutting out the other two, his mouth taut with earnestness, his blue eyes wide—pleading to be taken seriously.

"O.K., Inspector Bliss, shoot. What's your problem?"

The others spluttered into stupid laughter, "Problems, problems."

"In private," he added, catching the sergeant's sleeve.

Sergeant Jones shook him off and puckered his lips for a drink. "Oh come on, Sir. Spit it out, I haven't got all night. We've got serious work to do."

Bliss hesitated, pivoting around, checking for eavesdroppers. Len had made himself scarce, washing glasses further along the bar, hoping they'd get the message. No one else was close, though two men arguing at a small table set into an alcove caught his eye. Instinct and twenty years experience alerted his senses. When he'd wandered through the bar earlier the alcove tables, with room for two or three at a squeeze, had been the preserve of courting couples, some, he assumed by the tartness of the women, being paid for their services. Now, as he watched, the two men huddled together, quarrelling face to face. Putting it down to a lover's tiff, he turned back to the sergeant with a sobering stare. "I've lost him," he said forcefully.

Sergeant Jones critically examined the clarity of his beer against an ornamental bar lamp—an art nouveau knock-off masquerading as Lalique—then shrugged. "So what. We're on a ship, aren't we? He couldn't get off ... unless he's decided to swim to Amsterdam."

The other two roared.

"Have a drink Guv'nor and stop worrying," continued the sergeant, drawing the barman toward him with a crook of a finger.

"No, thank you, Sergeant. I'm on duty," Bliss countered pointedly, and stood in silence for a second as he contemplated pulling rank. Then, realizing the men would be of little use, decided to let it go. "I'm going to look for him myself," he said, moving toward the door.

"Miserable git," mumbled one of the others. "No wonder yer missus left yer."

"She didn't leave ..." he turned defensively, annoyed that he was still defined by a relationship that had sunk years ago; then decided not to waste his breath, not to salt his own wounds. Anyway, there had been others.

The argument between the two "lovers" in the alcove was briefly put on hold as Bliss passed. The second he was out of the way, Billy Motsom, a stubby, forty-something, professional enforcer, slinking behind the manicured facade of a mutual fund salesman, stabbed a finger at the other man, spitting, "The Arab wants this guy's head on a plate. You'd better deliver, or it'll be your f'kin head."

The other, Nosmo King, taller and decidedly unmanicured, rose determinedly, seeking a way out when Motsom slammed his fist on the table. "You lost him, so you'd better stop this ship and get him picked up damn quick. Understand?" King mopped his forehead with his sleeve desperate to gain thinking time, but Motsom's stare pierced painfully into his skull.

"O.K. I'll stop the bloody ship," he replied at last, shifting back into gear, telling himself his decision had nothing to do with Motsom's threat, that his only concern was LeClarc ... knowing he was lying.

Nosmo King, disgraced ex-cop turned private detective, jogged from the alcove, caught a glimpse of the three men at the bar and instantly summed them up. Scotland Yard detectives—probably on a taxpayer-funded goodwill junket to some unsuspecting foreign force. Memories of his days as a detective on such trips flashed to mind. Pissed most of the time, he recalled. The bloody foreigners were always so hospitable, and were used to drinking the local booze. Blurred memories of blurred visits—one boozy encounter followed by another—shot through his mind, alcohol greasing the flow of conversation between people of different nationalities.

They'll regret it, he thought, rushing the stairs to the upper deck three at a time. His mind was racing ahead. How the hell do you stop a ship? Shout, "Man overboard!," or is that only in the movies? Then a frigid blast of night sea air sharpened his senses as he forced open the heavy steel door to the deck. What the hell am I doing? I'm not even sure the poor bastard went overboard.

It was less than five minutes—five terrifying minutes—that Roger had been in the sea. Hope and despair had edged each other out a million times. The biting chill had numbed his body but stung his brain. How can it be this cold? It's the end of July—I think?

Death had visited him in the first few minutes as he'd struggled for breath against the iron hand clamped around his chest, but he'd fought off the spectre and his breathing had gradually eased. Who had claimed drowning was the least painful of all deaths? he wondered, recalling reading it somewhere—*Reader's Digest* probably. What did they know? Who had come back from drowning to tell their story?

He stopped swimming. "Why struggle?" said the small voice in his head. "You're drowning. Why prolong the agony?"

Twice he let go, allowing himself to sink slowly, but his will to survive brought him flailing, coughing, and spluttering back to the surface. So much for it being painless, he thought, as he re-fought the chest cramps. This isn't a hot bath or a jacuzzi; this isn't the Caribbean or Hawaii. This is the North Sea: Cold, bleak, and tempestuous. Nothing lives or dies comfortably here.

"Anyway," said the inner voice, rationalizing, "what about your parents? Maybe you should try for their sake."

His salt-stung eyes closed as he tried to conjure up images of them. A couple of featureless old people watching television in the sitting room of a three-bedroom semi-detached house in Watford was the closest he could get. Does Dad still have a moustache? he worried, becoming obsessed, convinced that failure to remember was evidence of death.

Pinch yourself.

He did ... Nothing. Total numbness.

Panic!

"Calm down," said the voice. "You can prove you're alive. Just remember what they look like."

Noises and smells rather than images sprang to mind. Old people's noises and smells—belches and farts, clicking false teeth, diarrhoea and disinfectant, and his mother's voice, grating, and demanding.

"Is that you, our Roger?" she'd sing out as he arrived home from the office each evening, her eyes glued to the television.

"No, it's a fucking maniac come to slice off yer head," he'd mumble *sotto voce*. "Only me," he'd call cheerfully, already halfway upstairs to his room.

"Yer late; yer dinner's cold," she'd whine.

"I've eaten," he'd shout, slam his door, and slump in front of his computer, safe and secure in his own world.

They won't remember me; won't even miss me, he thought and for a moment had a feeling of total freedom—thirty-one years old, finally escaping their clutches—even perversely revelling in the knowledge that his mother wouldn't have any say over his demise, and wouldn't be able to bask in the spotlight of sympathy. Drowning at sea wasn't the same as being hit by a truck on the High Street. No disfigured body in intensive care for her and her bingo friends to cluck over; no fearsome array of life support machines for her to shake her head at; no parade of weeping relatives commiserating over her impending loss. "Oh you poor dear— he was such a nice boy." And there would be no prognosis of survival given by an over-optimistic doctor, unable, or unwilling, to commit himself to the terrible truth. Without a body to view, weep over and bury, there would always be a question mark, a faint hope, a possibility. "Maybe he's run off with a bird—or a bloke—to get away from her," neighbours would tittle-tattle behind her back. And she'd hear them ... sniggering as she shuffled to the corner store wearing her loss in her downcast eyes. Instead of mourning a lost son for a few weeks, or months, her mourning would last forever. "Serves her bloody right," he said to himself.

Memories, however hazy, of his mother kindled thoughts of his room and the techno-shrine he had built there. And her jealous admonition: "You think more of that damn computer than you do of me." True, he thought, and promised himself the pleasure of telling her so—one day. It was an easy promise, now knowing he never would.

Thoughts of his beloved computer stirred images of his stubby fingers flitting across the keyboard. "My fingers!" he screamed and stopped swimming, just for a second, bringing both hands together, fingertip-to-fingertip. Feeling nothing, he whipped them out of the water, sank like a stone, and had to fight his way back to the surface. Catching his breath, he gingerly lifted his right hand to his face and peered closely. The total darkness that initially surrounded him had faded as his eyes had grown accustomed. His pallid fingers were silhouetted against the blackness of the sea, but their outline and colour blended into a grey miasma and, feeling himself sinking again, he dropped his hand back into the water to resume paddling. He hoped his fingers would be alright—prayed they would be.

A light flickered above the horizon then quickly disappeared. A few seconds later it was back, then out again. I'm hallucinating, he thought, and stared, intently, determined not to let it fade, but just as he concluded it was real, it went out again.

"It could be a lighthouse," he mused and headed in that direction.

Two minutes later, his mind, working in slow motion, caught on to the fact it was a distant ship. The light, flickering on and off like a dysfunctional advertising sign, was in rhythm to the lazy swell. Now identified, it held his attention. Is it coming or going? he wondered. His hopes leapt. They're coming back for me. Yes, that's it. Someone saw me go overboard and now they're searching.

Instinct overcame logic. "Help! Help!" he screeched. The ship was miles away. "Help! Help!" He had more chance of being heard by a passing jumbo jet.

His contracted vocal chords barely squeaked, his lungs pained with the effort, and the sounds that did escape were instantly grabbed by the breeze and scattered so quickly he wasn't sure he had made any noise at all.

Exhausted by the effort, he shut out the distant light, sank inside his mind, and found a procession of embarrassing memories parading past him: A ten-year-old with his head firmly jammed in the wrought iron banister—sore ears for a week; one from the fireman as he fought to free him, and the other from his mother's heavy hand. Plummeting out of the old oak tree on the common. "So not everyone can climb trees."

"Anyone can climb that one. My kid sister can climb that one." And that from a girl!

Then there was the goal post falling down during the school soccer finals—the saw marks clearly visible. Never picked, not even as a substitute, not for any team, both captains saying, "You can have the fatso." He'd shown them.

Mrs. Merryweather's Alsatian jumping out of the next-door upstairs window onto the greenhouse roof was a recurring vision. As a twelve-year-old, he'd been the first on the scene searching frantically amid the debris of glass, geraniums, and pulped tomatoes, trying to find the marrow-bone he'd tossed from his bedroom window moments earlier. The big dog bled to death in minutes and the bone, still clenched between his teeth, was buried with him. Various theories were put forward to explain Rex's fatal behaviour. "Rabies," suggested Roger, trying to deflect inquisitive stares.

"Nonsense," responded his father, but a worried look spread over his mother's face.

"You didn't get bit, did you?" she enquired quickly, checking his hands for signs.

"I 'spect he were chasing one of the cats," said Mrs. Merryweather through tears, then added redundantly, "Rex never done nothin' like this before."

Everyone had their own ideas, jaundiced eyes fixated on Roger, though no one was willing to risk his mother's wrath by pointing a finger.

As if waking from a dream to an unusual noise, Roger's conscious mind tried desperately to take control, and fighting through a mental fog to make sense of what was happening. It's true, he thought, your whole life does flash before you in death. Then reality struck—as far as he could tell he was dead.


Nosmo King, still smarting from his conversation with Billy Motsom, prayed otherwise, and was on the aft deck of the SS *Rotterdam,* desperately searching for some way of stopping the ship without becoming ensnared in the inevitable furore.

# *chapter two*

Detective Inspector David Bliss, still fuming at his colleagues, scooted around the deserted restaurants and coffee shops, frantically seeking Roger LeClarc. "There'll be hell to pay if we lose the fat git," Sergeant Jones had said, before he had discovered the duty-free bar and lost his senses. Yet, despite his size, LeClarc had slithered from sight.

Nosmo King had also searched for LeClarc; his motives were less virtuous, and he found himself being hauled to the bridge by a crewman who stumbled across him on the aft deck just as he'd launched a life raft in a final act of desperation. Looking like an anti-submarine depth charges, the cylindrical capsule descended spectacularly into the water, leaving King musing, "Did I do that?" The ripcord yanked tight, splitting it apart, the emerging life raft inflated like the wings of a newly hatched butterfly as carbon dioxide flooded its body.

Jacobs' voice startled him, "Oy! What'ya doing?"

Heart thumping, he looked over his shoulder to find the catering assistant heading his way.

"Man overboard!" he shouted excitedly, then turned to peer at the raft: a child's giant paddling pool bucking and leaping in a white-water thrill ride as it bounced repeatedly off the ships wake. His spirits sank. "Bugger. It's tied on," he muttered to himself, realizing the ripcord was tethered to a shackle at his feet. Jacobs' calloused hand grabbed his wrist as he reached down to undo it.

"I didn't see nobody fall overboard," said the young catering assistant cagily, his mind whirling at the thought that he might be dealing with a deranged lunatic or a dangerous drunk.

"Well I did," King lied. "Look, there he is."

The crewman, used to keeping watch, gazed into the blackness. "Where?"

"Over there. Look he's waving," said King with a positiveness that defied contradiction.

"Can't see no one," said Jacobs finally, although the flatness of his tone suggested his conviction was draining.

Nosmo seized the moment. "I'm not going to let the poor bastard drown even if you are. Help or get out o' the bloody way."

Jacobs let go of King's wrist, deftly unscrewed the shackle, and they watched for a couple of seconds as the raft was swept astern on the tide created by the propellers' thrust.

Jacobs shut the bridge door behind them and King found himself blinded by absolute blackness. A voice floated out of the dark. "Yup. What do you want?"

King froze, fearful of walking into something painful.

"Jacobs, Sir," called the voice from behind him. "This passenger says someone's fallen overboard."

"Well don't just stand there, come in."

Which way? wondered King. "Uh, I can't see anything."

"Don't worry, your eyes will get used to it in a minute," said the disembodied voice. "Bring him to the radar cubicle Jacobs, there's more light there."

Guiding hands on his shoulders propelled King across the bridge to an area cordoned off with blackout curtains. The invisible man explained, "We have to keep it dark so we can see what's ahead—no streetlights at sea. Lots of yachts have poor navigation lights. Some don't have any."

Squeezed together inside the tiny cubicle, the men took on an alien appearance in the luminous green glow from the radar screen, and King wilted under the presence of the officer. Six-foot-four and two hundred and fifty pounds, he estimated, and the man's smart uniform, contrasting sharply with the catering assistant's grease-streaked jeans and dirty shirt, added weight.

Pulling himself upright, Nosmo King strengthened his resolve and launched himself at the officer. "Why don't you stop the ship? Someone's fallen overboard."

"Sir, this isn't a double-decker bus. You don't just hit the brakes and stop. I've given the bos'n instructions, but I need to know exactly what happened."

This was someone used to giving orders, expecting to receive answers, and King's confidence crumpled. It's a good job the lighting's poor he thought, as beads of sweat broke out on his upper lip and the blood drained from his face. "Ah ... well. Ah ... like he told you," he stuttered, "I ... I saw someone fall overboard."

"How did they fall?"

That's sharp, thought King. "What do you mean, how did they fall?" he stalled, having given no thought to the physical difficulty of falling over a ship's rail, but realizing from the officer's tone it might be impossible; that it would need a jump, a push, or a violent lurch in a stormy sea.

Apparently the officer had similar thoughts and had no intention of helping out. "Sir, please explain to me exactly what you saw; how he fell."

King, cornered, backtracked. "Well ... I came out on deck and saw a figure disappear over the side. I dunno how it happened. Didn't notice what he looked like. It was over in a second. I just rushed to the back ..."

"Stern," corrected Jacobs.

"Yeah ... stern. I went to the stern and saw him in the water, so I chucked one of those life-thingies over."

"You launched a life raft?"

"Ah ..."

"That's when I saw him," Jacobs started, cutting King off. "He'd just launched an inflatable off the starboard upper boat deck."

With a doubtful look the officer turned questioningly to the catering assistant. "Did you see the man go overboard?"

"No, Sir. And I couldn't see him in the water neither," Jacobs shot back, his confidence buoyed by the senior officer's apparent scepticism.

Shit, thought King, if they won't stop the ship I'm screwed. "Sir ..." he began but the officer waived him off.

"Would you excuse us for a moment?" he said, catching Jacobs' sleeve and pulling him out of the cubicle.

Left alone, King's mind raced. How the hell did I get mixed up with this. The poor fat geezer's going to drown ... not such a bad thing, for him anyway ... but what else can I do, they obviously don't believe me. You know the rules, he thought. The catechism according to the locker room lawyers: Stick rigidly to the story, say as little as possible, and deny everything contradictory; even if they've got photos. He'd heard a similar phrase a thousand times, even uttered it a few. Whenever a fellow cop was in trouble for remodelling a prisoner's nose, creatively constructing a confession, or even lifting a few things from the scene of a burglary the advice of colleagues was always the same. "Keep your mouth shut and deny, deny, deny."

"But they've got the evidence!"

"Even if they've got video—deny it. Evidence can always get lost." That's a laugh, he thought; cops give exactly the opposite advice to criminals: soft voiced, persuading, "Why don't you tell me all about it? It'll go in your favour and I'll even put in a word with the judge."

How many times had he said roughly the same thing, knowing very well that ninety percent of criminals were only convicted because they'd blabbed. As for putting in a word with the judge: even the chief constable would be stretching the thin blue line if he tried that one. Anyway, the only reason he'd got mixed up with Motsom was because he'd believed his chief inspector, who'd persuaded him everything would be alright if he just told the truth. He'd blabbed, and where had it got him—prison, dishonourable discharge. I'll keep my bloody mouth shut in future, he'd thought at the time. But there wouldn't be a future. He was out of the force, unemployed, with a certificate of service that wouldn't get him a job as a bouncer in a daycare centre.

Jacobs and the officer crammed themselves back into the tiny cubicle, interrupting King's woeful thoughts, and his hand involuntarily sprang to his nose: Jacobs needed more than a clean shirt. His attention swung back to the officer who was insistently tapping his finger on the radar screen where numerous lights twinkled like stars in an alien sky.

"See all these dots. Do you know what they are, Sir?"

King's mind was adrift, still smarting from past injustices, and he queried glibly, "Ships?"

"No, Sir. These dots up here are ships," said the officer pointing out an area where there was only a smattering. Then he returned to a part of the screen where so many tiny points of light clustered together they melded like dots of paint in a Pisarro masterpiece. "This is clutter—caused by big waves or heavy rainfall. That's what this is—a storm, a big storm, and it's headed our way. I don't want to stop and look for a missing passenger unless I'm absolutely certain. Do you understand?"

King nodded thoughtfully as if re-evaluating his account of LeClarc's disappearance, then pulled his face into a funereal seriousness, deepened his tone respectfully, and pronounced, "I'm sure he fell overboard, Sir."

The officer made up his mind. "Call the captain," he barked, then rattled orders to the invisible crewmen on the bridge, while leaving King pondering over the mess of luminescent dots from the approaching gale. "Poor bastard," he breathed.

The captain, tie-less in a slept-in shirt, fly undone, and hair all over the place, looked as though he'd been dragged out of a brothel in a raid; he was not in the best of moods when he appeared in his brightly lit office, behind the bridge, a few minutes later. At fifty-nine, he'd been at sea long enough to know passengers would report seeing all sorts of things—usually UFOs or giant green squids—especially at night. He had hoped to get a few hours sleep before dealing with the impending storm, but now he faced the same dilemma as the officer: If he ignored King, and it turned out someone was missing, all hell would break loose—the press would have a field day. He was already envisioning the headlines: "Drowning Man Left to Perish." "Passenger's Pleas Ignored—Man Dies."

"What's your name, Sir?" he enquired in a no-nonsense tone, sitting at his desk and taking notes, while peering inquisitively over the top of his spectacles at King.

"Nosmo King, Captain," he replied without hesitation.

"Strange name ...?" he began, his words floating.

"Nickname," King obliged. "It's David, but everyone called me Nosmo at police college because I didn't smoke."

A look of confusion furrowed the captain's brow, his blood-shot eyes squeezed into questioning slits.

"Nosmo King ... no-smo-king," explained King, the urgency in his voice screaming, "For God's sake hurry up. There's a man drowning out there."

But the captain, refusing to be harried, echoed. "Police college?"

Another unasked question demanding an answer.

Big mistake, thought King, realizing instantly that he'd violated the criminal's code by volunteering information. "Long time ago," he shrugged, as if it had been of no consequence, and re-iterated his story. The captain's pen flashed across the log as they spoke, but he kept his focus on King, reading his expression, noting his tapping foot and wringing hands. Feeling the rising tension, King tried holding the other man's steely gaze, but found his eyes wandering to the porthole, his mind striving to deal with the possibility that his quarry was struggling for life in the cold, black ocean.

The wall clock ticked noisily as the captain took forever to scan his notes. He looked up. "How do you know it was a man?"

Now what? thought King as the captain, chief officer and Jacobs held their breaths, and he felt six eyes burning into him as tense seconds ticked by. "I only assume it was a man," he said eventually, reigning in his voice, feeling as if his chest were in a vice. "I suppose it could have been a woman. But I just have the feeling it was a man."

The search started almost immediately—02:34:17 according to the digital clock in the officers' wardroom where King had been told to wait. And each second ticked by with exasperating slowness as he paced in rhythm, willing the next digit to appear. Five steps one way and five back. Ten seconds! Is that all? Hurry up for Christ's sake; start turning the ship round. Motsom will kill me if we don't find him.

Kings' anxiety was echoed on the bridge, now a hive of activity. When King had first entered, its gloomily serene atmosphere had reminded him of the church he'd attended, early each morning, as a young altar boy. Even the smell had been strangely reminiscent—an amalgam of leather, varnish, and dampness—which to him, an eleven-year-old struggling with the concept of Christian faith, became the embodiment of the Holy Ghost. Now, the ghostly congregation of officers and crew stood at their allotted stations and watched as a halo of multi-coloured rotating lights, in the ceiling above the captain's head, indicated the ship was turning hard to port.

"Another ten degrees to port," the captain chanted.

"Ten degrees to port," echoed an acolyte in the guise of the chief officer.

"Ten degrees to port it is, Sir," responded a server whose job it was to turn the handlebars, which had replaced the giant steering wheel no longer necessary on a modern ship.

The acolyte took up the cry again, adding his own prayer for good measure. "Ten degrees to port it is, Captain. Heading now, two hundred and twenty-five degrees. E.T.A. 17 minutes."

"Thank you, Chief," said the captain who might just as easily have intoned, "Amen."

The service continued; litany and responses flying back and forth as a hundred details were attended to: Preparation of lifeboats and rescue teams—*For those in peril on the sea: Lord have mercy*—notification to coastguards and other ships; updates on the position of the approaching storm— *From lightning and tempest ... Good Lord deliver us*—requests to the port authorities in Holland, asking they delay trains, advise relatives, inform the police, and carry out a dozen other tasks—*Oh God, the Father of Heaven: have mercy ...*

A supplication, by ships tannoy, for information about any passenger whose presence was unknown, brought no response, and the captain considered holding a roll call of all crewmembers and passengers, even starting to give the chief officer an order, but then thought better of it. With over two thousand people on board, it would take hours to assemble them in a place where they could be counted with certainty. But, he realized, if just one were accidentally counted twice the man in the water would be left to drown. Yet, if the tally were accurate and showed no one missing would he risk his conscience by accepting the result?

Once committed, the captain—the High Priest of the ship—would do whatever he could to find and rescue the missing man.


Roger vomited and retched periodically as the salt water slopped into his mouth. Seasick, and sick of the sea, he struggled less and less for survival as his tired body sank deeper. The effort of climbing each successively higher crest had become too great, and the fast approaching gale whipped waves into a frenzy that tripped over each other and shot gobs of spray into his face. A fit, accomplished swimmer may have surmounted the ever-steepening sea, but Roger was not fit—had never been fit. Fat, even very fat, was the best possible description of his physical condition. Fat, but certainly not fit. In all probability it was his fatness that had kept him afloat for the past twenty minutes or so, although his eiderdown coat was definitely a contributing factor.

"Waste of bloody money," his mother had screeched when she'd picked the price tag out of his trashcan. "They must've seen you coming, you great dolt."

Although it was now gradually soaking up seawater, the coat, stuffed with waterproof duck plumage and sealed with a multitude of zips and ties, provided excellent buoyancy and protection against the cold. He had never regretted buying it, despite his mother's reaction; in fact, he was beginning to find it amusing to do things deliberately to aggravate her. Although lying about his homosexuality was perhaps the worst thing he could have done. Why did I say that? he'd wondered. She'd taken it badly, smacking him fiercely over the head with a plate. "Wait 'til your father gets home," she'd shouted. "You bloody poofter! Wait 'til I tell 'im."

He'd laughed it off. "I was only joking."

Am I? he'd wondered darkly.

Am I what?

Gay or just joking?

He'd been tempted, more through default than desire. If women didn't fancy him, and they didn't, then maybe, just maybe, he'd have more success with men. Rejection was both swifter and more painful—one false start in a park washroom left him with pants round his knees, his head in the toilet, and the contents of his wallet being divvyed up amongst a vicious gang of assertive gays. Failure to make his chosen team was bad enough without being rolled over by the opposition.

He'd deliberately upset his mother in other ways too—unnecessarily staying out until three or four o'clock in the morning, knowing she'd wait up for him, worrying to death he'd been attacked or hurt in an accident.

What is she thinking now? he wondered, as he was tossed mid-ocean in the darkness.

She's funny, he thought, his mind drawing a fuzzy picture of her: floury faced, heavily wrinkled—puckered almost—a large woman—not physically—she'd never been really big, but always managed to occupy more space than she should have done considering her size. As she had shrunken with age, she had seemingly grown larger and larger until she had taken command of the whole house. She's definitely funny, thought Roger—though not in any humorous sense. Funny how she doted; fretting at the slightest sniffle of a cold, panicking if the train was late—phoning the railway station, expecting to hear there had been a crash. Yet, when it came to his appearance—"Puppy fat," she called it when he complained about his diet of meat pies, chips, and chocolate.

"Mum, I'm thirty-one," he had protested.

"What d'ye wanna be skinny for?" she retorted.

She knows why, he thought, but couldn't bring himself to tell her. "I want a woman," he longed to scream. "I want to know what it's like to fuck a woman." But he'd never said it, strangely finding it easier to lie about being gay than admit his true desires for a woman.

The computer had caused a major rift. While other obsessive mothers might be insidiously sabotaging relationships between sons and their wives or girlfriends, Roger's mother picked a fight with his computer. The noise it made—"whirring like a maniac"—the space it took up, the electricity it used. She even complained it was causing interference on her television. "Snow," she called it. "Shut that thing off," she would shout up the stairs. "You're making snow on my telly." The television, "hers" through a jealously guarded remote, took precedence over real life and had been the leash she'd used to tie him to her side. "Don't go out our Roger, your favourite program's on tonight," she'd say at the mere suggestion he was planning an excursion. But the computer had changed all that. Now he could go anywhere in the world without leaving his room, and without her.

Her resentment had led to petty sabotage: "Bit of an accident," she claimed, when he'd left the computer on by mistake one day. He'd soon put a stop to that; protecting files with passwords, and locking the computer. He would even have locked his room if he could have summonsed the courage. "After all I did for you," she'd whimper, alluding to the pain of childbirth, stretch marks, cellulite, saggy breasts, and a slumped backside. "And now you lock your door!"

Her insignia of suffering had been used to ward off several of Roger's teenage insurrections, and now he lacked the strength to overcome the omnipotence of progeny guilt.

Roger was disappearing, and disappearing fast. Semi-conscious, and buffeted like a rubber duck in rapids, he'd withdrawn from the horror of his situation. He could do that: Switch off the rest of the world and reside only in the comfort of his mind.

"The lights are on but nobody's home," his father would mock.

But this time, his lights were going out. His will to survive was rapidly draining, and he was drifting toward death.

Everything aboard the ship had changed—so many lives shifted by a single thoughtless act. On the bridge, the captain was still in communion with his crew, even ordering hot chocolate and doughnuts for everyone. Most, dragged like he from the comfort of a warm bunk, were grateful for his consideration.

"Drink this in remembrance of me," he could have said, as he passed a steaming cup, heavily laden with sugar, to the chief officer. "How far John?" he asked, in an informal way. Just a friendly enquiry. The simple action of handing over a cup of cocoa bringing an instant bond between the two men, changing their relationship from master and servant to that of friends. But the relationship could flip back, instantly, should it be necessary. And both men knew it.

"About another four minutes to point Alpha, Bert, if the computers are right. Although God knows what chance we've got of finding the poor bastard in this weather ... assuming there is a poor bastard."

Point Alpha—the spot in the vast ocean where, according to the computerized navigation system, Roger's body should be found, alive or dead.

With a bridge resembling the flight deck of *Starship Enterprise,* the SS *Rotterdam* was equipped with all the latest aids: A satellite navigation system locked onto signals emitted by a dozen man-made moons; anti-collision radar tracked other vessels fifty miles or more away; and the auto pilot knew exactly where the ship was, where it had been, and where it was going. Apart from the intricate manoeuvres required to navigate congested harbours at each end of the voyage, the ship was perfectly capable of finding her own way across the North Sea. She could also retrace her steps, precisely, to any given point of the voyage.

Working backwards from the moment of King's arrival on the bridge, the navigation officer had calculated the moment Roger was believed to have disappeared overboard. The on-board computers turned that time into a location: Point Alpha—a mere pinpoint on the ocean's surface, yet a point defined with more accuracy than the distance between one wave and the next. Finding a needle in a haystack would have been child's play for this computer. Finding a fat man mid-ocean was well within its capability.

Many of the passengers were up; woken by the violent movements, which contrasted so sharply with the gentle sway, that lulled them to sleep just a few hours earlier. Few knew what had happened. Most remained in their cabins, a nasty surprise awaiting them in the morning when, at daybreak, they would peer out of the porthole expecting to see the familiar green landscape of Holland only to find a dirty, rolling sea. A few passengers, forced out of their cabins and onto deck by heaving stomachs, were surprised to find a large number of crewmembers hanging over the rails, studying the wave tops.

Searchlights lit the area around the sides of the ship, clearly illuminating each green wave as it smashed against the hull and climbed high up the superstructure before losing power and dropping back, only to be picked up and thrown back again by the next one. The ship, now almost stationery, rolled like a giant metronome marking time with the hellish cacophony created by the rising wind and crashing waves. Wave after wave attacked the ship, flinging spray high into the air, stinging the faces of the exhilarated passengers and disgruntled crewmembers lining the rails. But beyond the fringe of lights, the rest of the world had dissolved into the blackness of outer space.

Below decks, in the Calypso Bar, an alcoholic duo of detectives were still aggravating the barman. Nosmo King had been wrong in thinking they were en-route to a boozy goodwill convention. Their task, they believed, was almost complete and, in a few short hours, their Dutch counterparts would take over the mission and relieve them of responsibilities for the following thirty-six hours. A day and a half they planned to spend seeing the sights of Amsterdam.

"Hey. Barman. Whash your name anyway," slurred one of the detectives.

"It's Len, Sir."

"Yeah, Len, baby. Uh, what's happening. Can't you keep this bloody boat still." Detective Constable Doug Smythe, with many years of drinking under his belt and a maze of flamboyant capillaries on his nose, was sober enough to realize the swaying motion was not just in his head. But the other detective, a younger man with brush cut hair, and a goatee, which he believed fashionable, had flopped forward against the bar and wound his arm around a stanchion to prevent himself from sliding off the chair.

Sergeant Jones had ventured to the washroom, and was now making his way back across the deserted dance floor, waltzing back and forth in tune to the reeling of the ship. Sickness had left its mark—slicks of mucous stained his shirt and right trouser leg, and a large dollop of vomit perched on the toe of his right shoe.

The obstacle-free dance floor presented no real challenge to Jones, other than remaining upright with nothing solid to grasp. But the stairs, tables, and chairs of the bar area were an entirely different terrain, yet to be conquered. The Calypso Bar occupied the entire aft section of the ship—a cavernous auditorium of six semi-circular terraces overlooking the dance floor, each terrace reached from the one below by a wide flight of eight stairs. The bar itself was almost five decks higher than the dance floor, and only a ship's architect with an outrageous sense of humour could have placed the bar at the top of the incline and the washroom at the bottom.

Jones fell as he climbed the steps to the first terrace and was catapulted into a table by a particularly violent pitch. Grabbing a chair, he held on, bracing himself against the next lurch. Seconds later the ship slammed into another wave. "Hold tight!" he shouted to himself, grasping the chair tightly, but it was unattached and crashed with him down the eight steps to the hardwood floor below.

"Buggerin' ell!" he screamed, his words lost in the vastness of the almost deserted auditorium. He tried the stairs again, only climbing three before being shaken off balance, then lying on his back on the dance floor, swearing at the ceiling fifty feet above, unaware his left wrist had been shattered in the first fall.

"I think your mate needs a hand," said Len, watching from his perch at the bar, giving D.C. Smythe a poke.

"Oh shit," he replied, dragging his younger colleague with him to the sergeant's aid.

With the detectives no longer at the bar, Len seized his chance to escape and in less than thirty seconds ripped the cash drawer from the till, flicked off the lights, slammed and locked the bar grill, and was on his way to bed.

Disappointment awaited him at the purser's office, where he went to pay in the evening's takings.

"All hands on deck mate," the assistant purser said. "Didn't you hear the call? Some poor sod's gone for a swim."

He hadn't heard; didn't want to hear. Working late into the night wouldn't have been so bad if he hadn't done a day shift for his mate, a kitchen fitter, the previous day. Just for a second he considered sloping off to bed, figuring he'd not be missed, but the assistant purser, with more years at sea than he wanted to remember— waiting for a pair of dead purser's pants, according to his wife—saw the intention spread across Len's face.

"I'll tell the deck officer you're on your way then," he said, pointedly, as he picked up a walkie-talkie from the desk.

"Fuck you," Len muttered, ambling disgruntledly toward the boat deck.

"This is the centre of the search area," the deck officer was explaining as Len joined a group of crewmembers sheltering from the storm under one of the larger lifeboats. An audience of curious passengers were hanging about in the shade of the boat, listening to his performance, so the officer tuned his voice to a high pitched whine, sounding like a 1950s BBC radio announcer. "We believe the man should be somewhere in this area ..."

"Sounds as if someone's fallen overboard," relayed one of the passengers to his wife, shielding herself from the gale behind a storage locker.

"I hope we don't miss our train."

"He might drown."

"They'll be ever so disappointed if we're late for the wedding."

"Luv, there's a man missing!"

"I know ... but he's our only son ... sometimes I think you don't care."

"The weather's deteriorating rapidly," continued the officer, "so we must find him quickly. There's no description— report anything you see in the water. Any questions?" He paused long enough to scan the group—twenty men in fluorescent sou'westers hunching against the rain and spray, not an ounce of enthusiasm among them.

"Questions ..." he repeated, raising an eyebrow, pausing. "No? Good. We are relying on each and every one of you to do your best."

"Who does he think he is: Lord Nelson?" whispered a first-class waiter, but heard by many.

"Is there a problem?" shouted the officer in response to the gale of laughter, triggering more laughter.

"O.K., men. Go to your stations."

"Full of piss and self-importance," mumbled one of the engine room greasers, unhappy at being dragged from the warmth of the engine room and even more upset to discover his lookout station, on the starboard side, faced directly into the prevailing wind.

Detective Inspector Bliss, coming out onto the upper deck just as the men were drifting away, was unaware of the search, or its cause, and introduced himself to the deck officer. "D.I. Bliss, Metropolitan Police Serious Crime Squad. Can I help?"

"Oh Inspector ... Yes. We think there's a man overboard—perhaps you could help keep watch?"

Bliss jumped. "Man overboard." His eyes flashed wide. "Who is it? When was this? What happened?"

"Hang on officer, I don't know, you'd better speak to the captain. Let me just make sure everyone is at their post and I'll take you along to the bridge."

"Please hurry. I think I might know who it is."

Since leaving the others in the bar, Bliss had scoured the ship for Roger. His first stop, the purser's office, to locate Roger's cabin number had proved interesting.

"No one of that name," said the assistant purser, quickly running his finger down the passenger list, paying little attention.

"Let me look," said Bliss snatching the book from under his fingers. "There must be some mistake."

"No mistake, Sir," continued the assistant purser, grappling the book back with an air of certainty.

Bliss relinquished his grasp. "How can you be sure?"

"Never forget a name, Sir ... could tell you the name of everyone who's got a cabin, all two hundred and seventy-eight of 'em."

Bliss scanned the list and found the total. "Two hundred and seventy-eight," he breathed.

"That's right, Sir." said the officer, keeping his focus firmly on Bliss. "Starts with Adnam, ends with Yannus, and there's eight Smiths—but there ain't no LeClarcs, not tonight anyhow."

Bliss, impressed, awe-struck even, believed him. "I was sure he'd have a cabin," he muttered, starting to turn away, unsure what to do next.

But the assistant purser wasn't finished. "Ah ... It is possible that he's got a cabin, Sir ..." he began, nervously shuffling the list.

"How? I don't understand. You said his name wasn't on the list."

"You didn't hear this from me, but ... well maybe he paid cash and someone forgot to take his name."

"I bet they forgot to put the money in the register as well," said Bliss, quickly catching on, thinking it was an easy way for a crewmember to make a few extra quid every trip. He'd been in Serious Crimes long enough to know that whenever cash transactions took place, you could bet someone was taking a cut.

Without a cabin number, he turned his attention to the sleeping lounges. Hundreds of sweaty bodies, fidgeting on reclining chairs, formed a thick smelly carpet of humanity as he fought his way up and down the darkened aisles in between the rows—the stale odour of sleepers alternating with the stink of cheap perfume and the stench of an occasional fart. Backpacks, suitcases, even cardboard boxes stuffed with the belongings of the poorest passengers created an obstacle course in the tight aisles, tripping him repeatedly. Passengers, rudely awakened by his thrashing arms as he tried to steady himself, cursed him in a dozen languages. At the end of one row, between the last seat and the wall, he fell over a body lying on the floor. Pulling himself upright he began apologizing then, to his astonishment, saw he'd fallen over a young couple clearly engaged in oral sex. The woman, an attractive long-haired blond, on top of the young man, looked up with a fierce expression, as if to say, "Piss off," and carried on, quite unperturbed.

He quickly found the deck steward, a badly shaven unmade-bed of a man, with rotten teeth and a grubby red coat, slouched in the bright area between the two dimly lit lounges.

"There's a couple bonking in there," he said disapprovingly.

"I've seen worse mate," replied the steward, only half opening his eyes, making no attempt to move.

With the feeling that he must have led a sheltered life, Bliss walked away, shaking his head.

Bliss had been deep in the vessel's bowels, examining Roger's green Renault, while the ship had been turning around and had not noticed the change in direction. Brushing aside the sign warning of the danger of entering the vehicle deck during the voyage he'd slid open the heavy steel door and had been met by the acrid mechanical odour of engine oil, rubber, and hot metal.

Roger LeClarc's Renault, nestling amongst a raft of flashier models, was locked. He tried both doors, and the trunk, then peered through the driver's window and was surprised to see a suitcase and several smaller bags on the back seat. *Maybe he doesn't have a cabin after all.*

The small green car was familiar, very familiar. Bliss and the other officers had been keeping tabs on it for more than a week. They'd lost him a few times—round the clock surveillance of a target could be incredibly difficult, if not impossible. A moment's inattention, a little bad luck, or a run of red traffic lights was all it took for a vehicle to disappear, seemingly without trace. But, on each occasion, a quick analysis of Roger's regular pattern of behaviour enabled him to be located, either at his mother's or at the little terraced house near Watford railway station where he often spent his evenings before returning home in the early hours.

Details of his impending trip to Holland were well known. Roger, something of a celebrity in the computer world, had been invited to address a symposium of world leaders in The Hague: "Communicating in the Third Millennium," a two-day exposé of modern telecommunications, extolling the advantages of globalization and convergence. Ostensibly, Roger was an independent delegate, though few of the attendees would have been surprised to learn that he was the cyber-star of an aggressive multi-media equipment provider hell-bent on cornering the market.

Following Roger from his mother's house in Watford on the northern outskirts of London, to the ferry port had been straightforward. With the exception of a ten minute stop at the tiny terraced house on Junction Road, he'd poodled the Renault along at a modest pace to north Essex, sticking to main roads, avoiding bottle-necks.

Animosity between the detectives in the surveillance vehicle had flared during the trip, although there had been a number of times during their week of watch-keeping when they had volubly disagreed on tactics. As Sergeant Jones drove, with Senior Officer Bliss in the passenger seat keeping his sights on Roger's Renault, the other two detectives lolled in the back planning the excursion to Amsterdam.

"Red light district first, mate," said Wilson, digging Smythe in the ribs.

"I wanna try one of those brown bars,"

"What," laughed Wilson. "A Mars bar?"

"No you dork, one of those hash ..."

"I know you fool. I was pulling yer plonker."

"Leave me plonker out of this—I got plans for me plonker," he laughed. "I've heard the broads sit in windows starkers; showin' everything."

"Haven't you seen one before?" cut in Bliss.

"Bet it's a long time since you seen one," said Smythe, poking Bliss' shoulder, giggling stupidly.

Bliss ignored him, as he tried to shut out painful memories and focussed on the road. Concentrating on the green Renault half a mile ahead, he wondered whether either of them would actually pluck up the courage when faced with the opportunity. Regardless of the wares in the window, they'd probably be disappointed to discover one knocking shop to be much like another. The visual "sizzle," he guessed, would lure them to a steak cut from a tough old cow. Their ardour would be dimmed almost immediately by the request for cash in advance, and, having paid, and not before, would they discover the Venus in the window was unavailable—taking a break between rounds of sexual wrestling. Finally, after choosing an inferior model with a puritanically grim face and blubbery breasts, the fifteen minute performance would take place on a creaking bed in a room lit only by a couple of cheap candles. No amount of scent from burning wax would mask the chalky odour of spent semen from a thousand previous temple worshippers. The eternal triumph of hope over experience, thought Bliss, remembering his days on the morality squad and the universal sense of dissatisfaction. "You think I enjoyed it?" they would ask—pimps, whores and johns alike.

"You lot make me sick," he said, turning on the two detectives accusingly.

"You make *me* sick," shot back Wilson, unable to come up with a sensible response.

"You catch some poor hooker in Brixton with a few ounces of grass," countered Bliss, "and you think you've cracked the world's drug problem. Then off you go to Holland to get blasted, and get your leg over some whore young enough to be your daughter. You've got the morals of a tomcat in heat."

"Tomcats don't get in heat, Guv. Thought you'd know that. It's only the females that get in heat. Tomcats are good for a screw anytime."

"Precisely," replied Bliss, turning back to the road, his point made.

Sergeant Jones had stayed out of the argument, and Bliss had no doubt he would be with the others when the time came.


"I'll take you to the captain now," the deck officer was saying, but Bliss was miles away, still worried about LeClarc, and listening to the tannoy blaring overhead.

*"Attention all passengers. If there is a doctor on board would you please report to the captain's office, ten deck for'ard, immediately. Thank you."*

"Somebody must be pretty sick," he said as he followed the officer to the bridge.

"I bet the guy in the water isn't feeling too great either," replied the officer.

Roger was definitely not feeling great, he really wasn't feeling much at all. Numb from the cold, abandoned, hopeless, he'd retreated to his inner world and more or less made up his mind to die. Drifting into unconsciousness had been easy—managed without even trying—but the fierce winds and wild sea conspired to keep him alive, flinging him around like flotsam in the surf. The wind was his lifesaver, tearing apart the waves that bore him, surrounding him with fizzing foam—more air than water—penetrating every crevice in his coat, turning it into a balloon.

A heavy weight crashed on his head and sent him under for the umpteenth time. This is it. I'll go quietly, he decided, then fell out of the side of the wave as it exploded into a billion droplets and tumbled into the gulley below. He surfaced back to consciousness in time to feel the following wave pick him up—the uphill climb at the start of yet another roller coaster—and he'd almost reached the top when he felt the heavy weight crushing him down again.

"Get it over with," he shouted, but no words came as he slid back down; this time the weight stayed with him, pressing firmly against his left shoulder.

What's happening? he was yelling inside. What's happening to me? Look. But his eyes, stung once too often by the lashing salt spray, wouldn't open. Fear and the absolute blackness spun his thoughts back to his teenage years. He was fifteen or sixteen playing with himself in the bathroom with the curtains drawn, lights off, eyes shut tight, sitting on his hand until it went numb, then pretending it belonged to another—a girl perhaps.

"What'ye doing in there, our Roger?" she called, creeping up to the door unheard.

Oh shit! "Nothing, Mum."

"Liar! What are you doing? Open this door now."

"No."

"D'ye wanna clout?"

Tears welled. "No, Mum—please don't."

"Come on out then—hurry up."

"I love you, Mum," he cried, opening the door.

"Humph," she grunted, going back downstairs to *Dynasty*. "You'll go blind."

He stood at the top, pants round his ankles, watching her, hating her. Why had he said that? Why had he said, "I love you?"

"I hate you, I hate you, I hate you," he screamed inside. "I bloody hate you."

The painful memory reminded him he was still alive and he forced apart his eyelids, but a wash of blue-black Indian ink had painted the sea and sky into one. Then the huge weight shoved again and, spinning his head, he saw a phantom—a large patch of lighter coloured space, twisting and turning right behind him. The ghostly patch was misty, indistinct, but it had substance, he could feel it nudging and bumping into him. Intrigue overcame fear and he timidly reached out. "It's solid," he said to himself in disbelief, feeling resistance against his hypothermic fingers.

The ghost was tugging at his sleeve. This must be Death, he thought, trying again to get free, feeling his arm being pulled once more; Death's spectre coming to carry me off.

"Stop it," he yelled. "Stop it. I don't want to die—I'm sorry Mum. I'm sorry. I love you." But the ghost kept pulling, dragging him through the water, dancing in the wind, skipping over the waves.

Then, in an instant something changed—logic took control as the spectre smacked him heavily, bringing him to his senses. Suddenly conscious it was real, not part of some elaborate nightmare, he grasped for the smooth, slippery object. Understanding slowly filtered through his doziness. It's a life raft, he realized, amazed, as he was flung repeatedly against it, the sleeve of his left arm trapped by one of the many ropes looped along its side.

A hundred or more times, Roger and the life-raft were dragged up and down the watery hillsides as he desperately searched for a way to clamber aboard; then fate took a hand and he found himself on the crest of a wave, the raft in the valley beneath, and he flopped effortlessly onto it. Exhausted, yet relieved, he dropped back into unconsciousness, totally unaware that the SS *Rotterdam* was less than half a mile away, with a hundred and forty-three pairs of eyes straining into the darkness, seeking any trace of the raft or him.

"Something off the port bow—about ten o'clock," cried a female officer, catching a fleeting glimpse of lightness. Tension on the bridge instantly turned to excitement, men frantically adjusted binoculars and swung them from starboard to port, all eyes focussed in Roger's direction, but the huge waves conspired to keep him hidden. He and his ghostly chariot, wallowing from trough to trough, trapped under one breaking wave after another, would have been invisible even in broad daylight.

"Nothing," sighed the officer a few moments later, her disappointed whisper easily heard in the tension filled darkness of the bridge. "Sorry—my mistake."

"No problem," replied the captain. "We're well beyond maximum range anyway. He couldn't have drifted this far in thirty minutes."

The officers wandered back to their stations on the bridge, some taking the opportunity for a quick slurp of cocoa and a bite of doughnut. A couple made a dash for the washroom. The suspense was dissipating and everyone was grateful for the excuse to take a break, falsely justified by the apparent sighting.

"Captain, I've got a police inspector outside who reckons he knows the victim," the deck officer was saying to the captain's shadow in the gloom.

"That's interesting—must be some sort of outing," he chortled, "I've already got three in my office." He snapped the last thread of tension as he raised his voice, "Anyone else got a policeman? We've got four and want to make up a set ... Take over, Chief," he continued, stifling a few sniggers, "I'll be in my office if anything happens. Try to keep her head in the waves, bos'n, or we'll be up to our necks in vomit."

Sergeant Jones, together with his fellow drinkers, had fetched up in the captain's office in search of salvation, but had found little. Every lurch of the ship pulled his face into another grimace; the alcohol was wearing thin, just hazy vision, bad breath, and the persistent reek of vomit remained. He should have been hovering, contentedly, but the searing pain in his wrist and strong coffee had brought him down to earth. No doctor had come forward and the captain, dealing with lost sleep, a missing passenger, and an approaching storm, had kept the lock on the medicine cabinet. "No time for self-inflicted wounds," he'd muttered to the chief officer with a wry smile, thinking: A little suffering is good for my soul.

"After you, Inspector." said the captain, ushering Bliss into his office. "Do you lot know each other by any chance?"

Sergeant Jones looked up sheepishly and, with his good hand, pointed to his broken wrist, now in a sling. "Had a bit of an accident, Guv. Fell down some ruddy stairps." He should have said steps or stairs, but the words coalesced somewhere in the great void between his brain and mouth. The other two sat hunched, silently counting carpet squares.

"Captain, I wonder if I could speak to you outside. Would you mind?" requested Bliss, without acknowledging his sergeant.

"Bliss, old chap ..." pleaded the sergeant, but Bliss was already in the corridor.

"There's some cocoa and doughnuts in the Officer's mess if you're interested," said the captain, sliding the door shut behind him and cutting Jones off.

"Thank you, Sir. A cup of cocoa would be very welcome. Sorry about the Serg and the others, I think they've had a drop too much. I'll sort them out later, but I thought you would want to know that I believe the man you're looking for is named Roger LeClarc."

The captain stopped mid-pour. "Could you tell me why you think it's him?"

"Well, it's pretty hush-hush but, basically, we've had him under surveillance for the past week or two. He was on the ship but disappeared just about the time this guy went overboard. I've looked everywhere and can't find him."

"Is he dangerous?" enquired the captain, getting the wrong end of the stick.

"Oh, no ... He's not in trouble ... Well, maybe he is," Bliss added reflectively. "But he's not wanted—not by us anyway." He paused, sensing the confusion on the captain's face. "Sorry, I can't really tell you more at the moment, but with your permission I'd like to make some enquiries, see if I can find out what happened, that sort of thing."

"Well, I'd appreciate your assistance to be honest. Huh ... I didn't catch your name?"

"Bliss, Sir. Detective Inspector David Bliss. Serious Crime Squad."

His warrant card, produced from a black leather pouch, was brushed aside. "Fine, you go ahead. Oh, you'd probably like to start with the guy who saw him go over. I'd appreciate your opinion to be honest. He seems a bit vague."

The chief officer led D.I. Bliss to the Officer's wardroom and found Nosmo King cleaning the gaps in his teeth with a fingernail.

"Mr. King tells me he used to be a policeman. Isn't that right, Sir?" said the officer with a condescending tone, leaving King squirming as uncomfortably as a patient with dirty underwear in a doctor's waiting room, and wishing he'd found some other way to stop the ship—sabotage perhaps? He started to rise, but Bliss waved him down. "What force?"

"Thames Valley, but only for awhile—Oxford."

Bliss pulled up a chair and reminisced, "I did a course once with a bloke from Oxford ..." then cut himself short. "Tell me what happened, what you saw, Sir," he said, the policeman in him taking command.

King's account, now well practised, omitted only one detail; his meeting with Motsom in the bar following Roger's disappearance, before the fiasco with the life raft and his brush with catering assistant Jacobs.

"So where were you before you went on deck?" asked Bliss, unaware of the timing of events, recognizing King as one of the men in the bar.

"Just wandering around really. Here and there, you know."

"In the bar?" asked Bliss, his tone offering no clue as to the correct response.

"No," he shot back, much too quickly, much too aggressively. Instantly regretting the boldness of his statement, he tried to soften the punch. "I don't think so ... I don't think I was in the bar ... but," he added, covering all his bases, "I suppose I might have popped in at sometime."

Bliss, confounded, couldn't fathom a reason for King's wavering, or why he would lie—unless it *had* been a lover's tiff and King was embarrassed. "Funny," he said, "I could've sworn I saw you in there with another bloke."

Perspiration reappeared on King's upper lip, his mouth dried, and his legs crossed themselves without any conscious thought on his part. "You ... you must be mistaken," he choked, but as he said it, his right hand flew toward his mouth, attempting to gag the lie. Realising what was happening, King consciously diverted his hand, giving his ear an unnecessary tweak.

Gotcha! thought Bliss, recognizing the tell-tale gestures of a liar, and pressed his advantage, asking again about the bar. King eventually conceded he'd been in the bar just before he went on deck to throw the life raft. "I forgot," he added lamely, "what with all the commotion—the bloke falling overboard and all."

"And the other man?" continued Bliss, pushing King into a tight spot.

"No one ... a stranger."

"Didn't look like a stranger to me."

King took a few seconds, his mind racing, then came out with a rambling explanation, putting Motsom down as a quidam he'd mistaken as an old school chum. Their "tiff," he claimed, had been nothing more than a heated denial by the other man, annoyed at being disturbed.

Entering the SS *Rotterdam*'s bridge twenty minutes later, Bliss walked into the same black wall that startles everyone the first time they visit a ship's wheelhouse at night. The captain spotted him immediately and beckoned, unseen, in the darkness. "Ah, Inspector, if you'd like to come over here, I'm about twenty feet to your right."

Bliss turned, started walking, shuffling each foot forward a few inches at a time.

"Mind the ..."

The warning came too late. He'd collided with a slender pole then reddened as a giggle ran round the bridge. Thank God it's dark, he thought as he sidestepped the pole and continued blindly, but his eyes gradually brought fuzzy shapes into view until he made out the pale sphere of the captain's face.

"Well, what do you make of our Mr. King?" asked a set of teeth, glowing like the Cheshire cat's grin.

"I'm not sure, Captain, to be honest. Although the good news from my point of view is that the man overboard isn't my man—at least I'm pretty sure it isn't."

"How do you know?"

"It's a question of timing, Sir," replied Bliss recalling his interview of King. "I don't know why he's lying, but I can vouch for the fact he was with someone in the bar for at least two minutes before he went on deck and saw the guy jump, or fall ... Anyway, that pretty well lets my man out. It must've been someone else," he concluded. "Assuming King hasn't made the whole thing up."

"Whoever it is," the captain responded, "I don't fancy his chances. Thirty minutes in this water is about all anyone can take. It's been well over an hour now."

The chief officer, with an ear to the conversation, was anxious to continue the voyage. It would be his job, along with the purser, to deal with the complaints of passengers angry at missed train connections and delayed business meetings. "Should we call it off, Captain?" he asked, hopefully.

"We'll give it another fifteen minutes, Chief. One last sweep, and then we'll just pray no one's missing when we dock."

Fifteen minutes later, the SS *Rotterdam* resumed her voyage and the pale glow of the sun, still far below the eastern horizon, started to lighten the sky, but no sun would shine that day, or the following two days—not on that part of the North Sea. The storm headed north, its sights set on the offshore oilfields and the coast of Norway, leaving in its wake a large bank of cloud, and a confused and jumbled sea. Roger unconsciously rode his inflated chariot, like a thrill-seeker on an inner tube behind a speedboat, face down, arms flung forward grasping the rope. He was on the canvas roof, his great weight forcing it down. Beneath him the raft was full of water, and had he scrambled inside, he would certainly have drowned.

He stirred, briefly, long enough to assess his predicament. Fearing he might tumble off, he gathered together several ropes and lashed himself into position as firmly as his frozen fingers would allow. Now, feeling safer, he let exhaustion take over, started to doze, and began thinking of his other life, the one he'd left behind just four hours earlier, wondering if he would ever return. He thought of his the little green Renault, his beloved computer, and the house. His house. The little terraced house on Junction Road, in Watford; that would really send his mother crazy if she ever found out. He'd forgotten all about the house.

And then he thought of Trudy.

"Oh my God," he screamed, suddenly wide awake. "What will happen to Trudy?"

# *chapter three*

A strident, demanding tone of a car alarm was echoing along Junction Road, Watford; the noise coming from an old Volvo abandoned on a patch of wasteland where number 33 had stood until a bomb had blasted the two-up and two-down terraced house to smithereens in 1940, at the height of the Blitz. The owners had never rebuilt. A volunteer fireman had found their mangled remains—still sheltering in the cupboard under the solid wooden stairs in strict accordance with the Ministry of Defence *Air Raid Manual*. But what to do if a direct hit collapsed the staircase on top of you? "Pray. And be damn quick about it," was the only advice the fireman had to offer a scared sorrowful neighbour: a thirty-year-old housewife wearing the wartime cares of a fifty-year-old in her mother's polka-dot pinafore dress, with her prematurely greying hair pushed up under an old beret. "That's all you can do m'luv if they drop one right on top of yer," he said. "Put your hands over yer ears and pray."

The dead couple's nearest relative, a son packed off to his aunt in Australia—"For the duration," in the jargon of the day—had intended to return home one day to sell the land, or even rebuild the house as a tribute to his parents. Now he was too old to bother, and too rich to care.

It was only 3:30 a.m. in Watford, a full time zone to the west of the SS *Rotterdam,* and the rising sun was still an hour shy of trying to brighten up Junction Road, with its tarnished terraces of turn-of-the-century red brick houses.

Finally, fed up with the constant whining of the car's alarm, Mrs. Ramchuran, at number 70, slipped a dressing gown over her silk pyjamas, tied on a scarf, and stepped into the chilly pre-dawn air. With uncanny timing, her next door neighbour, the "guardian" of Junction Road, readied himself with an arsenal of advice for the offender and snapped open his door.

"Is that your's, Mr. Mitchell?" his neighbour enquired, nodding to the Jaguar.

Caught off-balance, he laughed, and even his laughter had a clipped cockney ring. "Bugger off, will you. Nah, I've not seen it afore. 'T'aint anyone's round here."

"Have you called the police?"

"Nah, waste of bloody time. They can't be boverred with this. Anyhow, they've got more important fings to do."

Mrs. Ramchuran wondered, aloud, if either of the residents on the other side of the road, closest to the noise, had phoned the police.

"Doubt it," said Mr. Mitchell, an elderly widower who could have turned his knowledge of the street into an entire category of *Trivial Pursuit*. "There's no one in at 34, and old daft Jack at 35 would never hear anyfing. He's as bloomin' deaf as a post."

The alarm stopped, mid-sound, as if an unseen hand had wrenched off the battery. Mrs. Ramchuran was startled by the sudden silence. "Oh," she gave a tiny jump. "Thank God for that."

Mr. Mitchell, George to his friends at the British Legion, was uncharacteristically wrong about his neighbours—there was someone in at number 34. Trudy was there, Roger's Trudy. She'd been there nearly a week, although George had not seen her and, as he and Mrs. Ramchuran went back to their beds, hoping the noise would not recur, Trudy was lying in bed, Roger's bed wondering where Roger was and what he was doing.

"I'll only be away for a couple of days, Love," Roger had said the previous evening, "I'll miss you, Trude."

Sitting on the floor at the foot of the bed, sorting through computer discs, choosing those that might come in handy as he prepared for his Dutch trip, he repeated, tenderly, "I'll miss you."

She didn't reply.

"I'm sorry ... I know you hate being on your own but I don't have any choice," he continued, still shuffling discs. "The company says I have to go. I wish you could come with me though. Maybe next time, eh? When you're feeling better."

She nodded slowly. Her sad young eyes pleading, "Take me ... Don't leave me here alone." But she could not ask.

"I'll be back Friday," he explained, as he packed selected discs into an old brown briefcase.

She'd been alone before—most days—with Roger at work in the city. But this wasn't just another day at the office; this would be three days and two nights—it would seem like a week, or a month.

She projected a silent plea to the back of his head, but her thoughts failed to sink in, and he continued,

"I'm getting the ferry to Holland tonight. That'll get me there tomorrow morning about seven ..." Pausing to examine the label on one of the discs his brow furrowed in concentration, then he blew down his nose. "Hum ... What do you think, Trude?" he asked, showing her the disc. "Do you think I should take this?"

She looked away, fraught with fear—every young partner's fear: fear of abandonment, fear of someone else—someone prettier, sexier, more exciting, more willing, perhaps; fear he might never return.

"Don't go—please don't go," she willed inwardly, knowing she could not ask.

"I'll have plenty of time to drive to The Hague," he continued, unaware of her desperation. "I don't have to be there until eleven. My speech is at two. Then I'll get the ship back tomorrow night and, bingo, I'll be back before you've even missed me."

As if suddenly aware of Trudy's needs, Roger paused in his task, brought his face close to hers and ran his fingers across her cheek. Perfect, he thought, absolutely perfect, as he sensed the softness of her fresh, young skin, then stroked her long dark hair and exposed a delicate ear. He loved her ears, adored them—could play with them for hours, gently stroking, teasing, and squeezing, as he controlled his computer with his other hand. But now, as he bent to kiss her ear, she twitched, like a horse bothered by a fly and lashed his face with her ponytail. He shrugged off the rejection and turned back to sorting his computer discs. "It's exiting isn't it," he said, meaning his trip, the tone of his voice matching his words. "Are you excited, Trude?"

She nodded again, but her dark brown eyes swelled with tears.

Roger packed the last of the discs, gave Trudy a triumphal glance, then turned back to his computer—more important things on his mind. Behind him, Trudy's silent tears kept flowing, glistening droplets trickling down her cheeks, congregating into little puddles on the wide band of foul-tasting sticky tape plastered over her mouth.

Trudy, now wide awake, felt disembodied—her thoughts hovering in mid-air, refusing to be part of the carnage that lay below her on the filthy bed—wondering what had hit her, and how she'd been stupid enough to get in the way. Beneath her, the bruised and bleeding body was in agony; hands and arms the worst: Blood and pus oozed from a huge blister on the side of her fist where she'd pounded against the rough brick walls; her shoulders and upper arms were blue from being repeatedly slammed against the solid wooden door—a living battering ram which had rebounded as readily as a tennis ball off concrete—and the wreckage of her nails, used as screwdrivers on the door hinges, stung constantly. But, at least Roger had left her unbound and had even pulled off the tape—once she'd promised not to scream for help or try to escape.

The hands of her watch ("Happy sixteenth," her mother had said giving it to her a few weeks earlier) were stuck at 6:23, the time she'd first crashed her fragile body against the door—Roger's door, the door to the outside world. Now, as she stared at the smashed watch, she found a mirror of her fragmented life in the few sharp shards of glass still held in place by the square gold frame, and screamed. Pain, torment, fear, and loss merged into despair with the subconscious realization that the last strand of her mother's umbilical cord had been severed.

The computer could have told her the time had she really wanted to know; the only lighting in the room came from its screen; the only sound, its constant "shhhhhshing." She stared at the screen, detesting it for what it had done, yet pleading with it to help. "What the hell is his password?" she shouted across the dimly lit room, then waited, almost expecting it to respond.

An idea eased her off the bed, drawing her to the computer, and she winced as she pressed a few keys. The message "ENTER PASSWORD" flicked onto the screen and she typed her name. "TRUDY"

"INCORRECT PASSWORD PLEASE TRY AGAIN"

"Shit," she shouted, convinced she had been right. "What about, 'Trude'?" she asked, trying again. The computer responded soundlessly, "INCORRECT PASSWORD—PLEASE TRY AGAIN"

"This'll never work," she muttered. "There must be millions of different words."

After several more rejections, she quit. Without his password she would never be able to connect with the outside world. Finally, frustrated and angry, she typed. "ROGER—PLEASE COME BACK. PLEASE LET ME OUT. I'LL DO ANYTHING YOU WANT. I LOVE YOU."

Sitting back, drained, thoughtful, she changed the typescript to a larger font and wrote again. "ROGER— I LOVE YOU—COME BACK"

Roger was not coming back—not at the moment, anyway. His floppy body was still trampolining up and down on top of the life raft mid-ocean. He was alive, conscious, and still wondering why the SS *Rotterdam* had not returned for him. They threw me a life raft, he reasoned, so they must've known where I was.

Nosmo King felt the shift in momentum as the search was called off. No longer wallowing as it steamed slowly round the search area, the ship was now leaping and bucking as it ploughed through the water, back on course toward Holland; as anxious to make up the lost time as the passengers and crew. Ignorant of what was happening, and with a nagging feeling he were being deliberately shut out, King slipped out of the little office and poked his head around the bridge door.

"Come in Mr. King, I forgot all about you," called the captain, noticing the tired, unshaven and dishevelled man, thinking now he would have looked at home in an airport following a crash—pacing amongst a crowd of worried relatives, anxiously awaiting news.

King moved toward the captain with his eyes captivated by the huge, green waves breaking over the bow. He jumped as a streak of lightning lanced down into the water right in front of the ship. Isolated from the mayhem by huge armour plated windows, the bridge seemed a tranquil place in comparison.

"It's like watching a movie of a storm," he breathed, mesmerized, then turned to address the captain. "I was just wondering if you needed me any more. Only I'd like to get a bit of sleep before we arrive."

"I don't think we need you Mr. King. Hang on a minute though, I'll just check with our detective."

D.I. Bliss, unseen by King, was in the radar cubicle, still studying the screen for signs of the missing life raft or the missing man.

"Inspector Bliss, do you need Mr. King for anything?" the captain sang out and Bliss emerged from the cubicle with a puzzled expression.

"Um," he hummed, "I'm not sure," and turned to King, "G'morning Nosmo. Ahh ... Could you just hang on for a minute. There's one or two things I just want to check with the captain. Do you mind?"

The unspoken words hung in the air for a few seconds as King struggled for an answer. Did he mind? Yes, he minded, minded very much; minded being left out of the loop, minded being ostracized. There was a time ... he was thinking when he realized that the epithet, "ex-police," carried with it a connotation of exclusion incomprehensible to someone who had never been in the force. His mind was in turmoil; desperately wanting to know what was going on; what they were saying about him; what they thought about him; how they had taken his story. But Bliss and the captain were watching and waiting.

"I'll just have another look at the radar." King acquiesced eventually, breaking the stalemate, and he wandered toward the cubicle, his head pounding with the knowledge that somewhere on the ship, Billy Motsom, his client, his tormentor, would be searching for him, desperate for news about LeClarc.

"Something's going on," Bliss whispered, nudging the captain to the far side of the bridge. "He knows more than he's saying."

"How do you work that out?"

"Well ... Did you tell him we'd called off the search?"

"No."

"Exactly. So how come he didn't ask? All he asked was, did we need him 'cos he wanted to get some sleep. So why's he suddenly lost interest in what happened to our man?"

The captain grasped the point. "I agree, but I don't see what we can do. He's stuck to the same story right from the beginning."

"Do me a favour, Captain. Just keep him here for about ten minutes, will you, then make sure he leaves by that door over there." The captain nodded as Bliss continued, almost to himself, "I've got to make some arrangements." Then, as an afterthought added, "I've also got to find LeClarc before we dock."

Precisely ten minutes later, Nosmo King left the bridge, following a compulsory guided tour. "He was as jumpy as a jib in a hurricane," the captain told Bliss later. "I've never known anyone turn down a chance to have a few minutes at the helm before."

"You were right, Sir. He's gone to a cabin," D.C. Wilson's voice crackled over the radio a few minutes later, as Bliss was back at the purser's office, still trying to find LeClarc on a list—any list.

"What number?" he called back. "I'm at the purser's office, I'll look it up."

"2042."

Running his finger down the list he found the cabin number. "The name on this list says "Motsom" but I wouldn't guarantee it," he said, then caught a nasty look from the purser as he added, "These guys don't seem too sure what they're doing."

"What do you want us to do, Sir?" asked the other detective, sobered by time and the sergeant's accident.

"I don't know. Just find out what's going on. Use your loaf if you've got one."

Bliss snapped off the radio and turned back to the purser who had decided he may as well take command of his office early. Roused out of his bunk in the middle of the night, like everyone else, he wanted to make sure his records were straight, just in case there was an inquiry.

"O.K., Sir," said Bliss. "So how soon will we know for sure if someone's missing?"

The purser scratched his stubbly chin, realised he'd forgotten to shave in the upheaval, and thought deeply. "Hum. It's not quite that simple. You see, in theory we know exactly how many people are on board, but, aah," he hesitated, "in practice ..." Pausing, he threw up his hands, shrugged his shoulders, and picked his nose before committing himself. "Anybody's guess really."

"What are you saying?" Bliss questioned, incredulously. "Are you saying you wouldn't miss the odd one?"

"Oh no ..." he started, then stopped, tilted his head to one side, threw open his hands, and disclaimed all responsibility. "Well yes, I suppose so, if you put it like that. With nearly two thousand passengers you can never be sure. It's not like an aircraft—we don't assign seats, and we often get strays."

"Strays?" enquired Bliss. Dogs, cats, what? "Strays?"

"Yeah ... friends of crewmembers smuggled aboard for a freebie; hitchhikers in the back of trucks, even people hiding in car's trunks so they can avoid the fare. The vehicles aren't searched by British Customs on the way out, and the Dutch authorities don't care if you bought a ticket as long as you've got a valid passport."

"So, how will we know if you lost someone in the night?"

The purser's shrug told the story, but Bliss heard him out. "You won't. Not unless a friend or relative reports them missing, or we find luggage in a cabin, or a car on the car deck after everyone's left."

Billy Motsom, cabin 2042, tired, furious, and very worried, was having similar thoughts and had a spotlight on King. "So, Mister, what are you goin' to do if the poxy little shit did go over the side, eh?"

"Look, I was hired to follow him that's all. Nothing else—nothing dodgy. I don't know why you want him and don't care. You paid me ..."

"Correction," cut in Motsom. "We was going to pay you."

"You'd bloody better, I've done my job. I followed him around for three bloody weeks. It was me that found out about this trip. There's nothing else I can do."

King rose toward the door but was forced back with a snarl. "You ain't goin' anywhere until I tell you—now sit down."

He sat, sensing the simmering violence. Not that he hadn't been warned. "Real nasty piece of work," one of the few ex-colleagues still prepared to talk to him had said, "though he hasn't got any serious convictions."

"O.K., let me put you in the picture," continued Motsom, sounding helpful. "This ain't no game of hide and bloody seek, it's big business and you're part of it, like it or not. So we may as well be friends. O.K.?"

King said nothing, unsure whether to be more fearful of Motsom as an employer or a friend, and he buried his head, mumbling into his hands, "Why did I get mixed up in this?"

"Money—Nosmo. Just like me."

"No. Not like you ..." he started, but Motsom cut him short.

"The only difference between you an' me," he sneered, "is you've done time. You're an old lag, an ex-con, a bent cop."

King, stung by the suggestion, stared into his fingers, thinking: First I get shut out by a snotty D.I., then a piece of dog turd calls me bent. Who's the criminal here? I didn't take back-handers; I wasn't shaking down drug addicts for part of their stash; I'm no crook. But he had no answer, he was trapped by his past.

Motsom took his silence as agreement and, with the air seemingly straightened, softened his tone,

"LeClarc has some computer stuff the Arabs want, that's all, and we was hired to get it, O.K."

King tried to butt in, "I wasn't hired ..."

But Motsom held up his hand, now the cop, saying, "Wait, I ain't finished," and he continued firmly. "We was hired, both of us. It's just that I only told you what you needed to know."

"Bollocks! You knew I wouldn't do it if you told me the truth."

"Maybe yeah. Maybe no. Who knows. Anyhow it's too late, you've lied to the captain."

"And the police," added King, absentmindedly.

"The police?" Motsom exploded, shooting upright, nudging over a beer, which flipped onto the floor and rolled back and forth, spilling drops on the mottled blue carpet.

King quickly bent to pick up the bottle, but Motsom grasped his shoulder and hauled him upright.

"Leave it," he ordered. "What did you say about the filth?"

King winced at the derogatory term, then shrugged, matter-of-factly, "There's a bunch of cops on board and one of 'em, a snotty inspector, was making noises about the missing bloke, that's all. Just routine. Couldn't resist poking his nose in."

"Why didn't you tell me you idiot?" he shouted, "What are they doing here anyway?"

"They're going on some sort of visit," he shrugged, his imagination running away with him. "Stop worrying, I didn't tell 'em anything. They've no idea who's missing and even if they did, they couldn't connect him to us."

It was true that D.I. Bliss didn't know who was missing, if anyone, though he shivered at the idea of any man struggling for survival in the ship's wake. From his perch in the first class restaurant, high in the ship's stern, he stared pensively at the evil sea, then slit open another croissant (baked on board every day according to the waiter) and poured coffee for the two contrite constables.

"Drink," he ordered, and they drank.

Sergeant Jones had not joined them, his purple swollen wrist making movement of any kind painful. He was, in any case, pre-occupied—working up a story to cover his backside.

"Right, you two," said Bliss, noticing how well the green of the sea reflected in their faces. "We're docking in half an hour. I've looked everywhere on this damn ship and I can't find LeClarc, so he's either hiding 'cos he spotted us, or it was him who went over the side and that private dick is lying about the time."

"So what's the big plan, Inspector?" asked Wilson, with caustic undertone.

Bliss picked up the sarcasm and twisted it around, "I could always follow your example ... get legless, break my wrist ..."

"You lost him ..." Wilson started, accusingly, but Smythe touched his arm. "Leave it Willy, let's wait and see. Anyway, what are we going to do about the sergeant?"

Bliss picked up his coffee. "An ambulance will be on the quayside and he'll be going back on tonight's ship once he's been plastered."

"Good old Serg," sniggered D.C. Smythe. "Plastered two nights running."

All three laughed—like a team.

A hollow "boom" from the tannoy system echoed throughout the ship and a singsong voice rang out, "Will all car drivers and passengers please re-join your vehicles for embarkation."

"That's us," said Bliss, downing his coffee as he rose. "Grab our bags and chuck them in the car, then wait for me. I'm going to see if I can spot him getting into the Renault."

The narrow companionway to the car deck was swamped by a tide of sweaty, struggling, fed-up passengers, with fractious kids screaming, "Are we there yet?" and fractious parents screaming, "Are we there yet?" Bliss squeezed his way as far as a stairwell but his descent was blocked by a vertical wall of miserable humanity. "Police. Let me through," he called hopefully, but a truck driver inflated himself into a road block, mumbling, "Push off and wait your turn. You're not in England now." Bliss retreated, tried two other stairwells without success and was finally swept down to Car Deck B with a crowd. He wanted to be on Deck A—where LeClarc's car was. Weaving in and out of the slowly moving cars, he reached the deck just in time to see Roger's green Renault driving off the ramp onto the quayside.

"Quick, follow him," he shouted to Wilson, as he leapt into the back of their car. Wilson slammed it into gear, stared ahead, ignored the angry horns and voices of maddened motorists, and forced a path off the ship.

They closed up on the Renault approaching the immigration booth, just as the driver's passport was being handed back. Only two other cars separated them but the immigration officer was in no hurry, his day's plan ruined by the ship's late arrival. They inched forward as the Renault disappeared into the custom's hall. "Hurry up," muttered Wilson, drumming the steering wheel, waiting for the smartly uniformed officer of the Koninklijke Marechaussee, a Dutch Marine, on immigration control. But Bliss wound down his window impatiently.

"Officer, we're in a hurry," he called, flourishing his warrant card. "Someone from your police force should be here to meet us."

The officer's English was good, not perfect. "Oh yes, Sir. Over zhere," he said, pointing toward a dark blue Saab parked against the custom house wall with two men in black leather coats idly blowing smoke rings at each other. Bliss leapt out of the car, warrant card in hand, and ran over to the men.

"What did they say?" asked Wilson as he returned, breathless.

"Everything's arranged," replied Bliss. "They've really gone to town. They've got four units to pick him up as soon as he comes out of Customs.

"Shit," said Wilson, "The Dutch must've money to burn. Four double-manned cars to follow a fat geezer in a poxy Renault, and we only had one."

"Well," responded Bliss, "Maybe they're not as good as us."

They laughed in relief, their task finally over and, with Roger's car emerging from the Custom's shed with the Saab in tow, Wilson mused, "I wonder if anyone did fall off the ship."

"Don't know," replied Bliss, his eye on the departing Renault. "But thank God it wasn't LeClarc."

Trudy, in Roger's house, in Roger's bed, instructed herself to go back to the beginning, to her first words with Roger on the Internet. Reasoning that he must, at some time, have said, or done, something to give her a clue about the user I.D. and password she now needed to access his Internet server.

They'd "met" four months earlier—Easter weekend—in a chat room—an ethereal cyber-venue where weightless messages pass simultaneously between any number of correspondents; people who have never met, have little in common and, in most cases, nothing better to do.

"Your dinner's getting cold. What on earth are you doing?" her mother bawled up the stairs as she left for work that evening.

"Won't be long—just browsing," Trudy replied, mesmerized by the tiny black and white screen. An hour later she was still there, her foil wrapped dinner balanced precariously in the fridge, on top of a chicken's carcass.

The chat room emptied as guests drifted away in search of greater stimulation—like an entire fleet of Flying Dutchmen destined to endlessly surf the vastness of cyber-space, destined never to be satisfied—leaving Trudy and Roger almost alone.

"SO, ROGER, DO YOU THINK ONE DAY COMPUTERS WILL CLONE THEMSELVES," she typed.

"THEY ALREADY DO. WE CAN'T MAKE COMPUTERS WITHOUT COMPUTERS," he replied. "ITS LIKE PEOPLE. YOU CAN'T MAKE PEOPLE WITHOUT PEOPLE."

"LIKE—SOMEONE'S GOT TO GET BONKED," added the only other contributor, a man with the unlikely name of CyberBob, who'd added sexual innuendo all afternoon.

"THANK YOU CYBERBOB AND GOODNIGHT," flashed onto Trudy's screen as Roger gave him a hint.

CyberBob didn't give up and, after a few more exchanges, Roger and Trudy crept out of the chat room to communicate through a private chat client. One-to-one private messages supposedly inaccessible by anyone else.

"I've met this really super guy, Marg," she stage-whispered to Margery, her best, best friend, in social science class the following day. "He's gorgeous and he's twenty-seven."

"Bit old for you, Trude. More my age."

"Yeah, but I told him I was nineteen, so he reckons that's O.K."

"And ... when he finds out?"

"I ain't going to tell him am I? And it's not like we're going to meet or anything."

"Well what's he like? You know: How tall is he? What's his hair like? His eyes? Hey, what's his star sign? My mum reckons you can always tell what a bloke's like from his star sign. She says Sagittarius is best. My dad's a Pisces, that's why she reckons he's so wet."

Trudy had no answers, but anticipated each evening's "meeting" with Roger with the heart stopping palpitations of a waif dragged out of a screaming pack of groupies to have dinner with a teen-star. Dashing home from school, frequently brushing off Margery in her haste so that by six o'clock, or a quarter after at the latest, she was made-up and ready for her date. But Roger never came on-line before seven-thirty, even eight-thirty—she'd wait. Her e-mail message, "HI ROGER—GIVE ME A CALL," would sit, unopened, in his inbox until he could escape to his room, switch on his computer, and wait for the three most important words of the day: "You've got mail."

A crease in the filthy sheet on Roger's bed irritated her aching left shoulder but, as she manoeuvred into a more comfortable position, pressure on her blistered hand made her cry out in pain. Once settled, she went back to her thoughts and recalled the evening, just a week after their original meeting, when "love" first appeared.

Coming home from school, she'd surrounded herself with a tide of cookies, crunchies and chocolate, which flooded the table and swept over the cereal bowl, still containing a few soggy cornflakes, which she'd abandoned in order to check her messages before school that morning. A sheet of writing paper, wrenched from an exercise book, had been brushed off the bowl by a pack of pretzels and now lay on the floor. The lipstick message, a random mix of upper and lower case letters, looked more like a suicide or ransom note than a mother's message to her daughter. "I'n NOT clearing up AGAIN—I've WARNED you. You left the MILK out again. the cat got it. I'll be back at ten—MAYBE."

Their messages flew back and forth that evening. "At lightning speed," according to Roger.

"HOW FAST IS THAT?" she enquired, but found little interest in the possibility of her written thoughts zipping round the world six times a second.

"WOW," she wrote—who cares, she thought.

"I DID MY HAIR RED," she wrote

"WOW," he replied—who cares, he thought.

Hard-drives, soft movies; gigabytes, teen-TV; RAMs and ROMs, music and make-up. Their words crossed though never met.

"I GOT A NEW Z360," he wrote.

"WOW," she wrote.

"I'M GETTING A WATCH FOR MY BIRTH-DAY," she typed.

"WOW," he replied.

The stilted conversation continued, the cut and thrust of debate, perfected by Senators before Christ, now blunted by the lightning speed of twentieth century technology—what truly masterful advertising genius had persuaded people that progress was to turn a thirty second phone call into an hour-long marathon of typing and reading?

Later, much later, in their exchanges, with all meaningful information exposed, she fished for his thoughts, his feelings.

"I THINK YOUR REALLY NICE," she typed, her misspelling unnoticed by either. "WHAT DO YOU THINK OF ME?"

"U ARE REALLY SUPER TRUDE. I'VE NEVER MET ANYONE AS NICE AS YOU. I WISH I COULD SEE U. I BET U LOOK LOVELY. I THINK I'M FALLING IN LOVE."

"Oh my God," she breathed, feeling a warmth as the words sank in. What would Margery think of that? Margery with her string of admirers; Margery always knowing the right thing to say to a boy; Margery with her cool clothes, "in" lipstick and the right footwear. "Height matters," she'd said, flaunting her new four-inch chunky heeled boots.

Trudy saved the message log on her hard drive, would have printed a copy but was out of paper. "I think I'm falling in love," she read, and re-read, luxuriating in the words; listening to them roll off her tongue; watching her expression in the mirror; imagining Roger saying them: "I think I'm falling in love."

"TRUDY—R U STILL THERE?" Her screen was saying.

"YES." she typed back quickly, suddenly realizing that she'd not responded to his earlier message. "I'M HERE, AND I THINK I'M FALLING IN LOVE TOO."

They could have picked up the phone, spoken directly, said what they wanted to say, heard what they wanted to hear, yet neither did, preferring to add another veil to the eternal dance. Lovers, fumbling in the dark, excited by the uncertainty of what they may find, deliberately delaying gratification—or disappointment.

Trudy called for Margery the following morning, something she rarely did of late, but she was unable to contain her excitement. Margery's cigarette-thin mother, a length of ash dangling precariously, answered the door to Trudy's cheery, "Hi—is Mar ..."

She got no further. "Hang on, Luv," she said, flicking the ash past her onto the street. "It's for you Marg," she shouted, turning to face the stairs.

"Go on up, Luv. It's time she was up for school," she called over her shoulder as she turned back to the kitchen.

Margery was miffed, "I thought you'd found a new friend," she sneered, dived under the bedclothes and buried her head in the pillow. One foot stuck out, her azure toenails—"Chic" according to one of her mother's magazines—contrasting sharply to the chalkiness of her skin.

"You're still my best friend, Marg," Trudy tried soothingly, closing the bedroom door behind her. "But Roger *is* sort of cute."

"Cute! Cute! You don't know what he looks like for gawd's sake," she shot back.

"I do so."

"Bollocks you do."

"Yeah, well that's where you're wrong, see."

Margery leapt up, almost knocking Trudy off the edge of the narrow little bed—a cheap standby bought for a nine-year-old eight years earlier. "You've met him?" she asked excitedly.

"Not exactly, Marg. But I know what he looks like, and he's sending me a photo. He's tall, well fairly tall anyway, and he's got dark skin. Not Paki or anything like that—just sort of tanned. Oh, and I nearly forgot, he's got brown eyes the same as mine. He's got a really posh job as well—some sort of computer programmer in the city."

Margery, stirred into momentum by Trudy's excitement, decided she might as well get up. She'd slept naked under the bedclothes, and now stepped, unashamedly, in front her friend, to examine her neat little body in the cracked, full-length mirror on the back of the door. "I think they're getting bigger, what do you reckon, Trude?" she said as she turned to face her friend, her hands pushing under the little mounds of flesh, squeezing every available gram of fat into her breasts.

Trudy, her mind fixated on Roger, raced ahead. "He commutes, you know." *Is that an achievement or what?* "He gets the train. Reckons he travels first class 'cos his firm pays. Oh, and wait for this, he's got his own house. Sounds pretty posh, too. And you'd never guess where it is."

She didn't wait for Margery's guess. In any case her friend was showing little interest, more concerned with retrieving various bits of clothing from around the room, carefully sniffing each.

"It's in Watford," she concluded triumphantly. "Not bad. Eh!" she added, carefully emphasising each individual syllable, and then repeating them for even greater emphasis, "Not bad. Eh!"

Margery didn't think it was bad, not that she thought it was good either, so said nothing. Her choice of knickers selected, she put them on, coyly turning away from Trudy as if she'd suddenly discovered she had something to hide.

"Just think, Marg. Watford on a Saturday," she said dreamily, her mind on the famous soccer club.

"Didn't think you wuz interested in football, Trude," Margery said at last, just to be annoying.

"Don't much. But I might get to see Elton John. They reckon he's there nearly every week."

Margery was not a John fan, never had been, couldn't understand anyone of her own age idolizing a strange little bald man old enough to be her grandfather. "Oh great!" she mocked, "Just what I always wanted."

Trudy's conversations with Roger had continued. Becoming longer; more intimate, more revealing, and even more desperate, as the tentacles of two lonely souls reached out to mesh with each other. Her mother, concerned mainly about the rising cost of the phone bill, had warned her about getting too involved. "You don't know anything about him really, Trudy love," she'd said, kindly, when her daughter had been explaining, excitedly, about some clever remark Roger had made. "Just be careful, that's all. He might be married, or weird, or ... or, I dunno. You're only sixteen, plenty of time for boyfriends yet. Anyhow, you know what blasted liars men are. Remember your father?"

Of course she remembered her father, how could she forget her father; although, thinking about it, she was surprised to discover she hadn't visited him for more than a year. His new wife, younger and definitely prettier than her mother, didn't like her, had never liked her. "It's like going to see him in hospital," she had complained to her mother after her last visit.

Her stepmother had fussed around them all afternoon like an over-attentive ward Sister, insisting they do nothing. "You two have a nice little chat," she had said, bustling in and out with cups of tea, finicky sandwiches, and fancy cakes from Marks & Spencer's on a silly little silver coloured cake stand, that, Trudy thought, looked as though it had been pinched from a one-star hotel. Her stepmother, the "Sister" was determined Trudy would go home to tell her mother how much better her father was being cared for now. But, beyond the smiles, and the seemingly kind words, there was a coldness, a distance, a chasm, and her father was being slowly drawn across it. Trudy was left standing on one side of the ravine as her father was being led by his new wife to the other, and by five o'clock her stepmother had had enough, repeatedly checking her watch, hinting about the bus times, anxious to ring the bell to mark the end of visiting time.

"Remember the time we caught him?" her mother was saying now. Though Trudy, only ten at the time, didn't feel she'd been personally involved in catching her father—although she'd certainly been there when he was caught.

"You should have seen his face," her mother continued, dreamily, forgetting for a moment that Trudy had.

He had been sitting at a corner table in a little Indian restaurant; she, her stepmother-to-be, stroking one of his hands with both of hers. The flame from the flickering pink candle warmed both their faces as they held each others' gaze, unwilling, or unable to let go; neither of them bothering to examine the plates of sizzling food the waiter was carefully placing on the pink tablecloth in front of them.

"Please be careful, Sir. It is very hot," warned the waiter, wondering why he was wasting his breath, before retreating. Trudy's mother wasn't retreating. She'd watched from across the room and now marched to attack. "So this is 'working nights,' is it?" she accused, her mouth taught with emotion. Then she swung on the other woman, biting out the words, "I'm his wife—I'm his day shift. I bet he hasn't told you about me." Without leaving any opportunity for a reply, she continued, in a sort of singsong voice. "And this is Trudy his little girl. Say hello to Daddy, Trudy."

Trudy, confused, upset, alarmed by her mother's uncharacteristically powerful performance, mumbled, "Hello Dad." Then, watched, terrified, as her mother reached out with both hands and tipped the plates of sizzling food into their laps. The startled lovebirds shot backwards, and the woman's chair tipped over, her legs spread-eagled and flailing in the air as her head hit the floor with a noticeable "thud." Panicking, she screamed, and scrabbled at the table in an effort to pull herself up. Catching only the tablecloth, she pulled hard and sank under a deluge of crockery, cutlery, and the single red rose, which he had so lovingly given her ten minutes earlier. Trudy's father rushed to rescue his new love and, as the waiters came running, Trudy's mother caught her hand, instructing calmly, "Say goodbye to Daddy," as if nothing had happened.

Pink was how Trudy would best remember that event. Everything seemed pink. Even her father's girl-friend's dress had been pink, although it had clashed with the pink of the tablecloth and the pink of the wallpaper. Her father's face had been the pinkest of all as she looked up at him and snivelled, "Goodbye Dad," then felt the tug of her mother's hand, dragging her from the devastation.

A spider, one of many in the tiny room, climbed onto Trudy's left leg. She twitched involuntarily to dislodge it, and woke sufficiently from her daydream to remind herself it was Roger she was trying to recall, not her father. It was Roger's password she needed now.

"Roger," she called forlornly into the gloom, "what's the password?"

They'd started dating almost immediately—meeting daily through the electronic wizardry of their computer modems. His wit and repartee were puerile—funny, she thought—and his crudeness gave him a slightly dangerous edge, adding to his mystique while re-enforcing her self-perceived adulthood.

"It's your own fault, Trude. You shouldn't have told him you were nineteen." Margery warned her, when she bragged of his sexual innuendos.

"But you always lie about your age, Marg," riposted Trudy. "You told that bloke in the pub the other night you were twenty-one and he believed you."

"That's 'cos he wanted to believe it, Trude. Anyhow, it's different when you're talking to someone. They can see when you're lying. Roger doesn't even know what you look like for certain."

Trudy lay thinking about her conversations with Roger, realizing that, after what had happened, nothing he'd said could be relied upon. They'd even discussed passwords once. She'd told him her's in a flash. "IT'S MARMY," she wrote. "THAT'S OUR CAT. HIS NAME IS MARMADUKE REALLY BUT WE CALL HIM MARMY, LIKE MARMALADE, 'COS THATS WHAT COLOUR HE IS. SORT OF ORANGEY, GINGER. WHAT'S YOUR PASSWORD ROGER?" She sat back, staring at the blank screen, until she worried he'd logged off without warning, and sent him another message. "U DONT HAVE TO TELL ME IF U DONT WANT 2. I DONT MIND, HONEST."

Her screen flicked back to an incoming message almost immediately. "I DON'T MIND TRUDE. IT'S JUST THAT I USE LOTS OF PASSWORDS AND SOME R A BIT RUDE. I'LL TELL U IF U WANT."

She typed back. "GO ON. IM AN ADULT REMEMBER. NOT A KID."

Instantly, her screen scrolled as a long list of words appeared. Beginning with "ass" and ending in "wank"; he'd included every crudity she knew, and several she didn't. She'd giggled as she saved the file, naming it "password@roger," and sending it to her *Wordperfect* directory.

"It's disgusting, Trude," said Margery. "Better not let your mum see it."

"Don't worry," she replied, "Mum doesn't know what I do on the computer."

Willing herself back to the present she posed the question, "What if he was telling the truth?" Completely awake now, her mind raced with hope as she started the painful process to raise herself off the bed. "What if one or more of those words were right after all?"

It was 8:30 a.m. in Watford as Trudy tried to reconstruct Roger's list from memory. The damp streets were alive with the noise of traffic and the sounds of children going to school, though Trudy heard none of it. The railway station, at the end of Junction Road, was still crowded with commuters lucky enough to start work in the city after the nine o'clock rush hour, or unlucky enough to have overslept. A discarded newspaper lay next to a litterbin on platform 4 and a young bank clerk—a late starter—held it in place with his foot as he idly read the headlines. "No trace of missing 16 yr-old. Police are still mystified over the total disappearance last week of Leyton schoolgirl Trudy McKenzie." He moved his foot an inch or two and examined the accompanying photograph. "Not bad," he said under his breath.

At precisely the same moment it was nine thirty in Holland, and D.I. Bliss, with his two constables, set off past the lines of waiting cars as they tagged along behind the Dutch police Saab. Custom's formalities had been waived for the visiting officers, and they found themselves being guided through a gate in the security fence, emerging directly at the exit lanes.

Bliss glanced to his left—there, just as he expected, was the little green Renault leaving the Custom's shed; a blue Ford with two Dutch detectives tucking in neatly behind it. There was Roger on his way to The Hague. Roger LeClarc—computer expert; Roger LeClarc—the man who'd unwittingly caused such a commotion on the ship; Roger LeClarc—safe and sound. Bliss let out a self-congratulatory sigh, gave his front seat companion a thumbs-up and took one last confirming glance at the Renault's driver.

"Oh Fuck! Stop, stop."

Bliss didn't wait, couldn't wait. Leaping from the still moving car, arms waiving madly, he dashed across the road, leapt the fence and almost threw himself onto the bonnet of Roger's Renault. Dutch police officers came running from all directions. And in the driver's seat, terrified beyond speechlessness, sat Nosmo King.

# chapter four

"Zo, Mr. King. I wish you to tell me once again, your story about the missing man," said the Dutch inspector, straight-backed—no-nonsense, his nationality barely discernable from his accent.

Nosmo sighed, "Look I've told you and told you. I've never seen him before. I don't know his name. He paid me two hundred pounds to drive his car off the ship. Then I got arrested. That's all I know."

"And you met this man in ze ship's bar. Is zhat what you said?"

"Yeah, that's right."

"And somebody stole the money from ..."

Nosmo interrupted, "Not all the money. I've still got a hundred."

"Oh yes," continued the inspector with a sarcastic sneer, "I forgot. Somebody must have stolen some of the money because now you have only one hundred and seventeen pounds and four pence. Is zhat correct Sergeant?"

"Correct, Inspector," barked the sergeant, taking notes across the desk from King, a role that seemed a complete waste of his enormous physical attributes.

"And finally, Mr. King, just for our records please, the man who fell overboard, the man whose car you were driving, the man who is now missing—who is he?"

"I told you, I don't know. I didn't even know if it was his car. He paid me to take the car, and then he must have jumped off the ship."

The sergeant threw up his eyebrows and gave a one-nostrilled snort, as if to say, "A likely story."

But the inspector's straight face gave nothing away. "Well Mr. King, I think you are in a lot of trouble. I cannot believe a man would pay you to take his car because he is going to die. It is not sensible."

"Well that's what happened. You'd better ask him if you don't believe me."

Impatience took its toll; the desk took a pounding. "Tell me where he is, Mr. King. Tell me where he is and I will ask him."

King started to smile, regretted it, and straightened his face, "I guess he's out at sea somewhere. Let me know if you find the poor bastard." He started to rise, "Can I go now please?"

A fierce look from the monstrous sergeant intimidated him back into the chair, but he kept a bold eye on the inspector.

Getting nowhere, unsure if anyone was actually missing from the ship, and handicapped by the absence of witnesses, the inspector played for time. "We have enquiries to make zo you will stay with us in prison ..."

King tried protesting, "But I didn't ..." then he let it go and slumped into the chair, washing his face in his hands in frustration. Twenty-four tension–filled, sleepless hours had taken their toll. Then he had an idea.

"Can I speak to the English detective, the one who stopped me?"

The inspector picked up the phone and prattled in Dutch, leaving King to wonder whether he was ordering lunch, a firing squad or Bliss' presence. Leaning menacingly over the back of King's chair, he said, "I have asked for the detective to come. Perhaps you will tell him the truth, Mr. King."

Nosmo snapped his head back, looked the inspector straight in the eye and lied, deliberately, "I am telling you the truth."

Seconds later a muffled knock brought the sergeant to his feet and his boots clunked across the flagstone floor with a noise familiar to King: Steel tipped toes and heels—an old army trick—much more impressive than leather hitting the parade ground. And the sharp toe-piece could make a nasty mess of an uncooperative prisoner's shins.

"This police station's huge," said D.I. Bliss, standing in the doorway, stunned by the height of the ceiling and the enormousness of the windows. "How old is it?"

"The Bosch built it," spat the sergeant, inflating himself to full size, making it clear the Nazis would have thought twice if he'd been around at the time.

"Thanks for coming, Dave," said King.

Bliss continued his inspection of the ceiling.

"It was a military barracks," added the sergeant, "Defences for the Rhine."

King tried again, "What's happening, Dave?"

The sergeant, in full historical flight, glared at King and finished his lecture. "When the British came in 1944 they made it their headquarters."

"Very nice," said King, applauding, "Now can you tell me what the hell is going on, Dave?"

Bliss snubbed him—*don't get familiar with me sonny*. "You asked for me, Inspector. Can I help?"

"Mr. King actually asked to speak to you but you can help, yes. Perhaps you can explain to him that our laws are very strict in Holland. He can go to prison for life for murder. Would you explain that to him please."

"I didn't do it," yelled King, leaping to his own defence. "I haven't killed anyone." He turned to Bliss, eyes pleading, voice cracking. "You know it wasn't me, Dave. It couldn't have been me that threw him overboard, could it?"

"How do I know? You're the only one who claims to have seen him go, and you certainly stole his car. Right now I'm not about to believe anything you say."

King was miles away, malignant thoughts of Motsom burning into his brain—*the bastard set me up*.

"Nosmo—are you listening?" said Bliss, prodding him.

"Sorry, Dave ..."

"I said, why should I believe you?"

"Because I told you what happened. I told you I didn't see who went over." Dropping his face into his hands in exasperation, he pleaded innocence, "I wouldn't have been stupid enough to push the guy over, then try to save him, would I?"

"You might have ..." started Bliss, pausing to think of countless analogies: Firemen setting fires then dashing heroically to the rescue; masked bandits ripping off their disguises and joining the pursuit; child abductors painstakingly searching the back woods and, most appropriately, murderers leading the hunt ... *"See, it couldn't be me ... I wouldn't be helping if it was me ..."* "You might have," he repeated without explanation.

"What, and then be daft enough to pinch his ruddy car?"

The Dutch inspector didn't wait for Bliss. "Then explain how you got his car key?"

It was true. Motsom had given him keys to the Renault, together with instructions to drive the car ashore if LeClarc failed to turn up. "If he has gone overboard," Motsom had said, "he's probably long dead, or, if he ain't dead, there's bugger all anybody can do to save him. Plus, if he ain't dead, I want to make sure our people find him, not theirs. So, we've got to get his car off or they'll know he's disappeared. O.K.?"

Nosmo's fervent prayer that LeClarc would turn up when they reached Holland wasn't answered. Now he was being accused of murder, car theft at the very least. And where was Motsom?

Billy Motsom had hidden his own car amongst hundreds of others in the port parking lot, and walked to a bar in town. The bar, a stones throw from the police station, doubled as a meeting place for leather-faced trawlermen—a few, the younger ones, still holding on to all their fingers. The stink of stale fish vied with smoke from a dozen pipes, but the smell of brewed coffee was overweening and Motsom took a cup with him to the payphone in the corner.

"Get me a boat, a big one," He spat into the mouthpiece. "King's been arrested, but he's safe, he doesn't know the plan ... The fat boy? ... How should I know? Swimming I hope ... Just get the eff'n boat."

Slamming down the handset, he turned to the room and realized he had brought everything to a halt. Like characters in a still from a forty-year-old black and white movie, everyone was now glaring at him: Cups, pipes, cigarettes, and hands frozen in mid-air. He smiled, a false toothy grin, jerked his shoulders as if to say, "Oops, sorry," and the room gradually restarted.

Just two streets away the imposing facade of the police station gave D.I. Bliss and his two colleagues a window on the entire dock area, and the giant slab-sided ferry on which they had arrived.

"It's bloody mayhem down there," said Smythe, with a hint of glee. "I bet they're pretty pissed off. First we're two hours late, then every bloody car and truck gets pulled to pieces. They could riot."

Bliss continued gazing out of the gargantuan window, captivated by the enormity of the situation. "Nothing else we could do," he shrugged. "He's either in a car, truck, or container, or he really did go for a swim."

Wilson stepped in, "What about the vehicles that have already gone? He could have been in one of them."

"Possible," mused Bliss. "But the locals have set up road blocks on the two main roads. They're checking everything that could have come off the ship."

"No point in starting a big sea search until we're sure," ruminated Wilson, staring at the grey horizon— sea and sky as one, thinking: helicopters, lifeboats, rescue Zodiacs, coastguard cutters.

Bliss was on the point of saying, "Correct," when a Dutch constable approached. "The captain is ready for you now, Sir."

Another equally vast room; a hurriedly assembled group of Dutch officers, two women and eight men sitting on long, brown leather, settees—five either side of an enormous low table scattered with coffee cups, cigarette packets, and the debris of some hastily eaten pastries. Each officer, note-pad at the ready, eagerly followed Bliss to the head of the table where Captain Jahnssen met him.

"Call me Jost," said the captain, ramrod straight, greeting Bliss like a foreign dignitary. Eager to impress, he continued effusively, "I have been to the headquarters of the British police at Scotland Yard," as if in doing so he had worshipped at a great shrine—The Vatican or Taj Mahal, perhaps.

Introductions were brief, though Bliss wondered why they bothered. All the men seemed to be called Caas or Jan, and both the woman were Yolanda.

"Right," Bliss started, feeling it was expected of him, knowing that neither of his officers were in a state fit to talk. "I know some of you have been involved with this case for the last few days but I'll quickly give you a .. " He stopped, mid-sentence. One Yolanda and a couple of Jans were attempting to write down everything he said. He lowered his tone and made eye contact with the female, a Scandinavian blonde with huge blue eyes that seemed to trap him—snake-like: Kaa captivating Mowgli in the Jungle Book. "I'll tell you when to take notes."

Continuing, he broke the attraction by focussing on D.C. Smythe who'd started snoring, exhausted, at the back of the room. "In the past three years we have lost eight of our top computer experts," he explained, personally shouldering responsibility for the entire population of the United Kingdom. "Eight of our most valuable assets in the field of computer technology have either been murdered, committed suicide, or simply vanished." Pausing for effect, he checked the face of each man in turn, skipped the blonde, and ended with the captain. "I won't bore you with unnecessary details," he added, "but you might want to take a few notes." Then he looked up, found Yolanda's eyes and lost his momentum. "Um ... eight ... um ... eight computer experts ..." he mumbled, froze, then got his act together by carefully checking his thumbnails. "We've lost eight and the Americans have lost some as well ...

The first one was ..." he paused again and looked at the captain, "Maybe I won't bother with names, they're irrelevant really. The first one disappeared without trace. Brilliant man—just developed a new process for making chips ..." He stopped, briefly examining their faces. Did they understand? Unsure, he interpreted: "Computer processors." Yolanda's wide blue eyes signified comprehension. Damn! Trapped again.

"He went for a ride on his bicycle and was never seen again," he pushed on, careful to avoid looking to his right, Yolanda's side.

"Number two ... It was put down as a suicide. Drove his car straight off a bridge into the front of an express train. Only bits and pieces were ever found and they were burnt to a cinder."

"Cinder?" she questioned, her voice striking him like a tenor bell—he knew which bell.

"Um, yes. Ashes, nothing left," he said, struggling to answer without making eye contact. "The body was never properly identified. The car exploded like a bomb when the train hit it—a huge fire, the train driver was burnt to death as well."

Kidding himself that he'd broken her spell, he risked a quick glance and immediately regretted it. She was waiting for him—her soft eyes drawing him in, holding him, mesmerizing him. I don't need this, he thought, breaking free, but with a quiver in his voice continued. "Number three—encryption specialist, another complete disappearance. Went for a stroll with his dogs one Sunday afternoon. The dogs came back. No trace of him ... Number four was different. The only female. She was working on an ultra-high speed system to connect banks around the world. She did kill herself, even left a suicide note. It seems she was being blackmailed but we never found out why ... Numbers five and six were friends. Two of the most seasoned computer boffins ..." he paused and translated, "two of the world's top computer experts. Worked for rival companies but were responsible for some major advances in computers. They disappeared on a fishing trip off the south coast. One of them owned a forty-foot cruiser and it just ... aah! . . um." Flipping open his hands he made a "pt" sound with his lips. "Gone," he said, expressively, expecting everyone to understand they had simply vanished into thin air.

"Seven was a couple of months ago. A major loss to the industry. This guy had just developed an entirely new kind of processor, a complete revolution. He was on his way back from California for a presentation to the company president, but never arrived. His plane blew up over the ocean. His body was never found, neither were his plans or prototypes."

"I remember that," said a Caas, "I zink that was the plane crash that killed all those Americans."

"Correct," said Bliss. "Two hundred and forty-three—twenty of 'em kids."

"Do you honestly think they would do that?" demanded the other Yolanda in puritanical outrage, her dour face and lank, chopped, prisoner's hairstyle as austere as her tone.

Bliss shrugged, "I don't know—it's possible. Some people will do anything for money."

Now, with a sweeping glance around the room, he changed stance and tone. No longer the lecturer, he relaxed to being a fellow cop. "Those are all the one's we're sure are connected. There was an eighth one, a strange man who worked on his own and sold ideas to the highest bidder. He lived in an old farmhouse in the Welsh mountains."

"What is Welsh?" interrupted one of the Jans.

"Sorry ... Wales. You know, the little country stuck on the west of England ..." Jan's puzzled frown suggested that geography was not one of his strong points so Bliss tried making it easy, "It's part of England."

D.C. Wilson, hailing from Cardiff, roused with a start, muttering, "Bloody not part of England," but Bliss cut him short with a glare. "Anyway, this man disappeared sometime in the past three or four months. No one seems quite sure exactly when."

He looked around the room, checking the officers one at a time, taking in the fact they nearly all wore glasses, and all but one were smoking. Even Yolanda No.1, as he had decided to call her, had a cigarette in her hand, and he felt himself shudder at the sight of her nicotine stained slender fingers. "Now," he said, taking a deep breath. "Now to Roger LeClarc."

Memories of the briefing room at Scotland Yard just three weeks earlier zipped through his mind—the briefing room and the pompous superintendent from Special Ops.

"Right, listen up chaps," the superintendent had begun, imagining himself still in the RAF where he had been nothing more than a corporal. "This is a big one. Screw this up and you'll all be back in uniform." He stopped and glowered at Sergeant Jones, "Name?" he demanded with a nod.

"Jones, Sir. Serious Crime Squad."

"Well Sergeant Jones," he started, almost conversationally, "smoking is a serious crime when I'm in the room." Then he boomed, "So put it out—this isn't a bloody bar."

Jones sheepishly stubbed out the cigarette amid the jeers of his colleagues and someone flicked a remote control, unveiling a monster television. "Watch this," commanded the superintendent.

"Roger LeClarc, 31 years." said a caption under an unflattering close-up of a bloated face with unruly hair. "Senior I.T. Consultant, ACT Telecommunications 1999," appeared under the heading, "Occupation."

A series of mug shots followed—family album types mainly: holidays, weddings, birthdays, and people doing stupid things; then a short section of home movie—Brighton beach in front of the Grand Hotel, Roger's distended white belly and folds of flab flopping up and down as he hopped in and out of the surf.

Then a more sinister collection, including a couple of video clips bearing the hallmarks of police surveillance cameras: Roger squeezing himself into his Renault; Roger on a train—asleep, snoring; Roger in his office—through a window; Roger eating; Roger's parents house in Watford; Roger coming out of the old terraced house near Watford station; Roger fumbling with his flies in a public toilet—"Don't ask," said the superintendent as a giggle rippled round the room. "O.K. Chaps," he added, as the video wound down, "everything points to this fat git as the target—in fact we've good info. he's next on the list. We've reason to believe that sometime in the next few weeks he will be snatched, and it's your job to prevent it—any questions?"

A youngish female voice piped up from the back. "Is he married, Sir?"

"Why ... Do you fancy him?" brought a hail of laughter.

"Have we got a full description, Sir. Address, date of birth, that sort of thing?" asked a young detective leaning forward in the front row.

"Naturally, Officer," he said, turning to his staff sergeant. "Pass out the portfolios, Sergeant, there's a good chap." He paused long enough for most people to get a blue folder with CONFIDENTIAL typed in the top right hand corner, then studied his copy. "You'll find everything you need in here, including rotas. Three teams of four—Inspector, sergeant, and two constables. Anything else?"

"Yes, Sir," queried one of the sergeants. "What's happening to them, the missing whiz kids—Do we know?"

Superintendent Edwards slumped in his chair and massaged his face in thought, taking time to decide how much to reveal. "We know for sure this isn't some two-bit ransom job," he began after a few moments. "Whoever's doing this ain't after their piggy banks. But, at this particular moment in time ..." He paused, still undecided, and finished by saying, "At this moment in time we have absolutely no idea.

"Dismissed," he shouted, above the buzz of speculation, stifling further questions.

"Wait," he commanded, stilling the crescendo of shuffling feet. "One last thing ..." then he paused while a couple of fleet footed officers were motioned back into the room. "LeClarc must not find out he is being watched under any circumstances. According to his boss he's a strange character. There's no telling what he might do if he thinks he's a target. So keep your heads down and jolly good luck chaps."

"Bombs away," shouted one of the officers, keeping his back to the superintendent.


Bliss, cautiously evading eye contact with Yolanda, completed his briefing, then reeled off a list of tasks for Captain Jahnssen and his officers. "You're already searching the cars as they come off but you'll need to search the trucks and containers. We'll need a complete search of the ship; interview crewmembers; photograph the possible crime scene—the railings on the aft boat deck; check LeClarc's car and all his belongings for clues; talk to as many passengers as possible—someone must have seen something." He looked up, had he missed anything? "Perhaps you could assign an officer to help me with translation and liaison duties," he said, then immediately realized what was about to happen. His mind raced back to the annual police sports day the previous August. Marty McLean, complete with kilt, threw the 20 lb hammer high into the air and totally in the wrong direction. He saw it coming as he stood on the track, warming up for the half-marathon. Rooted to the spot, not knowing which way to jump, he had watched with fascination as it hit the ground in front of him, bounced, and tapped his leg with little force.

Just like the hammer, he could see what was coming and stood, transfixed. Although not déjà-vu, the feeling was certainly similar as blue-eyed, blonde-haired, Yolanda No.1 slunk alongside and zapped him full force with her gaze. "Ze captain says I must do everything you would like, Sir," she said, and he felt a lump rising in his throat. Christ, he thought, this is bloody ridiculous, this sort of thing only happens in trashy novels and second rate TV movies. He swallowed hard, saying, "Dave, um, please call me Dave."

"Okey dokey, Dave," she replied, her English learned from CNN.

Bliss found himself staring again, but then realized he was on a two-way street. You must be almost old enough to be her father, he scoffed to himself; anyway don't be ridiculous—you're in enough trouble already; not to mention that you're still sinking in emotional quagmire from your last imbroglio—O.K ... *You win—don't rub it in.*

Quickly burying his head in Roger's subject profile, he sought an escape route in professionalism.

"I need a secure phone line to England right away," he said coolly, keeping his head down, "and a set of radios on the same frequency as your captain. And coffee, lots of coffee."

She didn't hesitate, "The coffee's over zhere, help yourself," she pointed, then headed off. "I'll get telephone and radios."

He watched as she left, her pert backside swishing elegantly from side to side, wishing he wasn't quite so curled round the edges, that his hair wasn't greying and tousled, that he had taken more care of skin, and that he'd put on a fresh shirt. No matter; some women still prefer the slightly wrinkled older man look—providing they're tall and reasonably slim, he thought, slicking back his hair, sucking in his stomach, pulling himself upright.

By the time he had poured coffee she was back with the radios. "Come with me please," she said leading him to a phone.

The, ex-R.A.F superintendent, Michael Edwards, was in a foul mood on the phone. "What an effing balls up, Bliss," he bawled, leaving no room for explanation or excuse. All he knew was what the Ops room had told him—that the team had lost their target—but the worst was yet to come. He still knew nothing of the possibility that LeClarc had jumped ship, or of King being arrested in possession of his car. "And where the hell is Jones?" shouted the voice in London. He didn't know about the sergeant's accident either.

Ten minutes later he had the answers, didn't like any of them, and was ruining what was left of Bliss' awful day. Finally, Bliss had taken all the abuse he could handle—it wasn't his fault, he told himself; Jones and the other two had screwed things up and let him down.

"Sir," he shouted down the phone, halting the superintendent mid-flight. "I am doing my best. I've been on duty for more than twenty-four hours. I'm too tired to argue. I need back up and co-operation. The Dutch are very helpful, but until we've searched every inch of the ship and every vehicle we just don't know where he is. I'll call you back in fifteen minutes;, I have to go now, Captain Jahnssen wants me urgently."

Edwards was still winding himself up when Bliss slammed down the phone.

"Ze captain doesn't want you," Yolanda corrected him naïvely, handing back his coffee.

"I know that," he sighed, slumping his backside against a desk.

"Oh," she exclaimed, catching on, waiving a finger in his face, "I zink you are a naughty boy."

"Ah shit, Yolanda, where the hell is he? The fat slob has probably found some bloody warm hidey-hole on the ship and overslept. Either that or he's playing a trick on us and he'll suddenly pop up and shout, 'April Fool.'"

"What is this April Fool?"

"Oh, never mind. Come on let's go and help search. The first thing I want to do is to go through King's possessions. There has to be a clue there somewhere."

Yolanda walked to the window and stuck her nose against it as she screwed up her eyes and stared down at the port. "Zair is zee Renault, by the port police office," she said, stabbing the glass with an index finger. "Mr. King's bags must still be in zair."

Bliss peered over her shoulder, his eyes following her finger, and he recognised the little green car though the fuzzy mist of her hot breath on the windowpane.

"Let's go back to the port then," he murmured, his mouth no more than two inches from her ear.

Activity at the port was simultaneously at a fevered pitch and a standstill. Customs, police, and Koninklijke Marechaussee officers were frantically searching each and every vehicle, while drivers and passengers idly stood around wondering what on earth was happening.

An impromptu press conference was taking place in the port manager's office. News of the situation was spreading quickly throughout the community where almost every household survived on the wages of at least one port employee. The reporter for the local paper and stringers for two dailies were hounding the ship's captain for more information, but he could offer little. "No ... We don't know for sure if anyone's fallen overboard."

"Why not?"

"Because there were no witnesses. Just one good citizen, an ex-policeman, who said he thought someone had fallen." The captain, unaware of King's arrest, knowing nothing about the stolen car, was happy to give him the credit. "He raised the alarm, even managed to launch a life raft, but in the rough seas it would have been difficult, almost impossible, for a swimmer to get into it without help."

"And his chances?"

"Without a life jacket, rough seas, middle of the night—he might have survived thirty to forty minutes, possibly an hour, no more ..." He shook his head from side to side just once as he finished his reply, "A thousand to one against—no chance really."

"And this person," queried the local reporter, a sombre beaky-looking man who spent most of his time nosing out obituaries, "He had no life jacket?"

"We don't know. I told you. We don't know if anyone actually went overboard."

A female stringer jumped at him, her deep masculine voice loaded with criticism as she did her best to lay the groundwork for a juicy controversy. "What would you say to people who might suggest you should have done more, Captain. After all, two hours searching was not very long."

He gave her a critical stare. Scheming witch, he thought, trying to make a catastrophe out of a disaster, trying to stir shit —wasn't the unfortunate death of a human being in itself enough to make the front page.

"Miss, as I have already explained," he began firmly, as if lecturing a fractious child, "firstly, we don't know for sure that anyone is missing. Secondly, if, and I stress the 'if', if someone fell overboard, they could not have survived more than an hour, and," his voice rose in crescendo, "thirdly, two thousand passengers would have been greatly inconvenienced and upset if we had wasted any more time."

The stringer sat back with a satisfied smirk. Now she had her story, and with it would have great delight in bringing this arrogant Englishman down a peg or two. The headline was already buzzing around in her head, the story already written, all she needed now was to top it with a few quotes from the local police, a few facts from the shipping company, and she would be ready to e-mail her editor—Priority: "Man sacrificed to please passengers."


Roger had not been sacrificed, not yet anyway. Alive, but not well, he was still bouncing along on top of his personal watercraft, waking from time to time, but never managing to achieve full awareness. Each time his mind neared the surface his eyes would float around, checking the ropes and peering in search of a rescue vessel. One sweep was all he could manage on most occasions, but as he drifted back into a coma-like state, he would always think of Trudy and mentally cry out for her.

Trudy's mother, Lisa McKenzie, had been crying for Trudy for seven days, four hours, and thirty minutes. She had counted every one as she sat on an old wooden chair in her apartment kitchen, surrounded by goodwill cards from relatives, friends, and people she'd never met, never even heard of. One, from a complete stranger in Scotland, had even contained a cheque for £5,000 with a wish she should spend it to find her little lassie. The signatory had added a postscript: "I lost my lassie twenty years ago and hope you don't suffer the same way as I." She'd cried for hours, holding it in her hands, feeling the heartache in the words. Crying for the man and his suffering; not for Trudy—Trudy would come home.

The chair had become her universe. She rarely left it, rising only to use the toilet or, occasionally, to relieve the unbearable cramp in her legs. Even then she would wait, deliberately punishing herself with excruciating pain as her limbs were starved of blood and oxygen. The chair was her whip—she a flagellant. Suffering so her Trudy would not have to. Suffering so she would not forget Trudy, even for a moment. Suffering because she loved her daughter so much she wanted to suffer for her. Suffering because she was a mother.

The chair had also become the symbol of her determination, as well as a tangible reminder of the past and of normality. The dependable little chair: a variety of small Windsor with graceful arms, and a seat hand carved to accept a pair of buttocks, had been her father's, and possibly his father's before him. It was a depository of unforgettable memories: Bouncing on Daddy's knees in front of the fire; Father

Christmas sitting to eat his mince-pie and drink his milk; a ladder to reach the cookie jar. Upside down, covered with a sheet, it had become a tent, a play-house, even a rocketship. And at least two daddies, her's and Trudy's, had used it as a bed, falling asleep, exhausted after supper, too worn out to make it as far as the couch.

The phone rang for the thousandth time and disap-pointment struck for the thousandth time—Trudy's father. Her racing heart sank.

"No news Peter. Nothing," she replied to his query, the fifth today as far as she could remember. He sounds worried to death, she thought, strange, considering the way he abandoned her; abandoned us.

"Of course I'll call you," she continued, answer-ing his plea. "I'm sure she's alright ..." she began, then wished she hadn't as her voice cracked and the tears flowed.

Is he crying too? she wondered, hearing the hollow silence as he held his hand over the mouthpiece. "Peter, don't worry ..." she started, then paused, questioning: Why shouldn't he? I'm scared shitless; why shouldn't he worry?

"Peter I'll call you—the moment I hear anything."

He made her promise, as he had done at the end of every call.

"I promise, Love," she said, then questioned—Why did I say that? Why did I say "Love" like that? It's just a an old habit, she told herself, a very old habit; but something deep inside her told her to straighten it out, that it wasn't right, that she still hated him, that he did-n't deserve niceness—certainly not from her. "I promise I'll call you, Peter," she added coolly then replaced the receiver without awaiting a response. It rang again before she could remove her hand.

Damn! she thought, picking it up straight away. It's him again, wanting to know what I meant. What did I mean—why the hell did I say it?

"Yes?"

"Mrs. McKenzie?" queried a strangled far-off voice. "This is Margery, Trude's friend. What's happening?"

It took a second to sink in as she struggled to clear away the notion that it was Peter, then a flashbulb went off in her mind. "Margery!" A dozen questions flooded her thoughts and she started three of them all at the same time. "What ...? When ...? Where ...?" she stammered, then started again, taking a deep breath; slowing herself down. "Where are you? The police have been trying to find you for a week."

"Holidays with Mum and Dad—camping in France. What's happened to Trude?"

"She gone missing. It's in all the papers."

"I know, I saw her picture," she screeched, breathlessly, a well-thumbed copy of *The Daily Telegraph*, nearly a week old, in her hand. "I'm in a phone box and my token thingies are running out," cried Margery, in a panic.

"Where is she?" exploded Lisa, fearing they would be cut off, or Margery would somehow be struck dead without revealing Trudy's whereabouts.

"I don't know, Mrs. McKenzie. I've no idea ..." she started, then hesitated in thought for the briefest second. "What about Roger?"

"Roger who?" responded Lisa, having forgotten all about Trudy's computer contacts.

"My money's almo—" was all Margery could say before a metallic clunk and a continuous buzz chopped her off.

An hour later (a lifetime for Lisa, sitting motionless in agony, screaming inwardly for the phone to ring, unable to call anyone for fear of tying up the line), Margery phoned back, this time from a police station.

"Who's Roger? Where does he live?" she screeched into the phone.

"He's some computer guy she's always going on about; reckons he loves her; say's he's got a ..."

Lisa had heard enough. "Where does he live? What's his phone number? Who is he?" Anxiety and hope intermingled as she reeled off the questions.

"I don't really know," replied Margery, vaguely, not sure which of the questions she was answering. "But he lives in Watford somewhere and works in London." She paused, "I've got a picture of him ..."

"Where?" she cut in, desperate for information.

"Probably at home. It's only a photocopy. Trudy's got the photo. We was just mucking around on the school photocopier ..."

"How can I get it?" she shot back, uninterested in technicalities. "When are you coming back?"

"Hang on a minute, I'll ask Dad."

The line went quiet and she panicked fearing another disconnection, but by ramming the handset tight against her ear caught the echoes of an altercation. "Don't argue. Please don't argue," she pleaded uselessly, then Margery took her hand off the mouthpiece and sobbed, "I want to come and help, but Dad say's he can't afford a plane ticket. It'll take three days to drive back."

Lisa McKenzie's heart leapt a little. "It's O.K. I'll pay," she said, remembering the Scotsman's £5,000. "Give me the phone number of the police station and stay there."

Taking down the number with exaggerated care her mind was telling her she was missing something, that Margery must know more, that she shouldn't let the girl go without getting more information. Trudy was out there somewhere—Margery must know more.

"Where is she?" she cried angrily.

"I don't know honest Mrs. Mc ..."

"I don't believe you ..." she started accusingly, then broke down, "I'm sorry Margery ... it's just that I'm so worried"

Calming herself, apologizing again and again, she checked the number with Margery three times before ringing off, then instantly regretted putting the phone down on the crying girl. Oh my God, she thought, I don't even know where she is.

Stunned, confused, and overwhelmed by the situation, she vacillated between Peter, an airline, the police, and the bank. Each time she looked up one number she would convince herself to call another. At last, a full two minutes later, she plumped for the police.

"She's in France, eh, Mrs. McKenzie," a familiar voice responded, "O.K. we'll be round to see you right away. Just stay there."

"I'm not going anywhere, officer. Please hurry," she replied, slumping in the chair and finding support, even comfort, in the curved backrest.


Junction Road was quieter now it was mid-morning in Watford. The commuters and children were all safely huddled in their offices and classrooms. In just a week or so Junction Road would become a different place. School holidays would begin and the little street would be turned into the Wild West, Wembley stadium, or a Mighty Morphin adventure park, depending on which group of kids happened to be most active at that time of day or night.

The two Watford police detectives had been given little information about Roger LeClarc.

"Just get down there and make a few door-to-door enquiries," their sergeant had said, without enthusiasm. "Apparently this bloke disappeared off a ship last night in the middle of the North Sea, right under the nose of a Met. police squad. God knows how they think he might have got back here by now."

"What are we s'posed to be looking for Serg?"

"Buggered if I know, lad. It seems as though the Met. had him under surveillance for awhile—seen him go to the place a few times ... Just as long as you put in some sort of report ..." he trailed off. Helping another police force out of an embarrassing spot wasn't a high priority.

They parked opposite Roger's house and sat in the car watching it for awhile—killing time. Like a loaf of bread with the crust sliced off one end, the terrace's architectural equilibrium had been unbalanced by the bombing of the last in the row. It now appeared incomplete, no longer matching the opposing terrace backing onto the railway cutting. The rubble of the amputated end house had been cleared, but, without anyone to care for it, the land had grown wild, and was now the local waste dump—an eyesore or an adventure playground depending on perspective.

"Bit of a shit-hole," said one of the detectives easing himself out of the car, advancing on the front door of the end house.

The other detective, a forty-something Roger Moore look-alike, scrambled over the bombsite alongside the house, making his way to the rear. He paused, part way, to look up at the wall which now formed the end of the terrace. It had no windows, none being needed for its original purpose, but the outline of three bricked-up fireplaces, one upstairs and two down, could clearly be seen. Black bitumen had been lathered over the wall, and replenished periodically, to provide a weatherproof coating.

"Can you see anything?" shouted the other detective, poking his head around the corner of the house, his knock on the front door bringing no response.

"Hang on a minute. I've just got stung," he replied irritably, shaking and rubbing his hand, then lashing out with his foot at the offending nettle.

"The back wall's fallen down, I can get over the bricks," he called a few seconds later, after kicking a path through the nettles.

Another voice joined in, "Oy. What are you two doing?" The ever watchful George Mitchell at No. 71, a veteran of the Royal Engineers and frightened of no one, was on his doorstep, ramrod straight and chest puffed out in a no-nonsense stance. "I'm going to call the law," he continued, his confidence wavering ever so slightly.

"It's O.K., Granddad. We are the law," said the detective in the street, producing his warrant card and strolling over to George.

"What do you know about the people in the end house," he asked casually.

George Mitchell, eyed the card critically, saying, "Don't know much 'bout 'em mate, to be honest. Used to be a family of Greeks or Turks there ..." he paused, concentration furrowing his brow, "I think they was Greeks, nice family. Papadropolis or some such name. Moved out about a year ago ..." he paused, spotting Mrs. Ramchuran out of the corner of his eye, the voices drawing her to inspect the sheen on her front doorstep, and he dragged her in. "I was just saying, Mrs. R., the people over the road, Greeks, nice people, you remember?"

She looked up at the suit-clad detectives in feigned surprise, thinking: Mormons, encyclopaedias or debt collectors. "Yes I remember the Greeks, Mr. Mitchell," she began defensively. "But they been gone a long time. There's a new man there now. I don't know him; hardly ever seen him."

George took up the conversation again, sticking rigidly to facts, but twisting each into a complaint. "Young bloke, funny looking bugger, works odd hours, never does nuvving to the place, comes and goes all times of the night but he's not there now. His car's not here." He searched the street. "Little green foreign thing." Another complaint. "It were here yesterday."

Roger Moore's double had fought his way back to the street and came alongside his partner. "Can't see anyone in there," he said, nodding back over his shoulder. "If I'd banged any harder on the back door it would have caved in."

George Mitchell, *Neighbourhood Watch* personified, beamed . *See, I told you he weren't there*. "I could've have saved you mucking up your suit if you'd asked," he said, inspecting the detective's trousers.

"Oh shit," moaned the officer, backing away, scrubbing at a greasy mess with a handkerchief, spreading the stain even further. "This is the second suit I've ruined in a week, my missus'll kill me."

"If I could get a few details," said the remaining detective, attempting to restore professional integrity by pulling out his notebook. "Perhaps you would call if you see anyone go in. Would you mind?"

"Not at all, Officer," said George, beaming with importance—*this is the life ... helping the police with their enquiries*. "But, ah, what's he s'posed to have done?"

"Oh nothing, Sir, it's just routine enquiries. We're not too sure where he is, that's all."

"Roger Wilco," said George Mitchell, thinking: You expect me to believe that? Fifty-five million people in the country and you're worried about the odd fat freak—I don't think so. But he shrugged off the snub. "It's none of my business, but he ain't in there I can assure you of that. There ain't nobody in there that's for definite."

Trudy would have disagreed had she been awake. And had she been awake she would have cried out to the detectives to rescue her, but, although less than twenty feet away, they would have heard nothing.

As the men drove away, one still engrossed in his trousers, muttering, "She'll bloody murder me," another police car was headed in their direction from across town. The driver, the "ex-RAF" superintendent's staff sergeant, had his boss on the radio. "I've seen LeClarc's parents, they're as much in the dark as us. His mum reckons he's never been in any sort of trouble, believe it or not she actually called him "A good little boy." Shit Guv! You've seen the size of him and he's thirty-odd. Anyhow, he lives at home; no close friends, so far as they know; goes to work, comes home, usual crap. We went through his stuff and, as far as they could tell, nothing's missing, only the stuff he took with him. He told 'em about the thing in Holland but sort of played it down. Oh ... this is a bit weird ... they reckoned they knew nothing about the house on Junction Road—you know the place ... I'm on my way to there now to take a shufty."

Roger's mother did know the house on Junction Road, had even been there with him, one Saturday afternoon, though he'd made her stay in the car. "It's a friend of mine," he'd told her as he parked outside, the Renault loaded with groceries. "I won't be a minute."

He'd waited ten minutes, spying on her from an upstairs window, letting her stew in the stifling afternoon heat with the ice-cream, butter, and frozen peas. Curiosity and impatience finally forced open the car door and Roger flew down the front steps. "Sorry,

Mum," he said bundling her back into the Renault and driving off.

"Who were it?" she demanded, craning to peer into the blank windows, suspecting a female; suspecting she was being cheated on.

"Just a friend," he repeated, knowing it would drive her insane.

"Sergeant 247639, Mitchell," George introduced himself to the sergeant at his door, thinking—"Quite a day." "I've just been talking to your lads, Serg. Nasty stain one of 'em had. Doubt if it'll come out."

"Yes, Sergeant Mitchell," he started, then changed his tone and added conspiratorially, "Mind if I call you George?"

He hadn't minded, placing the policeman from London as a peer, and they sat in his kitchen like a couple of old soldiers, chin-wagging over a cuppa for fifteen minutes before getting around to Roger.

"Like I told the others," he said, "Funny looking bloke—he looked like the snowmen we made as kids; just two balls, one big'un for the body and a little'un for the head; no neck to speak of and stubby little arms and legs."

That's our man, thought the staff sergeant, nodding in the direction of the house on the other side of the road. "Who does it belong to George— who owns the place?"

"It's his of course, as far as I know. I saw him talking to the real estate bloke the day it were put up for sale."

What's going on? puzzled the policeman; his mother would have known surely ..."Are you sure it's his?"

George, affronted, went on the offensive. "It's his I'm telling you. I can even give you the name of the estate agents if you like," and, without waiting for a response, he did. "It were Jefferson's up the High Street."

"Interesting," the staff sergeant mused, mulling over Roger's motives, wondering why he'd never told his parents. "What do you know about the place George?"

George Mitchell knew a great deal, most of his knowledge first hand, the wartime holding his most vivid memories. "It were August 1940, in the Blitz, the end 'ouse got bombed," he recounted. "A lot of people round here reckoned it was one of our own. See, there weren't no real air raid that night, not so far as we knew anyhow. Oh the sirens went off all right, dronin' on and on, but no one heard nuvving else until, 'Bang!' Bloody near shook me old mum's false teeth out it did." He paused long enough for a chuckle at his joke—and the memory. "Then we looked out and the 'ouse were gone. Just like that. 'Course it were the blackout so we couldn't do nowt 'til the morning. Then they found 'em hiding under the stairs, only the stairs were right on top of 'em." Clapping his hands in emphasis he added, "Flat as pancake."

"It was never rebuilt?"

"Nah. The son had been sent to Australia," said George, his strong cockney accent turning the country into something sounding more like a horse-trailer. "'Course the big tragedy were next door, where that bloke of yours lives."

Ears pricked, the sergeant leant forward.

"Oh yes," George continued, now deeply lost in the past. "The poor bastards," he said slowly. "The whole family went. Trampled to death in that underground disaster. You remember?" he said, as if it were an order.

"No, I don't actually."

George, puzzled, gave him a look, then smiled, more to himself than the sergeant. "Silly me, 'course not—you ain't old enough. Anyhow it were about a year later, maybe more." He paused, searching the floor for the exact date, "I dunno. Anyhow it ain't important," he said finally, giving up. Then continued, "Anyhow, after what happened to the couple on the end—flat as a pancake ... under the stairs—the family next door were petrified. They had three kids and they was worried to death the kids would get killed. So they took 'em down to 'is brother's in Hampshire for a holiday, to get away from it, the bombing that is, and they was all coming back by Tube. Brother, wife, and all." He stopped, took a long swig of tea and swilled it noisily around his mouth, puffing out his cheeks, as if deliberately allowing the tension to rise, then gulped it down and finished his story. "They was just coming up the stairs to change platforms when a bomb, a big 'un, dropped straight down the hole. It didn't go off, but everyone panicked and they all got crushed to death. Hundreds of 'em were killed, maybe thousands. They never got the bodies out you know, just buried 'em all together ... Tragedy ... Poor bastards."

Closing his eyes for a second, he sat back, breathing deeply, recalling every macabre detail as if he had been there. A notion he dispelled with his next words. "I was in Africa at the time. Rommel and El Alamein, you know. " A faraway look glazed his eyes and the crease of a smile warmed his mouth for a few seconds, then he straightened up. "It were a tragedy—poor bastards."

"And after the war?"

"Oh, there's been eight or ten different families since then. Most of 'em foreigners." He hesitated, "Not that I've got anything against them you understand. Nice enough, most of 'em anyhow. Take Mrs. R. next door, good as gold she is, she'll do me washing ..."

The police sergeant started to rise. "Thank you, George, most informative. Now, I don't suppose you'd know anybody with a key to the place would you? I'd like to have a little snoop around."

George fumbled in his pocket sheepishly. "Well, I shouldn't let on really, but the Greeks gave me a key when they moved out. Just to let the water and the 'lectricity people in. 'Course he might have changed the locks, but we could give it a try."

Slivers of faded saffron yellow cracked off the front door as it opened with an arthritic creak and the odour of abandonment—fungus, damp earth and musty clothing— signalled to it being unoccupied. A pile of mail lay swept to one side by the door and the staff sergeant scooped a handful. "Anybody home," he shouted, making George jump, dropping it back on the pile. "Junk."

There was no reply. Trudy was there but she couldn't hear.

They searched the entire house; it didn't take long. Two rooms upstairs and two down, plus the cupboard under the stairs, and the poky little bathroom tacked onto the back in the early 1950s, at a time when the combined introduction of running water, piped gas, and electricity turned personal cleanliness from a chore to a pleasure. Each room contained more or less the same. "Garbage," according to the policeman. "Just a load of old garbage." And everywhere the same powerful smell, the exhaled breath of billions of unseen creatures all busily devouring the fabric of the place.

"Look at it, George," he said scornfully. "Nobody's living here. Scraps of bloody firewood, that's all there is. Look at this chair," he exclaimed. "A fly couldn't sit on this without breaking it." And to prove his point he put his foot on it and pushed. "Oh Shit!" he exclaimed, as the chair splintered into a half a dozen pieces.

"I'm buggered if I know what he's been living on," said George, obviously dispassionate about the damage. "There's no furniture to speak of, no food, there's not even a bed."

There was a bed—Roger's bed—hidden in Roger's secret room. It was an oversized single bed; an expensive bed with a floral patterned pocket sprung mattress, and it had a very solid looking fancy brass bedstead. Trudy was lying on it, dreaming of somewhere else— anywhere else. Trudy, bruised black and blue, exhausted and bleeding, was sleeping, and had fallen asleep praying that her mother would rescue her when she woke. Trudy was there alright, but neither George nor the sergeant saw her.

After carefully locking the front door behind him, and giving it a little shove with the palm of his hand, just for good measure, the sergeant pocketed the key and thanked George for his assistance.

"Happy to help Sergeant," he replied, desperately wanting to ask for the key, too embarrassed to do so.

"Call us if he comes back," the sergeant shouted getting into his car.

"That's bloomin' weird," mumbled George, scratching his nose, staring at Roger's house, then he headed for Mrs. Ramchuran's to bring her up to date.

As soon as he turned out of Junction Road the staff sergeant punched the "recall" button on his phone and was patched through to Superintendent Edwards. "Nothing here, Guv, nothing at all as it turns out, though the nosy old bugger across the street reckons the house is definitely our boy's. If he's right, I'd like to know why he didn't tell his family he'd bought it—that's pretty odd. Anyway, I'm on my way back. Any news from Holland?"

The superintendent had no news from Holland and was still attempting to contact D.I. Bliss, who had failed to call back as promised nearly two hours earlier and was verbally abusing a frightened secretary in retaliation. "Stupid girl—is this the best you can do?"

Bliss was far too busy to deal with Edwards and, in any case, was delaying the call until he had better news. He had none. They had been in Holland for five hours and he still didn't know if Roger LeClarc had been kidnapped, drowned, or twigged, he was being followed and gone into hiding. His Renault had provided few clues, although, as Bliss explained to Yolanda, while standing beside it tapping his fingers on the windshield, "The most significant evidence in any case is often the total lack of evidence."

Yolanda's pinched eyes and furrowed brow suggested she was having difficulty with the concept, so he explained, gripping an imaginary wheel, "King was driving LeClarc's car. Right? But none of King's belongings were in the car." Comprehension turned her frown to a smile and they started to laugh.

"Christ!" he shouted. "That means that wherever King's things are we might find LeClarc. King wouldn't have taken LeClarc's car and just abandoned his own stuff. He hasn't got anything with him because somebody has got it for him, somebody else must have brought it ashore." Then he completed his train of thought, speaking almost to himself. "Motsom—it has to be Motsom."

Yolanda had no idea what he was talking about as he reflected on what had occurred. His eyes, wide open, were not looking at anything as he scratched an imaginary itch on his forehead. "King was talking to a man in the bar," he began slowly, pausing for thought between each phrase.

"King went on deck and saw, or said he saw, a man fall overboard ... I know he lied about the man in the bar ... He went to Motsom's cabin as soon as he left the bridge ... He drove LeClarc's car, but why?"

Catching Yolanda by surprise he grabbed her arm, looked her straight in the eye, and said triumphantly, "Motsom paid him. And," he continued enthusiastically, "I bet Motsom has got his luggage. And I wouldn't be surprised if Motsom has got LeClarc, or at least knows where he is."

Yolanda, managing to keep up with him for the first time, cut into his deliberations. "So, where is Motsom and what car does he drive?"

Taking her hand, he dragged her across the dockside toward the car deck of the ship. A crewmember tried to stop them. "You can't come on this way, Sir. No passengers are allowed on the ..."

"Police," shouted Bliss, refusing to stop, but having to yank Yolanda's arm to prevent her being hit by one of the huge containers manoeuvring off the ship. Once inside, they ran along the empty steel deck, their footfalls reverberating like automatic fire around the massive chamber, taking the elevator to the purser's office.

The purser was expecting them. "Saw you on the monitor," he said, nodding in the direction of a bank of security screens. "A lot of people get killed on the car deck," he added, as if it were a daily occurrence.

Ignoring the admonishment, Bliss breathlessly asked for the list of registration numbers from the voyage.

"He knew exactly what I wanted," protested Bliss, as he and Yolanda headed to the captain's office a few minutes later. "He was just being bloody awkward."

"Would that be ship's registration, crew registration, Custom's ..." the purser had started, but got no further.

"Passenger's cars and trucks from last night," Bliss had shot back angrily.

With the list of vehicle numbers obtained from the captain, Bliss and Yolanda had made their way back to the main police station in her white BMW 325i convertible.

"Company car?" he asked, impressed.

"Mine," she replied, as if it were a Ford.

The entire ship had been searched, "bow to stern, mast to bilge," according to the captain, when they found him in his cabin, and no trace of LeClarc had been found. "I don't see what else we can do," he had said, clearly anxious not to be delayed further. Failure to sail within the next two hours would make it impossible for the ship to ever regain its schedule, he explained. An entire two-way crossing would have to be scrapped, leaving more than four thousand people stranded—two thousand each side of the North Sea.

Bliss had considered his request gravely, as if he alone shouldered responsibility for releasing the vessel. "I don't see any point in holding you up any longer," he had said authoritatively. "We can search the vehicles and containers once they're ashore."

Back at the station, D.C.s Wilson and Smythe were snoozing off the alcohol when Bliss found them, spread-eagled on the leather benches in the room where he'd first met Yolanda. He would have woken them, annoyed he was still working to clear up the mess that had been, in large part, due to their negligence, but Yolanda restrained him. "The poor things, zey are exhausted."

Bliss relented, conceding there was little left for them to do. The list of vehicle registration numbers had been faxed to Scotland Yard for a search of the massive computer database; inspection of all the passengers' cars had been completed, apart from those that had got through the Custom's control point before the alarm was raised. "Zhey will be picked up at the check points," explained Yolanda; and the Dutch police were now concentrating on the massive trucks. Sniffer dogs, more used to searching for dead bodies than live ones, had been brought to assist.

Fresh coffee was brewing in the briefing room. "I need that," said Bliss as a phone rang. Yolanda tapped him on the shoulder, he turned, still stunned by her looks, half wishing she would stop touching him—no intention of saying so. "It's for you," she said, glancing in the direction of the man holding the phone.

"Detective Bliss?" he introduced himself into the mouthpiece, listening attentively in case the voice should have a foreign accent. Then a dreadful noise exploded in his ear and he felt his hands shaking, his heart pumping, and the heat rising in his face as it reddened.

"Bliss. What the bloody hell are you playing at?" Superintendent Edwards screamed into phone.

"Sir ..." Bliss tried, but was cut off immediately.

"It's taken me two effing hours to get hold of you. What the hell is going on? Why didn't you call me?"

"Sorry, Sir," he lied, not in the least sorry, "I couldn't get to a phone."

"I'll have you court marshalled for this you pompous little git," the voice on the phone was carrying on, forgetting he was no longer in the armed forces. "How dare you put the phone down on me. You are relieved of duties immediately, do you understand?"

"Yes, Sir," he replied, feeling relieved. "Thank you, Sir."

"Put one of the others on. Let me speak to Wilson."

Bliss glanced at the figure crashed out on the couch—it's tempting, he thought, but inexplicably decided against it. "Sorry, Sir. He's not here at the moment."

A grunted blast of disbelief came down the line, so Bliss added, "They're busy searching."

"Right, Bliss. It's one-thirty here. What time is it there?"

"Two-thirty," he replied quickly, and avoided the temptation of adding, "As any schoolboy could have told you."

"O.K. I'm on my way over. Flying to Schiphol Airport. Arriving six p.m. Get someone to meet me. Car and driver. How far is it?"

"Damn," said Bliss, his hand held tightly over the mouthpiece as he turned to Yolanda. "Edwards is coming. How far to Schiphol?"

She held up one finger and her lips mouthed the word, "Hour."

"About an hour, Sir," he said, his eyes glued to her lips, realizing the shape of the word "hour" had formed a perfect kiss.

"Right. Make the arrangements and don't muck anything else up."

"Sir ..." he started, intending to rat on Sergeant Jones and his drinking companions, then deciding against it. "Will do, Sir."

"And hold that ship until I arrive. I want to examine it personally."

Bliss looked out of the huge window and saw the first of the passengers' cars trickling down the ramp into the belly of the ship. Smoke billowed from the huge chimney as the engines fired up, and the dock below was a hive of activity as workers scrambled to load everything as quickly as possible.

"No can do, Sir," he said quickly, with no intention of returning to disappoint the captain. "She's just leaving."

Yolanda was touching him again, tugging insistently at his sleeve, trying to draw his attention to a fax just in from England. Motsom's car had been identified on the list from the ship. He grabbed the sheet, stared at it, and could scarcely control his excitement. Thinking quickly he noisily scrunched the paper into a loose ball next to the mouthpiece and mumbled, "Bad line, Sir. Better go. Meet you at six."

Then he replaced the receiver as Yolanda was saying, "You are a very naughty boy." They laughed together—again.

# chapter five

*I*s *this a dream? This is a dream: Is a dream this?*

Trudy, chasing the words in her mind, fingered the rough sheets of the bed beneath her, Roger's bed, and was gashed by the sharp edge of reality.

"It's not a dream. It's not a dream. It's a FUCKING NIGHTMARE."

Stop screaming—you're screaming again. Stop screaming.

Why ?

You're wasting breath. No one hears you.

Roger might.

You want him to hear?

"No ... yes ... maybe ... I dunno ..." she bawled.

Now look at the mess you've made of your face.

How ... how can I look? It's pitch black in here and I can't move.

"I CAN'T MOVE!"

You're screaming again.

You'd scream if you couldn't move.

Am I dead?

Can you smell that stink?

It's awful. What is it?

You.

Me? Yuk ... I stink that bad. I must be dead.

YOU'RE NOT DEAD.

I need to pee.

Get off the bed then—get to the bucket.

"I CAN'T"

Stop screaming. You can get up if you try ... Oh ... Now you're wet again.

Told you.

You might as well go back to sleep.


She woke with a mouthful of cotton wool, minutes, hours, days, later—gulping mouthfuls of air until her chest rose and fell with reasonable rhythm.

"Where am I ... I can't breathe."

The smell from the old plastic bucket in the corner suddenly caught up to her, made her retch, and put her mind in place. Tears trickled down her cheeks as they had so often in the past week; she would have wiped them away if only her hand would co-operate.

"You can do it," the voice told her. Whose voice she wondered—God?

Finally taking control, her mind forced her hand into motion, but the pain of movement turned a whimper to a scream. "Keep trying," said the voice, and her right hand swam slowly into view through the mistiness of tears.

What's the time? she wondered, in sudden panic. What's the day, or week? She twisted her wrist for her watch but its smashed face brought back too many memories, too much anguish, too many nightmares, and she started crying again. Misery dissolved to fear. "Oh God," she cried, "I don't want to be here when he gets back."

She scanned the darkened room, her eyes seeking the glow of the computer. It was still there, her only hope, but useless without his password. I must try some more, she thought, willing herself off the bed to crawl toward the luminant screen in the corner of the room.

Her hands, arms, and shoulders hurt most, but her whole body ached in one way or another. Each movement brought new pain as the sharp ridges of the rough flagstone floor sliced into her hands and knees. Reaching the computer she collapsed on the floor, breathless, and lay panting like a dog after a good run. Turning to lay face up she bit at the putrid air, forcing it into her lungs, never seeming to get enough. The exertion of the crawl, just two strides for a fit man, had drained her resources and left a snail-trail of blood and urine. I wish I'd used the bucket, she cried in disgust, as the wet denim skirt clung coldly to her backside. Even with Roger in the room, watching out of the corner of his eye, she had still managed to get to the bucket to pee—desperation overcoming modesty.

"Air," she gasped, "I need air." And awareness came like a lump in the breast as her dazed brain battled against accepting the obvious: She couldn't breathe because there was nothing in the air that was breathable. Most of the oxygen had already been sucked out of it and the effort of breathing itself sapped the dregs, making her light headed.

I must get fresh air, she thought, pulling her mind together. But how? She turned to the computer, somehow expecting it to help, and dragged the keyboard onto the floor so she could type without having to get up.

"ROGER. PLEASE COME BACK AND LET ME OUT," she typed, then erased the line and started again.

"DON'T COME BACK ROGER. PLEASE DON'T COME BACK. JUST TELL MY MUM WHERE I AM. PLEASE, PLEASE, TELL MY MUM. SHE'LL BE EVER SO WORRIED."

She stopped, overcome by the exertion of typing and thinking, and waited a full minute, breathing slowly, consciously, listening to the grating of exhausted air rushing in and out of her lungs. Her energy regained, she started again, being careful not to overtax herself, beginning at the top of the screen, aborting her plea to Roger.

"DEAR MUM," she typed, paused, considered, and deleted the "Dear."

"Too formal," she mused, and tears welled as she realised she'd never written to her mother before.

"MUM," she continued. "I'VE BEEN KID-NAPPED BY ROGER."

The phrase absorbed her for several minutes as she mulled over its ramifications and, although concluding it wasn't strictly true, could think of no better way to adequately express what had happened.

"Marg," she had said, excitedly, a couple of weeks earlier, "Roger wants to meet me—what do you reckon?" They had bumped into each other in Quickmart on their way to school. Trudy, buying lunch—a couple packets of crisps and a can of coke; Margery—conscious of her waist—choosing twenty Benson & Hedges.

"Dunno," answered Margery, with mock disinter-est. "You still ain't shown me his photo."

"Came this morning," lied Trudy, who had been sleeping on it for nearly two weeks.

"Let me see," said Margery, delving uninvited into Trudy's schoolbag.

"Get out," she cried snatching it away.

"One pound eighty, Miss," demanded the store-keeper tetchily, wise to the possibility that the squabble over the bag might be cover for the half dozen teenagers loitering near the candy display.

"Blimey, you should get done for overcharging mate. I'm only a kid," And they giggled as they slipped out of the store.

"Come on Trude, let's see it," nagged Margery, pinning her against a bus shelter.

"I left it home," she said nonchalantly, clutching the bag to her chest in case Margery should see it stuck into her Math book. "I'll fetch it at lunchtime."

"When are you going to meet him?"

"I dunno. He wants to take me for a ride in his Jag. Reckons if I get the train up to his place he'll bring me back in it."

"Yeah, as long as he gets inside your pants," Margery laughed, "otherwise he'll leave you stranded. I've met blokes like him before."

"You don't know nothing about him. He ain't nothing like that. In fact, he doesn't agree with sex before marriage."

Margery threw her head back, "Humph—say's who?" But didn't expect a reply.

The photograph smouldered in Trudy's bag all morning. Not that she wasn't dying to flourish it in Margery's face. But what would Margery say? *"What's a hunk like him see in a girl like you?"*

Finally, too hot to hold on to, she flipped the picture under Margery's nose in the photocopy room at lunchtime.

"Streuth," the girl exclaimed enviously. " What a looker."

"Yeah—he's pretty gorgeous."

Grabbing the photograph on the pretext of holding it up to the light, Margery slipped it into the copier and pushed 10 before Trudy could stop her.

"Here I don't want everyone after him," screeched Trudy, whipping it from under the lid as the machine spat out the first print.

Margery caught the single copy and tried to run. Trudy slammed the door and stood guard. "Give it back."

"It ain't yours. It's a photocopy."

"Marg," she implored, "Please don't show it to no one."

"What's it worth?" she teased, holding it high, out of reach.

"I won't tell your mum about the condoms I saw in your purse."

"Silly cow. Me mum gave 'em to me. Hasn't your mum given you any?"

"Please, please don't show it Marg," Trudy begged, but her concern waned as her mind shifted to other thoughts. How come Mum never gave me condoms? How come she never told me about sex?

"O.K.," said Margery, giving in as if it were of no consequence, "I won't show no one." But she kept the photocopy.

Trudy dragged herself back to the present and re-read the phrase, "Mum. Roger kidnapped me." It's not right, she thought, it's not fair, and the little curser scooted back across the screen at the touch of her finger as she deleted "kidnapped" one painful letter at a time. The effort required her total concentration and, as she considered what to type in its place, her mind wandered back to her meeting with Roger.

It was a Friday, the same day Margery left for France with her parents. Trudy saw them off. "Looks like you're goin' on safari," she laughed as Margery packed herself into the hired campervan next to the kitchen sink, under a box of emergency rations: Kellog's Cornflakes—cost a bomb in France; All Bran—gotta keep everyone regular, says her mother; a hunk of Cheddar cheese—can't stand that stinky French muck, says her father, complaining simultaneously about the French, the language, the toilets, the prices, the beer, gnat's piss; and the Germans?— "Bloody jerries think they own the beaches."

"Shut up and drive," says her mother, sliding into the navigator's seat, her hair rollers turning her headscarf into a porcupine. "But wait 'til we get to Paris and I show them poncy *boulevardiers* a proper hair-do."

Trudy waved goodbye with a tinge of jealousy, although Margery had confided in her the previous day that it would be disastrous. "D'ye think my dad'll let me get within a mile of any decent French bloke?" she'd scoffed. "Not likely." Anyway, Trudy had her own plans. She had a date with Roger.

School officially finished at 4:30 p.m. but she left an hour early, telling the office secretary she'd "come on" unexpectedly. Dressed in her new denim skirt, with a white cotton top, she checked herself in the mirror. "I should have had the ciggies," she mused, pummelling a few surplus inches into her bra.

The note for her mother was simple, and truthful, as far as she knew. "Going out with a friend. Back late. Got my key. Love Trude."

She arrived in Watford early, very early, but decided she might as well wait in the railway refreshment room where they had agreed to meet at seven. For nearly an hour her eyes were glued to the door, terrified she might not recognize him, and every few minutes she refreshed her memory from his photograph even though she knew each feature by heart: Mediterranean tan, chestnut eyes, toothpaste advertisement grin, stylishly short hair, and the unmistakable dimple in the left cheek.

Time clicked by in unison with a huge clock—a curio salvaged from the platform of an abandoned railway station—a tick so intrusive that everything else appeared to be keeping time with its measured pace, including the dumpy waitress whose far-from-sensible stiletto heels tapped in perfect rhythm as she plodded back and forth on the wooden floor. Diners chewed in time to the beat and the timer on the microwave "beeped" synchronously, signifying the successful "zapping" of a limp pasty or sausage roll.

Awareness of someone behind her started as a feeling of unease which she put down to nervousness as she waited for … what? Excitement, pleasure, romance. Love? There's no one there, she told herself, scratching the back of her neck, unwilling to take her eyes off the door lest Roger should arrive. There's no one there, she insisted to herself when the feeling intensified, and found herself fighting the desire to turn around.

As the minute hand on the railway clock clunked to 6:55 p.m. she made up her mind and turned suddenly, giving no warning, catching a man at the table behind her. "What are you staring at weirdo?" she spat, nastily.

His head dropped, and concentration puckered his features as he fidgeted with some crumbs on the tablecloth, then he pinched them between thumb and forefinger and arranged them on the rim of his plate.

Trudy, turning the tables, stared at him until his cheeks were as livid as port-wine birth marks, then backed off, thinking: Loser! It was his hair mainly—spiky translucent threads sticking straight out of his scalp without concept of direction or fashion. By the time he looked up Trudy was carefully examining the clock: 6:58 turned into 6:59 with a clunk as she peered anxiously at the door, beginning to wonder if there were perhaps two railway stations in Watford.

"Excuse me," a voice was saying in her ear. "Are you Trudy?"

Her head shot round and she found herself peering straight into the eyes of the strange-looking man. Her face was twisting into a mask of horror as the door opened and her head whipped back praying it to be Roger. Four people came in, three smartly dressed women in business suits and an older man in a blazer, none of them remotely resembling the five-foot ten, twenty-seven year old she was expecting.

"Who are you?" she enquired, careful not to look.

"Um ... Um ... I'm Matt. Um ... short for Matthew," he explained slowly, adding nervously, "I'm Roger's friend."

"Oh," was all she managed, thinking there was no diplomatic way of saying, "Sorry about your face."

"He ... um ... Roger asked me to meet you 'cos he's going to be late," he continued, warming to his story and moving around so he was now almost opposite her.

"Where is he?"

"Um ... At work. He's got an important job to do. He'll be home soon and he said I should take you straight to his house."

Trudy woke with a start and realized she had drowsed off in front of the computer. Damn, she thought, I must concentrate or no one will ever know what happened to me, then she re-read the start of the letter to her mother.

"MUM. ROGER ...ME."

I know, she thought, and painstakingly inserted the words "lied to."

"There," she said contentedly, "that's right."

Now the little screen read, "MUM. ROGER LIED TO ME," and she wrote the rest in a frenzy.

"ROGER LIED. I DON'T KNOW WHY I BELIEVED HIM. YOU SAID MEN WERE LIARS. DAD LIED. HE SAID HE WOULDNT LEAVE ME. WHY DID HE LEAVE? I DIDNT WANT HIM TO GO. IT WERENT MY FAULT MUM, HONEST, IT WERENT MY FAULT. PLEASE DONT BE CROSS WITH ME. PLEASE DONT LEAVE ME AS WELL, DONT LEAVE ME HERE."

Gasping, breathless again, she fought desperately for air. Confused and disorientated by the lack of oxygen in her brain, she willed her fingers to keep in touch with her mother, almost believing her mother was linked to her by the Internet. And a hazy reflection of her own face in the computer screen momentarily deceived her, "MUM—I CAN SEE YOU," she typed furiously, then stared intently, shaping her mother's features out of nothing, with the certainty of a believer chancing on an image of the Virgin Mary or Mother Theresa in a dusty window.

"MUM," she typed, "I DONT WANT TO DIE," THEN PAUSED, TAKING SIX OR SEVEN SHARP BREATHS, before adding. "I MUST GET AIR. WHERE IS ROGER?"

Roger was about thirty miles from the nearest land, alone and dejected. Although now mid-afternoon, fourteen hours after his disappearance, no search had commenced and he was still not officially missing; nevertheless his situation appeared to be brightening. Globs of black cloud still hung out of the sky, but the rain was infrequent, and the wind no longer tore the tops off the waves. The waterlogged clothing next to his skin had picked up some body heat and was acting as a wetsuit, insulating him against the cold seawater. He sat up from time to time, gazing around the horizon for signs of rescue, but had seen no ships all day. Some he missed while asleep, some were concealed by the steep waves and most were simply too distant.

Trudy was still uppermost in his mind and he kept thinking to himself: Why did I do it? But he knew why. Deep down he knew the simple inescapable truth, knew he loved her, would have done anything for her. Yet everything had gone wrong the day he met her. The railway station refreshment room had been almost empty when he arrived at five o'clock. He knew he was two hours early but, after four months of dreaming, what was a couple of hours? He had no photograph, only her description and his own imagination and, when Trudy arrived a little after six, he dismissed her as too early, too short, and not slim enough to fit the verbal portrait she had painted of herself.

By ten minutes to seven his nervous anxiety was at fever pitch. He could actually feel the blood pumping through his veins and hear his heart beating, fast and hard. The blood vessels in his cheeks were on fire and his whole body tingled with anticipation. He looked again at the neat little head of the girl in front of him almost wishing she were Trudy.

As seven o'clock approached, with no sign of Trudy, anxiety finally overcame reticence and he decided to approach the girl, but then she turned with disgust on her face and venom in her voice and his world crashed—it is Trudy!

As Roger's front door loomed, a small voice warned her that something was amiss, but the lure of the *real* Roger drew her on until she found herself pinioned against the faded yellow woodwork by his huge belly. Reaching over, Roger's pudgy hand inserted the key, and his bulk propelled her forward into the dismal hallway.

The light faded as the door slammed behind them and the nightmare began. "I'm Roger," he pronounced, without explanation, apology, or opportunity for her to get used to the idea.

She screamed.

"Stop," he cried in panic.

She screamed louder.

"Please stop," he implored, at a loss.

She kept screaming.

"Stop," he ordered.

She didn't stop; one high pitched, hair-raising scream after another. He clasped his hand over her mouth—she bit deeply. He cried out in pain and the screaming started again. He clasped his hand tighter. Screaming through his fingers, biting and kicking, she jerked her head free and smashed a fist into his podgy face. But he held on, squeezing harder and harder—and she was still screaming. A fistful of fat fingers wound tightly around her throat and she let go. Sagging to her knees she went limp, fooled him into loosening his grip, then turned, slamming a knee into his groin, and started screaming again. He grabbed her, more roughly now, forcing her face against his huge belly, holding tightly, his puffy palms covering her ears. She couldn't breathe; couldn't hear. Suffocating in a soft pillow of flesh, she lost consciousness.

"Oh my God! She's dead," he breathed, his voice echoing hollowly in the empty hallway, and he buried his face in his hands and burst into tears. Everything he had ever loved—dead. His pet rabbit had died, only a few weeks old. His favourite uncle had died—even the pallbearer carrying him had dropped dead with a heart attack. Mrs. Merryweather's Alsatian had died, and he was only teasing it. And now Trudy. Sliding apart his fingers he peeked at the crumpled figure in disbelief, willing the clock to turn back just two minutes, hoping the dishevelled pile of laundry would simply rise up and walk back out of the door.

Anguish, distress, grief, and utter misery coalesced into a single emotion and was replaced within seconds by sheer terror. What would his mother do if she found out? He couldn't let her find out. She didn't know about Trudy or the house, and certainly didn't know about the secret room: his room; his secret.

His tears dripped onto Trudy's limp body as he bore her to his secret room, then he tenderly placed her on his bed and knelt on the floor, praying by her side as she slowly came to, hearing him saying, "Please God help me. I didn't mean to ..." then he stopped, transfixed. "You're alive," he breathed, and she coughed and spluttered as her asphyxiated windpipe fought to recover.

"I love you Trudy," he wept, squeezing her hand and stroking her face. "I didn't mean to hurt you, honestly."

A laser beam of sunlight, the first and only that day, sought out the life raft and startled Roger from his daydream. It flashed on and off as quickly as a lightning streak as it skipped over his face and, by the time he had opened his eyes, it was gone. The laceration in the cloud had patched itself and Roger had no idea what had disturbed him. Struggling to heave his body higher in the raft, he quickly explored the horizon, but couldn't keep his stinging eyes focussed, so he slid back down and re-lived happier times—the discovery of his house and the secret room of which he was so proud.

It was early one Friday evening. The spring sunshine had heated the interior of his car, which he had left all day in Junction Road to save fighting for a space in the station car park. He was just opening the window to let out the baked-plastic smell when someone tapped.

"Excuse me mate," said the young man, more a boy really, his spotty fresh face peering down into the car, "do you live here?"

"No," he replied. "But can I help?"

"Well," continued the youth, "I need someone to ..." His words faded as he re-evaluated his idea. "No. It's O.K. mate." But then he started again. "I just thought ... if you lived here ..." He stopped, another sentence unfinished.

Roger eased his bulk back out of the car, grateful for an opportunity to talk to someone—anyone. "What do you need?" he offered helpfully.

"It's just that I have to put up this sign and I want someone to hold the ladder."

"Sure, no problem. What's the sign?"

Flipping around an estate agent's "For Sale" sign, he quoted, "For sale," quite unnecessarily, and continued confidentially. "It's my first one. I only started this week," then fished in his pocket. "Here's my card."

"Jefferson & Partners, Estate Agents," the card announced, "Michael Watson. Associate Salesperson."

"How much?" enquired Roger, scanning the scruffy terraced house.

"Forty two thou—" Michael hesitated, failing to finish yet another sentence. "I'm supposed to tell you about it first, before I give you the price. That's what they taught me at Jefferson's."

"That's O.K.," responded Roger, "I can see what it looks like. How much did you say?"

"Forty two thousand ... but I might be able to get them down a bit."

"Don't bother," said Roger, "I'll take it."

Michael's laugh turned into a nervous giggle. "Are you having me on?" he enquired, hardly able to conceal his delight—*Wait 'til I tell my mum*.

"No," said Roger, retrieving a chequebook from under the mat in the front of his car. "Who do I make it out to?" he asked, never having bought a house before.

"I ... I ... I don't know," stammered Michael, never having sold one. "But if you're serious, maybe we should go back to the office."

"O.K.," Roger replied, "but I don't want to be long. My mum will have supper ready and I don't want her to know yet ... It's a surprise," he added quickly, noticing the renewed cynicism on Michael's face.

Two weeks later, the first Saturday in May, he unlocked the front door and carted in his sparse possessions: his computer, and a rickety wooden table from a High Street junk shop to stand it on. The brand new bed—the one on which Trudy was lying—with pocket-coiled interior springs and brass bedstead, was delivered that afternoon. The shiny brass bedstead was the most expensive in the store, but the cost hadn't bothered him. His offshore account, overseen by the company's financial adviser, was as healthy as a rock star's bar bill, and a trickle of cash dripped into his local bank—the one his mother kept her eye on. His chequebook from an international bank, the one he bought the house and bed with, was another of his secrets. The concealed room was his biggest secret of all.

It was a stray electricity cable, which led him to the secret room. He hadn't been searching—he had no need. Everything he required was in the front room and, at last, he was able to enjoy the freedom of communicating with Trudy without his mother poking her nose in. But George's continual prying ate into his privacy and forced him into the back room, where the antiquated power socket wouldn't work.

The electrical supply panel, in the cupboard under the stairs, was part of a mysterious parallel world not usually inhabited by Roger. However, a cursory inspection revealed an old cable, insulated with frayed brown fabric, disappearing through a hole in the cupboard's floorboards. It must be the one, he thought, for no good reason, and pulled until it snapped, the loose end hurtling out of the hole and attacking him like a spiteful snake. Leaping away, he slammed the cupboard door and stood, sweat-soaked, in the dingy hallway, trying to catch his breath.

Armed with a screwdriver from his car's toolkit, he returned to the fray and, in the murky light filtering through a filthy transom window above the door, he tried to prise a floorboard to get at the broken cable. The screwdriver slid easily between two boards but, when he exerted pressure, the entire floor lifted. Releasing the tension he tried again, this time prising the board at the other end until he could catch his fingers underneath. The floor was a trap door and, as it swung upwards, he noticed a hook on the angled ceiling underneath the stairs, and was surprised when the hook grasped and held the door in place. Then he looked down and was startled to find a pitch-black shaft festooned with spider webs.

Dark and dank, the rectangular adit was the size of a small grave, although its depth was lost in the murk. Someone with imagination might have concocted an intriguing tale to explain its presence—may even have written a book: *The Rat, the Goblin and the Cupboard Under the Stairs,"* perhaps. But Roger shut the door and would have forgotten about it had his neighbour not persisted in peeping.

It was three days before he plucked up the courage to descend into the pit. Driven by George's constantly twitching curtains, he lifted the trap door, checked that nothing had altered, then felt his way down the robust wooden ladder. The dirt floor met him out of the blue and he gingerly tested it with his weight, fearing it might be a ledge—but it held. With his feet solidly planted he fished a flashlight from his pocket, spun to search for the broken cable, and came face to face with a solid wooden door. His nervous system went into overdrive, quivering his muscles and sucking the saliva from his mouth, and the flashlight fell from his hand with a thud that made him leap.

"Who's there?" he shouted in panic, scrabbling for his lamp, and he froze, certain he'd heard a reply. Then the doorknob started turning and he wasn't altogether sure whether it was him or some unseen hand on the other side. As the door swung open the vacant room made a mockery of his anxiety.


"MUM, I'VE FOUND A WAY TO GET SOME AIR," typed Trudy, the only inhabitant of Roger's secret room in more than half a century. "I WANT TO TELL YOU WHAT HAPPENED."

Trudy sat almost motionless on the stone floor, only her damaged hand moving as it painstakingly picked out each key from memory.

"IT WERENT ALL MY FAULT MUM, HONEST-LY. ROGER TOOK ME TO HIS HOUSE, HE TOLD ME HIS NAME WAS MATTHEW."

She stopped, thought, decided.

"MUM I HAVE TO GO. BACK IN A MINUTE."

Trudy rolled her body sideways, twisted into a crawling position, and dragged herself slowly across the room toward the door. It was only ten feet, no more than the width of her bedroom back home in Leyton, but the crawl took her weakened body near-ly two minutes. Five minutes later she was back at the keyboard.

"MUM, IM STILL HERE. I SUCK AIR THREW THE KEYHOLE, BUT ITS A LONG WAY. MY HANDS AND KNEES HURT."

Her stinging hands, especially the right one with a blister turning septic, were so painful she used her wrists and forearms to pull herself from the computer to the tiny air hole in the door. Two minutes there, two minutes back, and a minute to breathe in between.

"IF I SUCK REALLY HARD IM ALRIGHT FOR A WHILE," she added, wanting to explain everything.

The keyhole, her lifeline, had also been her focus of hope for the past week. She had stared at it a thousand times a day, waiting for the grate of Roger's heavy iron key in the lock each morning before he went to work, and then each evening as he came home.

"IM IN A ROOM UNDER ROGERS HOUSE," she painstakingly typed. "ITS IN WATFORD, BUT I DONT KNOW THE ADDRESS. HE TOLD ME HE HAD A BIG HOUSE—BUT ITS LITTLE." She paused, exhausted, and panting for breath, then slowly eased herself onto her stomach and started another journey toward her lifeline.

"ITS ME," she announced five minutes later, unthinkingly writing the expression she had always used to announce her arrival from school. Her routine had rarely varied. Pushing her key into the lock she would throw open the door, drop her school bag on the floor, sling her coat optimistically toward the hall cupboard and shout, "It's me," as if she had been away for a month. Before her father had left she could expect her mother's answering, "Hello Trudy, I'm in the kitchen," but afterwards, she rarely received a response.

"ROGERS GONE AWAY," she continued, "HE SAID HE WOULD COME BACK BUT I WASNT VERY NICE. I BIT HIM AND KICKED HIM WHERE IT HURTS, AND I SCREAMED A LOT. THEN HE SUFFOCATED ME."

Writing "suffocated" reminded her it was almost time to go back to the door. The journey itself consumed most of the energy acquired, so by the time she returned to the computer she was already craving more air.

"HE LEFT ME BISCUITS AND BOTTLES OF WATER," she continued, as if she had not been away. "BUT NO PROPER FOOD. THERES NO TOILET— JUST A STINKY BUCKET." She paused, breathless, and considered starting another round-trip to the door, but decided she could manage another line.

"THIS ROOM WAS DUG BY SOME PEOPLE IN THE WAR. I FOUND A DIARY AND SOME THINGS IN A TIN."

The square metal Oxo tin had a picture of a bull on the top and an insignia printed in red, "1,000 Oxo cubes, halfpenny each or 6 for two pence." It had caught her eye as soon as she regained consciousness. The dust covered rusty tin had been abandoned in a corner and she lay on the bed, staring at it in the pale glow of the computer screen. After Roger left the first night, she gingerly opened the hinged lid to examine the contents; hopeful it might contain a spare key for the room, though would have been surprised if it had.

"It's just a school exercise book," she muttered, taking out the old fashioned book with green marbled cover. "G. A. Blenkinsop. Diary of War," had been penned in the spaces for name and subject and, with great curiosity, she opened the wrinkled yellowed pages.

*August 25th, 1940*

If you are reading this our plan failed. Yesterday, the Willards, next door, were killed by a bomb. One of Churchill's. Part of his campaign of terror against his own people to incite them to fight against the International Fascist Party. We will not be defeated.

*August 26th, 1940.*

Started work on underground shelter today. Made trap door under stairs. Children must not tell anyone— sworn to secrecy.

*August 27th, 1940.*

Air raid last night. Worked all night. No problem with noise—big raid. Children helping nicely.

*August 28th-September 2nd, 1940.*

Too busy to write everyday. Working overtime at the office for the war effort. Then dig most of the night. Martha digs in the day as well.

She skipped forward a few entries, each much the same. Digging, digging, and more digging. On many days there were no comments at all.

*September 10th, 1940.*

Everybody working hard. 2 big air raids on 6th and 9th. Hid in our new shelter, felt safe. Throwing dirt onto bombsite next door. Warning of invasion given on the 7th. Operation Sea Lion is under way. Liberation is coming.

*September 18th, 1940.*

Digging finished. Using bricks from bombsite next door to make walls. Will take a long time. Battle of Britain officially over on 15th. Churchill lied—he didn't win. The Fuehrer is re-grouping to liberate us.

*September 29th, 1940.*

Walls almost done. Stones for floor very heavy.
Still no word on advancing army. Air raids stopped.

*October 15th, 1940.*

Room finished. Door seals well. Going to Hampshire for a few days rest.


Trudy idly flicked pages but there was nothing more. Just five pages explaining why her prison had been constructed. Reading and re-reading the neatly written notes, she wondered what had happened to the family— What plan? How had it failed? Her muddled brain couldn't work it out and she was just putting the book back when something glinting in the bottom of the tin caught her attention. In the gloomy light she hadn't at first noticed the five silver swastikas encrusted with diamonds, but now she carefully examined them; turning them over in her hands, wondering at their intricate beauty. Then, worrying Roger might catch her and take them away, she shoved everything back and squirreled the tin under the bed.

"MUM, ARE YOU STILL THERE?" enquired Trudy, kidding herself that the typewritten words were somehow breaking out of the computer and surging through the Internet; inwardly knowing that without Roger's password, they could not. "I HAD TO GET MORE AIR," she continued, almost apologetically.

"I TRIED TO GET OUT AT FIRST, I DIDNT KNOW I WAS UNDERGROUND. ROGER SAID HE WOULD LOOK AFTER ME. I SAID I WANTED TO GO HOME. HE CRIED AND SAID HE WANTED ME TO GO HOME TO. I PROMISED NOT TO SAY WHAT HAPPENED IF HE LET ME GO. HE SAID HE WOULD THINK ABOUT IT."

She closed her eyes for a second, as if considering whether or not she should tell her mother anything else; then her sore fingers started again. "HE KEPT SAYING HE LOVED ME AND I SAID, IF YOU LOVE ME LET ME GO, BUT HE DIDNT. WHEN I SCREAMED HE PUT HORRIBLE TAPE ON MY MOUTH—AND HE TIED ME UP SOMETIMES, WHEN I KICKED."

Suddenly finding herself short of breath she hurriedly added, "GOTTA GO," and started another excursion to the tiny vent in the door.

"MUM, ARE YOU STILL THERE?" she continued, returning ten minutes later, her delusional mind unable or unwilling to accept that her message was going nowhere. "IVE BEEN GONE A LONG TIME COS I NEEDED MORE AIR. IVE BEEN SUCKING FOR AGES AND AGES AND I THINK I CAN STAY WITH YOU LONGER BEFORE I GET DIZZY AGAIN."

"MUM," she started again, pounding the keyboard fiercely, insisting her mother should listen, "WHEN I GET DIZZY ITS LIKE WHEN YOU BEND DOWN AND STAND UP TOO QUICKLY. KNOW WHAT I

MEAN?" Without awaiting a response, though none was forthcoming, she changed topics and typed. "I DONT THINK HE RAPED ME. PAULINE ADAMS WAS RAPED BY HER BOYFRIEND AND SHE SAID IT HURT BAD. I COULDNT FEEL ANYTHING WHEN I WOKE UP SO I GUESS I'M O.K. BUT IT HURT WHEN HE TIED ME TO THE BED." She closed her eyes thinking of the time she was sure she had escaped—the second day of her captivity, when he'd caught her—then continued typing.

"He tied me up because I nearly got out. I'd hid under the bed and kept very still."

Roger, paying his usual morning visit before catching his train to the city, had unlatched the trap door in the cupboard under the stairs, scrambled down the ladder, and slipped his key in the lock with the anticipation of a birthday-boy. But the gift box was empty.

"HE DIDN'T SEE ME UNDER THE BED," she carried on, caught up in the excitement of her tale, "SO HE WENT BACK UPSTAIRS. I CREPT OUT AND GOT RIGHT TO THE TOP OF THE LADDER, BUT HE SAW ME. HE WAS AT THE BACK DOOR AND HE SAW ME IN THE HALLWAY. I RAN TO THE FRONT DOOR AND GOT IT OPEN, THEN HE CAUGHT ME. I KICKED AND SCREAMED AGAIN BUT HE WAS TOO STRONG. THEN HE TIED ME TO THE BED AND LEFT ME FOR AGES."

She hesitated, her fingers hovering over the keys, deliberating whether or not she had the strength to tell her mother what else had occurred. Eventually, she made up her mind. "MUM. HE LOOKED AT ME. YOU KNOW—DOWN THERE," she wrote finally, after erasing vagina and fanny, twice. "MY FEET WERE TIED TO THE BED AND HE PULLED MY

KNICKERS DOWN AND JUST LOOKED AND LOOKED. THEN HE SAID SORRY AND PULLED THEM BACK UP. THEN HE STARTED CRYING AND IT MADE ME CRY AS WELL."

Trudy suddenly found herself sinking and pumped herself up with a few sharp breaths. "MUM. ARE YOU LISTENING TO ME?" she typed, with a fervour that smacked of shouting. "I'LL HAVE TO GO AGAIN IN A MINUTE, BUT I WANT TO TELL YOU THAT I LOVE YOU EVER SO MUCH. I REALLY MISS YOU. PLEASE COME AND GET ME SOON. GET ME BEFORE ROGER COMES BACK. I LOVE YOU, I LOVE YOU."

She stopped, and slumped gracelessly onto the hard floor, landing heavily on her left arm. The damaged and tender shoulder muscles registered no pain, the nerves too starved of oxygen to care. Totally exhausted, she momentarily slipped into unconsciousness, but, just a few seconds later, an explosive bout of coughing wrenched her from oblivion and forced her to start another journey across the room. She had woken from a dream to a nightmare.

"ITS ME AGAIN," she wrote nearly an hour later, thinking she'd taken only a few minutes. "SORRY I TOOK SO LONG."

Her crawl to the door had been interrupted by several bouts of torpor; when her mind had refused stubbornly to register anything other than the whooshing of useless air as she hyperventilated on a fetid atmosphere almost devoid of oxygen.

"IM GOING TO TAKE A BREAK MUM. DO YOU MIND? IM SO TIRED ," she typed laboriously as her mind and body continued to slow, while her biological clock sped up, racing toward midnight.

A moment later she jerked back to consciousness; something important nagging her brain. "MUM— WAKE ME IF IM ASLEEP WHEN YOU GET HERE," she typed, then movement stopped, time was suspended. No more letters jumped onto the screen for more than a minute as her fingers, drifting aimlessly above the keys, awaited further instructions. To her befuddled brain, the minute seemed less than a second before she questioned, "MUM, IF I FALL ASLEEP WILL I BE ABLE TO BREATHE?" And another momentary pause was followed by a short burst of movement as her fingers howled, "HELP ME MUM."

# chapter six

"Ze captain has called a meeting in twenty min-utes at the port." Yolanda glanced at her watch. "At two-thirty."

Detective Inspector David Bliss followed her gaze and his eyes popped: chunky gold—inlaid with rubies and diamonds. "Cartier," he mused, praying she'd not noticed his Timex.

"It's still only one-thirty in England," he mumbled, more to himself than her, his battered old watch still behind the time. "God. No wonder I'm tired I've been up since six o'clock yesterday morning, that's ..." his eyes closed in concentration, "that's more than thirty hours."

"The ship's gone," she said, confirming the obvi-ous, as they drove down the narrow cobblestone street, overlooking the port, a short while later.

"Nice leather," he muttered, sliding his hand over the BMW's white doeskin seat squab.

"A bit foggy," she replied.

He let her misunderstanding pass with a smile and scanned seaward, looking out over the salt marsh to the wide estuary. But the SS *Rotterdam* had already dissolved into the thick moisture laden air.

The cobbled street was almost deserted, as were the three bars, which they passed just before the rail tracks. "Heineken, Carlsberg, and Royal Dutch," proclaimed their towering signs without need of further explanation. On any normal day each bar would have been packed with its supporters. But today was abnormal. Although the hubbub of the ship's departure had died, groups of disgruntled workers were still gathered on the damp quayside awaiting further instructions. Rumours had spread from one group to the next that every truck and container off the ship would have to be unpacked and physically searched. Carefully circumnavigating deep pools from the night's storm, Yolanda parked on the edge of a large gravelled area amongst clumps of spiky sea-grass, polystyrene cups, and cola cans. Driftwood signposts, eaten by wind and wave, warned of the tide's upper reach.

"Zis is an old castle," announced Yolanda, indicating a heavily fortified beachside bunker. "The meeting is here."

Captain Jahnssen was waiting for them. "Detective Bliss," he called excitedly. "We've got Motsom's car."

"What about Motsom?"

"He can't be far away," he replied, sheepishly dusting off his shoes with a handkerchief, knowing that one of his officers had been sitting on the information for an hour in the hope of catching Motsom single-handed. "We will soon have him caught." added Jahnssen with more confidence. "We have detectives watching him now ... This was built by the Germans in the first war," he went on, segueing conveniently to a more comfortable subject as his right hand swept around the concrete blockhouses.

"Impressive," agreed Bliss, pointedly checking his watch, anxious to move on; anxious to start a proper search for LeClarc; anxious to have some answers for the dreadful Edwards on his arrival at six.

"This is the outer defences, where the guns were," Yolanda explained as they reached the seaward side. "Look," she instructed, pointing to horizontal slits where gun barrels had once dominated the Rhine estuary.

"The wall's three meters thick ..." Captain Jahnssen started, when Bliss headed him off.

"Captain—the meeting ... shouldn't we ..." Then the voice of a junior officer came to his aid, calling insistently that everyone was assembled and waiting.

"Thank God," sighed Bliss, eager to have the investigation in full swing ahead of Edwards' arrival. They were ushered into the armoury, which had been transformed into a modern conference room. A hundred or more men and women, drawn from half a dozen stations, chatted amiably, renewing old acquaintances, catching up on gossip—"You'll never guess who she's screwing now ... Have you heard about ..."

"Alright gentlemen," the captain began, attempting to gain attention, but the commotion persisted until someone plunked a chair heavily on the old wooden floor and the meeting brought itself to order.

Bliss understood none of the captain's address, and was idly examining the intricately patterned brickwork of the huge vaulted ceiling when he heard his name mentioned. "Detective Bliss from Scotland Yard will speak to you now."

Shit! he thought, caught unaware—I wasn't prepared for this. Raising himself nervously, mind churning, he furtively glanced around and was immediately struck by the number of people crammed into the circular chamber. Yolanda had taken a front row seat directly facing him, and he sought inspiration and reassurance in her face. She smiled and gave a little nod, as if to say, "Go on."

"You were very good," she whispered later, as he sat down after outlining the circumstances of LeClarc's disappearance.

Very good—very good?. What does she mean? he wondered, trying to evaluate the strength of her words, worried that his address had flown over many of the officers' heads. But they'd smiled ... it couldn't have been too bad.

"Mr. Bliss ..."

Yolanda nudged him.

"Sorry," he said, realizing that Captain Jahnssen wanted him again.

"I was asking ... Do we have pictures of Motsom yet?"

Bliss rose. "Not yet Captain. I've asked criminal records to fax them over. But I've got some background on him." He paused, shuffled through his papers, found what he was looking for, and gave details: "William John Motsom. forty-eight years old; a few minor convictions, not serious, but he has a bad reputation. Nothing provable, but his name has cropped up in several gangland hits."

"I have information about his car," continued the captain, thanking him, then speaking to the audience in Dutch for a full two minutes, leaving Bliss with the distinct impression he was telling them what bungling idiots this English detective and his colleagues had been in losing LeClarc.

As Jahnssen sat down an impatient voice barked in English, "How do you know he's been kidnapped?"

The question forced Bliss to his feet once more.

"First," he answered, "a crewmember named ..." He flicked through his notebook, desperately seeking a name, but failed to find it, so repeated, "A crewmember was on deck when King claims LeClarc fell overboard. The crewmember," the catering assistant's name came back in a flash—"Jacobs, didn't see anyone else, only King. So we're fairly certain no one fell off the ship. King told me he didn't know Motsom, but I saw them together. And King went to Motsom's cabin after reporting LeClarc missing. Finally," he said, his voice rising in a crescendo, "King drove LeClarc's Renault off the ship." Feeling it was time to take some credit, he continued, "They knew their plan had gone wrong when I spoke to King. He knew I'd linked him to Motsom, so the only thing to do was to get LeClarc's car off the ship without anybody noticing. That way everyone would assume LeClarc must have arrived safely. Everybody would be happy, and no more enquiries would be made until LeClarc failed to turn up in The Hague for the conference." He sat down triumphantly, the case for the prosecution complete.

"But where is LeClarc?" enquired a spoilsport in the front row.

Bliss stumbled, "We ... ah. We ... ah ... think he's been put inside a truck or container. Drugged probably."

The captain was quick to step in. "We've searched every car, but he's a very big man ..."

"Fat man," sneered Bliss, getting in a dig, mindful LeClarc had given him the slip and caused him untold aggravation.

"Quite ... He's a fat man. So it would be foolish to hide him in a car. We're sure he is in one of the trucks and we must search them all carefully. We should have photographs of him for everybody soon."

A comedian made everybody laugh with the obvious. "Do you mean we might find more than one fat, drugged Englishman hiding in a truck?"

Then a deep thinker sitting next to Yolanda, scratched his head and asked a question in Dutch, which the captain translated before answering. "He wants to know— if LeClarc is in a truck, where's Motsom?"


Billy Motsom was still on the phone. He had changed bars for fear of attracting too much attention, and was now in the one under the Heineken sign. A few of the regulars had managed to keep their daily vigil—nuclear warfare might have stopped them if close enough—but the place was much quieter than normal, and the landlord would have assumed one of his competitor's was having a fire sale had he not known of the uproar at the port over a missing passenger.

Motsom stood by the payphone in one corner as he watched the landlord expertly slice the foam off the top of a dozen glasses with a wooden spatula. Why do they do that? he pondered, as he listened to a busy signal for the tenth time. Putting the phone down, he retrieved his florin and tried his cellphone again. The "low battery" signal beeped, so he slammed it shut and went back to the payphone. "It's me. I've been calling for ages. What's happening?"

He listened intently for a second, then exploded, "I don't care how fuckin' rough it is. Get a bloody boat even if you've got to buy one." He paused long enough for a response. "No, I don't know what they cost. And I still need a car. The cops are swarming all over mine. I nearly ran into a bloody ambush. Hang on," he said, stuffing more coins into the slot. "I don't know how they got onto me," he continued, "unless that clown

King has blabbed—thank God he doesn't know which truck we're using or we'd really be in the shit ..."

The barman interrupted nosily, enquiring if he needed more coins. Waving him away, he continued, "Yeah, he knows what we're doing, 'course he knows. He worked it out. He ain't that stupid. Anyway, forget King, we've got to get LeClarc if he's still alive, and I've got to get away from here before they find the truck and pin it on me."

The meeting in the fortress, less than a quarter of a mile away, was dissolving in a degree of chaos with search leaders showing a certain amount of cronyism as they began constituting teams in an adult form of "One for me—one for you." Bliss and Yolanda fought their way through a dark passage thronged with twenty or more Dutchmen all yakking at the same time, and emerged into the fresh air. Bliss looked up at the sky with surprise, he'd lost track of time and had not expected daylight.

"Christ," he said, in a sudden panic. "The super's arriving at six. I nearly forgot. I'll have to get going, I've no idea how to get there." He turned to Yolanda, "Where is it again, Ski-pole?"

"It's *shkeepol*. But don't worry, I'll take you; we've got plenty of time."

He checked his watch. "I'd like to talk to King again. I'm sure he knows a lot more than he's letting on."

"Okey dokey Dave," she said. "Let's go."


"Hello Nosmo. Want a ciggy or a coffee," he started cheerily as he entered the bare cell a few minutes later.

"I still haven't got a bloody lawyer," moaned King.

Bliss plunked himself informally on the end of the slatted wooden bench like he was taking a break. "I'll ask the captain again, but the trouble is I'm only a visitor just like you."

"Yeah well you ain't stuck in jail, are you."

"True, Nosmo. But you wouldn't be, if you told me what was happening."

"Are you offering me some sort of deal? Turn Queen's evidence as we used to say. Do you still say that, Dave?" He sneered.

"No. We call it grassing or bubbling now."

"I know. The trouble is I ain't got anything to offer. I've told you ... I ain't done nothing, and I don't know nothing."

"No one thinks they're bad, Nosmo; you know that," said Bliss, letting his eyes wander around the spacious cell. The high stone walls had been whitewashed recently he thought, but graffiti had spread like poison ivy as each temporary occupant had sought to immortalize his stay with a few hatefully inscribed monosyllables beginning with "F" or "C" on the nearest available space. The expanse of blank wall beyond arms reach from the bunk was relatively unscathed, although some joker had written, "Do not write on this wall," along the bottom.

"See that window?" said Bliss pointing to a heavily barred slot.

"Yeah."

"Unless you start talking, that's all the daylight you're going to see for a long time."

"And how are they going to keep me Dave? Claim they found a condom of cocaine up my bum?" he scoffed. "They haven't got any evidence—you know that. And since when is it a crime to try to save a bloke's life?"

"It ain't Nosmo. But you weren't trying to save anyone's life. The way it looks to them is that you chucked the guy overboard to steal his car. Is that what happened?"

"You know it ain't Dave. I didn't chuck anybody overboard. And I didn't steal a car neither."

"Well you'll have to try telling the judge that, but the evidence looks pretty good from where I'm standing."

"You're sitting Dave, not standing," he said, sarcastically. "Anyway I've told you. I'm not saying anything without a lawyer, and I won't be saying anything with a lawyer either."

Bliss changed tack. "What about your missus, Nosmo. Do you want me to call ..."

"I ain't got a bloody missus, so don't waste your breath."

The cynicism of a disenchanted romantic empathized Bliss momentarily, asking, "Divorced?"

"Sort of. She pissed off years ago. I s'pose we're still legally married but I ain't seen her in ages."

"Kids?"

"Couple. Grown up. One's nineteen, the other's twenty-one. They've got their lives sorted out. No point bothering 'em. There's nothing they can do anyway."

"Is there anyone ..."

Yolanda's voice interrupted, "Dave can I talk to you please?"

She was standing in the doorway, silhouetted against the bright light in the corridor.

"Lucky old Dave," said King under his breath.

"I'll be back. Don't go away Nosmo," he said, slipping out of the cell and pulling the huge wooden door closed behind him.

"They've found the truck," said Yolanda, impatience overcoming discretion.

King, with an ear to the door, muttered, "Oh shit."

Back at the port, just three minutes later, Bliss and Yolanda had no difficulty in finding the relevant truck. It was swarming with uniforms. Captain Jahnssen, in darkest blue with a smattering of gold stars, detached himself from the melee as they approached.

"Found it," he beamed, pointing to a red and white truck with a matching forty-foot container on its back. "In here somewhere."

They caught up to him, "How do you know?"

He stopped, now alongside the juggernaut. "One of the custom's dogs smelled the air vent. Here," he said, pulling Bliss under the truck, shooing away a cluster of inquisitive officers.

"Look," he said, shining a flashlight upwards to a tea-plate sized wire grating. "This is where the air comes out."

"Where's the entry?" enquired Bliss, escaping from underneath the monster and carefully examining the joints and seams of the panel work for hinges and a doorway large enough to accommodate LeClarc.

"Probably concealed behind the cargo. Some dockers are coming to unload it."

They walked toward the giant double doors at the rear as the captain explained. "It's a load of plastic bags going to Istanbul according to the manifest."

Fifteen minutes later the area looked like a freeway truck crash. Pallets piled high with boxes were strewn haphazardly over the dockside, and dozens of uniformed officers wandered amongst the wreckage seeking signs of life. A throng of officials were inside the container, examining remnants—bits of broken pallet, shreds of cardboard, billows of plastic wrap— picking over each artefact with the solemnity of a philatelist searching for a first-day cover. Nothing: No neatly constructed cubicle in the middle; no false wheel arches; no carefully camouflaged chunk of cargo containing a hideaway—absolutely nothing.

Disappointed, they began jumping down as Bliss, still on the ground, seized the flashlight from the captain and stooped under the truck. Emerging quickly he poked his head around the rear doors and peered at the floor.

"The vent doesn't come up inside the truck," he said, to no one in particular. Some of the uniforms stopped moving and he repeated himself. "Look. the vent doesn't come up through the floor." Diving back under the truck he checked again, then scrabbled around for a probe; a piece of stiff wire a foot long would be ideal, he thought, and he spotted something fitting on the ground and excitedly lunged for it. A violent overhead explosion caused him to shriek, and his right hand snaked upwards, too late to ward off his attacker—a sharp corner of the chassis. Staggering from under the truck he was caught by familiar hands.

"What's happened Dave?" enquired Yolanda urgently.

"Hit my bloody head."

"Let me see," she said, gently prying his fingers from his scalp and tenderly parting the hairs. "It's only bleeding a little," she lied, quickly putting her hand over the wound to stem the flow. "I think we'll get someone to look at it."

Reeling noticeably, he allowed Yolanda to guide him toward her car. "Wait," he cried without opening his eyes. "Tell the captain the air vent goes forward to the front of the container."

Another pair of hands, bigger and firmer than Yolanda's, caught hold and eased him into the car as he swooned; fatigue, pain, and blood loss sapping his will.

Bliss would have seen Motsom walking back from the port to one of the bars had he been alert as they shot past. Motsom, knowing the truck had been discovered, scurried to the nearest phone. It was only a matter of time before the driver was induced to talk, warnings had to be given, arrangements made.

Twenty minutes later disillusionment awaited a drowsy Bliss as they returned from the port medical clinic. "Just one stitch should do it," the doctor had said, muttering about the apparent epidemic of injured cops—Sergeant Jones with his broken wrist, Bliss assumed, though he hadn't asked, believing Jones had already received more attention than he deserved.

With the truck's cab detached, a concealed door into a hidden compartment had been exposed, but the forlorn look on Captain Jahnssen's face warned him not to expect good news.

"Empty," Jahnssen shouted "He's not in there." Then he turned to a group of officers lounging against one of the pallets, lighting cigarettes from a common Zippo lighter, and angrily fired a volley of Dutch at them. The cigarettes were grudgingly stubbed out, one man making a performance by dropping his on the tarmac and defiantly dancing it to pulp with a flamenco. They ambled away, joining the ragged snake of uniforms heading toward the offices, seeking coffee or a cold beer.

"Look here," said the captain leading Bliss and Yolanda to the secret door they had discovered; he pointed out the professionalism of the construction, the way the riveted seams of aluminium had been used to mask the door's outline, and inside, three narrow collapsible bunks hung on the back wall.

"That's a false wall," Bliss pointed out, quite unnecessarily, giving it a tap and noticing the hollowness as the sound bounced around the empty container behind it. The entire front end of the container was a narrow compartment invisible from inside or out.

"Very clever," muttered Bliss to himself. "But where's LeClarc?"

Some plastic storage containers of food, and several plastic jugs of water, had been pulled out by the officers and, as Bliss bent to examine them, dizziness struck again. Yolanda grabbed him, eased him back to a standing position, then opened each container and patiently displayed the contents: Bread, steak & kidney pies, and an assortment of chocolate cakes. Enough for several days, he thought, even for LeClarc.

"Where's the driver?" asked Bliss of the captain who was still nosing around inside the compartment.

"Arrested," he said, jumping down. "They've taken him in for questioning."

"Shit!" spat Bliss, "You know what this means?"

Yolanda shook her head for the briefest of seconds before he continued. "LeClarc isn't here. He didn't drive his car off the ship ..."

"So ..." she started to say, but he beat her to it again.

"So, he must have fallen overboard. King was telling the truth after all."

The captain tried to butt in, but Bliss didn't give him a chance. "Oh God! That poor sod's been in the water all day; nobody's done anything and we were supposed to be protecting him."

"There could be another truck with a hidden compartment," the captain suggested implausibly, offering Bliss some defence. "Anyway, it's too late to start a rescue operation now. It will be dark in a few hours. All we can do is ask shipping to keep a good look-out."

Alerted to the time, Bliss sneaked a look at his watch. "Four-thirty," he said, keeping his shabby timepiece under his cuff. "We should get to the airport, Edwards will be here soon."

"Let me see," she said, grabbing his wrist.

Oh no! A nightmare—a scratched supermarket special; its vinyl strap shedding threads—damn!

"That's English time Dave. It's five-thirty here."

He let out a squeal. *Had she noticed?*

"Don't worry. We'll be there in time."

"You said it would take an hour." *Maybe she'd not seen his chronically challenged timepiece.*

"Quicker than that," she said, thrusting him hurriedly toward the BMW, adding, "Your watchstrap's falling apart."

*Shit!*

They sped in silence for awhile. Yolanda, driving fast, concentrated furiously as she snaked along a narrow road, which twined itself along the banks of a canal, green with algae. Several cyclists leapt off their machines in response to the blare of the BMW's klaxon, and a lone fisherman angrily aimed a wooden clog at them as they passed. Bliss watched her with a dozen questions on his tongue but decided against saying anything. She clearly knew what she was doing and was totally absorbed in controlling the car. Woman and machine in complete unison, yet it was obvious which was in charge. The questions could wait.

"Radio?" he suggested, reaching for the control, then burst into laughter as a familiar melody washed over them.

"Recognize it?" he asked.

Her shrug said, "No," but the touch of a smile suggested otherwise.

"It's Wagner's Flying Dutchman overture," he laughed, then exhaled in surprise, "phew—that was less than five minutes." A sign which clearly meant "airport" in Dutch had caught his eye as she stood on the brake, skidded toward a six-foot mesh fence, and slid to a halt inches from a gate. Sliding a magnetic card through a slot, she punched in a security code, and scooted through the gap as the gate opened with a metallic whine.

"We are not there yet, Dave," she said, stamping her foot back on the accelerator and roaring along a perimeter road toward a cluster of hangars at the other end of the runway.

"Let's go," she said, expecting him to work out what was happening for himself, as she stopped amid a cluster of small planes.

"Yours?" he asked, staring in awe at the twin-engine four seater.

"My father's," she said as she flicked open the door, slid into the cockpit and pulled him up into the plane with a powerful hand.

Donning a headset, she jabbered into a microphone while simultaneously checking meters, flicking switches, punching buttons, wiggling controls, and watching bits of the aircraft stir into life. Her head and eyes moved at lightning speed as she tore through the pre-flight routine then, satisfied, she gunned the engines and the whole plane danced noisily to life.

"Okey dokey, Dave?" A question?

He nodded and, with a slight jerk, the plane gathered speed then juddered to a stop at the end of the concrete strip.

"Waiting for clearance to land at Schiphol," she commented casually, as if sitting in a car at an intersection waiting for the lights to change.

"What does your father do?" he forced himself to say, attempting to control the wobble in his voice—telling himself that it was just excitement, like the start of a roller coaster ride.

"Glasshouses," she replied with a shudder.

"Glasshouses," he repeated, surprised, having expected tulips or cheese.

"Are you O.K.?" she asked, noticing his pallid complexion, wondering if his wound was still causing lightheadedness.

"First time," he admitted, meaning: in a small plane. Idiot, he thought, why tell her that?

"There's a first time for everything, Dave," she said, mischievously, and caught the edge of his smile as her light turned green. Playing the throttles like a virtuoso on a rare instrument, Yolanda increased the power to fever pitch. Then, with a quick check left and right, she released the brake.

Aloft, a minute or two later, Bliss squeezed his eyes shut them popped them open. It's really happening, he concluded, trying to keep his feet on the ground while having a hard time escaping from the notion that the bump on his head had made him delusional. The land was dropping away and, within seconds, they were skimming over the little town. The dock was empty apart from a couple of tugboats. The giant cranes stood idle, their jibs erect awaiting the arrival of the next ferry. And the car parks around the port were beginning to fill with continental holidaymakers en route to England and Englishmen on their way home from the Continent.

Climbing slowly brought more and more of the North Sea into view, and the white-topped breakers crashing onto the beaches were easily visible for several miles up and down the coast.

"Maybe we should go and look for him," said Bliss peering out to the horizon.

"Not in this," she answered, smoothly manipulating the controls so that the plane banked around and straightened up parallel to the coast.

The plane banked again without any apparent effort on Yolanda's part, and headed inland. "We should be there in about twenty minutes. Do you want a drink Dave?" she asked, taking her eyes off the esoteric pathway she had been following. His eyes urged her to look where she was going but, unperturbed, she reached behind to open a minute refrigerator.

"Coke or pop?" she said pulling out a can dusted with ice mist.

"No thanks," he replied, a slight burning sensation in his groin painfully reminding him he hadn't found time for a pee since leaving the SS *Rotterdam* at breakfast-time. Resolving to keep his mind off the subject of liquids until they reached Schiphol, if he could, he asked, "Why are you in the police, Yolanda?"

"For the excitement; for adventure. My father wanted me to go into his business, but I hate it. I have no brothers or sisters. I am, how you say ... A lonely child."

"An *only* child," he corrected, although, being a singleton himself, couldn't help thinking she may have been correct.

"Okey dokey—*only* child. Anyway my father gave me everything to make me want to be a glasshouse builder—it's boring. Every glasshouse is the same—there's no soul in a glasshouse; no passion, no excitement—just metal and glass; it doesn't even have an engine."

"Not like a BMW."

She glanced out of the corner of her eye, pleased he had caught on, "Yeah—nothing like a BMW ... So, what would I do Dave—the same as my father: Meetings with farmers, salesmen, engineers ...?"

"But," he interrupted, "your father must have made a lot of money."

"Yes, and now he is too old to spend it ... and what has he done all his life? Pah," she spat derisively, "Glasshouses. Now my mother has died he is lonely; wants me to join the business, but I won't ... Glass," she spat, as if it were a dirty word.

All this and an inheritance—interesting, he thought, studying the slender manicured fingers of her left hand as she deftly flipped open a Coke, finding a confusing assortment of rings—none looking particularly binding.

Keep your mind on work, he thought, asking, "Will he leave you the business?"

"Yes," or "No," would have sufficed, but she flicked switches—on/off, up/down—checked meters and craned her head around the sky as if searching for the answer. "He already has," she confessed eventually, sounding like someone admitting to having a sexually transmitted disease. "Technically it is already mine, but I don't tell many people. I like being a cop, especially a detective."

"And you'd have to leave if they knew?"

"No, but it might be difficult," she answered without elaboration, and they flew in silence for a almost a minute while Yolanda pondered the wisdom of her decision.

"What about you ..." she started, but he quickly interrupted. "Yolanda," he said, the pain in his groin becoming unbearable, "I've just thought—in the truck, we found plenty of food and water, but what about a toilet?"

"There was one, on the floor in the corner."

"Really," he said, kicking himself for being so unobservant.

She understood, and excused. "It's O.K. You had a nasty bump on your head. How is it now?"

"Okey dokey," he said, and they laughed together, again.


"Shut your eyes if you are scared of landing; I always do," she teased as they touched down on a short runway, well away from the colossal passenger jets and giant freighters. They took a cab from the group of shabby huts reserved for owners and pilots of private planes, arriving at the glossy marble floored main terminal at Schiphol in time to pick up Superintendent Edwards from the arrival gate.

"Perfect," Bliss mouthed to Yolanda as he moved forward to greet the senior officer. "Detective Inspector ..."

"Bliss ... Yes, I remember," Edwards said stonily, adding, "Get that bag. Where's the car?"

Tote that barge, muttered Bliss *sotto voce*, saying, "The car's just outside, Sir."

"Thank Christ for that. I hate fucking flying. I'm getting the ship back even if it does take all bloody night."

They marched toward the exit, falling in step behind the superintendent, then he abruptly stopped and spun round, "Excuse me, Miss. What ..."

"Sir," Bliss jumped in, just in time to prevent the superintendent from making a fool of himself, "this is Detective Constable ...ah ..." The realization that he had no idea of her surname caused him to fumble for a second until she rushed to his aid.

"Pieters, Sir, Yolanda Pieters."

"Delighted to meet you, Miss Pieters. I am Edwards," he said with a weak smile and an implausibly strong aristocratic accent. "Bliss," he hissed, pulling him to one side with a glare and dropping the accent, "You're in enough shit already—I hope you're not pissing around with a bloody woman."

"Sir, Miss Pieters is their top detective; she was assigned to me." He lowered his voice, "I can assure you we are not pissing about."

"Better not be," spat Edwards, as he marched off expecting them to catch up.

The cab was still waiting at the curb as Yolanda had instructed, and the superintendent's bag and briefcase were loaded in the trunk before he realized it was not a police car.

"What's this?" he queried, as if he'd discovered a lump of dog turd on his parade square.

"A taxi, Sir. We, um ..." Bliss stalled, realizing that he still had to break the news about Yolanda's plane.

Yolanda stepped in magnificently. "A police aircraft is waiting to take us directly to the port. Our captain knew you would be anxious to take command, so he personally ordered it for you."

Edwards beamed, then spun on Bliss. "Why the devil didn't you say so Inspector?"

"Sorry, Sir," he mumbled, opening the cab's front passenger door before slipping in the back with Yolanda.

"I hope you won't mind flying again so soon?" Yolanda asked, keeping a perfectly straight face, nudging Bliss in the ribs.

"No. I won't mind," he replied with a slight wobble in his voice. "Good pilot is he?"

Bliss suddenly had a thought. "You were in the air force weren't you, Sir?"

"That's right Bliss. That's why I hate flying. I've seen so many of them so-called hotshot pilots. Couldn't fly a fuck'n ... Oh sorry, Miss ... Couldn't fly a kite."

"Well I can assure you we have an excellent pilot, Sir."

"Glad to hear it. Now tell me what the bloody hell's happening. Where's LeClarc?"

Roger might have wished he had an answer. Steep choppy seas had replaced the violent breakers left in the wake of the storm, so, instead of riding up and down each huge swell he was now being jiggled about, constantly changing direction. There was no longer any danger of being thrown bodily off the raft, but the jerky flip-flop motion made it impossible to stand, even for a second, without being bowled over. The wind had died completely, not even the whisper of a breeze ruffled the wave-tops, and a blanket of water vapour hung heavily above the surface and was quickly arranging itself into a cold impenetrable fog.

The memory of Trudy was the only thing keeping his will to survive alive. For the first time in his life he had been happy, really happy, then everything had gone awry. A few vivid memories of the past week played constantly in his mind, like a movie collated from clips off the cutting room floor: The expectation, the thrill of their meeting, the look of disgust on her face, the struggle in the hallway, her "dead" body, the nightmare task of getting her down the steep ladder, the temptation to touch her bottom when her skirt had ridden up as she hung over his shoulder ... a temptation he had succumbed to, thrusting a finger inside her knickers to feel the baby soft flesh in the crease of her buttocks. Then he'd recoiled, feeling the sting of his mother's palm across his face and the sound of her voice rampaging in his brain—but it was an old memory coming back to haunt him. "Stop that you dirty little bugger," she had yelled. "I told you never to touch girls there."

"Sorry, Mum," he had cried, an eleven-year-old schoolboy exploring the meaning of life with the little girl who lived three doors away. She was ten, and quite willing, but his mother had surprised them in the garden shed. His father, when he came home from work early—summonsed by his mother—had taken a powerful stand; words were not enough—his mother had said. Ten lashes with a leather belt on his expansive bare backside had stung for days and he had seen the red welts in the mirror a full week later.

The movie continued: Trudy crying—it was her crying which disturbed him the most.

"Don't cry, Trude; I love you. I'll look after you," he had told her over and over. Through the tears, she'd plead for him to call her mother;. he'd promise—anything to stop her crying—but he always found an excuse ... "I tried Trude, honest. She must've been out."

"Stop crying and tell me you love me, Trude," he would often say, "then I'll take you home."

"I love you, Roger," she eventually replied, her resistance sapped by his persistence and her desire to escape. But he didn't take her. "I've got to go to work Trude, I'll take you tonight."

Filled with hope and expectation she dashed off a note to her mother: "Love you mum—see you tonight." But the day stretched to eternity as his promise gradually faded in the thinning air. Then, when she was close to despair, her heart leapt as a blast of fresh air revived her. But he had another excuse. "The car's broken. I'll have to take you tomorrow." Each day a new excuse—then he started making demands.

"Trude," he said one evening just after he came in from work. "If you show me your thingy I promise to take you home."

"No," she shouted, firmly clenching her skirt between her thighs as she sat on the bed in the glow of the computer.

"I won't touch," he pleaded. "I just want to look."

"You looked before. You tied me up—remember."

He remembered, but if only he'd looked closer—touched maybe. Rueing the missed opportunity, he implored, "Please let me have another look."

"Will you really, really promise to take me home if I do?"

"I promise," he lied. "Scout's honour."

"And you won't touch?"

"Promise."

With a sigh of condescension, she lay back and wriggled her knickers to her knees. "Promise?" she said, making one final check.

"Promise," he said.

Like a stripper teasing a group of randy partygoers, she eased up her skirt, and, as his hand snaked toward her, kicked him in the mouth, leapt off the bed, and hauled up her knickers.

"I wasn't going to touch honest," he whimpered through his fingers, his lip already swelling, then his tone changed to that of a spiteful brat. "I was going to take you home, but I'm not now." *I'm keeping the ball if you don't let me play.*

The four-minute taxi ride from Schiphol to the private airfield had been heavily weighted by Superintendent Edwards' presence, and sunk further when he spotted Yolanda's small plane.

"Doesn't look like a police plane," he grumbled.

"Unmarked," said Bliss, with a flash of inspiration.

"This way Edward," Yolanda sang out, her voice bouncing with enthusiasm.

Edwards stopped and glared. "My name is Superintendent Edwards," he stressed, dragging the mood even lower.

"Oh ..." she began, confused. "I thought you said your name was Edward."

Bliss strolled between them carting the senior officer's luggage and made light of the situation. "Where shall I put Superintendent Edwards' bags, Detective Pieters?"

"In here, Detective Bliss," she responded, quickly catching on.

Bags loaded, the superintendent was on the point of boarding when he had second thoughts.

"Is there a bathroom here anywhere, Inspector?"

Relief swept over Bliss, he had almost forgotten his own desperate need. "I expect so, Sir. I'll come with you, " he replied, turning to Yolanda for directions, but she shrugged.

"Maybe in that building," was the best she could offer, turning to the nearest Quonset hut.

"We'll ask," shouted the superintendent, already ten strides away. Bliss caught up. The granite-faced superintendent sensed his presence and without looking, launched into him. "So, let me get this straight, Bliss. You were guarding LeClarc?"

"Me and the ..."

"Shut up," he ordered nastily, his teeth clamped tightly. "I'll tell you when to speak."

"Yes, Sir."

"As I was saying. You were guarding LeClarc—correction—you were being *paid* to guard LeClarc. And he disappeared under your fuckin' nose."

Bliss considered the merit of interrupting further but lost his chance as Edwards spat. "You useless little shit. Do you realize what they're saying about me at H.Q.?"

He didn't, but could guess.

Edwards stopped and stared him straight in the face. Bliss, a good six inches taller, shrank several feet. "You screwed up," the senior officer barked, "and I suggest you start thinking of some bloody good answers for the discipline board. As far as I'm concerned this will be all your fault. You failed to do your duty. The press are lapping it up. It'll be all over the evening papers. Even the P.M.'s office has been on the phone wanting to know if it's true. 'Lost another one have we?' the bloody press secretary said, as though we lose one every day. Heads will roll Bliss, but I shall make sure your's goes first. Got me?" Then, re-enforcing his fusillade, he yanked open his fly and defiantly pissed on the ground.

Bliss, fuming, could think of nothing worthwhile to say and they walked back to the plane in silence to find Yolanda sneaking a cigarette. Squeezing it out, she dropped it on the ground and opened the passenger door.

"Where's the pilot?" Edwards blared, baulking at the doorway. He was not having a good day—why should anyone else?

Bliss and Yolanda looked at each other, but were saved the need to explain as Edwards spotted a uniformed man walking toward them. Satisfied, he climbed into the rear seat and was still fidgeting himself into place when the man, a security guard, veered off to continue his rounds.

In the air, eventually, Yolanda concentrated on the flying, while Edwards concentrated on quelling his stomach. Bliss sat quietly, entranced by a white carpet of greenhouses and the endless ribbons of canals and roads, while steaming under the threat of disciplinary action.

"How much longer?" Edwards queried gruffly after ten minutes in the air; ten minutes of edgy silence when neither man had said a word.

"Fifteen minutes," Yolanda replied cheerily, glancing at him in the rear view mirror, thinking: He looks awful. Mr. Bliss looks pretty rough too, she thought, stealing a look at his darkly pensive face out of the corner of an eye. "We might run into some turbulence soon," she continued. "We often do around here." Her right eye winked at Bliss and he caught the look. "It's something to do with the sea, " she added for effect, noticing just a touch of brightness around his lips.

Edwards moaned, saying nothing.

Thirty seconds later her right hand eased its way across the short gap in between the seats and slid over the top of Bliss' thigh. Her fingers gently squeezed into the soft flesh near his groin and all hell broke loose.

The plane dropped like a stone and started spinning wildly. Her grip on his thigh increased. A scream came from the back. The plane crashed against an invisible cushion of air, then bounced off in the other direction. Her fingers bit into his flesh an inch from the end of his growing member. She stabbed at the controls and the nose shot upwards as Edwards was smashed back in his seat. Then the plane skidded onto its side forcing Bliss' body to slide across the cockpit in her direction. Her fingers held his leg tightly as his world tumbled upside down. Bliss wanted to scream— terror or excitement? Before he could decide, Yolanda gave his thigh an extra little squeeze, let go, put both hands on the controls, and resumed level flight.

"A bit bumpy," she said nonchalantly.

Superintendent Edwards slumped in the seat, a paper tissue held firmly over his mouth. He said nothing, the fear in his eyes said everything.

Captain Jahnssen was waiting on the tarmac as they touched down. Yolanda had alerted him on the radio. "Pleased to meet you, Sir," said the captain, unsure of the correct address to use for a foreign officer of equal rank—sticking with "Sir" as the safest bet.

"Michael," he snapped, gratefully collapsing onto the rear seat.

"We'll see you back at the port, Detectives," the captain addressed Bliss and Yolanda together. "Why don't you stop and get a meal. You two haven't eaten all day. I'll bring the superintendent up to date."

"Any news?" enquired Bliss, hopefully.

The captain shook his head as he climbed in beside Edwards, and the car sped off with Yolanda slumping in relief and Bliss dancing on the spot.

"What's up Dave?"

"Won't be a minute," he shouted, running for a nearby building.

# chapter seven

Lisa McKenzie paced frenziedly outside the Flightpath restaurant at Stanstead airport, a few miles north of London, not far from Watford. Her ex-husband sat inside chatting to the police constable who had come with them to meet Margery. Peter poked his head out the door for the fourth time. "Come and have a cup of tea, Luv."

A smile failed in the attempt and she shook her head. "I'm alright." Abstinence had become a penitence: *How can I eat when my baby is ...?* And to have eaten or drunk when not in her chair would have been doubly sacrilegious.

The moment she'd left her chair in the apartment in Leyton the feeling came over her that she was doing the wrong thing: Believing that leaving the chair would somehow break the bond tying her to Trudy's spirit and that, without a tether, the spirit would simply drift away.

"You don't have to come if you don't want to," the officer had said, detecting her reluctance. "Me and Mr. McKenzie can get her and bring her straight back here."

She was torn, desperate for news, desperate to see Roger's photograph and even desperate to see Margery, who at least embodied some link between her and her only daughter. "I'll come," she decided at last, after declining twice. "What time does she arrive?"

"The plane's due at seven twenty-eight," the policeman said, with annoying precision. "We've arranged for Margery to be brought straight through immigration and customs, so we should be back here by half past eight at the latest."

It was now nearly eight-fifteen. "Delayed," was the only information provided on the huge arrivals board, but they already knew that. The constable had contacted the control tower as soon as they arrived a little after six-thirty. "Two hours late leaving Avignon due to a puncture," he had told them. "They might be able to make up a little time but they said we shouldn't expect her much before nine-thirty."

"Damn," swore Peter, well aware a couple of national papers had promised to run Roger's photograph, as long as they had it before ten.

"Let's keep our fingers crossed shall we," continued the policeman. "Anyway, another day won't make much difference." The immediate look of horror on Lisa McKenzie's face alerted him to his faux pas and he fumbled to correct himself. "Ah ... I mean. I know it does make a difference. But, um ... It would give us more time to make sure the picture's printed properly." Her face was unmoved. "Anyway," he placed his trump firmly on the table, "more people read the papers on Saturdays than they do on Friday."

Lisa McKenzie, convinced they were already too late, buckled under the weight of yet another setback. Her face scrunched and she started to cry. Peter flung a sympathetic arm around her and pulled her to his chest.

"Sorry," mumbled the policeman.

"It's O.K. Not your fault Constable. My wife's very emotional at the moment."

Looking up, she caught the innocence in his vacant expression and realized the possessive term was just a slip; his troubled thoughts a banana skin for his tongue. Another wave of emotion rippled across her face and she wept more loudly.

They had spent the first hour at the airport in the depressing waiting room at the police office, but had run out of conversation in the first five minutes. Aside from Trudy, any other topic would have been facile. The constable, an infatuated chrysanthemum grower, longed to tell them about the propagation of his latest creation, a huge double pink he was certain would win major prizes.

"Do you like flowers Mrs. McKenzie?" he asked, with a bounce of brightness in his voice, hoping to take her mind off Trudy.

"Not much." Her apartment was overflowing with bouquets from well-meaning well-wishers—three since Margery's call at lunchtime—and mention of more flowers immediately crumpled her face in thoughts of funerals.

Lisa had spent most of her time in the waiting room staring bleary-eyed at a bulletin board, strewn with pictures of missing people, culled from the *Police Gazette*. Some bore inscriptions that terrified her: "*Missing since October 15th 1982*," was boldly printed under the smiling face of one little boy, forever four years-old in the minds of his distraught parents.

Another said. "Last heard of in 1991—stated intention of visiting friend in Morocco." "That's ten years," she mused, biting furiously at the quick of her nails.

"She's not here," she screamed suddenly, "Trudy's not here."

Peter leapt at her scream, flinging aside the seven-year-old *National Geographic* he'd been scanning.

"Look," she ordered, her head zipping back and forth in a desperate search for her daughter's likeness. Peter looked.

The constable came up behind them. "It's too soon," he said, with quiet authority. "It takes at least a month for the photos to be in the *Gazette*. Anyway," he lightened his tone, "I'm sure we'll have found her by then."

Finally, after refusing an offer of tea from a grumpily indifferent sergeant, who had made it clear he would be sacrificing some of his own personal supply, they decided to take a walk around the airport. Everywhere she looked Lisa saw Trudy; every girl with long dark hair grabbed her attention; every female face, and some male, had familiar features. And what if she'd disguised herself? What if she'd cut her hair, bleached it, changed style, altered her entire appearance? No one escaped scrutiny without at least a cursory inspection, irrespective of age, size, or colour. The airport lounges were filled with potential Trudies and an embarrassed Peter eventually dragged her, fairly forcibly, away from the busiest areas.

"She won't be here Luv," he said, firmly taking her arm. "The constable has gone to enquire if there is any more information, I said we'd meet him in the restaurant."

"What about that girl over there?" she tried, refusing to give up.

He looked. "She's at least forty. Come on. Let's go and wait for Margery."

A dark ponytail bobbed in the distance—she struggled in its wake. "Stop it," he commanded sharply, dragging her toward the restaurant.

"Nothing new," the policeman said as they met a few minutes later. "I'm sure we'll find her easily once we've got the photo," he added with a smile to Lisa, hoping to make up for his previous insensitivity.

"Roger might not know anything," she replied coldly, refusing to get her hopes up. Disappointment had knocked her back into the old kitchen chair too many times already.

Peter stepped in. "We won't know if we don't try. Trudy has to be somewhere, and you know how mad she was about that computer. Maybe this guy will know something, or some of his friends might."

Roger certainly knew where Trudy was, though had no idea what she was doing.

Trudy was typing again. Sending another message to her mother that would get no further than the little green screen. The first message in nearly five hours.

"MUM. WHERE ARE YOU. PLEASE HURRY ..." Her fingers paused, the flurry of activity had sapped her energy. Every movement she made away from her breathing hole in the door now requiring more and more effort. She was already completely drained by the time she had crawled to the computer but, with her lungs screaming for air, she willed herself to stay just long enough to keep in touch with her mother.

"GET DAD," she added, in desperation, and then she was gone again. Her painful pilgrimage starting once more.

"Do you like the herring?" Yolanda enquired, stuffing a large prawn into her mouth, peering at Bliss through the trio of tall white candles, which formed the only barrier between them as they sat in one of the few remaining Dutch restaurants in the tourist resort, a few miles to the north of the port. The ride in the BMW had taken twenty minutes but, as Yolanda explained, they had no choice, unless he preferred Indonesian, Chinese, or American; all of it fast and foreign. Bliss looked at the partially exposed fish skeleton on his plate, debating how and when to finish it; wishing he'd opted for a burger or chow mien.

"Every visitor to Holland must eat at least one raw herring," she continued as if reading from a Michelin guide. "It is the law." She kept a straight face and for a moment he could have believed her.

Then he laughed. "You're joking."

She smiled, admitting nothing.

"Anyway," he said, "if they are that good, why didn't you have one?"

She pulled a face and pretended to spit on the floor. "They're disgusting. We only give them to visitors."

"Now you tell me."

"If you are a good boy and eat all of your herring," she said, slowly lifting a huge prawn to dangle tantalisingly in front of his face, "you can have another one." Laughing, she quickly popped the prawn, whole, into her mouth.

The candlelight flickered between them as he studied her. Analysing her face carefully, without staring, trying to identify the one or two unique features that would distinguish her from any other woman. Fashionably unruly short blond hair, baby blue eyes, nicely formed white teeth and a pair of lips some men would kill for.. But such a description could fit thousands of similarly attractive women. As a detective he searched for something more noteworthy, more uniquely identifiable, more defining: The deep dimple in her left cheek, not reflected in the right, was certainly striking, though hardly conclusive. Her nose was perhaps a little bulbous; not unattractively so. But the feature which struck him so positively lay either side of her mouth, where her flesh creased deeply, and perfectly, into a pair of delicately curved parentheses, bracketing her lips and accentuating her smile.

Tiredness dragged him down as his eyelids drifted together and, giving his head a quick shake, he renewed the conversation. "I wonder what has happened to LeClarc."

"They threw him off the ship," she replied casually.

"But why? They obviously planned to put him in the truck ..."

She interrupted, laughing. "I know, but he was too fat and they couldn't get him in."

Bliss laughed with her, "No, I don't think so ... although ...?"

Yolanda's face became serious. "What's he worth?"

"What do you mean?"

"He must be valuable or they wouldn't want him. People steal things because of what they are worth."

"Sometimes," he agreed. "Usually ... But sometimes they take things because they are jealous, to get revenge, or ... or lots of reasons."

"What about the other eight missing people?" she asked, changing tack. "How many of their bodies were never found?"

He thought for a moment while the waiter collected their plates. The herring's eyes had been staring accusingly at him for at the past five minutes and he was pleased to see it go. "Only one for sure—the woman; the one who committed suicide. There were a few burned bits left from the guy who hit the train, but it must have been like trying to identify a pig by examining a barbecued pork chop.

She shuddered. "Dave, I'm eating."

"You asked," he said, and continued, in revenge for the herring. "I've seen the photos. All the identifiable bits were so badly burned you couldn't be sure they were human."

"DNA?" she enquired, knowing he would understand.

He shook his head slightly. "Doubt it; they might have tried, but they had no reason. His wife said it was him, recognized his clothes and car. The inquest said it was an accident: lost control and crashed through the fence. It was just bad luck the train was there at the same time."

"Bad luck or very good timing," she mused. "Zo, the other six," She leaned forward earnestly, seeking information in his eyes, a balloon glass of Chardonnay cupped in both hands like a crystal ball suspended mid-air between them. "Where are they?"

He shook his head again, but his eyes remained riveted to hers. "No one knows," he replied. Their eyes stuck. His face tingled. Her lips parted, just a fraction. Time stopped.

Then the waiter broke the spell and they leaned back while he scurried around removing bits and pieces of unwanted cutlery to make room for the main course.

"Steak and chips," Bliss had insisted, having been coerced into the herring; feeling one native dish would be sufficiently politic. She had chosen a warm chicken salad with an unpronounceable name for herself.

"Nobody really took any notice of the disappearances until we got the tip about LeClarc," he said, as soon as the waiter was out of earshot.

"Why not?" she enquired, then pushed a forkful of food in his direction. "Try this it's wonderful." He opened his mouth, almost involuntarily, and she slid the fork in.

"Mmm, that's good," he mumbled, though was glad he had chosen the steak. "Lots of people disappear," he continued, returning to his theme. "Most turn up sooner or later. If they are adults and there is no real suspicion of foul play, we don't go out of our way to look for them."

Considerately, she held her next question until he had eaten a few chunks of steak. "But these people were important. Somebody should have made enquiries."

The implied criticism stung and he went on the defensive. "It's not that simple. Two of them, the woman and the guy hit by the train weren't missing: they were dead. One man disappeared in the Atlantic. The loner who lived in the Welsh mountains was eccentric."

Yolanda's head cocked to one side. "Centric?" she questioned.

"Weird—a bit crazy," he explained.

"Okey dokey. But that leaves four."

He chewed thoughtfully trying to remember what had happened to the others. "The two men in the boat," he said, between bites, "could have been an accident. It could've sunk, caught fire, hit by a whale ..."

"Eaten by a herring," she proposed, and made him laugh again.

"Seriously," he continued, straightening his face, "anything could have gone wrong."

"And the other two men?"

He shrugged. "Run off with their secretaries; scarpered with the social club Christmas fund; fell in love with each other and started a gay bar in California."

Yolanda laughed.

"Who knows," added Bliss, "but the point is, nobody linked the cases together. The M.O. was different in each case."

He stopped—checking her face for comprehension—then carried on. "All the informant said was LeClarc was going to be kidnapped, nothing about the others, they might not be connected at all."

Yolanda stared meditatively into her wineglass for sometime, then began slowly. "This was well planned; would have cost a lot of money. King, Motsom, and the driver had to be paid, and the special truck had to be on the right ship. If that crewman ..."

"Jacobs?" suggested Bliss.

"Yeah ... If he hadn't been on the deck at the same time as King, it would have been another accident—like the others."

Bliss tried to interject but her mind was pre-occupied—the answer seemingly at her fingertips. "Whoever took them went to a lot of trouble and, in most cases, wanted you to believe they were ..." She paused. "Dave, Dave."

He had fallen asleep, his head slouched on his chest. Thirty-six hours of uninterrupted wakefulness had finally taken its toll.

She drove delicately back to the port, easing the powerful car gently around the sweeping curves of the narrow road on top of a polder, more than fifty feet above the sea. Below her, the mist was condensing into fog, and the huge breakers had been crushed into a low undulating swell by the weight of the heavy still air. Only the remnants of the storm remained, smeared across the sky in thin grey streaks and tinged pink by the setting sun. Bliss slept motionless on the reclining seat by her side.

Captain Jahnssen was waiting for them and came flying out of the back door of the police station the moment he saw the white BMW.

"Yolanda, Yolanda," he shouted, his hands forming a megaphone around his mouth, as she started to get out. She stopped, somewhat startled, and stared. He shot twenty words of Dutch in her direction and, without a word, leapt back into the car and drove away.

Slipping calmly back into his seat in the staff dining room a few moments later, the captain returned to his chocolate gâteau with the nonchalance of the innocent.

"Was it them Jost?" enquired Edwards.

"No ... No. I expect Ms. Pieters will take him straight to a hotel. He'll be here in the morning I am sure."

"I wanted that little snot back on board the ship tonight," Edwards snapped icily, feeling cheated.

A chill had permeated the relationship between the two senior officers from the moment they had driven away from the airfield. Superintendent Edwards was on the offensive before the captain had even fastened his seat belt.

"Captain," he had started, formally.

"It is Jost."

"Very well, Jost," he said, sounding like a sergeant major, "I think we should understand each other, start off on the right foot, keep everything square. D'ye know what I mean?"

"Yes, Michael," he replied, concern immediately detectable in his voice.

Edwards continued forcefully. "I want to make it clear. I am the only person who gives orders to my men. Bliss should be working, not gallivanting around with some ..." he nearly said "tart," but switched in time to, "woman," adding, "Even if she is a detective."

"Superintendent," responded the captain, visibly shaken by the attack, "that man has done a terrific job. I'm not sure about the others, especially the sergeant, but you shouldn't criticize Inspector Bliss."

"It was his bloody fault they lost LeClarc in the first place. Where are the others anyway?"

"Your sergeant with the broken wrist has gone back on the ship. The other two, we have taken to a hotel."

Edwards snorted his disapproval, fuming at the notion his men were luxuriating in a hotel when, if he had his way, they would have been on jankers—shackled in a guardhouse on iron rations.

"Can you tell me more about this case, Michael?" Captain Jahnssen asked, attempting to fill the awkward void.

Edwards shot a glance at the back of the driver's head. "I'll tell you in private. You never know who you can trust these days."

Five minutes later Superintendent Edwards had flung himself into an armchair in the captain's office and started dragging papers out of his briefcase.

"Drink, Michael?" offered the captain.

"Coffee—milk, two sugars."

"I have some excellent Scotch," he said, flourishing a bottle of single malt, like a parent trying to placate a fractious child with the offer of a toy.

"I am on duty, Jost," Edwards replied stonily, refusing to be bought—then relented. "Maybe later ... What a bloody fiasco," he said as he slapped a thick file onto the captain's desk. Have you any idea ...?" He paused. "How much do you know about this case?"

"I know a few computer specialists have disappeared, or been killed, and this LeClarc man was a target. It seems they pushed him off the ship for some reason. That's about all really."

"Do you know why they wanted him, or the others?"

"Not really. But if you would excuse me for a moment, I must order your coffee. Oh, do you have a photograph of Motsom? We still haven't received one by fax."

He picked up the phone as Edwards rummaged through his briefcase, turning up a photograph stamped "Central Records 1986." "The only one we've got," he said, handing it to the captain.

Edwards shuffled a few papers, waiting while the captain finished his call then asked, "What's Motsom's role in this?"

Jahnssen put the phone down and perched on the corner of his desk. "We don't know, but we do know that the main suspect, David King, was in touch with Motsom on the ship, and Motsom's car is still at the port."

A polite rap on the door interrupted them and the officer delivering the coffee took the photograph.

"He's going to get some copies out to all our men. They'll make enquiries around the port and the bars. Usual routine. Motsom must be here somewhere."

He was wrong. Billy Motsom had left town nearly an hour earlier.

"Right," said Superintendent Edwards, clasping his hands together and thrusting them high above his head, "let me explain." Then, pulling himself upright in the chair he took a deep breath as if preparing to deliver an earth shattering revelation.

"What we are dealing with is potentially more dangerous than the atomic bomb." Exactly the same words the Minister of Defence had used to him at a cabinet briefing two weeks earlier. "Let me repeat," he continued, pulling himself forward in the chair, "potentially more dangerous than the atomic bomb."

His arms dropped. He lowered himself back in the seat and his eyes gazed skywards in their sockets, checking his brain to see if he had missed anything. The captain, feeling an answer was expected, if not demanded, could only manage an astonished, "Aaaah."

Edwards brought his fingertips together in front of his face, and toyed thoughtfully with the end of his nose. "The fact is, these nine people, together with half a dozen Americans, potentially pose a threat to world peace."

The captain was way behind, though catching up. "So you are suggesting, whoever controls these people, whoever's kidnapped them, could somehow use them to control the world."

"Far-fetched, I know, Jost, but precisely. Together they could hold the entire world to ransom. Even a nuclear bomb can only be targeted against one country at a time. Information can destroy the world."

The captain slid off the desk back into his chair, then laughed. "You're crazy.

Edwards, for once, seemed unconcerned. "I said exactly same thing when they told me, but think about it for a moment, Jost. Do you remember what happened a couple of years ago when half the phone systems in America went on the blink for a few hours?"

The captain's face was a blank.

Edwards continued without awaiting an answer. "Chaos, absolute chaos: Stock markets tumbled; emergency calls went unanswered; banks ground to a halt; transportation systems crashed; air traffic snarled up— took nearly three days to sort out." He paused, leaned forward and added, conspiratorially, "Not to mention the interruption to inter-governmental communications and defence systems."

"Do they know what caused it?" asked the captain, lamely.

"Publicly they blamed it on a power failure, but," he lowered his tone to a stage whisper, "the people at the Pentagon have other ideas—a trial run. Somebody accessed the computer system of the telephone company, screwed the whole thing up just to see what would happen."

The captain wasn't convinced and risked Edwards' ire. "This sounds, how do you say: Off the wall. I don't believe a few computer people could do that."

"The right people could."

"But there are security systems."

Edwards sat back and dealt an ace. "Twice in the past three months the U.S. National Defence computer has been seriously compromised ... Twice," he added for emphasis.

"But ..." began the captain, losing confidence.

"And," continued Edwards without waiting for the captain to finish, "at least two communication satellites have been knocked off course in the past year alone."

"Yes, but as I was saying, were any of the missing people involved?"

"We have no idea. We don't know where they are or what happened to them."

"Inspector Bliss said two were dead," responded the captain, attempting to weaken the superintendent's case.

Edwards slowly sucked in his breath, released it as an explosive "Pah," and admitted, "We're not sure now that they are dead."

"What about the woman who committed suicide? Bliss said she left a note."

His reply was guarded. "That's true, there was a note ..." Edwards hesitated as if holding onto something important, keeping Captain Jahnssen on a leash. "Dogs," he added mysteriously. "I wasn't involved in the case but apparently she lived on her own with a couple of Dalmatians and a snappy little terrier of some description. Anyway, it was about two weeks before a neighbour called the police, thought the woman was away on holiday, and when they broke in there wasn't a lot left."

"I've seen a couple of cases like that."

"At the time nobody questioned it; they cremated the few bits that were left and the dogs were put down."

The captain figured out the possibilities. "So you think the woman they ate was a different woman?"

"It's possible. The same sort of thing with the bloke that smashed into the train—was it him, or was it some poor sod who had been picked off the streets and stuck into his car wearing his clothes?" He smiled wryly. "He was cremated right away, the train driver went up in flames with him."

The captain stuck his forefinger in his left ear, twisted it, and carefully examined the result before enquiring, "How sure are you these cases are linked?"

"We're not. In fact until we got a tip about LeClarc a few weeks ago we hadn't even considered it. But, according to certain people, the biggest threat we face today is global destabilization. Whoever controls the telecommunication and computer networks effectively controls everything: commodity prices, money supply, what we see, what we hear, who talks to whom. Not to mention all our defence and transportation systems." He warmed to his theme and continued as if he had worked everything out for himself. "You know what happened at the end of the last war?"

Captain Jahnssen nodded obligingly, but his puzzled expression showed signs of information overload.

"You know what happened to the German scientists and rocket builders? The Yanks snatched half of them and the Ruskies snatched the rest. Do you think anybody would have got to the moon if it hadn't been for German scientists? Never."

"Yes, I know that, but what has that got to do with this case?"

Edwards gave him the same look he might have given a ten-year- old school-kid with a snotty nose. "Brains" he shouted. "That's what it's all about. You don't need to control the resources if you control the brains. The brains today are computers, and the way to control them is to control the programmers; they're the rocket scientists now. Whoever has them is amassing an arsenal more powerful than all the world's armies put together." He relaxed slowly into the chair and closed his eyes. "I'll have that Scotch now," he said, his mission complete.

An urgent knock at the door interrupted the momentary peace.

"Enter!" shouted Edwards—force of habit, forgetting he was a guest.

"We've found Motsom, Sir," babbled the uniformed officer as he burst into the room flourishing the photograph. He spoke English, but his eyes flicked back and forth between the two men, unsure which of the senior officers he should be addressing.

"Where?" they both questioned at the same time.

The officer, a tall young man in a smartly pressed uniform, continued in Dutch until the captain stopped him with the command, "English."

He switched immediately. "The barman at the Rhine Tavern recognized him from the photograph. He's been there all afternoon."

"Is he still there?" asked the captain, taking the photograph and examining it with interest.

The officer's face fell a little. "He left about seven o'clock. But the barman remembered the car—a black Saab. I've put the description out to all forces. I'll keep you informed."

"Let's eat Michael," said the captain, seizing the opportunity, "and I can explain what we are doing."

## chapter eight

"GIVE ME A DRINK," demanded Trudy, her bloodied fingers taking more than two minutes to select the correct letters from the dyslexic jumble on the keyboard. Another bout of coughing doubled her over and left her gasping for breath. The rancid air had rasped her throat for more than a week, but at least it had been freshened a couple of times a day when Roger visited. Now, for nearly thirty -six hours, she had breathed the same stale air, supplemented only by what she could laboriously suck through the keyhole. The constant effort of sucking was itself painful as her swollen and cracked lips kissed the cold metal escutcheon. Yet, she instinctively knew stopping would mean certain death.

"WATERS GONE," she added slowly on the next line, without troubling the apostrophe key.

Roger had left plenty of water, but she had used it more to ease her pain and discomfort than to quench

her thirst; splashing it liberally onto her face to cool
sore lips and flush away salty tears; bathing blistered
and bloody hands; washing herself after peeing.
Following her abortive and painful efforts to escape, it
had been too much effort to use the bucket. In any
case, the only time she was really aware of wetting herself was when the acidic fluid ran down her legs, aggravating the cuts and sores on her knees. An entire bottle
of water had been used to rinse out her knickers the
first time she failed to reach the bucket. Too wet to
wear, she had draped them over the computer where
she hoped the warmth would dry them. Without underwear, the wet, course, denim of her new skirt rasped
the tender flesh of her behind with every movement.

"MY BOTTOM HURTS, MUMMY," she typed,
with the tears of a toddler suffering diaper rash. Crying
again she decided it was time to go, slithered to the
floor, and let her lungs drag her back to the life-sustain-
ing hole in the door.


Superintendent Michael Edwards and Captain Jost
Jahnssen dined alone in the imposing staff room, the
highly polished floor and oak panelled walls acting as a
sounding board. Almost everything in the room
remained the same as it had been when the original owners left, hurriedly, in 1944. Only the chairs and language
had changed. The Senior Officer's Mess, as it had been,
would have been instantly recognizable to any of the
German soldiers stationed there at that time. Indeed, several had returned over the years, greeted politely as
guests, though never as friends, by the new inhabitants
of their barracks on the hill overlooking the port.

Superintendent Edwards salivated over the menu.
Twenty-five years experience of British police canteens

had never yielded *Coquilles St. Jacques Ostendaise* or *Rognons de Veau en croute avec sauce Bordelaise.* Greasy fish and chips or liver and onions with mash was as close as they'd come.

The captain caught the look of astonishment. "It is from the restaurant next door."

Edwards relaxed and lied, "I guessed it was." Then he settled on the fish and chips masquerading as *Filet de Sole (au Mer du Nord), Meunière avec Pommes frit.*

"Let me tell you what we have done," began the captain, their dinner orders taken by a surly filing clerk with a ring in her nose and a hairstyle from hell, making no pretence of being a waitress. "We've interviewed King, he will say nothing. We will keep him overnight then take him before a magistrate tomorrow on charges of murder and stealing a car."

Edwards' head jerked up. "Murder?"

"Well. That's how it looks at the moment. If he didn't push LeClarc over the side why was he driving his car?"

"Good point," replied Edwards, "What do we know about King?"

"He say's he is a private detective but can't prove it. He didn't have a car on board and we have not found any of his belongings. There was no cabin booked in his name but we think he was travelling with Motsom." Reminded of Motsom, the captain retrieved the photograph from his file and studied it for a second. "I think this man is the key to the case, Michael; what can you tell me about him?"

Edwards sifted through his papers and came up with a single sheet. "Born 1955, Birmingham, England. William John Motsom, alias Billy. 5'11", brown hair, brown eyes, muscular build." He glanced up. "This was ten years ago Jost, he might have gone flabby since then." He returned to the page. "Right ear-lobe missing," then pulled a face, "Tattoo: naked woman on left forearm." What is it with villains and tattoos of naked women? he thought to himself.

Scanning the page, he skipped to the pre-cons section. "A few juvenile convictions: possession of weapons, robbery," then mumbled, "that's interesting."

"What?"

"He was interviewed in relation to one of the missing computer people. The one who disappeared on his bicycle. Motsom's car was seen in the area that day." He flipped the paper over, the blank side stared at him. "It doesn't say what happened, just that he was interviewed. I'll get someone to look into that. Now what's happening with LeClarc."

"We've asked shipping to look out for the body, but the fog's quite thick I understand," said the captain, splashing another shot of whisky into each of their glasses.

"I got the forecast before I left England. There's a fog warning in the North Sea for at least twenty-four hours. Maybe longer."

"It could last a week or more," added the captain, with the voice of experience. "Sometimes we don't see across the river for two or three weeks."

"Is there any chance of finding him alive?"

"No—impossible. He could survive a few hours at the most, but in a rough sea without a life jacket he would be dead in thirty minutes. He probably died straight away."

"What about the life-raft?"

"King threw it over the side. He probably thought the crewman had seen him push LeClarc overboard, so he pretended he was trying to save him. Quick thinking, but too late for LeClarc."

The first course arrived—prawn cocktails in delicate glass tureens shrouded with plastic. The co-opted waitress dumped them on them table, still wrapped, and stomped off without a word.

"What about the truck?" enquired Edwards.

"Yugoslavian registered, or it was, before Yugoslavia broke up. Impossible to trace the owners now ... could be Serbian but we're not sure. The paperwork looks O.K. but there's at least four different official governments issuing documents, and several unofficial ones."

"The driver?"

"Austrian—says he knows nothing about it. We'll have to let him go unless we can link him to Motsom or LeClarc. He's scared. Claims he just picked up the truck and was paid cash to deliver it. There was nothing to prove LeClarc was going to be put into that truck—just a hunch. The fresh food and water suggests there was going to be a passenger, and we think the truck was designed to get refugees out of Bosnia or Croatia, but someone hired it for this special job. It has certainly been used before. Mr. Bliss found the compartment. He is a very good detective, I think."

"He shouldn't have lost LeClarc in the first place. It's all his bloody fault," Edwards shot back, his face immediately reddening. This was one hook Bliss wasn't going to wriggle off. Edwards needed a scapegoat. Word had already filtered back to him that he was being personally blamed. The assistant commissioner, according to the rumour picked up by his secretary in the lunchroom, had called the deputy commissioner to discuss a charge of neglect. There were several old scores to be settled and the rumour had followed an acrimonious 9 a.m. meeting with the A.C., which had lasted all of thirty seconds.

"What's happened?" the Assistant Commissioner had enquired blackly, without inviting Edwards to sit down.

"We seem to have temporarily lost LeClarc, Sir," he had said with false bravado.

"Well I suggest you temporarily find him again, Mr. Edwards."

"We are trying, Sir."

"Try harder Mr. Edwards and, just for the record, how did eight detectives manage to lose one fat man on a ship?"

Flustered, he mumbled "Ah ... I'll get onto it right away, Sir."

"You do that Mr. Edwards. I shall expect your report in twenty-four hours. Good morning."

The waitress returned noisily with the main course, her heavy boots clumping halfway across the room. The captain yelled they were not ready so she plunked the tray of food on the nearest table and clumped back out. Despite the noise Edwards didn't notice her, his mind still stuck on the morning's meeting and, with mounting fury, his fists clenched, his muscles tensed, and the blood pumped in his temples.

"Bugger. You'd think four of them would be enough on board one bloody ship," he exploded, slamming a fist onto the table and catching Captain Jahnssen completely off guard.

"I. Um ...," started the captain, but was immediately cut short by Edwards violently smashing his right fist into the palm of his left hand as if stabbing himself.

"What could go wrong, eh?" he yelled, but gave no time for an answer. "How could they have been so stupid?" Then the tension abated and he looked across the table at the captain, "Sorry," he said, "I wonder if I could have a drop more whisky." He spoke as if nothing had happened and the captain poured him a generous shot before rising to fetch the dinner plates.

They ate silently for more than five minutes—an explanation brewing. "There was a second team," Edwards began eventually, "back- up—but Bliss and the others didn't know about them. It was just a safety measure in case anything went wrong."

"Something did go wrong," interjected the captain, then wished he hadn't.

"I know," screamed Edwards, "I pulled the second group off when LeClarc got safely on board. I didn't want to lose two teams for forty-eight four hours. What could happen on a ship? It was only an eight hour crossing for Christ sake." He paused for a second, then pleaded with Jahnssenn. "I was just trying to keep expenses down."

"Oh," was all the captain could muster.

"So," continued Edwards in a lighter tone, "what's our plan now?"

Captain Jahnssen really didn't have a plan, the events of the day had taken their own course and he, like everybody else, had simply reacted. Thinking for a second he ad-libbed, "I thought you would want to interview King and the driver yourself," he began, then paused hoping Edwards would say something to give him more time to think.

"And ...?" said Edwards expectantly, then had an idea of his own. "What about the truck, do we know where it was going?"

"Istanbul according to the documents, but that would take three or four days by road, maybe more."

"Perhaps we should contact the Turkish police, although I doubt if LeClarc would have been taken there. They would probably have stopped the truck en route and hauled him out into a car."

An idea seized the captain. "What if I put a couple of men into the truck and let it go, he might lead us to the kidnappers."

Enthusiasm brightened Edwards' face as he envisaged the scheme. "I could send two of my men with two of yours in the back of the truck. We'll have to hope the kidnappers have no way of knowing LeClarc isn't inside."

Jahnssen frowned, "It might be dangerous. I think we should send a car as well, another two officers." He paused for thought, "Maybe four, these men have already murdered two innocent people if what you say is correct."

"I've only got two men here."

"And Detective Bliss?"

Edwards felt his blood rising—Bliss had twice put the phone down on him in one day, in addition to losing LeClarc. "Mr. Bliss will return to England first thing tomorrow," he replied firmly—further discussion unwelcome. "We will make do with the men we have."

The chocolate gâteau had been excellent. "A definite cut above the canteen at Scotland Yard," Edwards was saying when an officer crashed into the room and blasted the captain with a volley of Dutch.

"They've spotted the Saab," translated the captain excitedly, "near Rotterdam."

"And Motsom?"

"Quick. We'll go to the communications room and find out."

They half ran down the long corridor, round a corner. Run up a staircase or wait for the elevator? They chose the stairs, climbed six and heard the ping of the elevator behind them. They kept going, the decision already made. Two steps at a time they made it to the next floor, turned left and flew into the control room.

Stopping for a second Edwards familiarized himself with his surroundings—no different from any other police control room: A jumble of telephones, radios and computer terminals; walls covered with banks of alarm panels and enormous maps; desks strewn with scratch pads, instruction manuals and coffee cups.

The loudspeakers were alive with unintelligible words, shooting back and forth with the rapidity of a foreign TV quiz show. He couldn't understand a word yet knew exactly what they were saying.

"They're chasing the Saab," the captain said rapidly in English, not wasting time for fear of missing something important. "We've got two cars behind him."

Edwards pictured the chase in his mind. The tension of the police drivers and co-drivers: adrenalin pumping, muscles taught with anticipation, breathing heavily, hearts beating loud enough to hear. Each man speaking in one-word commands: Right. Left. Faster. Stop. The controlled power and emotion—two highly charged men and more than two hundred horsepower in one car. The excitement; the exhilaration; the thrill. And the risks: Cornering too fast; braking too late; jumping lights; squeezing through impossible gaps.

Captain Jahnssen listened intently, interpreting what he could, the important bits. "They're driving fast—two hundred kilometres an hour."

There's nothing like it, thought Edwards, exhilarated by the excited babble on the radio, nothing compares to the thrill of a police chase: Seat of the pants driving; controlled skids, sudden direction changes. The risk taking. Guessing—no, not guessing—calculating the way the target will turn. The rush; the sheer speed; the way everything flashes past in a blur. Total concentration on the target and the road to the exclusion of everything. Mind and machine in perfect harmony.

The voices on the radio bubbled with excitement as they closed in. "Big intersection ahead," explained the captain.

Edwards pictured it: Red lights rushing toward them—stab the brakes; jab the clutch; wrench the gear stick; thrust the throttle to the floor; twist the wheel; feel the tires sliding and bouncing, losing grip. Pedestrians and cyclists out for a jaunt suddenly caught in the midst of a life and death struggle. Blast the horn; hear the siren screaming overhead, your siren; other sirens joining in. Take the corner; pray the truck can stop; hope the pedestrian isn't deaf or stupid. Feel the car protesting; shaking; vibrating, over-revving. Hit the wrong gear in a panic; slam it back into second, ram the throttle to the floor, hear the engine's screaming; feel the acceleration as the tires bite. Look ahead: is he turning; stopping; shooting?

Edwards listened—one guttural voice after another; fast talking in a foreign language reminding him of fighter pilots in war movies—fear and tension released by shouting single words or staccato sentences. The captain translated, his words becoming as crisp as the chasers.

"Lights are red. They've gone through."

"Who?" asked Edwards.

"The Saab." He held up his hand, "Wait," he commanded, they've hit a car." He listened intently, "They're still going." A moment's silence. "They're turning left, they won't make it." He paused. "They did." A second later, "They've hit another car." He turned to Edwards with a quick explanation, "They're on a busy street, we've got three cars behind and we're setting up a road block ahead."

Edwards imagined the speeding cars weaving in and out of traffic; pedestrians running into doorways; terrified parents dragging fascinated kids off footpaths;

cars sliding to a halt. Hunted and hunters skidding on two wheels, fishtailing around corners and bouncing off parked cars.

The voices on the loudspeaker became louder, tension increasing and the captain almost whispered, "The road block's coming up."

Edwards saw it—two cars blocking the road— amazing how fast they came toward you.

"He's not slowing."

Five hundred metres, guessed Edwards, plenty of time.

"Still going."

Edwards knew the fear, the panic. Passengers and co-drivers praying silently, even aloud. "Oh Christ! Stop you, bastard. Stop!"

"Not stopping."

Two hundred metres. The swearing, "Oh Fuck! For fuck's sake stop. STOP!"

"They're shooting."

The worst. Don't panic. Don't lose control. Decide quickly: If you weave you lose control; drive straight and you hit a bullet at 100 miles an hour.

Jahnssen barked an order.

The loudspeaker reverberated with the sound of shots then fell silent. Edwards held his breath. The control room hushed.

The loudspeaker rattled back to life, the captain translated. "They hit the road block, they're still going."

Edwards imagined the scene: The Saab ramming first into one police car, bouncing off into the second, scattering policemen and sending debris in all directions.

A barrage of voices sprung from the loudspeaker. The captain looked relieved. "No one killed. We are still after them."

Edwards' mind was racing, thinking of the co-drivers

and the fear of not being in control, the fear he felt when flying. Too frightened to look, too scared not to. Unable to do anything but pray, trust the driver, and occasionally swear out loud to release the tension. "Bastard. Get out the bloody way," or "Fuck—that was close." Wanting to scream, "Slow down. Stop! Stop! Let me out." Breathing a sigh of relief as each danger passes then immediately worrying about the next.

Jahnssen was translating again. "It's a bridge."

"A bridge?"

"A canal bridge, it's lifting."

Excitement mounted in the voices on the radio, like derby commentators near the finishing post.

"Not stopping."

"The bridge's still going up."

"They won't make it."

"STOP! STOP!"

The whole room held its breath. The radio went dead. Twenty seconds later it chattered back to life. The captain turned to Edwards with a look of dismay, "They've got away. They jumped the gap."

Disappointment filtered through the room. Policemen and civilians drifted back to their duties, or slunk quietly away with the disillusioned expression of footballer players losing the Cup by a single last minute goal. Some passed a few words as if commenting on strategy or team spirit, most remained silent.

Edwards looked at the captain, "Well Jost, what happens now?"

"We'll keep looking for them but I think we should go ahead with our plan. I'll arrange for the men to go in the truck and the back-up car. Perhaps you would interview King and the driver. You had better start with the driver so we can release him as soon as the truck is prepared. Two hours should be enough."

"What's the time now?" Edwards asked of himself, checking his watch which still read 9:05 p.m. Glancing up he saw the control room's illuminated digital clock blink from 22:05 to 22:06 and he reset his watch to Dutch time.

9:06 p.m., said the flight information board clock at Stanstead airport as Margery, bottle-bronzed, still in beach shorts with her breasts bubbling out of a skimpy T-shirt, walked through the arrivals gate, saw Trudy's mother, stopped dead, and erupted in a torrent of tears. The accompanying stewardess, unaware of the situation, tried to comfort her, but Margery twisted out of her grasp and flew toward Lisa.

For several minutes they moved back and forth in a slow dance, blocking the narrow exit, neither wanting to be the first to break away in case the other should accuse them of caring less about Trudy. The constable, with a tremulous voice, suggested moving out of the way, but the joint outpouring of pent-up emotions made them deaf. Trudy would have found it strange, even amusing, to see her mother and Margery locked together this way. How many times had her mother trashed Margery? "That girl's bad news. I wish you'd find a nice friend" she would say.

With Margery's hastily packed bag over his shoulder, Peter nudged them through the main doors toward the police car, the policeman urging them to hurry. Peter, grabbing his arm, whispered, "Don't worry constable, it's too late tonight."

"Not quite," he replied, looking pleased, explaining that a friend at the *Daily Express* had promised to hold a space as long as they had Roger's picture before midnight.

Peter swung round in his seat as soon as they hit the main highway. "Margery, Luv. What do you know about this Roger bloke?"

Margery distanced herself a little from Lisa. "Trude said he was twenty-seven, I said that were too old. She didn't say a lot about him really." She paused for effect, as if trying to think of what to say next, though she had thought about nothing else since seeing Trudy's picture in the paper. "He's got a big house in Watford and drives a Jag."

"That's it. That's where she is," cried Lisa. "Why didn't you stop her you stupid girl?"

Margery had found a prickly seat and squirmed. "I told her not to go. Honest. I told her that all he wanted was a fu ..." she stopped, suddenly aware she was not talking to her peers, "You know?" she finished, with uncharacteristic shyness.

"Have you any idea of the address?" enquired the constable, feeling it was his responsibility to ask the questions.

"I've thought and thought, but she never said."

"Did she say if she was unhappy at home?" continued the constable, treading on thin ice.

She quickly replied, "No," then looked sheepish. "I don't know if I should say this ..." she paused, fidgeting uncomfortably, her eyes roaming back and forth between Lisa and Peter, then she took the plunge, "Trudy doesn't like her stepmother—reckoned it was her fault her dad left home."

Peter said nothing but Lisa stepped in quickly. "Come and stay with me Margery, 'til your parents get back."

"Is that alright Mrs. McKenzie?"

"I want you to," she pleaded forcefully, then added, "Please."

"Mum said I should ask if I could. She's worried as well."

"Anyway, I wouldn't feel happy with you on your own after what's happened to Trudy." The admission that something had "happened" to Trudy dispelled all remaining optimism and immersed Lisa in macabre thought: Her lips quivered, she squeezed them together tightly; her eyes misted, she shut them; her body started shaking, she clenched her muscles. But the emotion continued building until the pressure became too great and she exploded into a violently sobbing mess.

Peter leaned over and quietly asked the constable to stop the car.

"It's dangerous here."

"Please."

He stopped. Peter leapt out and, changing places with Margery, quickly bundled Lisa's jerking body in his arms and pressed her face to his chest.

Nobody spoke for a while, the car was filled with the sound of Lisa's sobs and an occasional breathy, "There, there," from Peter, who would have added, "Everything will be alright," had he not known she would immediately see through the lie and weep even more. They were travelling fast, without dramatics. The constant buzz of the engine and the ever-changing hum of the tires, were the only sounds for many miles, as each occupant unsuccessfully tried to come up with something to diffuse a further explosion of grief. Then the constable decided to offer some hope to Lisa, judging it was time to end the silence. "Mrs. McKenzie?" he called, in the rear view mirror.

She responded with a sniffled, "Yes."

"You don't know anything bad has happened. She might have just gone away with this bloke on holiday and didn't tell you 'cos she knew you'd say no."

"Trudy wouldn't do that."

"Are you sure?"

"Yes!" she snapped, but wouldn't have bet her life on it.

"Were you close?" he continued kindly, hoping to ease the tension.

"Yes, Well ..." she wavered—he caught the waver. "Not as close as we used to be. I work evenings, and she's at school all day, so we don't see too much of each other."

The memories of how life had been were too much: tears started again, quietly this time, tiny droplets dribbling down her cheeks. Tears of guilt, regret, and remorse shed by every imperfect parent; tears for the missed opportunities; tears for things said and unsaid. But Lisa's tears were magnified a thousand fold by the fact that, unlike other parents, she might never have the opportunity to say: "Sorry daughter. I did my best."

Wiping the tears, Lisa leaned forward and touched the constable's shoulder, insisting he should pay attention. "She wouldn't leave her cat, she adores it," she sniffled.

"What if she was only planning on going for a few days?"

"She wouldn't."

He uttered, "Ah ... hah," which could have meant anything, but Lisa chose it to mean he didn't believe her.

Why wouldn't they believe her? The first policeman who came to the house had been the same. He'd started off compassionately enough, taking Trudy's description, names and addresses of her friends and relatives, things she took with her—nothing really, just her handbag, places she liked to visit,; hobbies, even the things she liked to eat. Then he started. "Are you sure you didn't have any trouble with her?"

"No."

"'No,' you didn't have any trouble or 'no' you're not sure?"

"No trouble."

"You didn't have a fight?"

"No, we never fought."

"Never?"

"Hardly ever. Well not physically anyway."

"But you did have rows?"

"Yes," she was forced to admit. "We did have disagreements. Doesn't everybody?" She sought confirmation in his face but saw a different look; could see what he was thinking—How do I know you haven't killed her and dumped the body somewhere?

Twenty times at least she felt like saying, "Get out if you're not going to do anything." But she didn't say it, knowing he would claim that proved her guilt. Then he brought up the drugs, "Was she?"

"No."

"How do you know?"

"I just know."

"Does she smoke?"

"Yes. They all do, well most of them anyway."

His look said, "Hash," but she carried on before he had a chance to say it. "So what does that prove. I like a drop of Martini, does that make me an alcoholic?"

"No," he admitted. Then, after a pause, asked, "And what about sex?" Giving her a questioning look, too embarrassed or too sensitive to come clean and ask if Trudy were a virgin.

"I don't know," replied Lisa, looking away.

"Has she ever ..."

God, she thought angrily, this man's a copper and he's frightened to ask me if my daughter's ever been bonked. "No ... Yes ... Possibly. I don't know. She never told me."

"Could she be on the game?"

"How dare you?"

"We have to ask."

"No you don't."

"Look, I'm sorry but we've got to have some idea where to start looking. I'm not saying she's on the game ..."

"She's not," Lisa shouted straight into his face, her eyes not more than three inches from his.

He remained calm. "Like I said, I'm not suggesting she is ..."

"Good!" she yelled.

"All I'm saying is that I need to know ... If there were the slightest possi—"

"There's not," she shot back before he could finish.

"I'm just asking, then we'd know where to start looking, Kings Cross railway station for instance."

She stared at him coldly. "I'm not going to tell you again. She's not a whore. O.K."

"O.K.," he replied, unconvinced.

"Anyway, I don't suppose you'd bother to look if I said she was," complained Lisa. He glanced sideways at her, doubt written all over his face—she could have throttled him. "I told you, she is not. Got it."

He got it.


"The Historic Borough of Leyton," proclaimed the sign proudly as they neared Margery's home. "Asshole of the World," had been added, unofficially, in fluorescent red, and the artist would have been gratified to know his work reflected well in the headlights of the car. Directed by Margery, the constable pulled up outside the darkened house and looked at the dashboard clock. "Ten-oh-five," he said, pleased with himself for making good time.

"This is Roger," Margery said, triumphantly flourishing the folded sheet from the centre of a biology book a few moments later. Lisa grabbed it and the others stared over her shoulder. Peter quickly shook his head, and Lisa said, "No," but continued staring, surprised by the lack of malevolence in the man's eyes, thinking that she herself might have difficulty resisting his obvious charms.

"You are quite sure this is Roger?" the policeman asked in an official tone, holding the photocopy up for Margery to see. She nodded seriously. And, mindful of the fact the picture could one day become an exhibit in a murder trial, he carefully placed it in a plastic evidence bag and wrote on the label "Roger??? Last known address—Watford."

Fifteen minutes later he was on his way to the *Daily Express* office with a creased photocopy, and verbal description of someone who might well have come from a different species, or planet, than Roger LeClarc.


Roger would have recognised the man in the picture, although his swollen eyelids would have made the vision somewhat blurry. In any case he was submerged in darkness, darker even than his first night as a castaway, the sky completely shut out by a cold wet blanket of fog.

Things had brightened just a little by late morning, the great globs of black and slate-grey cloud rushing northwards, leaving a wash of translucent white with the brush strokes clearly visible. But, just as the heavens were being re-painted sky-blue, a swirling mist began wafting around the life raft, shutting out the horizon and coating Roger with tiny beads of water.

Several ships had slipped by in the fog, only the penetrating tones of their foghorns signalling their presence and, by late afternoon, he had convinced himself that a particularly close horn was that of a lighthouse. It must be a bay or inlet, he thought, deceived by the calmness of the water, and dreamed of a wide sandy beach garnished with bare-breasted nymphets and a hundred hamburger joints. The prospect of hamburgers jerked him awake—food, I need food, must have food. "There must be food inside," he mused and sat on the edge of the giant rubber ring with his feet dangling speculatively into the opening, weighing the pros and cons of venturing inside, into a water-filled paddling pool.

His stomach won, and a minute later he was floundering helplessly as his bulk dented the flimsy bottom and a deluge of water knocked his feet from under him. His thrashing flushed him further from the inflated rim and, within seconds, he was drowning again: His weight, sodden coat, the water, and gravity, conspiring to drag him under the canopy toward the centre. He sank to his chest and sat forlornly in the middle with only his head and shoulders above the water, the canopy draped over him like a huge deflated parachute.

Once the water, and his mind, had calmed, he used his hands as flippers to inch back toward the opening, then his right hand collided with the box of emergency rations and he clung to it thankfully as he clambered back onto the roof and collapsed, exhausted.

The blanket of fog hanging motionless above the sea intensified hour by hour. By early evening the cold white swirling mist of the morning had become a uniform grey wall. Night appeared to fall several hours earlier than it should otherwise have done and Roger slept.

Night was also falling in the Dutch port where preparations were being made to keep tabs on the truck bound for Istanbul. A knot of officers, English and Dutch, stood around the rear of the trailer receiving instructions, then Detective Constable Wilson dropped a bombshell. "Sorry, Guv," he said, "but I'm not volunteering to go in that." He hesitated momentarily, adding, "With all due respect," a fraction too late to have any sincerity, and he kept his eyes on the ground, away from Superintendent Edwards.

"I wasn't asking for volunteers," snarled Edwards, his clenched teeth chattering in anger as he hissed, "Come with me."

Turning his back, he strode smartly away, leaving Wilson looking to his colleague for support. D.C. Smythe pulled a face—*you're on your own mate,* and an embarrassed silence built with the possibility of a showdown. Edwards broke the spell. "Wilson," he barked, the single word somehow encompassing the phrase, "Come here you bastard."

"Yes, Sir," Wilson replied, half running to catch up with his senior officer.

Edwards turned on him as soon as they were out of the group's earshot. Making eye contact he flew at him, "You will go in the truck you little snot," he spat. "How dare you show me up in front of the captain."

"But, Sir ..." Wilson tried to explain.

"Don't you 'but' me you little runt."

"Sir, I have an important engagement," he managed, before Edwards could stop him.

"Nothing, I repeat, nothing is more important than this case to you, and your career, at this moment," he said, adding with venom. "Do I make myself abundantly clear?"

Wilson wouldn't give up; couldn't afford to give up, "Sir, I promised my wife ..."

Edwards cut in with a sneer, "You promised your wife what? I bet you promised you wouldn't get pissed, or wouldn't get a dose of AIDS from a whore in Amsterdam. Wouldn't have stopped you though would it?" He paused for breath and a change of tone. "That reminds me, I still haven't found out what you and the others were doing when Bliss lost LeClarc on the bloody ship. Where were you? How come Bliss was the only one on deck? What was Sergeant Jones doing when he fell over? Trying to hold up the bar was he? Or, do you expect me to believe Bliss lost him all on his own?"

Wilson spluttered, "We were ..."

"I should warn you mister, I've already spoken to Sergeant Jones. Just in case you were thinking of telling me porky pies."

"I'm not sure what we were doing," Wilson replied hesitantly after a few moments of prudent thought.

Superintendent Edwards, an experienced interviewer, knew the signs; knew very well that Wilson remembered precisely where he was and what he was doing at the material time. "I'll tell you what Mister Wilson," he began, offering a backhanded compromise, "you get in that truck with Smythe and the others, and by the time you return I'll have forgotten all about what went wrong on the ship." Still staring, he raised his eyebrows, "Do we understand each other?"

Wilson understood. "Yes, Sir."

Edwards marched stiffly back to the truck with Wilson, slack-shouldered, in his wake. "Now Captain," said Edwards as if they had never been away, "please continue with the briefing."

Fifteen minutes later, unaware he was carrying three passengers, the driver gunned the huge truck life and, after warming the engine for a few minutes, dropped the rig into gear. Destination—Istanbul.

"What do you think, Michael?" asked the captain as they watched the big rig rocking violently as it rolled over the railway lines on its way out of the port, carrying Detectives Wilson and Smythe together with Constable Van der Zalm.

"We shall soon find out," replied Edwards. "The driver may be lying, especially if he was paid enough—or scared enough. He was certainly nervous, but wouldn't you be if you were arrested in a foreign country; particularly if you hadn't done anything wrong?"

The captain nodded, "I suppose I would ... That reminds me, you haven't spoken to King yet."

The truck swung hard to its right just outside the dock and accelerated toward Rotterdam. An unmarked dark green police car, waiting out of sight just beyond the dock perimeter, took up its position and the two-vehicle convoy set off.


"David King?" Superintendent Edwards enquired of the lone occupant in the cell.

King was tempted to say, "No," just to be awkward, but nodded without getting up. "What?" he replied defiantly.

"I'm Superintendent Edwards, New Scotland Yard. I'd like to have a few words with you."

King studied him critically, rising slowly—thoughtfully—saying nothing. Edwards turned to the captain, still standing in the cell doorway. "It's O.K. Jost. I'll call if I need anything."

Edwards swung on the substantial wooden door, heard the solid clunk of the lock dropping into place behind him, and turned to face King, now standing a good six inches taller than he.

"Sit down please, Mr. King," he said, feeling ill at ease under the weight of King's stare.

"I'll stand," replied King coldly.

Edwards dropped to the bench. "Sit down," he instructed with a wave of the hand, somehow managing to make his order sound like an invitation.

King stood defiantly, and an uncomfortable feeling prickled the back of Edwards' neck. "I really think it would be better if you sat," he persisted, forcing himself to stay seated.

"I said I'll stand."

"Sit," he commanded, as if ordering a dog.

King glared, "Do you always get your own way?"

Edwards, realizing he was at a severe disadvantage, pressed his hands firmly on the bench and started to rise, "I'm here to ask the questions, Mr. King. I said sit down."

King made his move, towering over Edwards, making no attempt to sit. "Why don't you go screw yourself?" he said, spitting malice.

"How dare you?"

"Don't pretend you've forgotten ..." continued King, and a horrified look of recognition spread over Edwards' face.

"Nosmo King?"

The scream of a siren pierced the air, reverberating sharply along the tunnel-like corridor, bringing the captain and officers running. King's cell door flew open and he handed Edwards' slumped body to them, saying, "Mr. Edwards had a little accident." And he shut the door himself.

Edwards, holding his hand over his mouth, mumbled, "I'm O.K., I just slipped."

Confused, the captain tried to help. "Let me see?"

"No, 'I'll be O.K., I just need a toilet."

"What happened?"

"Like I said: Accident—slipped and fell against the bench."

The captain shook his head in disbelief. "I've never heard of a policeman slipping in the cells—prisoners sometimes."

Blood was oozing from between Edwards fingers and he winced as he gingerly ran his other hand over the back of his head. "There is always a first time," he managed to reply as he allowed himself to be led to the washroom.

Two minutes later the cell buzzer sounded again. Returning, the captain warily unbolted the observation flap. "Yes—what do you want?"

"I want to talk to D.I. Bliss," demanded King, with new found arrogance. "Is he still here?"

"What happened to the superintendent?" asked the captain, sceptical of Edward's explanation.

"Slipped and fell. Is he alright?"

"I don't know," he snapped. "Anyway, why do you want to see Detective Bliss?"

King thought, for just a moment, as if he were considering telling, but then decided against it. "Just get him. O.K."

Captain Jahnssen shot a look at his watch. "It's after midnight. You'll have to wait 'til the morning."

Slamming the hatch shut, the captain marched off to find Edwards. "Should I get the doctor, Michael?" he asked a few minutes later, as Edwards continued spitting blood into the sink.

"No, I'm fine really," he replied with difficulty, his swollen upper lip already protruding like a small red balloon. Then he tilted his head back and regretted it as the pain brought tears to his eyes.

"I wish you would be honest with me Michael," said the captain, reigning in his anger. "I can't see how you fell and hit your head and face at the same time."

Edwards made no attempt at an explanation. "I'll be alright in the morning Jost."

"King has asked to see Bliss again," he said, a query in his voice.

"Has he," replied Edwards; neither an answer nor a question.


The two-vehicle convoy processed slowly toward Rotterdam amid the sparse evening traffic. Wilson and the other two officers were being flung around amongst the towering skids of boxes inside the little den, like riders in a crazy ride. Illuminated only by a small battery-powered lamp, they had no choice but to sit tight. Constable Van der Zalm, a dour Dutchman even in good weather, sulked in a corner and made it obvious that being cooped up with a couple of Englishmen for four days in a truck was about as appealing as being castrated by a madman with a plastic knife. And Wilson, still smarting from his brush with Edwards, worried what his wife would do. Her ultimatum still nagged— "Once more, just once more," she had said, coldly. "If you let me down once more ... that will be it."

"I'll be back early Saturday," he'd promised.

"You'd better be. I mean it this time."

"I really, really promise," he'd added foolishly.

"The christening's at ten o'clock. If you're not back ..." she'd left the sentence unfinished. She didn't understand—but how could she. A teacher, always a teacher, only a teacher, for whom anything other than nine to five Monday to Friday, was an infringement of personal liberty.

A profound change in engine noise signalled a transformation of landscape. "We are coming into the city," declared Van der Zalm, hearing the exhaust reverberating off houses and walls. Wilson had just picked up the radio to tell the car driver to start closing the gap when the truck driver suddenly slammed on his brakes. Without warning, tires squealing in protest and bouncing off the road, the trailer slowed rapidly, shimmying from side to side as if trying to overtake the cab. The radio flew out of Wilson's hand and Smythe looked up just in time—the pallet of boxes behind them was being forced over by its own momentum. He shouted a warning as he leapt to his feet and began pushing against the stack with all his weight. The others scrambled to their feet and together they held it, not upright but straight enough to stop it falling.

"What the hell is he playing at?" shouted Smythe as the trailer ground to a halt and they were surrounded by an unexpected calm. The total silence, and almost tangible stillness, contrasted so sharply with the noisy motion of a few seconds earlier that the three occupants were temporarily stunned. Then Wilson thrashed his way past the boxes to get to a spy hole in the side of the truck. "We're at a junction," he called to the others still holding onto the stack. "I can see the traffic lights." The lights changed, nothing happened. "Call the car," he shouted. "See if they know what's going on."

Van der Zalm had an animated discussion, in Dutch, on the radio, then turned to Smythe. "We're completely blocking a main intersection. They don't know what to do. They can't drive by and they can't see the cab."

"Shit," shouted Wilson, angry at their lack of initiative. "Tell one of them to get out and see what the driver's doing."

Almost a minute later the back doors rattled as the giant bolt slid back. A familiar face peered in. "The driver's run away, " said the officer.

Wilson leapt out and took control. "He can't have got far. Split up and get after him. You," he pointed to Van der Zalm, "get on the radio and ask for assistance." He looked around—tall apartment buildings clustered at each corner of the junction; a dozen alleyways and driveways radiated in all directions. A plaza of six stores at the foot of one apartment block had attracted a small group of people and he ran toward them in the hope they had seen something. The other officers fanned out without any thought of organizing a proper search.

Wilson reached the group to find a hostile alliance of prostitutes and junkies congregating outside an all-night pharmacy, seeking a snort or a shot from a legal addict. None admitted being able to speak English apart from one woman wearing an indecently short skirt over a seam-splitting backside. "You wanna good time big boy?"

A cacophony of shrill sirens splintered the group and within minutes a dozen or more officers were milling around the truck. The junction was completely blocked, the driver had taken the keys and even locked the doors to make the task of clearing the obstruction as difficult as possible.

"I guess this means Edwards will send us back on the next ship," Wilson said to Smythe with a broad grin.

Two hours later, the search abandoned but the truck still firmly in place, the six officers returned to the police station and reported to the captain in the control room.

"Where's the super?" enquired Smythe, who had been psyching himself up to expect a major meltdown.

"Gone to bed," replied the captain. "He's had a bit of an accident."

"Nothing trivial I hope," muttered Wilson.

"You may as well get some sleep," he said, equally grateful for Edwards' absence. "I am sure he will want to see you in the morning."

# *chapter nine*

Billy Motsom placed himself squarely next to the skipper in the smelly wheelhouse of the herring trawler. No other boats were moving as they slipped out of the harbour at first light and headed slowly along the river toward the sea. The ancient skipper, as short and stocky as his boat, sporting an obligatory beard and embroidered peak cap, was adding to the fog with his pipe. The scented tobacco smoke hung listlessly about him in the still air, creating his own personal cloud of fragrant smog, which followed everywhere

"Bad veather," he spluttered for the nth time, and gave three short coughs as he did at the end of almost every sentence.

"You got your money," replied Motsom tersely, not eager to recall he had already paid ten thousand dollars and had promised a further ten if they found LeClarc alive.

"I know you vant to find your brother Mr. LeClarc, but it will be difficult in this fog."

Motsom managed to look crestfallen, although the skipper could hardly have noticed in the poor light. "We must find him—his poor wife and children ..." His voice, dripping with anxiety, trailed off, and the merest suggestion of a tear appearing in his right eye was swiped away with the exaggerated brush of a hand.

The anchor-chain capstan, on the forepeak below the wheelhouse drifted momentarily into view as the fog thinned a fraction, then disappeared again just as fast. The bow of the vessel remained permanently out of sight, the other side of the murky wall into which they continually pushed. With dawn, just a hint of daylight had seeped through the gloom and changed the black of night to the smoky grey of day. Only the booming foghorns penetrated the thick fog. Their sonorous tones, muffled further by the water-laden atmosphere, came from all directions at the same time. Some from ships, others from lighthouses, and some from navigation buoys along the waterway.

Stretching above his head, the skipper pulled a switch and the foghorn on the roof of the wheelhouse rumbled through the entire boat. Motsom reached up and flicked it off. "Too noisy," he said, his tone daring the skipper to challenge him. Concern and anger met in the skipper's eyes, but he said nothing, quickly turning his attention to the radar screen. The x-ray vision of the radar saw through the fog, mapped out the riverbanks and marker buoys, and occasionally a large blip indicated a ship at anchor. Rows of little blips showed the location of a string of trawlers and pleasure craft firmly tethered to moorings, their skippers too wise to venture into the murk.

The marine radio, humming quietly to itself on a shelf above the console, suddenly buzzed with the crackly voice of a coastguard. The skipper reached for his microphone to respond—Motsom seized the arm, "What are you doing?"

"They vant to know why we are going out in this veather."

"Leave it," he commanded, relaxing his grip.

The skipper pushed his hand forward. "I must answer."

"Why?" Motsom's grip hardened again.

The radio cut in, the voice insistent.

Glancing at Motsom the skipper jerked his arm free and reached for the microphone. "It's the coastguard. They vant to know the boat's name. They see us on radar."

Motsom smacked the arm away. "I said, leave it."

Deep concern spread over the skipper's face as the atmosphere between the two men darkened, gloomier even than the surrounding fog. "I have to answer," he said. "They will send a boat to stop us."

"In this weather," said Motsom," I don't think so. We'll take the risk."

Making up his mind, the old skipper grabbed the microphone and said two words before a single bullet ripped clean through the radio, embedding itself deep into the solid woodwork of the wheelhouse.

In panic, the skipper spun the wheel and the trawler's invisible nose veered shoreward as the vessel leaned on its beam.

"Straighten up," yelled Motsom, the muzzle of his gun in the skipper's back and the gnarled, scarred hands gripped the wheel to a stop, then swung it back the other way. The small boat gradually hauled itself upright as the rhythmic puttering of the old diesel engine shook it from end to end, and dirty black smoke poured out of the chimney to mingle unseen with the fog.

The muffled crack of the pistol shot penetrated the thick wooden deck timbers and alerted the only crewmember—Willem, the seventeen-year-old tidying ropes on the aft deck. Only three weeks at sea—still green, still finding his sea legs—he was drawn to the wheelhouse to report the noise and was surprised, alarmed even, to discover it locked.

"What do you want?" the skipper shouted in Dutch, his voice hardly audible through the thick wooden walls and armoured glass, and his face barely visible in the gloomy light. Motsom slipped the gun back in his pocket and said, threateningly, "Tell him to go away."

The skipper started in Dutch, but Motsom stopped him with a hand gesture and commanded, "Speak English."

He started again, shouting this time, "Everything's O.K. Go and make some coffee."

Willem's young face clouded as he clambered down the short ladder into the tiny cabin. The two occupants, Motsom's compatriots, glowered intimidatingly at him, and he bustled around uneasily occupying himself with the kettle and stove.

The local news headlines the evening before had carried the story of the ferry's missing passenger and it was quite understandable, he thought, that the man's brother and two friends would be prepared to hire a boat to try and find him. Motsom, masquerading as Roger LeClarc's brother, had gone straight to the wheelhouse to chart a plan of action, but Willem had watched with misgiving as the other two cased the boat: Peering into the fish hold, delving under the tarpaulin covering the dinghy on deck, lifting the hatch on the tiny engine compartment.

"Coffee?" Willem enquired as pleasantly as his taut face would permit, showing the container. Both shook their heads.

"Rather have a scotch. This stink's making me fuckin' sick," snarled Jack Boyd, the taller of the two, a man in his mid-fifties who might have blended at a criminal lawyer's convention, though the dark stain of stubble shadowing his long chin and his gritty diction would have put him on the defence bench.

"Haven'a got any," replied the other, his speech heavy with a rough Glasgow accent.

"You've never got fuck-all."

Willem felt the eyes of the two men boring into him as he made the coffee. The water took forever to boil on the single propane burner with its dancing blue flames, but a sense of normality and consolation returned with the pleasant aroma rising from the percolating grounds. Thankful when it was ready, he climbed from the claustrophobic cabin juggling three stained cups, a coffee pot, and a metal jug of milk. The heavy wooden wheelhouse door was still locked so he gave It a vicious kick. The skipper looked at Motsom questioningly.

"Open it," he ordered, tapping his gun pocket. "And no funny business."

Keeping one hand firmly on the wheel the skipper reached over, unlatched the door, and drew Willem in without speaking.

The skipper's uncharacteristic coldness immediately caught the youngster's attention. The old man was usually so chatty, more like a good mate than someone old enough to be his grandfather: Football, the Spice Girls, and a new movie could often keep them going to the fishing grounds, and the old man wasn't beyond recounting hair-raising tales of long past sexual encounters or wartime exploits when he'd smuggled the odd allied ser-

viceman to a rendezvous with an MTB off the coast
under the German's guns. Now his worried eyes flicked
nervously back and forth, ever watchful of Motsom's
hands, and he said nothing to his young assistant.

"Where shall I put it?" he asked the old man in
Dutch, and the skipper caught a rebuke from Motsom
as he started to respond.

"English."

"He doesn't speak much English," he lied, glancing
repeatedly at the smashed radio in the hope the boy
would notice.

"Don't say anything then."

"I must tell him to check the engine, if that's alright."

"O.K. but no tricks."

The skipper spoke, leaving Motsom in the dark, but
the boy left with a cracked smile, apparently satisfied.

"Are there any other radios?" asked Motsom as
soon as the boy had gone.

"No. None at all."

A red navigation buoy the height of a house suddenly loomed alongside the wheelhouse, coming
sharply into view and then disappearing in an instant
as the tide and engine swept them past. The skipper
yanked hard on the wheel, cursing himself for taking
his eyes off the radar.

"What was that?" asked Motsom, unaware of their
brush with disaster.

"The channel marker. We are now in the sea."

Motsom pulled his gun. "Keep straight and don't
try anything—I'll be just outside."

Sidling out of the wheelhouse door, his eyes and the
gun focussing hard on the skipper, he shouted,
"McCrae. Where are you, you Scots git?" but his free
hand remained grasping the wheelhouse door, ensuring
the skipper couldn't slam it shut behind him.

"Here Billy," said the shadow of a head popping up almost at his feet. "What's up?"

"Where's the boy?" he demanded urgently.

"Don't know. He made some coffee ..."

Motsom cut him off. "Find him and stick with him. Be nasty if you have to. They know something's going on so he might try to be clever."

Motsom slid back into the wheelhouse, never having completely left. "O.K. Captain. Let's get going,"

The skipper looked confused. Motsom realized that he did not understand. "Hurry up," he insisted, his right hand whizzing around and around like a windmill, the gun twirling dangerously on his fingers. "Go fast."

"I can't," replied the skipper nervously. "It is impossible. I can't see."

"Use the radar. That's what it's for."

"We might hit something."

"I'll risk it. Now get going. Full speed ahead, or whatever you say."

"But where are we going?"

"Like I told you. Follow the ferry route to England." Then he pointed the gun directly at the skipper's head and continued, menacingly, "You have ten seconds to speed up. One ... two ... three ..."

The old skipper leaned on the throttle and the vessel lunged for the open sea. An instant later the door was whipped open and McCrae dragged a simpering Willem into the wheelhouse, throwing him to the floor at Motsom's feet.

"Got a fuckin' radio."

"Where?"

"In the lifeboat on deck. Sending a message."

The skipper screwed his pipe into his mouth and sucked fiercely to stifle a smile.

Motsom swung on the boy and pressed the muzzle to his temple. "What did you say?"

The skipper answered for him, his eyes glued firmly ahead into the fog, "He doesn't speak English. I told you."

"Take him below and tie him up," shouted Motsom waving his gun at the figure on the floor, "I'll deal with him later." Then he turned on the skipper with a malevolent sneer, "You had better pray he didn't say nothing."

As the last echoes of land slipped slowly off the edge of the radar, the trawler, engine at barely half throttle, headed due west out into the smooth waters of the North Sea—a journey it had made several thousand times in search of herrings, but never before in search of a lonely, cold man on a life raft.

# *chapter ten*

A shrill buzz pierced its way into Yolanda's sleep and stung her sluggish limbs into action. Fighting her way through the duvet she came close to identifying the source of the noise when it stopped, and she sank back toward sleep, hoping it had been part of a dream, knowing it was not. A second buzz brought a slender arm, snake-like, groping for the phone, and she seized the handset and dragged it under the duvet. "Hello."

Two minutes later she slipped out of bed, replaced the handset on its cradle, flicked on the bedside lamp, and stretched naked in front of an expensively framed full-length mirror—a masterpiece in glass. What a mess, she thought, horrified at her sleep-tousled hair and yesterday's face. Shower first, she decided, but changed her mind. I'd better wake Dave. Captain Jahnssen had sounded unusually agitated on the phone, "Get Detective Bliss here right away—Edwards wants him."

The bathroom's fluorescent light was less forgiving than the bedside lamp and one glance in the harsh mirror convinced her to make hurried repairs before waking him.

"Dave," she whispered, but thirty-six hours of high tension needed more than one night's recuperation, and she stood quietly, studying the sleeping face in the half-light, listening to the peaceful song of his gentle breathing. She bent closer. "Dave," she cooed, watching for movement in the laughter lines etched into the side of his face; listening for a change in his breathing. His fair skin showed the shadow of a beard in the dim light, and the crooked nose, seemingly at odds with an otherwise symmetrical face, tempted her to reach out and smooth it straight.

"Dave," she tried, a touch louder and smiled, amused by the thought of this man sleeping in her guest room. "Dave," she called, then leaned in and brushed her mouth lightly against his. The tip of his tongue darted out to run along his lips.

"Dave," she sang, laughingly, in his ear.

His eyes opened slowly. "Ah—hah."

She moved away a fraction so he could see her. "Dave, you have to get up. Superintendent Edwards wants to see you."

"Shit," he shouted, then, looking up into her face in the soft dawn light found an angel. "I must get up," he said, hoping to break the spell and was half out of the bed before realizing he was nearly naked and, looking down, found a morning swell beneath the bedclothes. One inch further and she may have seen everything.

"Here, have mine," she said, turning from him to slip the dressing gown off her shoulders, and he watched, mesmerized by the two humps of her buttocks wriggling beneath her filmy nightgown as she

made her way out. Peeping provocatively from around
the door, her body now hidden from view, she joked,
"It'll look better on you than me." Then she was gone.

Fifteen minutes later, wide awake, showered,
dressed in his own clothes—found neatly folded on an
antique dressing table—he entered the cathedral-sized
living room, its movie-screen sized window staring out
over the ocean. Drawn inquisitively to the window, he
swiped his hand across the glass to clear the condensa-
tion then stopped, feeling foolish, realizing the moisture
was on the outside where the impenetrable fog was
blotting out both sea and sky. His movements caught
her attention. "I'll be out in a minute," she shouted
from her bedroom. "The coffee's hot. Get it yourself."

"Can I bring you some?" he enquired, angling for
an excuse to see her again in her nightgown.

"I'm not dressed," she replied saucily, but he misunderstood the invitation and bumbled an apology.

By the time he had drank his coffee she was ready
and slid alongside him at the kitchen counter.
"Breakfast?"

"Not bloody herring."

"I promise," she laughed, opening the fridge.
"Eggs, bacon, and cheese. Is that alright?"

"Cheese?" he queried. "With eggs and bacon."

"This is Holland, Dave."

"O.K.," he said. "Sounds good to me. Now I wonder what the hell Edwards wants?"

An hour later the white BMW eased into the parking
lot at the rear of the police station and Captain
Jahnssen looked down from his office window. "Here
they are Michael," he sighed, seeing an end to the persistent whining that was driving him crazy.

Superintendent Edwards checked his watch, mumbling, "Bout bloody time," through his swollen lips, and strolled to the window in time to see Bliss emerging from the driver's side. "Why's he driving?" he asked accusingly. "He shouldn't be driving one of your cars."

Janhssen cringed, then struck back in exasperation. "It's not ours, Michael. It's Detective Pieters' own car. She can let him drive if she wants to."

"Up here Bliss," commanded Edwards hanging over the balcony outside the captain's office then, turning, he marched back into the office knowing his order would be obeyed.

Twenty seconds later Yolanda walked into Edwards' broadside. "Not you Miss, just Bliss," he hissed, as they entered the captain's office.

She would have argued, though the captain's look suggested she should not, and on her way out smiled sweetly at Bliss. "I'll wait outside, Dave."

"That won't be necessary," Edwards said sharply, his puffy lips adding additional venom. "Detective Bliss has one more task, then he'll be going back to England on this morning's ferry."

"I'll wait," she replied, shooting Bliss a confidence-boosting smile, then slammed the door, cutting off any response.

Edwards took a few moments to compose himself, not knowing which was worse, a thumping from King or insolence from a woman, and he concentrated on plucking some imaginary fluff from his sleeve as he allowed the temperature in the room to simmer.

"King wants to talk to you, Bliss. Why? "No "Good morning, Officer. Did you sleep well." Nothing pleasant.

"No idea, Sir."

"I don't know either ... but I expect you to report everything he says directly to me and to no one else."

"Right, Sir."

"No one. Do you understand?"

"Yes, Sir. If that's what you want."

Edwards closed in, locking eyes. "That is what I want," he said, emphasising each word individually. "Anyway," he asked again, "why would he want to see you?"

"He wouldn't tell me anything when I spoke to him before ... What happened to your face, Sir?"

"Nothing," Edwards' hand flew to cover the damage, waffled something about an accident, then changed his mind. "Mind your own damn business."

Bliss' look to Captain Jahnssen asked, "What did I do?" and Edwards jumped all over him. "I saw that look Bliss. You look at me when I'm talking to you. If I tell you to mind your own damn business that's exactly what you do. Do I make myself clear?"

Bliss chose not to answer.

Edwards' voice rose to a fevered pitch. "Do I make myself clear?"

"Yes." Impudence written all over his face.

"Yes, what?"

"Yes, Sir.'

The shouting brought Yolanda barrelling back into the room. "Anybody want coffee?" she called cheerily. Captain Jahnssen could have kissed her. "Good idea Yolanda. Let's all go to the dining room for coffee." Grabbing Bliss around the waist he started to propel him out of the door but Edwards was far from finished. "Wait. I ..."

"Come on," said the captain, ignoring the protest, "we all need some coffee."

Yolanda caught Bliss' hand and dragged him down the stairs, blatantly taunting Edwards who trailed behind, speechless.

Ex-police Constable Nosmo King, private detective, sometime acquaintance of Superintendent Michael Edwards, and now murder suspect, sat in the interview room waiting for Bliss. Two constables stood guard by the door and the giant sergeant filled the chair opposite him at the desk. They're taking no chances, he concluded, guessing correctly that no one had bought the story of Edwards' fall. Now labelled a violent offender he was not surprised when they'd roughly handcuffed him before dragging him the thirty feet or so from his cell to the interview room.

Bliss entered alone, oblivious to the reason for the heavy security, and waved the guards out. The sergeant hesitated, "I think we should stay."

"I'm sure Mr. King will behave. Perhaps somebody would like to stand outside the door? I'll call if I need assistance."

"Well Nosmo, you asked to see me," he said as soon as the door closed.

"What's the weather like Dave?" he enquired, testing the temperature while deciding his tack.

The coldness of Bliss' stare was enough—*Don't waste my time*. "Start talking or I'm off."

"Do you know Edwards well?" asked King.

"No—not really," he replied slumping non-committally into a chair, and quite unprepared to discuss a fellow officer with a member of the public—especially a suspected murderer—even if he was an ex-cop.

"He doesn't me like me very much."

"So what?" Bliss shrugged, unconcerned, assuming Edwards had given him a hard time the previous evening, then he sat upright with the sudden realization that there was a hint of familiarity in King's tone. "Do you know him?" It was a shot in the dark.

King drew a cigarette butt from his shirt pocket and made a performance of chewing it for several seconds before nodding slowly, "Yeah, I know him ... Sergeant Michael Edwards, shit-stirrer extraordinaire, as he was ten years ago."

Intrigued, Bliss' eyes opened wide as King continued. "Dave ... can I trust you?"

"Depends on what you're going to tell me. I can't promise that anything you say won't be given in evidence."

"I want you to believe me. I didn't push that bloke off the ship."

"Then why did you lie to me ..." he started, but changed tack, curiosity getting the better of him, realizing there was something praying on King's mind. "Wait a minute Nosmo. What do you know about Superintendent Edwards?"

"Have you got a light."

Bliss shook off the request impatiently. "What do you know?"

King, still deliberating, tried to scratch his ear but the handcuffs made it difficult. "If I tell you about Edwards will you promise not to tell him? It's nothing to do with LeClarc. Nothing at all."

"O.K.—shoot," said Bliss, his interest now piqued, "As long as it doesn't affect this case, I'll promise."

"Edwards was the bastard who got me fired from the force," King started bitterly. "He'd forgotten all about it. It didn't mean anything to him but he destroyed my life. That's why I hit him."

Bliss jumped in his seat, amazement all over his face. "You hit him?"

"Yeah," King laughed, "I smacked him in the gob last night. Then he remembered me. I bet he looks a mess this morning."

"He does," agreed Bliss, concealing a smirk.

"Does he still say it was an accident?"

Bliss nodded quickly.

"Thought he would," continued King. "He's too proud to admit someone bopped him and he wouldn't want to try to explain why."

"Why did you hit him?"

"Like I said, he ruined my life."

"But how?"

King thought for a moment, still not sure he should divulge his relationship with Edwards, but then began, telling his story as if he had rehearsed it a hundred times.

"We were on the same force: Thames Valley. He was a sergeant with a bad reputation—battering prisoners, planting evidence, fitting people up—but he led a charmed life. Word was he had a little black book and he kept a record of every bloody thing anybody ever did wrong."

Bliss interjected, "I've heard he still does."

King looked up, "I bet he does. Anyway," he continued with his prepared narration, "If he heard of an inspector screwing a policewoman or having a beer on duty, or a superintendent sloping off for a quick round of golf with his mates, he'd write it all down: Exact time, date, place, etc." He mimicked the actions of a person writing, as far as the handcuffs would permit, then added, "Anytime he was in the shit he'd pull out his book, flick through the pages, and remind some poor sod what he'd done. It worked like a charm. Everyone was scared to bloody death. He reckoned he had something on every senior officer in the force. That's how he got promotion, nobody wanted to upset him in case he pulled out his book."

Bliss stopped him, "But you weren't a senior officer, what did he have on you?"

"Nothing," replied King quickly, annoyed at being interrupted, annoyed that Bliss would think he had a shady past. "He didn't have nothing on me."

Bliss screwed his eyes in confusion. King explained, "It was a domestic case. Some bloke with handy fists clobbered his wife and Edwards just happened to be in the area. I got there first. The woman had a bloody nose and a cracked tooth—bit messy, hardly fatal. The husband was upstairs bawling his eyes out, couldn't believe what he'd done. Anyway, I was patching the wife up when Edwards arrived. 'Leave her,' he said, 'Go and arrest the bloke.'

"He ain't going anywhere, Serg,' I said.

"You arguing with me?' he said, real nasty. Anyway, before I could do anything, the woman's brother arrived, took one look and said, 'Where is he?' Edwards pointed upstairs and the brother went up like an express train. I tried to go after him but Edwards stopped me. Ten minutes later the brother comes down and chucks three of the husbands fingers and a handful of teeth on the floor. 'He won't do it again,' he said, and stalked out cool as a cucumber."

King paused for a long time and closed his eyes, reliving the horrific moment when he realised the blood soaked fingers and teeth had been physically wrenched from a living human being. They had rushed up the stairs to find the husband writhing in agony, several pairs of his wife's knickers stuffed into his mouth as a gag; the remains of his crushed fingers hanging limply, some dangling by threads. The bedroom door was awash with blood, lumps of skin, and flesh still stuck to the jamb where the fingers had been mashed to a pulp, or chopped off, as his brother-in-law had thrown his weight against the door, the fingers trapped between it and the frame.

"Didn't you hear anything?" asked Bliss quietly, seeing the sadness in the other man's eyes.

"Yeah, I heard a few shouts and some bangs. I thought he was just smacking him around a bit. Edwards thought it was bloody funny ..." He paused, unsmiling, "Until the brother came down with the fingers, then he went as white as a ghost."

"What happened?" enquired Bliss, expecting to hear how long the brother-in-law spent in prison.

"Me and Edwards were charged with conspiracy to cause grievous bodily harm," King continued, dealing with the side of the story which affected him the most. "I didn't know what to do. Everybody said keep quiet. Don't say anything—deny, deny, deny. Say you never saw the bloke go up the stairs. But that was wrong. It was Edwards' fault, so I went to my chief inspector and told him."

"What did he say?" enquired Bliss, helping the story along.

"He says, 'Go with your conscience. Tell the truth.' So I did. I stood in the dock, put my hand on the Bible, and told them exactly what happened. Then Edwards got in the witness box and came out with the biggest load of bull ... reckoned he arrived as the brother was coming down the stairs, when it was all over. Then the chief inspector pulled out the station log book and backed him up—calling me a bloody liar." He paused to cool down, then added the obvious, "Someone had fixed the log book."

Bliss raised his eyebrows—it could be done.

"I got six months in jail and Edwards got promotion," King concluded with a hint of irony.

"Why did the chief inspector lie?" enquired Bliss, guessing the answer but preferring to hear it from King.

"He must have been in Edwards' little black book," said King, his tone saying, "As if you didn't know."

Detective Inspector Bliss was at a loss, his loyalty trapped between a disagreeable fellow officer, and a man who was only a convict because his conscience had been stabbed by a betrayer's stiletto.

"I would tell you about LeClarc, but I'm scared I'm going to get shit on again," King said eventually, staring at the desk between them.

"I wouldn't do that to you Nosmo."

"I know you wouldn't. At least I don't think you would, but Edwards would." Studying his hands for several moments he found an answer. "There's no evidence I threw LeClarc overboard, and if l stick to my story about being paid to drive the car off the ship, they'll have to let me go." He searched Bliss' face. "Am I right?"

"Maybe yes, maybe no."

"C'mon Dave, you can do better than that."

"O.K., you're probably right."

"But then you won't find LeClarc or the others."

Bliss nearly leapt over the table. "You know where he is?"

"Slow down Dave ..."

Bliss couldn't control his excitement. "Are the others still alive?"

King nodded slowly, letting his eyes speak for him.

"Where are they?"

"Not so fast. I'm saying nothing until you promise Edwards won't know where the information came from."

It wasn't a difficult decision. "O.K., I won't tell Edwards."

King buried his face as if making one final attempt to keep his secret to himself, then opened his hands and let it all out. "I was the informer Dave," he started, "I called Scotland Yard and told them about the plan to kidnap LeClarc."

"You knew?" breathed Bliss with incredulity.

"Yeah. I discovered the plan was to kidnap him, but I wasn't supposed to know, and I wasn't involved ... not in the kidnap anyway, I swear to you." He sought re-assurance in Bliss' face, but found only cynicism. "Motsom hired me to follow LeClarc and find out where he was going," he continued. "I thought it was above board—straightforward surveillance. One of the girls from his office let slip about his trip to Holland and when I told Motsom he was chuffed— even gave me a bonus. I thought that was the end of the job, then he asked if I fancied a trip to Holland. I said, 'Sure. Why not. What do you want?' 'Just follow him, make sure he gets on the ship safely,' he said, and offered me five hundred quid plus expenses, so I took it. I've struggled ever since I got booted out of the force so I needed the money."

Bliss was confused. "So why the anonymous tip? Don't tell me you've still got a conscience."

Still got a conscience? queried King to himself, stung by the implication he may have lost it. "Yes, I still have a conscience," he wanted to scream, but didn't, fearing Bliss would cast a sardonic eye. Why else would I have tipped off Scotland Yard? I owed them nothing— they owed me everything. They stood by and cheered as Edwards robbed me of my reputation; family; friends and liberty. But yes, I've still got a conscience.

"Why anonymous, Dave?" he answered after a few seconds. "Because if I'd strolled into the Yard with this story I would have got the kid gloves and bum's rush combined. 'Thank you, Sir,' some snotty sergeant with two weeks service would have said, and filed my report in the nearest waste bin, mumbling, "Bloody informants."

Bliss nodded sympathetically, knowing there was respect in anonymity, that both sides treat informants as scum. Anyway, the proverbial, "anonymous tip," could be more useful than a cold-blooded informant. The motives of the anonymous were incontestable—not so with informants who always wanted something.

"Conscience," mused King, "I suppose it was. When I went to Motsom's place a few weeks ago to pick up my bonus I heard two of his goons bragging about how they'd chopped up a woman and fed her to some dogs."

"The Mitchell case?"

"Yeah," replied King, impressed with Bliss' memory. "I'd read about it in the paper and remembered she was involved with computers, so I did some digging and found out about the others. It was obvious LeClarc was next—that's when I tipped you off."

Bliss interrupted, agitated. "Where are they?"

"I'm coming to that, but I want you to know what happened to LeClarc."

"Hurry up then, I haven't got all day."

"After I'd lost him, Motsom told me he'd been hired by an Arab to get him. I saw some papers in his cabin with Istanbul on them and said, 'Is that where he was going?' He said, 'Yeah,' and we'd better get him there or there would be trouble. He was in a state. Whoever hired him has got some clout. Mind you, Motsom is no pansy. He had two shooters that I could see, one of them looked like a machine pistol. He wanted me to see them—giving me a message. That's the other reason why I don't want anyone to know about this chat. Motsom'll kill me if he finds out."

"Why didn't you tell me all this on the ship?"

"I didn't know you were following LeClarc. When I saw the four of you propping up the bar I thought you were on a piss-taking junket at the tax-payers expense. I thought somebody would be watching him but I assumed they'd be more professional—no offence Dave."

Bliss meditated on King's admission for a few seconds. Finally conceding, "You're right. But it wasn't me at the bar."

King began, "I saw ..."

Bliss headed him off. "I was only there to get the others to help me find LeClarc. Anyway I don't have to explain myself to you."

"You see why Edwards mustn't find out," continued King his mind racing and his voice rising in a panic. "It was my fault he drowned. I didn't know what to do. I wasn't sure he'd fallen overboard. I thought I saw him in the water, I just wasn't sure. I panicked, told Motsom, and he said stop the ship, so I chucked the life raft over, but the bloody crewman saw me and didn't believe me. It was all my fault ..."

"O.K., O.K. Calm down. It wasn't all your fault, we should have been watching him better. Anyway it's too late now. But where have they taken the others?"

King pulled a handkerchief from his pocket and spread it on the table. Neatly scribbled in one corner was an address in Istanbul.

Saturday's dawn had broken in Watford, England. The bustle of weekday rail commuters along Junction Road was replaced by families with noisy children off to the seaside, amusement park, or a day's shopping expedition, but Trudy still lay in the silent gloom of her underground tomb. Away from the foggy coast the brilliant July sunshine started to turn the milk left standing on doorsteps. And, across town, Roger's father, still wearing yesterday's shirt, felt the warmth on his arm as he fumbled around the partially opened front door, sweeping up the milk bottle with the daily newspaper in one go.

"Who is it?" bellowed Mrs. LeClarc from the sanctuary of her bedroom, anxiously anticipating a visit from a policeman to say Roger had been found alive and well, and that the two straight-faced constables who had called the evening before had made a horrible mistake.

"Only me dear, just getting the milk," he called up the stairs. "Do you want some tea?"

"Anything about our Roger in the paper?" she enquired.

He flopped the *Daily Express* open on the hall table and scanned the headlines. "Can't see anything."

Ten minutes later, after delivering tea and sympathy to his distraught, though still demanding, wife, Mr. LeClarc's eyes hit upon a single paragraph on page three of the paper. He read it twice before going on to page four. Halfway through page five he lost concentration and found himself thinking about the earlier article. Flipping back, he looked again at the poorly reproduced photocopy with its caption. "Do you recognize Roger?"

He drifted up the stairs, the newspaper held in front of him like an offering, re-reading the paragraph aloud.

*"Roger sought in missing girl case. Police have released this photograph of a man they are seeking in relation to last week's disappearance of 16 yr. old Trudy McKenzie. "He is not a suspect," stressed Detective Sergeant Malcolm Kite, (43 yrs.), but may be able to assist with enquiries. Roger, (surname unknown) is described as 5'10" medium build, 27 yrs. Known as a computer whiz he is believed to live in the Watford area. If you know this man etcetera, etcetera."*

"Maybe they've run away together," said Mrs. LeClarc, grasping at straws. "Give it to me," she ordered, snatching the paper from his hands. "Let me look."

She scanned the piece. "Our Roger ain't twenty seven," she whined immediately.

"Maybe the paper's got it wrong. They're always getting things wrong."

"He's not five-foot ten neither."

"I think we should call. You never know," replied his father, feeling the need to do something constructive.

"But look at the photo," she commanded, thrusting the paper back at him.

The grainy monochrome picture bore no resemblance to Roger, but he wouldn't admit it, even to himself. "Could be," he said, angling the paper against the window for better light.

"No it ain't," she shot back, offended anyone would suggest she couldn't recognize her own son.

"I think it could be," he continued vaguely, rubbing his forehead and leaving a dark smear of printer's ink, unwilling to let go of the thread of hope.

"Don't be an idiot," she hissed, and buried her head in the pillow.

"I still think we should call."

Her muffled words barely reached him. "Do what you like."

Detective Constable Jackson, the Roger Moore look-alike with stained trousers, strolled into the C.I.D. office at Watford police station with two paper cups of brown liquid strongly suspected of being coffee, despite having pressed the "Tea" button on the machine. "Is that the Junction Road case?" he asked, as his partner replaced the phone.

"Yeah, that was LeClarc's father. They saw the picture in the paper."

"It's a bit of a coincidence—two missing people called

Roger both from Watford," he said, placing one cup in front of his partner, still eyeing his own suspiciously.

"The descriptions don't match at all. I've already spoken to a D.C. in Leyton. Nothing fits, only the name. Anyway that team from Scotland Yard had LeClarc under surveillance. They would have seen if he was with a woman."

"I still reckon it's odd that a bloke called Roger from Watford goes missing in the middle of the North Sea and a girl from Leyton goes missing with a bloke called Roger from Watford.

"They don't know she went off with this bloke. It's only what her friend thinks. Anyway nothing else fits. The friend said he lived in a big house. She said he drove a Jaguar. He's 27, he's 5'10' ... Shall I go on?"

"She also say's he's a computer whiz."

His partner took a quick swig from the cup, screwed his face and spat the whole lot into a wire wastebasket. "Ugh. Sugar!"

"Sorry, I forgot. Anyway I still think it might be worth having another look at that place on Junction Road.

The phone rang. "Criminal Investigation Department," Jackson said augustly, hitting the "hands-free" key, speaking to the ceiling.

"Switchboard," yawned a female operator. "Bloke from ACT Telecommunications, whatever that is, wants to speak to someone about a missing person."

"Get uniform branch to deal with it, Luv; we're busy," he snapped.

"I'm getting pissed about here. I already tried— they said it were your case. I wish somebody'd make up there bloody mind."

"PMS," he mouthed across the desk to his partner. "O.K. put him on," he said, tiredly, no idea what missing person she was talking about, and switched to the handset. "D.C. Jackson, can I help you."

A polished Oxbridge accent jumped down the phone at him. "What the devil's going on Officer?"

Two can play at that game, he thought, replying snottily, "I have absolutely no idea what you are talking about, Sir."

"Have you got the *Daily Express*?"

What is this—twenty questions with attitude?

"That's my photograph on page three but my name is definitely not Roger and I am certainly not involved with the disappearance of any schoolgirl," continued the voice, not giving Jackson an opportunity to respond.

Grabbing the paper from his partner, Jackson came close to knocking over his drink. "Watch out!" shouted the other man, as Jackson stared at the picture.

"What do you mean, it's your photo?" he said into the phone as he scrutinized the face.

"Officer," the voice continued, "I do know my own face and so do a lot of other people. This is very embarrassing. My wife is very upset; so am I. I've called the *Express*. They say someone at your police station gave them the photograph and claimed it was this Roger fellow."

"Let me get this straight, Sir," he said, stalling as he jotted a few notes. "The picture in today's paper of the man we are looking for in the Trudy McKenzie case is you."

"That's right, and I'm not Roger. I haven't kidnapped any girl and I'm not very happy. In fact I shall be talking to my lawyers about suing someone for defamation of character."

"Lawyers," mused Jackson with his hand over the mouthpiece, feeling the weight of the plural, deciding it was time to take cover. "It wasn't us who gave *Express* the photo, it came from Leyton. I suggest you give them a call."

"Oh," he floundered for a second, "I thought it was you."

"Sorry, that case is nothing to do with us."

"But the paper says this Roger lives in Watford."

"That's correct, Sir, but the girl's missing from Leyton—it's their case."

A few moments silence left Jackson wondering if the caller had slammed the phone down. "Sir?" he enquired.

"Yes," replied the voice, thoughtful, less angry.

"Have you any idea how someone got your photograph?"

"Oh yes. Someone stole it a few weeks ago from the showcase at our head office. We knew it was missing—assumed it was a staff member's prank."

"Sorry I can't help you, Sir," Jackson said as he put the phone down. Then he looked at his partner. "There's something funny here. Let's take another look at that place of LeClarc's. I'm beginning to wonder if the two Rogers are connected."

He laid out his theory driving to Junction Road. "If the photo ain't Roger's, then the description's prob'ly wrong as well. What if LeClarc has run off with this girl." He thought for a second, going over the evidence in his mind, then reconstructed the case out loud. "This McKenzie girl deliberately gave her friend a photo of the wrong guy; gave a false description, and didn't tell her mum where she was going." He paused long enough to negotiate an absurdly parked truck, then triumphantly solved the case, "I bet Roger and this McKenzie girl have eloped. I bet her mum wouldn't have him in the house, so she came up with a dodgy excuse and sloped off to Holland with him. Now they're sunning themselves on the Costa

Bravo or a beach in Florida and laughing their pants off at us silly sods."

"Maybe," replied his partner, unconvinced.

George Mitchell was just leaving home for High Street, scouting for something interesting for his dinner, when the two detectives returned.

"Mr. Mitchell," Jackson called, as the sprightly eighty-three year old marched along Junction Road like he was still in command.

He halted and peered down into the car. "Good morning officer," he responded crisply, proving the strength of his eyesight matched his legs; then he bent and enquired seriously, "Did you manage to get the stain out?"

Jackson blushed as his partner jumped out and greeted the old soldier with a wide grin. "Morning Mr. Mitchell, lovely day."

"G'morning. Any news of your young man?" he nodded toward Roger's house.

"We were hoping you might know something."

"Only what I told you yesterday. He's not come back s'far as I know. I ain't seen 'is car for best part of a week."

Jackson, spotting a parking space, headed off as his partner and Mitchell wandered across the road into the warmth of the sun.

"Did he ever bring a girl here?" asked the detective, getting to the point as he scrutinized Roger's doorstep.

George Mitchell shook his head. "I never saw no one, but he kept funny hours like I told you. He'd come and go at all times."

"How did you know when he was here?"

"Sometimes he'd put the front room light on. Other times I'd see him go in."

"Mr. Mitchell never saw a woman here," called the detective as Jackson returned, then he ran up the two steps to the old yellow door and banged hard. "Just in case," he explained to George who was eyeing him as if he were deranged.

"I told you ...There's no one there," said George, visibly offended.

Trudy woke with a start. Her ears, sensitized by two days of total silence, had picked up the faint sound of the thump. For a moment she lay disorientated on the damp stone floor in the darkness wondering what had woken her. Then she slowly pulled herself up, carefully testing each joint and limb for pain, and stuck her ear to the keyhole—nothing. A few seconds later she fastened her mouth over the hole—like a baby sucking its mother's life-giving breast, and drank in the refreshingly oxygenated air.

Leaving George on the front doorstep, the two detectives fought their way to the rear of the house over the unofficial waste dump. Clambering through the garbage and debris they forged a path through the stringy vegetation, Jackson scything wildly at a patch of nettles with a length of rusty guttering, disturbing a frenzy of flies.

"Ugh. Want something for lunch," he called to his partner, finding the fly-blown carcase of a rat and poking it with his lance.

"Disgusting sod," replied the other as he climbed over the rubble of the dividing wall into the wilderness of Roger's backyard.

George Mitchell greeted him as he rounded the back of the house. "Bloody eyesore that mess is—council should get it cleared up."

"How the hell did you get here?" he enquired, astounded at the appearance of the old soldier.

"I came through old Daft Jack's next door," he replied, using his thumb to point at the gap in the decayed wall between Roger's house and his next door neighbour and, following the thumb, the detective found himself looking at the scarecrow figure of an old man, with wispy grey beard and antiqued leather skin. Jack grinned, and all three of his teeth shone green in the morning sunlight.

"He's not really daft," said George as if Jack were not there. "It's just that he's deaf, so the kids make fun of him."

Jack remained on his side of the dilapidated wall, fascinated by the unusual activity.

"Can he hear anything?" whispered Jackson.

"Oh yeah. When he's got 'is deaf-aid on. He 'as it off most of the time to save on batteries, so you have to tell him." He turned to the old man, put his right hand to his own ear and, with a twisting motion, yelled, "Earring aid."

Jack fiddled with the device until it let out a shriek that made him jump, spent two minutes adjusting it, and ten seconds saying he'd never heard or seen Roger. The excitement over, he promptly clicked it off and disappeared back inside his house.

The two detectives turned their attention to Roger's back door—still firmly locked.

"We really should get a search warrant," said Jackson for George's benefit, though he had already made up his mind not to bother.

"If it's empty we won't have a problem," replied his partner.

George overheard. "There's nothing in there, I can tell you that for now."

"How do you know?"

"One of your sergeants came by after you left yesterday and I let him in," said George, failing to mention that he too had been in the house.

"How?"

"With a key." Then he added sarcastically, "How do you think I let him in?"

Jackson's partner ignored the sarcasm. "Oh great, now you tell us—c'mon let us in then."

George carefully examined the highly polished toe-caps of his boots for several seconds. "I let 'im take the key," he mumbled, feeling guilty for some reason, as if he had been personally responsible for its safe-keeping.

A few minutes later they stood in the front hallway, just inches from the cupboard under the stairs, directly above Trudy's dungeon. The "accidentally smashed" kitchen window was letting in a welcome breath of fresh air.

"Sewer," said Jackson with a sniff, as his partner shuffled through the heap of mail squashed into a pile behind the front door.

"This one's undone," he lied, as his finger prised open the flap of an envelope that appeared to contain more than junk mail. Slipping out the contents, he recognized the letterhead from a furniture store. "According to this, LeClarc had a new bed delivered here back in May," he announced. "Phew, look at the price."

Jackson peered over his shoulder. "Well where is it then?"

George unintentionally gave away his previous incursion. "There's no bed in here." But the detectives overlooked his remark, intent on searching for more documentary evidence.

A letter from British Telecom fell open with some assistance. "There should be a phone here somewhere," said Jackson, skimming the printed page. "Here's the number. This was May as well—the fourth apparently."

His partner flipped open his cellphone and tapped in the number. The distant phone rang twice in his ear but no one in the house heard it, then a string of high pitched bleeps alerted him to the fact that he was trying to communicate with a machine.

"It's a fax or a computer modem," he said, with a confused look.

The computer screen, just ten feet below, leapt silently into life "STANDBY—MODEM CONNECTING."

The sudden movement caught Trudy's eye and, with only a moment's hesitation, sent her scrabbling across the room, oblivious to the pain in her hands and knees.

Detective Constable Jackson had shut the lid on his phone and cut the connection before Trudy even reached the machine. "CONNECTION—ABORTED," flashed three times before the screen went blank. Tears streamed down her face. "MUM, MUM, MUM," she typed frantically, then sat sobbing and coughing, staring at the screen, begging it to try again. "MUM HELP."

"There should be a phone jack somewhere," said Jackson's partner as he probed around the hallway and on into the front room where he discovered the recently installed socket. "It's here, and there's no phone plugged in," he called, as if that somehow explained the modem's response.

D.C. Jackson, rifling through the mail, needed more light and tentatively toyed with the ancient brass light switch before finally giving it a flick—whipping his hand quickly away as if it might bite. "The powers on," he pronounced unnecessarily, when they were bathed in the sepia glow of an ancient bare bulb, then he dropped to the floor and swept up a number of long black hairs.

George Mitchell took once glance and brushed them off, saying, "Mrs. Papadropolis," as if she'd lived there the day before.

"What colour was Roger's hair?"

"Almost white, sort of straggly and thin."

"Couldn't be his then," he said, dropping them carelessly back on the floor.

Some newly made scratch marks on the hallway walls caught his attention and he traced them. "Probably where they brought in the bed," he mused. " There's not a lot of room."

Five minutes later they'd searched the entire house, confirmed the bed was not there, and stood in the cramped hallway wondering what to do next. D.C. Jackson expressed his thoughts aloud, seeking ratification from the others. "There's no phone but the number works; the power's on; there's no bed but there should be; there's no furniture or belongings, yet LeClarc was living here—the Met. Team saw him, so did George."

"Sort of living here," corrected his partner.

"Yes. Sort of," Jackson reiterated. "It's as if he was living here but he wasn't. Like he's in another world, another dimension."

"You've been reading too many weird books," said George, steadfast in his belief that there was a rational explanation for everything.

"Hello," shouted Jackson, as loud as he possibly could, startling both his partner and George. "Is there anybody there."

"Don't piss about," hissed the other detective, mindful of the presence of a member of the public.

"I'm not," he replied, jumping up and down, his size 11 shoes thundering on the bare wooden boards. "C'mon out wherever you are," he continued, his loud voice filling the entire house. "C'mon—we know you're here."

"I shouldn't do that if I were you," said George worriedly, recalling the sergeant's demolition of the old chair.

The raised voices and banging easily penetrated Trudy's dungeon and, finding a hidden reserve of energy, she rushed the door and tried thumping. Her blistered and bloated hands were like water-filled balloons thwacking a target at a village fête. She screamed, nothing happened. Pulling herself up to the keyhole, pressing her lips hard against the metal plate, she willed her vocal chords into action. A series of squeaky sounds leaked out.

D.C. Jackson, nearest to the cupboard, heard. "Listen," he said. "What was that?"

"Mouse," said George, dismissively. "There's plenty of 'em around here."

"Or a rat," suggested his partner, remembering the dead animal outside.

No one thought it was Trudy and the detectives left the house by the front door a few minutes later, deciding that a photograph of the real Roger LeClarc, from his parents, would be useful; George volunteered to clean up the broken glass.

"Don't worry, Mr. Mitchell, we'll get someone to mend the window," said Jackson on his way out. "Not that there's anything of value in there."

The voices had stopped for Trudy and she rushed hysterically back to the computer on the other side of the room, some inner strength taking control, her dead nerve endings no longer registering pain. Still panting frantically. her fingers flew across the keyboard.

"MUM I CAN HEAR YOU. I'M DOWN HERE. MUM PLEASE HURRY."

Dragging herself back to the door she put her ear to the keyhole and heard nothing. "Please Mum," she sobbed. "Please Mum." Then exhaustion took over and she gradually collapsed back to the floor.

# *chapter eleven*

"**D**etective Constable Bliss," hollered Superintendent Edwards, his voice booming the length of the station corridor, as Bliss emerged from his meeting with Nosmo King more than two hours later.

Anticipating an ambush from Edwards, Bliss had spent the final five minutes of the meeting mentally preparing himself, yet immediately went to pieces. The relatively diminutive figure at the other end of the corridor, now beckoning with furious hand movements, exuded such an aura of control he felt his willpower being siphoned away. Everyone, and everything, stopped, like a confrontation scene from a wild west movie. Who would be fastest to the draw?

The superintendent fired the first volley, shouting, "Here!"

Adolf Hitler, who, for all Bliss knew, may have walked this same corridor fifty-odd years earlier, could never have commanded such authority in a single word.

Bliss capitulated immediately. Heart thumping and blood rising, he answered, "Yes, Sir," and started the lonely walk.

Yolanda fell in step—a henchman in a lemon yellow two-piece that would have been more at home on a catwalk. "I could kick him," she suggested from the corner of her mouth, and probably would have done had he agreed.

Reaching into his pocket, Bliss pulled out King's handkerchief and slipped it to her. "Thank you," was all she could think of saying as she grasped it, with puzzled eyes, peeling away just as they reached Edwards.

"In here," Edwards motioned to an empty room and Bliss fought desperately to get his mind under control in preparation for the string of lies he was about to tell.

Twenty minutes later the white BMW purred restfully as Yolanda concentrated on the face of the figure walking across the car park toward her. She had seen similar expressions before—faces of survivors fleeing the scene of a hostage taking. A vengeful postal worker had been pumping bullets randomly into his colleagues, his supposed tormentors, and the escapees all wore the same mask. Fear, anger, and disbelief combined with just a twinge of relief, producing a deadpan expression that said so little, yet hid so much. Any minute now he'll break into a little nervous smile, just to prove to me, and himself, that he came through it alive, she thought, and, on cue, Bliss' mouth widened, his teeth showed briefly, and he shrugged his shoulders lightly as if to say, "That didn't hurt."

"Hi," he said airily, jumping in beside her.

She smiled, genuinely, "Okey dokey Dave?" and dropped the car into gear without adding to his discomfort by asking what happened.

Heading back to her apartment in thoughtful silence she glanced at him a couple of times and recalled how most of the hostage survivors had quickly disintegrated into snivelling, whimpering messes. She guessed he would not.

Yolanda's expensive and well-travelled suitcase had taken her less than three minutes to pack and stow into the trunk of the car. Bliss had spent considerably longer gathering his few possessions. Deep in thought, he had moved around the apartment in a daze. The words, "Suspended from duty," were uppermost in his mind. Edwards' parting admonition, "Get your ass on that ship and be in my office nine o'clock Monday morning with a full report," also left a nasty sting that wouldn't go away.

"Have you got everything?" she enquired, creeping unnoticed into the bedroom behind him.

"I think so."

"What about this?" she held up his toothbrush and made him reach for it. Their fingers met. Neither thought it was an accident. The electric charge that leapt from flesh to flesh was purely imaginary, yet perfectly real. Her heart pounded and she felt an inner tingling sensation. Their eyes locked over their hands and the vivid blueness of her pupils held him prisoner. He couldn't escape; didn't want to escape; didn't even try to escape. Running his fingers along the length of hers, he found the wrist and held it while his other hand took the toothbrush and tossed it onto the bed. Pulling gently, he eased the outstretched hand toward his mouth and pressed the palm to his lips. An instant may have been a minute, or an hour, and neither of them could have guessed with any certainty how long they stood glued together by eye contact alone. Flustered, unsettled, he pulled away, grabbed the toothbrush and shoved it into his suitcase, saying, "I've got to go," with unnecessary harshness. "The ship sails in half an hour." Then they fumbled uncertainly around each other for a few minutes while Yolanda checked the lights, the taps, the answering machine, then locked the front door behind her.

Bliss' half-closed eyes took little notice of the route to the port. The coastal fog had thinned a little but after ten minutes he still could not see the ship. Then rows of humped backed greenhouses replaced the little terraced houses at the roadside and stretched into the murk.

"Where are we going?" he enquired almost casually.

"Istanbul."

His eyes went wide and his voice lifted an octave, "Istanbul?"

"Yeah. Istanbul."

He sat bolt upright and stared at her. "Don't be silly Yolanda, I'm in enough trouble already. Anyway it would take at least four days."

"We're not driving there."

"We are not going there," he said firmly.

"Why did you give me the handkerchief then?"

"Stop."

"No."

"Stop, or I'll jump out," he shouted, undoing his seat belt.

Her eyes stared straight ahead. "Go on then," she taunted, pulling a "couldn't-care-less," face.

"Please stop Yolanda," he said, trying hard not to get cross.

Her face changed; his seriousness had sunk in and disappointment dragged her down. She parked untidily, without indication, and suffered the angered blast of the following driver's horn as he barely missed rear-ending them in the fog. "Dave, What else can we do?" she began, trying to reason with him.

"Contact Interpol."

"Have you ever dealt with Interpol?" she asked in a way that made it clear she had.

"No," he admitted.

"Look at your watch Dave."

He looked

"What's the time?"

"Eleven-thirty."

With a confused look she quickly checked hers. "It's twelve-thirty, Dave. You've still got English time."

"Oh, right."

"So," she continued, "It's twelve-thirty Friday. If we work hard the request will be ready for Interpol by five o'clock. With any luck they'll deal with it first on Monday morning. They might have a Turkish translation by next Tuesday and by next Wednesday hundreds of Turkish police will go the address."

"That's useless," he cried, "They'll have cleared out long before then. They might have left already."

Bliss gnawed on a knuckle, deep in thought, for a few seconds. Istanbul sounded good; Istanbul with Yolanda sounded ... "Sorry," he said eventually, shaking his head from side to side, his speculations soured by malignant thoughts of Edwards. "I have to go back. I would lose my job. Edwards is determined to nail me." Putting his hand lightly on her arm he looked deeply into her face. "I really am sorry. You don't know how much I'd like to say yes, but I can't. Please take me to the ship or I'll miss it."

The roar of the ship's siren sounded a final warning as they drove into the port. Yolanda expertly navigated a maze of plastic traffic bollards, snubbed a "no entry" sign, and came alongside the ship.

Slinging his suitcase onto the end of the gangway, Bliss caught her up in his arms and their lips smacked together and refused to let go. A parting peck turned into a full-blown smooch. Her body swung limply in his arms, her mouth moved frantically against his, and his hands swam up and down her body.

The crewmember at the top of the gangway was waiting to give the order to lift, and yelled, "Oy! Get on with it mate. We're bloody late already."

Bliss broke away, grabbed his suitcase, jumped onto the bottom step and peered wistfully at her. "Sorry," was all he could say, and he really meant it.

Then she threw him a curve. "It's Okey dokey, I'll go on my own." Her face clearly said she meant it. "Goodbye Dave." Was there a crack in her voice? Her bottom lip quivered. He was sure he saw it quiver.

"Bye," he mumbled.

She tried a smile. He recognized a false smile when he saw one.

"Damn," he shouted, jumped off the gangway, marched back to the car and slung his suitcase on the back seat.

"Make up your bloody mind mate," shouted the crewman, giving the thumbs-up to lift.

Yolanda talked on her car's mobile phone with the same alacrity and excitement as she drove. Bliss sulked, his arms folded tightly across his chest. The fog had thinned a few miles inland and the powerful car negotiated the sweeping curves of the highway at more than double the speed limit.

"We'll have to drive," she had said as soon as they left the port, "It's too foggy to fly."

"All the way?" he'd asked, expressionless.

"No," she'd laughed, "only to Schiphol."

With a final burst of chatter she flipped the phone into its holder. "They'll hold the plane."

He tried to sound uninterested, "What plane?"

"To Istanbul."

"I don't believe you," he said frostily. "Why would they do that?"

The deep crescents on either side of her mouth accentuated her smile. "I told them a very important British police officer was pursuing an international terrorist and there would be a lot of trouble if they let it leave."

Bliss tried hard not to, but couldn't help smiling. Slowly unfolding his arms he enquired, "Does Captain Jahnssen know what you ..." he stopped and corrected himself, "What we are doing?"

"Sort of."

"What do you mean—sort of?"

"I said that as I was flying to Istanbul for the weekend anyway, I might as well snoop around a bit. He didn't believe me. He just said be careful."

A large truck in front of them was proving to be an obstinate obstruction. Yolanda blasted her horn several times although Bliss had no idea what she expected the driver to do. Finally she took an outrageous chance coming out of a bend, slamming her foot to the floor so hard the tires spun as they leapt ahead. Fishtailing, they shot pass the truck and forced an on-coming car onto the verge. "Weekend drivers," she shouted, forging ahead, another truck in her sights.

A wide stretch of dual carriageway with sparse traffic relieved Bliss' anxiety and he felt it safe to break Yolanda's concentration. "What's Istanbul like?" he asked, excitement getting the better of him. "Have you been there before?"

She had, several times, and talked animatedly for several minutes about the fabulous Blue Mosque; the sun rising over the majestic Bosphorus bridge; the bustling bazaars; and the mounds of deep purple figs and heaps of sugar dusted Turkish delight hawked by vendors at almost every street corner. "We might even try some of the famous bluefish," she added, as if they were a couple planning an adventurous holiday.

"I hope it's better than herring," he said, with the makings of a smile.

Now, only a few miles from the airport, Yolanda thought Bliss had relaxed sufficiently to answer a few questions. "What did Nosmo say about Edwards?" she enquired innocently.

He reflected, just for a moment, then recounted the salient parts of King's story without embellishment, though sparing her none of the macabre' detail. "Eleven teeth smashed as he kept ramming his brother-in-law's mouth into the metal door knob at full force," he said, and noticed her contemplatively running her tongue along the top of her teeth as he spoke. She shuddered thinking of the excruciating pain as the solid brass ball had smashed its way into the poor man's mouth. With the worst yet to come he considered keeping quiet about the chopped fingers, then perversely decided to punish her for forcing him to go to Istanbul. She swallowed hard and drove silently for a short while, staring intently at the road ahead. "That's horrible Dave," she said quietly just as they reached the airport.

Dumping the car across a pedestrian walkway, Yolanda leaned on the horn and caught the attention of a passing porter. Bliss grabbed his case from the back seat. "Mine's in the trunk," she shouted over her shoulder as she threw the car keys at the porter, flashed her badge and shouted a load of Dutch. The porter gave a weird sort of smile which caused Bliss to ask, "What did you say?" as they ran together across the concourse.

"Told him to take it to the airport police office," she liberally translated, totally ignoring the warning that, if she found the slightest scratch on her return, she would break his legs.

Although Bliss had certainly flown before he'd amassed few frequent flyer points, and felt an exhilarating rush of adrenalin as the giant plane stood on its tail and roared eastward. Settling back in the comfortable first-class seat—"Don't worry," Yolanda had said, "I'm paying."—he watched, fascinated, as Europe floated beneath him. Tiny blobs of cotton wool cloud drifted into view, seeming to keep pace with the plane, and Yolanda gabbled away, ten to the dozen, in Dutch with her stewardess friend. "We went to school together," she'd confided, as they scuttled to their seats. He sensed they were talking about him, and felt like a pedigree dog being discussed by a couple of trendies. "Glossy hair, nice teeth, well groomed, good proportions."

Something Anne said made them both giggle. "Is he house trained?" thought Bliss laughing to himself. Occasionally Yolanda dragged him into the conversation. "Anne says, would you like to go to the flight deck and meet the pilot."

He nodded, "Yes," he would like that.

"We've got plenty of time," she added, "It's about three and half hours to Istanbul."

Prettily arranged plates of hors d'oeuvres, together with a couple of miniatures of Mouton Cadet, appeared on the little tables in front of each of them, and they began toying with each other. Yolanda started it, playfully sneaking titbits from his plate, trying not to get caught. He grabbed her hand on the third occasion, the little caviar and smoked salmon roll still between her thumb and finger. Bending down, he forced her hand to his mouth and slowly crammed the whole lot straight in, food and fingers together, and wouldn't release them until he had licked the fingers clean. Still holding her hand, his eyes sought hers, they met and locked. Then he slid her fingers back to his mouth.

"Tell me about yourself, Dave," she said in a soft voice, retrieving her fingers, maintaining the gaze.

He picked at his plate and started slowly, almost shyly. "I don't know where to begin ... I 'm forty-two. I'm a cop, but you know that." He hesitated. "I don't really know what to say." But then added, "I'm not really dedicated to any particular sports or hobbies. I like to do lots of different things. I like to try everything at least once."

Yolanda smiled, "I thought all English detectives studied poetry, or classical music, or psychology."

"Only on television, Yolanda. Most of the ones I work with study beer, soccer and women—probably in that order."

The question, "Are you married?" slipped out as she tried to bite it back and she snapped, "Don't tell me." Her fingers flew to his mouth and pinched his lips tightly together. She studied him earnestly, her fingers digging into the flesh around his mouth, making his eyes water. "Promise you won't tell me."

"Um, um," he hummed trying to make it sound like "O.K."

"Promise," she demanded seriously, and slowly backed off without taking her fingers away.

"I promise," he mumbled as best as he could. "I promise."

She took her hand away a little, but left it hovering. "Promise again," she said, "Please promise you won't tell me."

"I will promise," he began, "but ..." she fiercely clamped his lips together again.

"You promised."

Wrenching her fingers away he gasped, "Alright, I promised, but what if I said I was ..." She tried to stop him but he caught her hand. "I'm not saying I am, and I am not saying I am not. I'm just saying what if you knew I wasn't married. How would you feel?"

She sat back. "It would be difficult for me to fall in love with a foreigner."

His head jerked up—a foreigner? He'd never considered himself a foreigner and was startled to realize that was exactly what he was.

She continued, "It would be too complicated—imagine the wedding, nobody would know what to say, what to wear, or where to have it. Then it would be a problem to know where to live. And the poor children—seeing only half of their relatives most of the time." She carried on with numerous other objections: religion, customs, education. "Food," she added, poking him in the ribs accusingly. "You don't like herrings."

"Neither do you," he reminded her, poking her back.

"Then there's sex," she concluded, giving a little smile.

"What do you mean—sex ?"

"Well, you might do it differently to us."

"We could always find out beforehand."

Her look was mischievous. "We could?"

"But what if I were married?"

"Oh, that would be exciting. Sort of thrilling and dangerous."

"Like flying?" he suggested.

"Yes," she agreed happily, "like flying," then paused to rearrange her face. "But afterwards I would feel guilty and feel sorry for your poor wife, or I would try to take you away from her and that would be bad as well."

The voice of experience, he thought noticing her pensive expression. "What about you," he enquired, "Have you ever been married?"

She thought intently, as if the answer required calculation. "I tried it once but it wasn't much fun."

Almost as if on some pre-arranged cue, Anne arrived with the main course—Beef Bordelaise strewn with plump white asparagus spears—and lifted Yolanda's mood. She teased him unmercifully, taking each juicy stalk of asparagus and sliding it slowly through her pursed lips with her head back, exposing the length of her slender neck.

"Witch," smirked Bliss knowing exactly what she was doing. Then her hand slipped into his lap under the table and brushed lightly over the bump of his erection.

"You are a naughty boy, Dave." she said demurely, and he closed his eyes and willed her to keep going but she stopped. A few moments later she slid out of her seat. "Bathroom," she said.

Ten minutes later, when she hadn't returned, concern clouded Bliss' face and irrational thoughts spun in his mind. What if something awful had happened to her—maybe she's fainted. Feeling slightly foolish he found his way to the solitary cubicle behind the curtain and tapped lightly on the door. "Yolanda," he whispered, "are you in there?"

"Yes," she sang out, opening the tiny door.

Dancing to the rhythm of their own music they manoeuvred into the minute washroom, their mouths fastened together. He saw what was coming and hesitated a fraction, a jumble of excuses racing through his mind: There wouldn't be enough room; other people might be waiting; someone might miss them; it wasn't professional. Bugger, he thought, slamming the door with his foot, it's not as though there's anyone else in my life at the moment. That's sleazy Dave, he chided himself, then relented. Alright then, if you must know, I think she's bloody gorgeous and maybe I'm not too old to try again.

Yolanda reached behind him and slipped the catch. His fingers fumbled with the buttons of her blouse while her hands played in his hair. "Quickly Dave," she said, without breaking the kiss, and helped him with the last button.

"I've never done this before," he breathed, as his fingers fought with the clasp of her brassiere.

"What?" she questioned laughingly.

"Had sex in an airplane," he whispered, his eyes eagerly seeking a glimpse of the pale fleshy mounds.

"You said you liked to try everything once."

Full, yet firm, her breasts yielded only slightly when he set them free from the lace trimmed half-cups of her bra. With a breast fitting perfectly into the palm of each hand, he massaged and moulded them, squeezing and teasing until she could wait no longer. Giving the inside of his mouth a parting wash with her tongue, her hands urged his face toward her chest. His head dipped and his lips brushed her nipples; his saliva lubricated them; his tongue traced their outline. Then he tweaked the hard pink erections between his teeth and felt her whole body quiver. His mind swam, this wasn't happening, this couldn't be happening.

Seized by a sudden urgency, her hands flew to his groin and she tugged insistently at the zipper of his trousers.

"Please, Dave, please," she urged.

He experienced again the sensation approaching take-off. The jet engines revving faster and faster; the vibration; the tension running through his body; the pent up excitement. Then the thrill of the rapid acceleration as the plane bounded toward the far end of the runway with more power than ten thousand horses. Then he felt the powerful thrust of take-off as her legs swooped around him and drew him in, both her hands pulling, insisting, guiding.

Absorbed entirely in their emotions, neither saw the sign on the wall flashing impatiently. "Fasten your seat belts."

Free as an eagle, but faster than a bullet, the giant flying phallus slipped through the air, its cargo of humanity hurtling toward a higher altitude. Bliss felt himself recklessly flying fast. Climbing higher and higher. Penetrating deeper and deeper into the warm, humid atmosphere. His body trembling with the thrust from the mighty engines of the plane; his excitement enhanced by the fear of crashing. Now his powerful upward thrusts were matched by hers. Eyes closed they raced together, higher and higher, faster and faster, piercing through the earth's envelope, penetrating the dark, mysterious, humid clouds. All thought of Edwards and LeClarc swept from their minds. Then, together, they burst jubilantly out into the bright clear blue sky and floated and soared above the clouds.

An insistent banging brought them down to earth. "Yolanda, Yolanda," Anne shouted through the door, "we're coming in to land."

"So are we," mumbled Bliss.

"Vienna?" queried Yolanda a minute later as they stepped out of the washroom, hot, sweaty, and hastily dressed.

"Thirty minute re-fuelling stop," answered Anne with a broad smirk that said she not only knew what they were doing, but would enjoy in gossiping about it to lots of other people. "Quick get in your seats."

Emerging from behind the curtain into the cabin, the weight of thirty eyes fell upon them with such force that Bliss almost staggered back. Everyone was staring, many with knowing grins. Yolanda giggled, but Bliss' face turned an even deeper shade of pink. Carefully avoiding eye contact, he kept his head down, scuttled to his seat with Yolanda in tow, and wouldn't have been surprised to hear a round of applause.

# chapter twelve

A noisy seagull dive-bombed Roger's raft, mistaking it for a fishing boat in the swirling mist, hoping to snatch some offal from the deck, and his thoughts of Trudy were interrupted as he fended it off with a lazy swipe.

"Clear off."

Returning to his daydreams, Trudy's aesthetically improved likeness appeared again and again in selectively recreated memories: The heart-pounding thrill of their first meeting in the railway refreshment room; the stolen glimpse of her vagina as she lay unconscious on his bed; her pink breast flopping out of the torn white top when he caught her trying to escape; her neat little body squatting over the bucket to pee.

From out of the swirling mist he conjured other images of Trudy—a vision of whatever and whoever he wanted her to be—before her spectre had transmogrified into a very solid, snivelling, sixteen year-old: The times he had sat in front of his computer with her loveliness, her innocence, her whole being, flooding through the Internet and appearing as words on his screen. And his face warmed at the way he had sat naked in his little room, his hand in his groin, as he read and re-read her often misspelled, and frequently misused, words.

Trudy's captivity had altered everything and, as he rushed home from work on the Monday evening, he missed the expectant thrill of meeting his true love—his computer bearing Trudy's E-mail message. It wasn't that he wanted to communicate with her, he wanted to *really communicate* with her, and would have been hard pushed to explain the difference.

"Come on Trude. It's just a game," he said enthusiastically, trying to pretend nothing had changed by her capture. "We can play it together. I'll leave a message for you, then you can send a message back to me."

Pouting, "No," she turned her back and sat cross-legged on his bed in the dungeon.

"Oh come on," he implored, his hand worming toward his groin.

"Sod off."

He begged ... "Please, Trude."

"Fat slob."

... insisted, "Come here."

"Asshole."

... ordered, "Get over here."

"Bollocks."

Losing control, he grabbed her long ponytail, dragged her to the stool beside him, and started to type. "I love Trudy McK ..." then a pang of remorse swept through him and his fingers shook as they wrote "I'm sorry, Trude. I didn't hurt you, did I ?"

"Screw you," she had typed valiantly in response, determined he should not see her weaken.

Just twenty feet above the water, the fog thinned and the seagull glided gracefully in the brilliant sunshine, searching for greener pastures. A trace of sunlight stole through the mist and Roger instinctively held his face up to bask in its grudging warmth. Staring at the inside of his eyelids, he formed a picture of Trudy which bore no resemblance to the bruised and battered body now lying on the rough flagstone floor beneath the house in Junction Road. His mind's eye could never have imagined the pathetic comatose figure with knotted hair, bloated eyes, and diarrhoea encrusted legs, though a sudden dark thought sent a shiver down his spine and shook his eyes wide open. Trudy's sleek image evaporated in the haze. "Trudy," he called softly, his lips hardly moving. But she was gone.

The dark memory clouded his mind with darker thoughts: Trudy's first morning in the little room under his house, the previous Saturday.

"Why are you keeping me here?" she had blubbered, as soon as he unlocked the door and let himself in. She was curled on the edge of the bed, head buried in hands, tears dripping uncontrollably off her chin onto the swell of her breasts.

"'Cos I love you, Trude."

"You lied to me."

"You lied to me too," he retorted, in a "tit for tat" voice.

"No, I didn't."

"Yes, you did."

"White lies," she conceded, in between wet sniffles. "I never sent you Marge's photo or nothing like that. And you said you had a big house."

"It is Trude. It is a big house," he shot back, deluding himself.

"Show me," she said, uncurling herself and starting toward the door, looking for a way out.

Ignoring her request, he blocked her path. "And I've got a car."

"A poxy Renault," she taunted, stabbing him with her finger and feeling the flabby flesh give way. "A poxy little Renault. What sort of car is that? You said you had a Jag."

He blushed. "I'll get one."

She poked him again, taunting, goading. "Like hell you will." Another poke. "You're just a fat slob with a poxy little Renault."

"Don't make fun of me," he cried, sticking his hands over his ears.

"Fat slob, fat slob, fat slob," she yelled.

The smack sent her reeling as she took a fall for a thousand previous tormentors, and her cheek stung as a torrent of blood gushed from her left nostril, but she didn't give up. "Bloody monster," she shouted, then scuttled into a corner and huddled into a miserable ball awaiting a further attack. Nothing happened. Her whimpers subsided, her breathing slowed, and she carefully raised her head, anticipating the thump that didn't come. Roger sat on the edge of the bed, his whole body heaving as he silently cried.

The deluded seagull swooped again, its battle cry piercing the haze long before its mottled grey plumage shot out of the murk and lunged. Perfectly camouflaged in the mist, the turkey-size bird buzzed the raft repeatedly, appearing from nowhere, screeching ferociously, then disappearing—only to re-appear a few seconds later from an entirely different direction. After a dozen or more fruitless passes, the bird showed its contempt with a badly aimed dollop of shit and vanished.

The shifting brightness of the early afternoon caught Roger's attention. A hint of movement in the water suggested a breeze. A slight lulling motion stirred the raft and one edge lost its grip on the water and dropped back with a little "plop." Balancing himself precariously, he raised himself as high as possible and strained his eyes into the surrounding sphere of mist. Then a stab of pain doubled him over and he sank back into the raft clutching his belly. Another cramp hit him as his stomach fought with the contents of the emergency ration box—three days provisions for ten, devoured by one person in five hours.

The thought of food reminded him of Trudy, but everything reminded him of Trudy. Warm, fuzzy memories of their evenings together swam into view but were bent beyond recognition. Candlelit dinners followed by sessions of passionate lovemaking were as fictional as the Barbie he'd fallen for. Most evenings he had munched a mountain of junk food while transfixed by the computer screen, watching it as if it were television.

"Do you want some chips, Trude?" he had offered one evening, without taking his eyes off the screen. She picked a few from his outstretched newspaper bundle but had little appetite.

"Happy families," he mused with the briefest glance and the thought of a smile. And he meant it.

It was Tuesday evening, the day before his departure to Holland. "It's nice having you here," he continued, still concentrating on the moving picture in front of him.

She mumbled, saying nothing.

"I'm glad, Trude."

"Ummh," she hummed and could have meant absolutely anything.

"It's nice having my own family."

"I'm not your family, Roger," she said reproachfully.

"You are now, Trude."

Her fight was gone. "Alright, Roger."

"I love you, Trude," he said, not taking his eyes of the screen.

"I love you, too," she responded mechanically.

Just like Mum and Dad, he thought, and wasn't so very wrong.

Following supper, he had a few minutes while a computer program downloaded and turned his attention to her. "I'll brush your hair, Trude." The brushing led to stroking, stroking to licking, then he made a clumsy stab at her ear with his tongue.

"Get off," she screeched. His sad round face turned back to the computer and he ignored her until a little after midnight when he rose to leave. Scared of being alone, frightened of waking, choking for breath, she pleaded, "Please don't go, Roger."

His face lit up. "I'll stay if you let me ..."

She sat quietly for a few seconds deep in thought then shook her head.

Roger locked the door on his way out.


Detective Constable Jackson, together with his partner from Watford police station, returned to Roger's house mid-afternoon to check on the glazier's handiwork, and surprised Edwards' staff sergeant as he was letting himself in.

"What the hell d'ye think you're doing?" enquired Jackson without subtlety, catching the man with the key in the lock.

"And who the hell do you think you are sonny?" sneered the sergeant drawing his warrant card and holding it up to Jackson's nose.

Jackson miffed, but outranked, introduced himself, "We've already searched the place Serg. There's nothing in there."

Unconvinced, the sergeant shoved the door and they piled into the familiar hallway. "I looked myself yesterday," he admitted. "But we may have missed something."

"Something about the girl?" enquired Jackson.

"What girl?" queried the sergeant. He'd not seen the newspaper and knew nothing of Trudy. Jackson briefed him while his partner idly sleuthed around, kicking the thick layer of dust into a cloud that split the shafts of afternoon sunlight into a million glittering motes.

Trudy lay beneath them, her breathless body now in a coma. Her frantic efforts of the morning had finally exhausted her dehydrated body, and she no longer had the energy, or the will, to keep her mouth glued to the keyhole. The computer screen in the corner still gave out its faint rays of hope and still bore her final entreaty to her mother.

"MUM, MUM, MUM," it flashed repeatedly and was programmed to do so until eternity.

The brief wartime diary of the Nazi sympathiser who had dug the shelter, together with his family's little silver Swastikas, remained in the OXO tin in a corner of the dim, damp chamber. The underground cell, abandoned for nearly sixty years, had failed to preserve the lives of the family who built it, and was now preparing to become the permanent resting place of Trudy Jane McKenzie, aged sixteen years and a couple of months.

In the hallway above, Jackson and the staff sergeant pored over photographs of Trudy and Roger.

"Have you shown the neighbours?" enquired the sergeant.

"Not yet," replied Jackson. "We've only just got the one of the McKenzie girl and we had to get this one of LeClarc from his mother. The picture in the *Daily Express* was one of LeClarc's bosses. That's why we're pretty sure there's a link between him and the missing girl."

"Sergeant," Jackson's mate shouted from the front room, "take a look at this."

"I bet this is where the bed was," he said, pointing out scuffmarks on the floor, and they followed the trail to the cupboard under the stairs, the entrance to Trudy's cavern. "It ain't in there," called Jackson, "I've already checked," so he shut the door and moved toward the staircase.

"Let me look at that picture again," requested the sergeant, sneaking it from Jackson's hand. "I thought so," he continued mysteriously, bending down to scrape a few long dark hairs from the floor.

"They come from a Greek woman who used to live here," explained Jackson's partner pompously, seemingly having an answer for everything.

"Who says so?"

"Bloke across the road ... Mitchell at 71, told me this morning."

"And you believed him?"

Doubt suddenly flooded the detective's face and reservation crept into his voice. "That's what he reckoned anyway."

The sergeant held the hairs against Trudy's photograph. "What do you think?"

"Possible," breathed Jackson and his partner reluctantly nodded in agreement.

The stiletto heels of the dumpy waitress clicked in time to the old station clock as the sergeant and the two detectives sat down to order tea fifteen minutes later. The railway refreshment room was busier than it had been when Trudy and Roger had waited a week earlier. The uniforms had changed as well: Board meetings, business luncheons, and bottom lines were far from the minds of the Friday afternoon mob in their ripped jeans and offensively decorated T-shirts. The smartly dressed commuters wouldn't be back for another two hours, leaving the refreshment room at the mercy of the unemployed and unemployable.

"At least they remembered LeClarc," said the sergeant, referring to several of Roger's neighbours who had identified him from the photograph.

"Old George Mitchell doesn't miss much," added Jackson. "You'd think he would have seen the girl if she'd been with Roger."

"Yes," demanded the waitress, making it clear from her stance that she was unlikely to stand any nonsense. "What do you want?" Her tone, and expression said everything: "No credit—don't even ask; if it isn't on the menu we haven't got it, and even if it is we might not have it, and pinch my bottom and I'll stuff your teeth down your throat."

Not intimidated, the sergeant laid his hand expressively on her tubby forearm, looked her straight in the eye, and addressed her as if she were his maiden aunt. "Now my dear," he said, "we'd like three cups of your finest China tea and some of your very best roast beef sandwiches."

She melted.

"Oh, and by the way," he added, "I don't suppose you'd recognize either of these two?"

She did—both of them.

One hour later, Junction Road, Watford had become a circus, with Roger's home the star attraction. Gaily coloured ribbons of red and yellow cordoned off the area outside the house. Brightly painted vehicles with flashing lights and musical sirens completely blocked the narrow street. The ambulance appeared to be entirely unwarranted but, as at any circus, somebody felt it wise to have one standing by. Why anybody summonsed the fire engine was unknown, but, in the initial panic following Detective Jackson's call for assistance, someone must have thought it a good idea.

The official audience of residents, reporters, and cameramen were augmented by an ad-hoc bunch of busy-bodies, excited children, and a couple of drunks who had stopped to heckle the uniformed policeman acting as usher. Patrolling up and down inside the police perimeter with a stone face, he minutely scrutinized every scrap of identification before lifting the flimsy tape, and allowing the artists into the ring.

George Mitchell and Mrs. Ramchuran were waiting to play a fringe performance to an audience of several dozen television and newspaper reporters denied access to the main attraction. The press had been unable to prise any information from the police beyond two comments: One, from D.C. Jackson, "Just routine enquiries," and the other, from a brash young sergeant, turned the face of the young female reporter prawn pink as he suggested an alternative use for her microphone should she stick it in his face again.

Now she wavered the microphone threateningly under George's nose and the cameraman gave a signal. The sideshow began.

"How long have you lived at 71, Junction Road, Watford, Mr. Mitchell?" she asked, attempting to cram as much information as possible in a single shot.

"Sixty years," he replied crisply.

"What can you tell us about Mr. LeClarc, at number 34, Sir?"

"Funny looking bugger ..."

"Sir, this is for national television," she reminded him.

George, with a vacant confused look, tried again, "Well he is a funny ..."

"O.K., Sir," the interviewer cut in quickly. "Can I ask you about the girl. Trudy McKenzie?"

"Never 'eard of her," he replied shirtily, wondering who on earth she was talking about.

"Is there anybody in the house now, Mr. Mitchell?"

"Loads of policemen," answered George truthfully, missing the point entirely.

The interviewer pulled a face and swung her microphone to attack Mrs. Ramchuran. She knew even less than George but at least she didn't waste their time. "I've only seen the man a few times. He was sort of fat with whitey hair. But I never saw no woman there."

Then a young newshound, in Bermuda shorts, spotted Daft Jack standing in the half-opened doorway of his house and the crowd of reporters and cameramen drifted in a wave in his direction.

In Roger's kitchen, hidden from the stare of the cameras, the main performance was in full swing. Superintendent Edwards' staff sergeant was running the show to the chagrin of the local officers—openly chatting while he tried to address them.

"Gentlemen," he started, clapping for attention. "First of all I can tell you Roger LeClarc, the owner of this dump, has drowned at sea. But," he stressed, "the press must not be told under any circumstances." A hush settled over the nine officers in the cramped little room as he continued with enormous solemnity, "Gentlemen—this case is much, much, bigger than two missing people."

Speaking for a few moments he laid out a short history of LeClarc's disappearance, making vague references to the potential for international catastrophe and general mayhem, then added, "Now that we have a firm connection between him and the McKenzie girl we want to know: If she was here, where is she now? She certainly didn't leave with him."

"How do you know?" asked the disembodied voice of a stubby officer straining to be seen at the back.

"Our men lost him once, possibly twice, in the past couple of weeks," admitted the sergeant, "but they always found him pretty quickly. They never saw the girl, and she definitely wasn't with him the day he left for Holland."

"Where do you think she is?"

"I have no idea son," he said darkly, "But if she came here with him and didn't leave then," he paused pointedly, "your imagination is as good as mine."

A civilian crime scene officer tried to squeeze into the crowded room but ended up poking his head round the corner and speaking as if he were being charged for every word. "Had a quick look in the hallway Serg: long dark hairs; clothing fibres, probably white; scratches on walls. Photographer's getting pictures— we'll take casts."

"Any idea what may have caused them?" asked the sergeant as the man paused for breath.

"Furniture ... fingernails," he suggested vaguely, then added a general accusation, "a clumsy cop." Then continued, "Fingerprints and footprints all over the place." His eyes swept the audience, "Mainly yours I suspect." He waited as if he had something to add but was reluctant to run up his bill.

"Anything else?" enquired the sergeant after a second or two, feeling it was expected of him.

He had deliberately kept the best to last—a conjurer building up his trick, then he pulled out the rabbit, "Several drops of blood."

"Blood?" the word was breathed around the room.

"Oh yes. Definitely blood."

"Whose?"

Peering over the top of his spectacles he gave the speaker a supercilious look. "How the hell should I know," he said dismissively, then studiously consulted his notebook for several seconds before adding, formally, "There are indications of a possible struggle in the front hallway."

"A definite maybe?" suggested one of the officers without sincerity, and was ignored.

"When was the struggle?" enquired another.

"I wouldn't like to theorize," he replied, but then did just that. "Judging by the state of the blood and the look of the scratches ... " he paused, meditatively and let his eyes wander to the ceiling, "several day's ago—could be week—not more."

The sergeant took command amid a speculative hum. "O.K. sort yourselves out—two men to a room. Check everything. Usual routine: floors, walls and ceilings. Don't disturb anything if you can avoid it but don't miss anything. Two of you can start in the garden before it gets dark—check for any sign of recent digging."

"What about the waste dump next door?" asked Jackson recalling his previous excursion over the wilderness. "It'd take a bloody month to dig that lot."

"We could try infra-red detection there," replied the sergeant. "But let's finish with the house and garden first. Let's do this quickly. We're probably too late, but my guess is she's around here somewhere."

The Dutch herring trawler had ambled all day to reach the area of Roger's disappearance despite Motsom's relentless urging. The sun was diving toward the western horizon before the skipper admitted they were close. "If your brother's still alive he should be somewhere near here," said the skipper, still paying lip service to Motsom's claim.

With the persistent fog making it impossible to see the water rushing past the hull, it was difficult to judge the speed of the vessel, or even the direction of travel, and Motsom had no idea the skipper had nudged the little vessel along at a mere 5 knots, hoping someone may have picked up the deck hand's brief mayday call from the lifeboat's emergency transmitter early that morning. Around mid-day, before the fog had begun to lift, Billy Motsom had stood in the wheelhouse next to the skipper when he had a nasty feeling something was wrong.

"How do I know we're going the right way?" he suddenly enquired after a long period of silence.

"We are."

"How do I know?"

"You'll have to trust me," the skipper replied, deliberately weaving doubt into his tone.

Shit, thought Motsom, we're going round in circles, and had visions of winding up alongside a police launch in the middle of the port when the fog lifted.

"Stop!" he yelled.

"What?" cried the skipper.

"Stop," he demanded, "right now."

The gun was unnecessary, the skipper got the message and eased back the throttles. "What's the matter?"

"Show me," said Motsom, roughly grabbing the elderly skipper's arm and spinning him to face the large map on the table at the rear of the tiny wheelhouse. "Where are we? Which direction are we going in?"

The old man hesitated for a second, as if considering giving false information, then ran his finger along a line marked, "Ferry," and said, "About here."

Motsom followed the line: a double row of red dots across the pale blue ocean—like a neatly stitched seam binding England to Holland.

"But how do I know we're going the right way?"

The skipper eased his arm free and pointed at the compass.

"Look," he said.

Motsom obeyed, and saw the little needle swinging gently back and forth through a short arc, undeniably pointing west. Satisfied, he ordered the skipper to get going, and faster, something the wily old man had no intention of doing.

Below decks, McCrae and his newly acquired partner, Jack Boyd, were getting to know each other. Boyd, known on the street as, "Jack the Sprat" or simply "Sprat," because of his skinny frame and slippery reputation, could list eighteen armed robberies among his accomplishments; questioned three times, charged twice, convicted only once—as a teenager—a rookie. He had been a fast learner. His murder record was better; a perfect score: Boyd—three, Police—nil. Apart from a short stretch in a juvenile detention centre for a kid's prank, and two years for the one unlucky robbery conviction, he might have been considered a model citizen. McCrae on the other hand would never have been considered a model anything—other than a hit man.

"You did that double wet job in Hammersmith in the sixties didn't you?" Boyd said, recalling the well-publicized murder trial.

"Got off with manslaughter," said McCrae gruffly, suggesting he was being unjustly accused. "Then I got parole when they found out the bastards I killed had tortured my auld man to death."

"Did they?" Boyd asked with a lift in his voice.

"Och no. 'Course they didn't you pratt, but they wasn't around to deny it, wuz they?"

Boyd laughed. "Nice one," and lashed out to kick the deck hand who was lying on the floor of the cabin. "Laugh son," he said, and laughed again.

The deck hand couldn't laugh, he had been bound and gagged by someone who'd had more experience in his field than many professionals in more traditional occupations.

"What are you going to do with this?" Boyd enquired, sweeping his hand around to indicate the boat. "And him," pointing down at the trussed deck hand.

"Och. I dunno yet, I havn'a decided."

"What about doing the same as you did with the other boat?"

"What do you know about that?" demanded the Scotsman, alarmed that details had leaked.

"I heard a rumour."

"Motsom told ya I bet."

"So."

"He should keep his bloody mouth shut."

"He said it were real funny."

McCrae's face relaxed, coming as near to a smile as it was ever likely. "It was one of these computer snatch jobs," he reminisced, "a couple of months ago."

"There were two of 'em weren't there," added Boyd helpfully, as if McCrae might have forgotten.

"Yeah, that's right—two birds with one stone. Motsom had the contract for both of 'em and it just so 'appens they go fishing together in one of them's boat."

"Were it a big 'un?" enquired Boyd with the excitement of a wide-eyed kid.

"Och. No. But it were very fast. Anyhow," he continued, "the idea was to snatch 'em afore they got on the boat, then take it out to sea and sink it. But it had to look like an accident in case anybody ever found the bloody thing."

"What about the bodies? You'd need bodies."

"Och aye, you'd need bodies," agreed McCrae. "But the plan was to ditch the boat in really deep water so by the time anybody found it, if they ever did, there'd only be skeletons left."

Boyd began to smile, he'd heard the outcome from Motsom, but didn't want to spoil its re-telling by the master.

"So," McCrae continued, "I figured why waste two good bodies, why not use skeletons." The distinct twist to his face could have been mistaken for an attempt at a smile. "Motsom and me snatched the two computer blokes and sent 'em on their way. Then we stuck the skeletons in the driver's seats and went out miles." He paused, the memory of the sight of the two skeletons dressed in the kidnapped men's clothes, including their caps, was too much for him. He almost laughed. Boyd was laughing already.

"Anyhow," he went on, exaggerating wildly, "there they was, two f'kin skeletons driving the f'kin boat a hundred miles an hour then 'boom!'" he slapped his hands together. "The f'kin thing explodes."

Boyd was laughing uncontrollably, having difficulty hearing what McCrae was saying.

"Then …" McCrae stopped and started again, "then, 'Whoomph,' one of the f'kin skulls comes flying through the f'kin air and missed Motsom by a f'kin inch … Whoomph," he shouted again for effect and tittered just a little. "Came flying right passed us, and we was a long way off …

Whoomph," he said finally, making sure Boyd had missed nothing. "Whizzed right passed Motsom's head."

Boyd almost wet his pants.

Above them, the afternoon sun was shining on the wheelhouse. The skipper and Billy Motsom could see ahead for miles, but nothing of the water just twenty feet below. A dense crust of fog remained glued to the sea's surface like a thick cotton-wool blanket and the wheelhouse of the fishing trawler gave them a ghostly outlook. An amputated mast, complete with rigging and sails, could be seen gliding along in the distance as if unattached to the yacht sailing in the murk below; the upper decks of a small freighter drifted across the horizon without the benefit of a hull; seagulls wheeled hungrily above them.

"I have to go to engine room," the skipper said as the afternoon wore on. "I must check the engine."

"O.K.," responded Motsom leerily, "I'll come with you."

The skipper had his answer prepared. "No," he said quickly. "Someone must stay and keep watch."

Motsom smelled a rat. The little ship had puttered along for hour after hour without any apparent assistance of the skipper, other than an occasional tweak of the wheel. A quick trip to the engine-room for a splash of grease was unlikely to make much difference. He put his hand on his gun, "I said, I'll come."

The skipper's plan was already unravelling. For several hours, drawing ever nearer to the search zone, he had tried to think of a way to save himself and his young mate, guessing that once LeClarc was found, or the search abandoned, Motsom and his hoodlums would have no choice but to dispose of them—a simple task in mid-ocean. But if he disabled the engine they would be marooned together until rescued. Motsom would surely realize the difficulty of explaining the absence of crew to the authorities and might think twice about getting rid of them.

Careful not to let his disappointment show, the skipper eased back the throttle, and tried again. "It might take half an hour," he warned. "We could hit something."

Motsom relented, stuck his head out of the wheel-house and yelled, "McCrae. Get up here will you, Sprat as well if he wants."

"So how are you going to sink this one?" the Sprat enquired of McCrae, as soon as they had replaced the skipper and Motsom on the bridge.

McCrae stared blankly ahead, concentrating on holding the wheel straight, his dour face suggesting he wasn't comfortable disclosing professional tactics. "Bomb I expect," he replied, with a shrug.

"Plastic or jelly?"

"Neither, you idiot. This sort of job ain't like doing a safe you know."

Boyd's surprise showed on his face, so McCrae gave him a lesson in the finer points of murder. "Look, when you blow a safe everyone knows what happened so it don't matter what you use. But if you blast a car or ship with plastic or jelly, or even bloody fertilizer, then the cops knows it's murder. There's bits of the bomb left everywhere afterwards."

Boyd nodded. He knew that.

"So," continued McCrae, "The trick in my game is only use the stuff that's already there."

Boyd wasn't sure what he meant, but wasn't going to say so.

McCrae sensed the lack of understanding. "Look," he explained, recalling a recent exploit, "if you're going to blow up a plane, use the stuff on board. Blow up a fuel tank or an oxygen cylinder. They'll think it was an accident. Do it over water and they'll never work out what hit them—might even think it was a f'kin missile or a laser gun of some sort, but they won't find any explosives 'cos you didn't use any."

Boyd understood. "The two skeletons in ..."

"Gas tank," replied McCrae, adding, "You heard about the computer bloke who crashed into the train?"

Boyd nodded. "Yours?" he asked, with an admiring look.

"Yeah, a classic," he said, and his eyes glazed as he stared into the fog recalling the event.

They had stopped the unfortunate man on a quiet stretch of country road on his way home from work, his computer disks and various files in two briefcases on the seat behind him. Motsom, dressed in a police uniform, stolen for the occasion from a real police-man's home, leaned into the car and accused him of drinking and driving.

"I've only had one, Officer," protested the hapless man.

"If you would just step this way, Sir," said Motsom guiding him toward the unmarked car with dark tinted windows. The naïve man suspected nothing and was neatly stripped, bound, gagged, and bundled into the trunk by McCrae within seconds. With the kidnap vic-tim out of the way, McCrae quickly set to work on his car—wiring an explosive detonator into the fuel tank and refilling the windshield fluid container and radiator with gasoline.

"Motsom had dragged a bum off the street," explained McCrae, recounting the event to Boyd. "Gave him fifty quid and told him he just wanted him to drive his car for some reason. And you should have seen his face when Billy gave him a load of new clothes, the one's we took off the computer bloke. He was really chuffed—sat in that car like he owned it."

"How do you like your new vehicle, Sir?" Motsom had teased in the tone of a car salesman.

"Very nice mate," the simpleton beamed, happy to go along with Motsom's fantasy.

"And would Sir like to go for a little drive."

The longhaired, unshaven, middle-aged bagman hadn't driven for years but remembered how, and Motsom sat alongside giving directions as they jaunted along the winding country roads. The short journey brought back memories of better days and the man tittered and clicked his tongue with pleasure as he stroked the soft leather upholstery, fiddled with knobs and switches, and admired himself in the rear view mirror which Motsom had obligingly tilted in his direction.

"Pull over here," said Motsom as they neared a narrow bridge over a deep railway cutting.

He stopped as requested, blind to the car with tinted windows sliding to a halt behind.

"Hang on there a mo," instructed Motsom, as he stepped out of the car.

McCrae slipped unnoticed into the rear seat, whipped a hood over his head and bound him to the seat with parcel tape in less than three seconds. Then Motsom, wearing surgical gloves, squirted the flailing hands with superglue and jammed them onto the steering wheel.

"Eight seconds," said McCrae, consulting his watch with a professional eye.

"We've got one minute," said Motsom calmly as he walked the few yards to the fence overlooking the fifty-foot ravine and, as McCrae inched the car forward checking the alignment of the wheels, Motsom frayed the three strands of rusty old barbed wire.

"O.K., let's go," said Motsom, his head tilted, listening for the train as he prepared to push. McCrae felt his pulse rising as he stood, battery in one hand, two wires attached to the detonator in the fuel tank, in the other. Then, the distant whine of the express, and Motsom flicked his eyes up and down the narrow road—all quiet.

"Ready," he breathed.

A wolf-howl scream marked the passage of a farm crossing and McCrae bent to push.

"Wait ... Wait ... Hold it ... Hold it ..." murmured Motsom, his shoulder to the back of the car, judging the train's speed and distance. Then suddenly he shouted, "Stop."

Confused, McCrae looked up to see Motsom dashing to the front of the car. In a flash he opened the door, snatched the mask off the driver and ran back. "Push! Push! Push!" he shouted and the car shot over the top, down the bank, and exploded into a huge fireball as McCrae touched the wires to the battery. Then the flaming steel coffin crashed headlong into the front of the speeding train and the screams of the car driver melded into the screech of steel on steel.

"I wanted the poor bastard to see where he was going," explained Motsom as they climbed back into their car, the computer specialist safely in the trunk.

"What's so bloody funny?" asked Motsom, returning to the wheelhouse with the skipper at gunpoint.

Boyd was the only one laughing and he brought his face under control long enough to start, "Mac was just telling me ..." then McCrae's elbow struck sharply into his ribs.

Motsom ignored them, waving at the pale-faced skipper with the barrel of his gun. "I caught him trying to sabotage the bloody engine."

"That's naughty ..." said McCrae.

"What's that?" interrupted Boyd, his attention caught by a movement outside the wheelhouse.

They turned as one and followed the direction of his gaze. In the distance a thin streak of fog had detached itself from the surface and was stabbing skyward. Then, as they watched, the top of the spear burst into a little red star and began lazily drifting back down on a parachute.

"It's a flare," commented McCrae.

"I can see that," replied Motsom nastily, "But where did it come from?"

"Over there ..." started Boyd, but was headed off by Motsom.

"I mean—who would send up a flare you idiot?"

They looked at each other; no one daring to mention the obvious. Then the skipper broke the silence with the words he had been dreading. "It could be him."

"Get over there," shouted Motsom, with a haphazard wave of his gun. "C'mon hurry up—get this tub over there before I blow yer brains out."

With long sweeps of his short arms, and a heavy heart, the skipper swung the wheel and, after a moment's hesitation, the trawler shook itself free of its lethargy and bounded toward the flare.

Roger's little boat was less than a mile away, sinking fast. One side of the inflated raft, the side supporting Roger's weight, flopped uselessly into the water with a gaping hole, dunking him to his waist. The flare had punctured it. Roger, alerted by the sound of the trawler's engine, fearing he would be missed in the fog, had frantically grabbed the flare from the emergency box and stupidly held it over the top of the raft's inflated side while pulling the red ignition tab. Nothing had happened for a few seconds as the fuse glowed invisibly inside the barrel, and he'd just convinced himself it was a dud, when, with a "Whoosh!" a frightening belch of burning gas shot seawards and the skyrocket roared out of his hand. Terrified, his eyes jerked upwards in awe as the rocket ripped a hole through the fog. Then the raft slumped beneath him and he looked down, horrified, to see a jagged puncture and the water rushing in. In panic, he fought to get away from the sagging side, but his exhausted limbs and swollen hands were of little use. To make matters worse, his stomach was still fighting the effects of seasickness and the overdose of emergency rations. Stomach cramps gripped him repeatedly and, as the hull of the trawler drifted into his circle of visibility, he was leaning over the side throwing-up again.

A shout from above startled him, "Oy! You there. What'ye doing. Kissing the fish?" Motsom was laughing and even McCrae came close to breaking his face.

"Save Trudy. Please save Trudy," was all he managed to say, then he collapsed unconscious into the water.


The old clock in the railway refreshment room clunked its way to 8 p.m. and the lumpy waitress stood by the door and flipped the "closed" sign. She'd had an unusual day and was anxious to get home to see herself on the news. Although the excitement had perked up her flagging energy mid-afternoon, she was now feeling the effects. In addition to interviews and photos, she'd still had to serve the dozens of press and television people who had lined up for endless cups of tea. And everybody had been in a rush, no one wanting to leave the circus at Roger's house for a moment longer than necessary lest they should miss the star attraction.

Walking up Junction Road, a minute later, she briefly joined the knot of sightseers staring expectantly at Roger's front door. Disappointed when nobody recognized her, she was just moving on when Roger's innocent looking yellow door cracked open a fraction and a man's face searched the crowd. Then the gap widened and a uniformed officer slid out and quickly pulled it shut behind him, heightening the speculation that they had discovered a house of horrors; an excited buzz went around the expectant audience—enough pressmen and rubber-neckers to fill a double-decker bus—this could be BIG!

Standing at the top of the steps, the policeman cleared his throat and flashed a hastily scribbled communiqué. Waiting, just long enough for the cameramen to fire up their machines, he balanced up and down on his toes, coughed a couple of times, then read from the sheet.

"Investigations into the disappearance of Roger LeClarc and Trudy McKenzie, sixteen years, are continuing. At present we have no clear evidence but we cannot rule out foul play."

A barrage of questions flew toward him but he ducked back into the house leaving the cameras with a picture of the closing door.

Detective Constable Jackson, looking more than ever like Roger Moore in the flattering warmth of the evening light, stood in the hallway with the staff sergeant and a handful of other officers.

"I don't think we can do any more," said Jackson, addressing the air as his eyes swept around making one last check. Every floor, wall and ceiling in each room had been poked, prodded and tapped; bright lights and pencil thin beams had shone into every crevice; magnifying glasses had magnified everything imaginable—but no one had even considered the floor in the cupboard under the stairs. The cupboard had been searched, almost everyone had poked their nose in at some time, some even fingering the hook in the ceiling thinking it to be a clothes hook, but no one had tugged at the floor.

"I think you're right lad," replied the sergeant. "If we have to, we'll get a builder in to take up all the floors, but there's no point until we get the lab tests on the hairs and blood. That won't be until Tuesday or Wednesday next week."

Jackson stamped his foot on the wooden boards and a quiver ran through the house. "If she is under here she won't be going anywhere in a hurry, so it doesn't matter."

Trudy was there—directly beneath him, just ten feet away; ten feet that may as well have been a mile, her emaciated little body scrunched into a lifeless ball against the prison door. The computer still bearing her final plea to her mother, humming happily in the corner, while countless little creatures nibbled away at the fabric of the room, and each other, in the moonlight of its screen. The constant struggle for life and death continued unabated.

"Alright lads," continued the sergeant, "let's call it a day. Make sure you take everything with you and nobody is to blab to the press. Got it?" His eyes scanned each face, waiting to see a nod of agreement before moving on. Satisfied, he opened the front door and heard the buzz of excitement as the remaining reporters pressed forward.

"Last out turn off the lights," said one of the officers jokingly as he made his exit.

"Wilco," replied Jackson with a smile, then he glanced at the conveniently placed electricity meter on the wall next to the door.

"There's a light on," he muttered to himself.

"What d'ye say lad?" enquired the sergeant.

Jackson indicated the meter with a nod, "It's still moving. There must be a light on."

"Don't think so," he replied.

Thirty seconds later, the entire house checked, Jackson and the sergeant stood in the hallway watching the tiny hand creep slowly around and around, and around.

"Well something must be on," said the sergeant.

# chapter thirteen

The atmosphere in the bustling terminal at Istanbul's Atatürk airport had all the qualities of a Turkish bath, forcing Bliss and Yolanda to fight their way out of the scruffy building through a smelly smog of sticky air. Attempts to mask the stench had failed, and the atmosphere suffered as much from the cure as the malaise. Sickly sweet antiperspirants, as nauseous as body odour, and ammonia disinfectants more noxious than the stinking toilets, competed for air space with exhaust fumes and the odour of roast goat.

"Taxi," shouted Yolanda at the snappily dressed chauffer of a sleek limousine, a dainty flag dangling limply from a little staff on the roof. The driver's half closed eyes ignored her as he jerked his head in a backwards nod and clicked his tongue.

"Tack ... see?" she mouthed, pronouncing both syllables, assuming he had misunderstood the universal word.

With a look of disdain, he lifted his nose in the air and flicked a finger toward a line of yellow cabs, the apparent losers in a recent demolition derby.

"I'd rather take this one," she said, determined not to be fobbed off.

"Sir," he replied, smiling directly at Bliss. "Please tell your wife this car is for the Minister of Antiquities."

"She's not my wife ..." he started, then stopped himself, noticing the phoney smile on the driver's face, recalling Anne's warning on their flight from Vienna. "You'll be alright as long as they don't smile," she had said, adding, "The only thing more dangerous than a growling Grisly is a smiling Turk."

"Sorry," he mumbled and dragged Yolanda away.

"Always some excuse," she moaned, as they lugged their bags toward the line-up of write-offs on the other side of the road.

The first cab reeked badly of garlic and, no sooner had they sat down than Bliss retched, and they shot back out. The driver of the second didn't speak English, Dutch, or Bliss' schoolboyish variation on the theme of French. Yolanda tried a few words of her native tongue and would have been stunned had they understood.

"Was that Swedish?" he asked, as they headed to cab number three.

"Nearly ... It's Danish—they're similar. We moved to Holland when I was two."

Well that explains the hair and eyes, he thought, with a glance.

"I speak Englees," said number three, addressing Bliss. "My name is Abdul."

Yolanda gave him an affirmative nod—the taxi and Abdul would not have been out of place in Amsterdam or London.

"Hotel first," she whispered, as Bliss reached forward with the address Nosmo King had given. "I need a shower," she added with uncharacteristic diffidence.

"Oh, I'm sorry—of course. I should have thought," he replied, reflecting on their exploit in the plane.

"Which hotel, Sir?"

Bliss, stumped, was readying to say, "Somewhere cheap," when Yolanda came to his rescue. "The Yesil Ev, please," she said, confidence restored. "I've stayed there before," she explained. "You'll love it, they have huge beds with beautiful brass bedsteads." Her eyes smiled. "We may as well enjoy ourselves now we are here."

And, in celebration, their lips crushed together.

"Sir. Sir. Sir. Please, Sir."

Bliss broke away reluctantly, "What is it, Abdul?"

"You must not do that, Sir. It is a crime."

"To kiss my wife is a crime?" he asked loftily, hoping his presumption wouldn't offend Yolanda.

"Yes, Sir, in public it is a crime. In private it is O.K. but it is forbidden in public in our country."

He leaned to whisper in Yolanda's ear.

"Sir, Sir," the driver warned, fearing another kiss.

"It's O.K.," said Bliss with a placatory wave, then continued sarcastically, "Would it be alright if I speak to her?"

"Oh yes, Sir, that is alright."

He didn't bother—he had caught a glimpse of Abdul's malicious smile in the rear view mirror.

The shanty-like suburbs of single story houses quickly gave way to modern apartments and office towers, and they sneaked glances at each other while Abdul gave a spirited impression of a tour guide.

"This the famous Topkapi Palace," he said with a wide sweep of his hand taking in four downtown blocks.

"Wow," said Bliss. "That's huge. Who was it built for?"

Abdul scrutinized the building carefully, seeking inspiration or a sign, and the car wandered hazardously until an irate bus driver caught his attention with a horn blast.

"It was built for very important man," he replied eventually, as if he had known the answer all along.

"Mehmet the Conqueror," explained Yolanda quietly. "It is where he kept his harem and eunuchs."

"That is correct, Sir," said Abdul, basking in Yolanda's glory. "And this, Sir," he added, introducing an enormous building topped by a crescendo of domes with the aplomb of the architect, "this is the Blue Mosque."

"It looks grey," responded Bliss as he stared in awe at the multi-layered building sporting a mass of towering minarets. "How old is it?"

"It is very, very, very old," said Abdul gravely, with little calculation.

"It's blue inside Dave. We'll go there tomorrow," said Yolanda with a little excited squeeze of his hand as they drove alongside the turquoise waters of the Bosphorus.

The hotel, was, "as stuffed as a pig," explained the desk clerk colourfully, scanning an incomprehensible ledger while wildly scratching his head. Yolanda slid a crisp twenty-dollar bill between the book's leaves and a miracle occurred. Apparently a cancellation had just been phoned in, and he had overlooked it. He was, he said, immensely sorry for the misunderstanding, then hinted that the cancellation of a more desirable suite could be arranged for another twenty. Bliss clicked his tongue in disapproval but stopped when the clerk broke into a smile. "It is just my little joke, Sir." Bliss didn't laugh.

A hire car had proved more difficult and Bliss gave up easily. "Taxi it is then," he said, with relief, having studied the driving habits of the locals for the past twenty minutes.

They quickly showered, dried, and dressed, and he made a stab at a kiss as they readied to leave, but she turned a hard face and spun away.

"Sorry ..." he mumbled confused.

She turned back with a mischievous grin. "It is a crime, Dave." Then laughed as she pushed him onto the huge soft bed and mauled his mouth until he cried, "I can't breathe."

"Get a cab. I'm ready," she called, disappearing into the bathroom to repair her lips.

Bliss stepped into the hot evening, sniffing the potent aroma of hibiscus, mimosa and diesel, and found that Abdul had anticipated their requirements.

"I say to myself. This nice man he needs Abdul, so I stay," he explained, obviously sensing the possibility of a landing a weekend's work.

Of course he could find the address Nosmo King had written on the handkerchief, but as to how far, and how long, his eyes took on a faraway look. "Ten minutes, maybe an hour," he said, his vacant expression adding, "Who cares."

Fortunately, it took only twenty minutes and they arrived while it was still daylight. The address was a warehouse, a windowless white concrete block, like an iceberg rising out of a jumbled sea of rocky pack-ice.

"Earthquake," explained Abdul, excusing the ramshackle industrial complex, where only a handful of small factories and the warehouse remained. A twelve-foot perimeter fence surrounded the warehouse and Abdul slowed at the gate. "It is closed," he said with hardly a glance, and was driving off when Yolanda shouted, "Stop!" He eased back on the accelerator and turned to Bliss. "Do you wish for me to stop, Sir?"

"I wish you to do whatever the lady says," Bliss shot back, infuriated by the driver's treatment of Yolanda.

"Yes, Sir. If that is your wish, Sir," replied Abdul with a vicious smile.

Two minutes later they were back in the car. The high mesh fence topped with razor wire and the conspicuously padlocked gates had dispelled any notion of breaking in for a quick sneak around.

"I told you," said Abdul. "Everywhere closed, I bring you back Monday."

"Maybe," replied Yolanda coolly. "But now we would like some dinner," and sought Bliss' agreement.

Abdul said, "I have excellent number one place. Trust me."

Bliss toyed with the idea of refusing, just to test Abdul's hunger, but the young Turk was already warming to a smile so he thought better of it.

As a tourist guide Abdul had been less useful than a local telephone directory, but he'd hit the spot with the restaurant.

"It's Russian," explained the maitre d'hotel, as they were led to an intimate alcove surrounded on three sides by intricately pierced screens. The atmosphere, heady with the smoke of a dozen ornate hookah pipes, was enriched by the scent of a hundred perfumed candles; the breathy cry of a reed flute added to the aura with exotic Arabian music, the sound barely fluttering the air. The shimmering candlelight, softened by smoke, shifted time, and the two detectives drifted into an ambience of nineteenth century romanticism.

"This is real gold," exclaimed Yolanda, fingering a piece of cutlery.

"The tablecloth's silk," replied Bliss and he reached for her hand, whispering, "No messing around O.K."

She sniggered, "Okey dokey Dave."

"The lamb's leg is good," interjected Abdul, wrecking the moment. He had insisted on escorting them. It was, according to him, his duty to do so. He would be there purely as gastronomic adviser he assured them, surely no less than they might expect of a good taxi driver anywhere in the world.

He took his new-found role seriously, ordering a sampler platter of local delicacies as a starter before they'd even opened their menus. They concurred out of politeness, but Yolanda drew the line at the choice of main course. She wanted the Bosphorus bluefish and said so. Abdul shook his head slowly from side to side, "Not fresh." He wagged a finger circumspectly. "Fishermen no catch on Friday." Pretended to spit. "Fish is no good today." Then smiled. "Lamb is good." They settled on the lamb, accompanied by Abdul's choice of vegetables, Abdul's selection of wine, and Abdul's recommended dessert.

The first course arrived almost immediately, and Yolanda gave Bliss a suspicious look while they nibbled on exotically presented tidbits, seemingly comprised entirely of bluefish.

"We must hire a car, Dave," she said pointedly, between bites.

Abdul missed the point. "I can drive ..."

"No, Abdul." Bliss held up his hand and spoke firmly. "The lady wants to hire a car."

"Of course, Sir. No problem, Sir. I get you car."

A look of astonishment crept over Bliss' face as Abdul pulled a cell phone from his pocket and tapped a well-known number. Thirty seconds later he said, "I take you after dinner. It is all arranged."

The leg of lamb arrived and was not what Bliss and Yolanda expected. A whole leg the size of a spring chicken sat on each of their plates. "Delicious," agreed Bliss to Abdul's enquiry, though Yolanda looked less enthusiastic.

"Are you alright?" he asked tenderly.

"It was only a few weeks old, Dave," she whimpered, gently poking the leg on her plate. A touch of moisture appeared in the corner of her eye and Bliss stroked it softly away. "I know love," he said, "But it's too late now, and what we don't eat will be wasted."

The frown blossomed into a little smile. "You're right, Dave. I am silly, and it is very nice."


Forty minutes later, finally free of Abdul and his instructions, advice and opinions, they found their way back to the warehouse in the hired car. The map given to them by the car's owner—loosely introduced by Abdul as a cousin—was as old as the car itself; about twenty-five years, they thought, although it was difficult to tell. The car hire office turned out to be a shack stuck on the back of a hovel, and Abdul's cousin was, according to Yolanda, at least two hundred years old. His habit of spitting, wetly, every three or four words as a form of punctuation, gave his guttural speech a physical dimension.

Abdul had translated, dispensing with the saliva. "The price is flexible," he said.

Taking this to mean negotiable, Bliss offered ten dollars a day as a starter, but Abdul said, "No, my cousin says you must pay him what you think it is worth when you return. He says he knows you will not cheat him because you are American."

"Sounds great to me," said Bliss with as much of an American accent as he could muster.

The warehouse had changed with the arrival of night. A gleam of light now shone from underneath the double doors of the truck entrance. Light seeped from vents high up on the walls, and floodlights made pools of light at the front and rear of the building. A car, not there earlier, was now parked at the building's front, inside the perimeter fence.

They stopped on the side of the unlit road, some distance away, and Bliss pulled another thread from the strap as he nervously checked his watch. "It's eight thirty," he whispered.

"Dave, please change your watch, it's ten thirty," she replied. "And why are we whispering?"

"I don't know."

"We'll have to get in there," she said, straining to see the compound in the darkness.

"We should call the local police," he suggested, starting the engine.

She turned it off. "Dave—think about it—some Turkish cop wanders into your station at midnight on a Friday night, doesn't speak a word of English, and tries to say he's chasing a gang of international kidnappers, and they might just possibly ..."

Bliss was shaking his head, "O.K. Yolanda, you're right. We'd probably lock him up until he was sober."

The lights of a large truck appeared in Bliss' mirror and lit up the car's interior. "Get down," he shouted illogically, and they ducked as it rolled passed. Slowing, it pulled up at the warehouse gates.

"Quick Dave, let's slip in with the truck."

"This is crazy ..." he started, too late. Yolanda had taken off and was way ahead as he ran the two hundred yards to the gate in the darkness. The truck had stopped and the driver was beeping for attention. Nothing happened for half a minute or more and they flattened themselves against the fence, as still as posts. Then the gates were opened by a shadowy figure who had appeared from nowhere and, within seconds, they were in the compound, their entrance covered by the truck.

The gates clanged shut behind them and a hand clamped the padlock in place. Hidden by the darkness, away from the floodlit doors, they crouched to the ground until the truck, and the man, had entered the warehouse, and the giant roller door had hummed to a close.

Raising his head warily, Bliss squinted at the squat building wishing he had x-ray vision. "We should try to look inside," he mused, though had no plan or intent.

"Okey dokey," Yolanda replied jauntily, willing to go along with him.

"How?" he asked, hoping she would know what to do.

They both stared. "What about ..." started Bliss, then Yolanda cut in, "There's some light in the wall up there ... Come on," she said, slipping her hand into his, dragging him to the wall, where, ten feet above the ground, a ventilation brick was sieving light through a mesh of tiny holes.

"I can't see anything," she whispered as she stood precariously on his shoulders a few seconds later.

"Get down then," he hissed, his voice straining as his legs shivered with the struggle to remain upright.

"Wait," she said, catching a glimpse of movement. Then the lights of a car suddenly swung in their direction and picked them out against the wall.

"Get down Yolanda. Please," he implored as the lights turned away, and she dropped into his arms. They crouched silently against the wall until the car had stopped at the warehouse door.

"What's happening?" breathed Yolanda, as Bliss peeked around the corner.

The floppy bundle picked out of the car's trunk could have been a rolled carpet, judging by the ease that it was manhandled into the building, but Bliss swallowed hard, saying, "I think it was a body."

"Dead?" she enquired.

"Or unconscious," he replied.

The gates clanged shut behind the departing car and the shadowy figure walked back toward the warehouse. Bliss had seen enough. "We must call the police."

She gave him a quizzical look, lost in the darkness. "How are we going to get out?"

The locked gate and twelve foot fence certainly presented a problem. "Let's take a look around the back," he suggested, hoping to find an exit.

The back door of the warehouse, with a bead of light running around its edge, caught Yolanda's attention immediately. The light, from a halogen flood lamp high on the wall, left the door itself in shadow. "Stay there," she whispered, "I'll go." and stepped toward the pool of brightness.

"No," he said, trying to grab her arm, but she slipped out of his grasp and sidled along the building.

This was not in his job description—not in anyone's job description—and he hissed warnings until she was out of earshot. "Obstinate bloody woman," he muttered as she inched along the wall and eased herself slowly toward the door. A sudden rustling at her feet startled her as a small creature scuttled from under foot. Scared, she stood gasping for air for a second before moving on. Taking a deep breath, she stilled her hand and slid her fingers over the door handle. It gave way with a jerk and a clunk loud enough to make Bliss jump. "Blasted woman!" he hissed, motioning frantically for her to return. She refused with a shake of the head, and thrust her weight against the door. Bolted, she guessed, as it held, but another door, beyond the circle of light, tempted, and her slender figure faded from Bliss' view.

"Stubborn cow," he moaned as he peered after her into the gloom, then the first door opened with a heart stopping crash and a figure jumped out. Yolanda threw herself to the ground in a split second and prayed. The gun in the man's hand swept back and forth aggressively as he scanned the lit area. Yolanda, lying beyond the pool of light, lay frozen to the ground. Bliss moulded himself to the wall and watched with horror as the gun swung rapidly. Greeted by silence, and the absence of a target, the gunman pocketed the weapon and, with a shrug, turned back into the doorway. The door started to close, the light from the doorway faded, Bliss let out his breath in a long silent sigh, and Yolanda started to move.

In a flash everything changed. Yolanda's foot dislodged a pebble and it clacked against a neighbour as loudly as a pistol crack in the tense air. She dived to the ground as the gunman leapt back out of the door, aiming wildly. Bliss froze, and a warning cry dried in his mouth as the gunman advanced. Yolanda squashed herself into the dusty screen as the gun found her and held steady. Bliss' heart stopped and his mind whirled in panic as the gunman strained forward, hesitating, momentarily unsure. Bliss sensed the hiatus and shot into action. Picking up a rock, he tossed it at right angles and sent it clattering across the ground.

"Excuse me, I'm lost. Do you speak English?" he squealed, his strangled voice struggling to be heard as his mind spun through options—duck, run, shake, or shit. "Get a grip," he told himself. "He won't shoot."

"Click."

He ducked, but it was Yolanda. She'd hit another pebble and the gunman was turning. Blood seeped from

Bliss' face, and he didn't need to see his knuckles to know they were white as he stepped out of the shadows into the circle of light. "I am sorry," he babbled, "but could you help me. " A blast of vicious Turkish hit him and scared him more than the gun, but he persisted, ignoring the weapon, walking forward saying, "Speak English?" Then repeating, "Do you speak English?"

"Yok," the man shouted, with a villainous smile that would only cheer an orthodontist's accountant.

Bliss stopped and threw up his hands, movie fashion. "Don't shoot. Don't shoot. I just ..." But he couldn't think of anything to say. His mouth froze, brain paralysed by fear, as Yolanda slowly rose from the ground and stealthily crept up on the gunman. Noise, Bliss thought, I must make noise to cover her, and he broke into nonsensical jabber, "I'm Engleesh, Inglees; No; Yes I come ... Don't shoot. Please don't shoot." Then, just as he expected her to clobber the gunman with a rock, she slipped into the open doorway and vanished. Idiotic woman, he thought, then fell silent as the swarthy man advanced, his potbelly and foul breath preceding him.

Flicking his gun like a deadly feather duster, and forcing Bliss backwards with a lethal blast of halitosis, the gunman swept him around the building and out to the road. "No Inglees," he spat, and made a performance of padlocking the gate.

Bliss crabbed quickly along the roadside, one eye on the gunman, and by the time he reached the car the small voice of his mind was hammering in his skull, "Go for the police." But his thumping heart was shaking his hand so much he couldn't get the key in the ignition. "Run," screamed the voice. "Stay and rescue her," pulsed his heart, sucking the breath out of his body 'til he felt faint. "How the hell can you get her out?" demanded the voice. "Get the police, it's her only chance." But his heart rooted him to the spot. "Go, and you'll never see her again."

He turned the ignition, then switched off. "This is stupid," he said, knowing it might take hours to get the police. The voice said, "twenty minutes," but he knew it was lying. "Get her now, don't wait, they'll kill her," thumped his heart, but the gunman was still there, by the gate, still staring, so he started again, turning quickly, and took off toward the city's glow. Five hundred yards and he switched off the lights, swung on the wheel, and sped back to the compound under cover of darkness.

Seconds later he was attacking the fence at the far corner like a maniac, muttering, "headstrong witch," with tears and perspiration streaming down his face in the darkness, as his hands grappled with the wire. He dug frantically at the rocks and sand; his heart pumping wildly as he dragged boulders aside; his muscles straining as he wrenched at the posts, and his hands burning as he pulled at the mesh, yanking it back and forth, worrying it out of the ground, grumbling, "Stupid, stupid, stupid, bloody woman." His mind spurred him with images of Yolanda: bound, gagged flogged, raped, murdered; each image making him dig faster, harder, more determinately, and all the time his tears dripped onto the parched ground and dust stuck to his sweat soaked clothes.

Fifteen minutes later, exhausted and distraught, he was still struggling with the obstinate wire, when a noise in the distance distracted him and he looked up to see the gates being opened and the truck easing out of the warehouse. Running furiously, he headed toward the gates, almost uncaring whether or not he was seen. The truck was out of the gates within seconds, he still had a hundred yards to run, the gates were starting to close, he was breathless. At fifty yards the first gate was already closed and the gunman was pulling on the second. His legs were giving out, his breathing heavy, he stumbled forward, then he crashed headlong into a body running the other way.

"Yolanda," he cried with joy.

"Quick," she yelled. "They're getting away in the truck."

She dragged him back to the car, the truck was already disappearing into the night. "Hurry, hurry," she urged and within seconds they were in the car and roaring after the juggernaut.

"He's in the truck," Yolanda shouted jubilantly. "It's like the one at the port with a secret door. I saw them put him in." She urged him faster, "Go, go, go, Dave."

He slammed his foot hard to the floor and sped in the direction of the truck, now well out of sight. "Alright, Yolanda," he said, close to laughter at the craziness of the situation. "But no more arguments. As soon as we find out which way he's going we'll call the Turkish police and leave it to them.

"Okey dokey, Dave," she replied softly, stroking the dust and dried tears from his face, adding, "Thank you," in a tremulous voice.

"What for?"

"For saving my life," she replied, tears of relief welling inside her. He shrugged it off, but felt a warmth as he drove ferociously along the badly made roads. "What did he look like, the guy in the truck?"

"I didn't see very well, but it wasn't Roger LeClarc."

It couldn't have been Roger LeClarc. He was lying asleep in the smelly cabin of the Dutch herring trawler, somewhere between Holland and England. A relaxed expression had spread over his face, his ordeal over. He had been rescued, and he had told them to save Trudy. He was at peace. His seemingly endless night had ended. Unfortunately for him, another was just beginning.

The old car seemed to understand the urgency of the situation and raced along under Bliss' guidance.

"Which way?" he shouted as they approached the first main intersection.

"Right," she said, "No ... Left." Her voice hovered, "Left ... I think." Then she came down firmly. "Left Dave. Go left."

He turned, ignoring the screech of brakes and the blaring siren of an approaching truck. The back of the old car tried to overtake the front as they swung onto the main road, then Bliss stomped his foot on the accelerator and the car straightened as the front pulled away. Yolanda egged him on. "Go, go, go."

He went—faster and faster. Swooping recklessly in and out of gaps in the traffic; skimming either side of slower vehicles; leaping traffic lights and laughing at stop signs. Bliss drove like a man possessed with an urge for an early grave. Warnings came thick and fast: Horns blasted, tires squealed, and fists threatened. He took no notice, his whole being concentrated solely on catching the truck. And Yolanda peered determinedly ahead, intently searching the rear of every vehicle, desperately seeking a familiar licence plate.

"There it is," she yelled. "Slow down."

She was right. Straight ahead. The innocent looking truck was hiding out in a herd of similar juggernauts, trundling along at a modest pace.

Their wild ride over, they slowed toward sixty miles-an-hour and felt as though they had stopped.

Then, as Bliss matched his speed with that of the truck, the old car tried to shake itself to pieces. "Tires need balancing," he said as the wildly bucking steering wheel fought to break free of his grasp. He touched the brakes and was disappointed at their reluctance, but, pumping hard on the pedal, he eventually caught their attention and the car slowed to a contented speed.

"Where are we?" he asked after a few miles.

"Istanbul," she replied unhelpfully.

"I meant, where on the map?"

Reaching over to the rear seat she retrieved the map and switched on the interior light.

"Oh my God!" she flinched.

"What? What is it?" he screeched, assuming he'd missed an on-rushing hazard.

"Your hands Dave."

He knew, but had said nothing. The frantic digging had cut and blistered his hands beyond recognition. She understood immediately and her face dissolved in tears, "You did that for me?" she blubbered.

He laughed it off. "Well I couldn't leave you. You hadn't paid for the hotel."

"Give me your hands," she commanded between sniffs.

"I'm driving!"

"Only one," she said, trying hard to smile.

Using a tear soaked tissue she did her best to soothe the tender fingers and lovingly caressed and stroked them for several miles.

"We're stopping," he said, noticing the traffic was slowing, and she released the hand with a brush of her lips.

"What's that?" she asked, looking ahead.

"I think it's one of the bridges over the Bosphorus.

I saw it on the map."

Her eyes searched the map and found the bridge, looking like a staple holding together a wound between Europe and Asia. "It's a toll bridge Dave. There's bound to be cops at the booths."

Bliss reached for the radio, having in mind something slightly tortuous ending in a triumphal flourish; Mahler's *8th Symphony* perhaps, but the knob came off in his hand and dropped to the floor as the radio burst into a terrifying screech. He bent, scrabbling at his feet, desperate to quell the radio's dreadful din, when Yolanda calmly bashed it with the side of her fist and, with a whimper, it died.


There had been no policemen at the bridge control, and Bliss had watched as Yolanda raced from booth to booth desperately begging help from the attendants, while he had been pressured onwards in the line-up by a dozen blaring horns. Then he looked up. "Yolanda," he yelled, realizing that it was too late; the truck was already climbing into the sky.

"Yolanda," he shouted again, catching her this time, and he beckoned furiously, then felt a bump as the following car shoved him forward.

She was breathless and downhearted. "Nobody speaks English and there's no cops," she said leaping back into the car as it was physically shunted eastward by the irate follower; "Trust in Allah," stencilled across his windshield.

Tossing a handful of coins and her nastiest look at the man in the booth, they were away, riding up into the sky, high over the black ribbon of sea that forms the perpetual rift between east and west.

"Asia," she said simply as they crested the summit,

and descended into a new continent, and the start of another day.

The old car easily kept up with the truck as the night hours ticked by. Following the truck was easy, the driver avoiding the spotlight by cruising in convoy. Although they had both concentrated furiously at first, determined not to lose their quarry, while desperately scouring the roofscape of every oncoming vehicle, eventually, it became apparent they would never spot a police car in the dark and, if they did, they'd never catch up with it, so Yolanda dozed off.

"We'll find a police station at first light," Bliss assured her, but she was asleep.

They had stopped once in the night, at the insistence of the fuel gauge and Yolanda's bladder. Bliss pumped the gas, to the annoyance of the young lad, who saw his entire career being jeopardized by westerners, more accustomed to self-service. Yolanda ran to the washroom—a bottomless bucket over a smelly hole—and to the store. Sweeping a handful of unrecognized and unpronounceable packets off the shelf, she gave the owner enough money to cause a fit of choking, and four minutes later they were back on the road. It took another fifteen minutes of Yolanda's break-neck driving to catch up to the truck, then it was Bliss' turn to sleep.

The sun's rays were just peeking over the mountains ahead when disaster struck. "Puncture!" yelled Yolanda excitedly, as the car began bucking and weaving uncontrollably on the rotten road surface.

"No brakes," she added in alarm and desperately fought with the kicking wheel while furiously pumping the pedal. Bliss was awake in an instant and his hand shot out and gripped the wheel alongside hers.

"Truck!" he shouted, wide eyed in horror. She had seen it—coming straight at them—its siren blasting a pathway ahead. They wrenched at the wheel and the car slewed sideways, tilting dangerously, flinging Bliss against the door. Yolanda held on and wrenched it back. The tires bit into the rough road surface and flung them the other way. Now they were headed straight for the truck again. The siren was screaming and the leviathan was snaking drunkenly from side to side as the driver wrestled with the wheel, guiding it one way then the other, trying to avoid the skidding car. Finally, the brakes gripped and locked, jarring them to a halt, ripping the deflated tire off the rim, leaving them stationary in the middle of the road as a front wing slowly dropped to the ground.

They stared, powerless, as the monstrous vehicle bore down on them, the driver's frantic face clearly visible in the early morning light. Then with a hurricane's blast it roared passed, skimming the car's purple paintwork and nudging it aside like an unwanted plaything. Without stopping, and with the same concern he may have shown to a squashed rabbit, the truck driver banged his foot back on the accelerator and fled. The two detectives sat motionless, drained and petrified.

Yolanda spoke first. "Did you see what was on the front of the truck?" she asked breathlessly.

He nodded, the huge gold letters forged into his brain. "Trust in Allah."

The old car limped off the road onto the verge like a mortally injured stag, and they climbed out to survey the damage.

"Superficial," muttered Bliss, but then he stared into the trunk and the empty space stared back. "There's no spare wheel," he said, shaking his head. "That's it Yolanda—this car's road kill. We'll never catch them now."

"I didn't like the colour anyway," she said, cheering him, then she leaped into the path of an oncoming car and flagged down the driver as if it were something she did every day of the week.

"I do not speak English," explained the driver, with a snooty Oxbridge twang; Aznalehu: Amarigna Alchilim he went on, in the Amharic of an Ethiopean camel driver. Then he proceeded to say he couldn't speak French, with the accent of a Parisian boulanger, and could not "Sprechen Deutch," with a guttural dialect obviously learned from a Münchener Braumeister.

Bliss and Yolanda sat in silent contemplation as they sped toward the sunrise with a man who demonstrated his linguistic prowess by explaining in at least thirty other languages that he couldn't speak any of those either.

Twenty miles and twenty minutes later, with no idea of where they were, where they were going, or how they were going to break the bad news to Abdul and his cousin, Yolanda glanced out of the window at a passing truck stop. "There it is," she screeched, catching Bliss and the driver by surprise. "Stop!" she cried. The driver gave her a blank stare. "Halte! Stoppen! Arret! Pausa!" she screamed desperately. He got the message and slammed on the brakes.

"The truck's back there," she said, stabbing the air furiously. Bliss peered at the row of big-rigs laying off to the side of a ramshackle roadhouse, and conceded one of them looked familiar.

"I saw the number, Dave. It's ours. Come on."

"I don't recognize anybody," she whispered, a few moments later, after furtively scouring the smoke-filled café. The chatter of coarse voices had died briefly as they entered, a blonde woman and a six-foot tall man giving pause for thought amongst a bunch of swarthy middle-eastern truckies. A few tables at one end of the room seemed to be reserved for misfits and foreigners, and the hubbub started again as they chose seats near a couple of hitch-hikers, festooned with stars and stripes.

"What are we going to do?" asked Yolanda, tiredness and worry etching lines in her forehead. "There's a kidnapped man in that truck. We must do something."

He had no idea and said so. "We don't even know where we are," he added, turning the map over and over in his hands. "We can't call the local police and we can't follow him." He paused for a second, "I could call the office from the payphone if ..." his voice faded. "That's just a waste of time. I've no idea where we are."

The coffee stuck to the cups. "Mud," protested Bliss, but drank anyway. The cakes cloyed to their mouths.

"Yesterday's," moaned Yolanda, but they ate—it had been a long night. She stared out of the window. "Too late," she said with defeat in her voice. "It's going." He looked. In the daylight he could see the white truck with red lettering pulling onto the highway and half-rose, saying, "We've got to do something," though had no idea what.

An expansive middle-aged man with a fiercely tweaked moustache and monks tonsure, inside a stretched grey suit—flecked indecorously with the ash of a thousand cigars—placed his coffee on the table next to them and re-established the Ottoman empire on the same territory conquered by his predecessor in 1281. Osman would have been proud as the Turkish businessman flaunted his self-importance by colonizing two tables, six chairs, and a windowsill, with a briefcase load of papers and files, an imposing ledger, plates of food, adding machine, coffee cup, and two laptop computers.

Yolanda slid the map from Bliss' hands and mouthed, almost silently, "Get ready to run."

"What?" he said, loudly, and she stuck her fingers to his lips and leaned forward, "Give me thirty seconds then drag me away."

Totally clueless, he nodded and hoped he would work it out when the time came.

With a flourish and a non-stop babble of Dutch, Yolanda threw the map wide-open onto the business-man's table. Sliding into the seat opposite him, she caught his eye and gave him a smile that could launch an entire fleet. "Where are we?" she tried in Danish. Bewildered, flustered and visibly drooling, he desper-ately tried to help. She encouraged him, grabbing his hand and guiding it over the map as she caressed his fingers. His blood pressure soared, sweat poured from his brow. She leaned forward and his eyeballs nearly exploded as he caught a glimpse of her pale white breasts down the top of her blouse.

"Show me," she pouted, leaning right across the table and toying with his nose.

"Come on Yolanda," called Bliss as instructed, irked at being left in the dark. Smiling provocatively into the businessman's eyes, Yolanda bundled the map.

"Nice talking to you," she said, with the hint of a kiss, and was still holding his gaze as they got to the door, guessing it would be a long time before he could safely stand up.

"What was that all about?" demanded Bliss gruffly.

"Arranging a replacement car," she replied mys-teriously, then waved a bunch of keys in his face and guided him around the corner to the businessman's Mercedes. Within seconds they were back in the hunt, the truck only a few miles ahead, heading toward Ankara.

"Shit, Yolanda, if we get ten years in jail, I want to share a cell with you. You'd get us out in no time."

# chapter fourteen

"Mrs. McKenzie?" the policeman called as he stepped from his car outside Trudy's home. It was nearly two o'clock on Sunday morning, and he and his young partner had been stooging around for nearly three hours outside the empty apartment.

Lisa swivelled questioningly, "Yes?"

"Mrs. Lisa McKenzie?" he asked, seeking confirmation in the dispirited eyes of the woman as she stood at the doorway, key in hand.

"Yes, that's right." And animation flooded back into her voice. "Is it Trudy? Have you found her?"

"Perhaps we should go inside Mrs. McKenzie."

The import of the dreaded words, "We should go inside," was not lost. Her hand flew to her mouth; well-practised tears flowed instantly.

"I'm Peter McKenzie," Trudy's father stepped in, gathering Lisa in his arms. "I was just dropping my wife ..." he stopped, "Just dropping Trudy's mother off.

Is there some news?"

Both frantically searched the seasoned face of the policeman for clues, but, apart from a persistent nervous twitch, there was no message.

"Let's just go inside," he said with the voice of experience, gently taking the key from her hand and inserting it into the lock. Trudy's cat Marmaduke flew out of the open door with a desperate "Meow."

"She loved that cat," said Lisa in the past tense, bursting into body-shaking sobs.

A young red-haired policewoman stepped out of the shadows and helped Peter propel his distraught ex-wife into the hallway. It was her first week of night duty; only her third week out of training school. The sergeant had said it would be good for her to get some experience delivering dreadful messages.

"It's the worst job," he had said with a pained look, as he'd flashed through a montage of distraught faces in his mind: Every person whom he'd ever had the misfortune to inform about the death of a close relative, or other equally devastating calamity. "One moment they're happy and smiling, saying, 'What can I do for you Officer?' then you tell them a husband, wife, kid or mother is lying on a stainless steel cart down at the morgue. Suddenly their whole life disintegrates in front of you." He gazed off into the distance and his voice floated. "It effects you for weeks. You never get them out of your mind." His bottom lip gave a little quiver, but he quickly straightened himself up. "Of course, some of 'em don't believe you. That's worse, when you have to try to convince someone their life's just been flushed down the pan."

The sickly smell of a thousand fading blooms struck them as they walked in. "I must get rid of these flowers," snuffled Lisa through the sobs.

"Kitchen alright?" Peter asked the officer.

"Fine," he replied, still not giving anything away.

"She's dead isn't she?" Lisa said as she slumped into the old wooden chair, finding neither comfort nor solace in its hard wooden arms.

The policeman hesitated long enough to pull on his most sombre face, and his downcast eyes and shuffling shoes told a dismal tale. "No," he began, "she's not dead ..." leaving the sentence ominously suspended.

"But?" demanded Peter, knowing someone had to ask.

Lisa's face lit up. "Not dead?"

The policeman's solemnity remained, though his persistent nervous blink added a farcical tone, "She is very, very sick."

"How sick?" she shot back, with pleading eyes. "Tell me," she screamed, wanting to throttle the words out.

"Shall I put the kettle on Mrs. McKenzie?" said the young W.P.C. remembering her training school days. "I'll make a nice cup of tea."

"How sick?" shrieked Lisa, blanking the young policewoman out.

Peter McKenzie dropped to the floor at his ex-wife's feet, clasped her hands in his, and looked up. "What's happened?" he implored, seeking clues in the policeman's face.

"She's on a life support machine," he replied, his uplifted intonation managing to put a positive spin to the news. "They haven't told me much but I understand she was found in some sort of cellar and couldn't breath very well."

"Where is she?" exploded Lisa.

"Watford General Hospital."

"We'll go right away," Peter said, standing up.

"Will you be alright, Sir. Can you find it?"

"Yes, we've only just got back from there," he said, easing Lisa out of the chair.

They had been in Watford all day, copies of the picture they believed to be Roger, clasped in their hands. Touring the suburban streets, scrutinizing startled strangers, enquiring in a hundred pubs, shops and restaurants. "Do you know him? Have you seen him?" Some had recognized him, they claimed, but no one came up with a surname or address. They had even been to the railway station refreshment room in the morning before the commotion caused by the detectives' visit. The dumpy waitress had not recognized Roger's boss, there was no reason why she should. He lived in Croydon and had never been to Watford.

Lisa wasn't finished. "What about Roger?"

The policeman shuffled again, holding back the details, protecting his backside. "It seems he may have locked her in a cellar," he said, then totally absolved himself from responsibility by adding, "but don't take my word for it. That's only what I was told."

"What sort of animal could do that?" spat Peter McKenzie. "And where is he?" Leaving unspoken, "I'll kill him."


The animal in question was still asleep in the cabin of the trawler, his limp carcass flopped untidily onto the bench. On the floor beneath him was the trussed body of the deck hand. Although somewhere on the North Sea, his exact geographic location was difficult to determine, thanks to the skipper's quick thinking earlier in the evening, at the time he was being dragged from the sea.

"He's smashed the bloody compass," McCrae had shouted, diving into the wheelhouse to investigate the sound of a crash. Then the back of his hand had lashed across the old skipper's face.

"We'll deal with him later, give us a hand with this fat lump now," called Motsom, struggling to manoeuvre Roger's heavy body from the deck down the narrow companionway into the cabin.

With Roger dumped in the cabin, Motsom, McCrae, and Boyd returned to the wheelhouse. The skipper's drawn face had lost its ruddiness, though the red welt of McCrae's hand was beginning to blossom on his left cheek; but at least he'd ensured his survival, for awhile. Without a compass the three hoodlums could never reach land, and they knew it. But the old skipper didn't need a compass. He'd fished the same waters for more than fifty years and could pinpoint his location by the stars, the run of the tide, the smell of the air, and the direction of the breeze.

"I should shoot you, Granddad," said Motsom, the barrel of his gun lodged in the skipper's left nostril. The old sea dog half smiled but said nothing. Then his face clouded as Motsom continued solemnly, "But I think I'll shoot the kid first."

"No. He's only a boy. Please don't ..."

"O.K. Granddad, let's do a deal. You get us back to Holland in two hours ..." he paused, sensing the alarm on the old man's face, "O.K. make that three hours, and I won't shoot the boy. Alright?"

"I ... I can't," he stumbled, frantically searching for a plausible reason.

"Fine," said Motsom making a move, "then I may as well shoot him now."

Motsom was half out of the door before the skipper stopped him with a pleading look. "I can't ... because we don't have enough fuel," he said, his voice quavering with fear.

"He's lying," said McCrae, idly picking at the shattered remnants of the compass.

Motsom scanned the utilitarian instrument panel. "Where's the fuel gauge?" he said, more to himself than either of the others. There wasn't one. A long dipstick on the engine room bulkhead was all the skipper needed to test the depth of oil in the tank, and he had no intention of telling Motsom about it.

The cold hard nozzle of Motsom's gun jabbed into the side of the skipper's head. "Which is the fuel gauge?"

"I don't have one. I know how much fuel I have and we can't get back to Holland."

"Where can we get to?"

"England ... maybe," he replied with deliberate vagueness.

"Get the boy," shouted Motsom, making them all jump.

A few seconds later Boyd dragged the deck hand into the wheelhouse and propped him against the chart table.

"I was just telling the skipper," started Motsom conversationally, "I want to get back to Holland in three hours."

The skipper tried to interrupt, "I told ..."

"Shut up," snapped Motsom, with a crooked snarl. "Like I was saying," he continued to the boy, his pleasantness instantly restored, "I want to get back in three hours or ..." he paused, "I will have to shoot you."

Motsom grasped the bundle of dirty rags that McCrae had stuffed into the boy's mouth, and wrenched them out. The boy coughed and spluttered and Motsom gave him a few seconds, then he seized him hard around the neck and stared him straight in the eyes. "Your friend doesn't think I'll shoot you."

The skipper tried again, "Leave ..."

McCrae smashed his gun into the old man's ribs. "Belt up."

Without breaking his stare Motsom continued, "Tell him you don't want to die, boy."

"I don't want to die," the boy whispered obediently.

Motsom stamped his foot, shouting, "Louder."

"I don't want to die."

"Louder," screamed Motsom, his face not an inch from the boy's.

"I don't want to die," he squealed as loudly as he could.

"Did you hear that old man?" Motsom said without taking his eyes off the boy.

"Yes," said the skipper calmly, his spirit apparently broken.

"Good. Now take him below," he said, as his hand on the back of the boy's neck propelled him toward Boyd. "Hurt him if you want to."

The skipper scowled.

"Only joking, Granddad. Right let's get going. Holland—three hours."

Boyd was half out of the door with the deck hand when Motsom added, "Call me if that fat turd LeClarc wakes up."

"O.K. Billy."

Temporarily out-flanked, the skipper eased the throttles ahead and spun the heavy wheel. Responding with a shudder, the trawler slowly picked up speed, and the last light of the day faded from blue to mauve behind them as they steered into the approaching night.

An hour later, now surrounded by darkness, the skipper glanced at the radar screen watching for the approach of familiar landmarks. A small blip, directly astern, caught his attention. Ten minutes later it was still there, closer if anything. Motsom, gun dangling, stared expectantly into the night ahead, searching for the first signs of land.

Fifteen minutes later a plethora of bright blips dotted the edge of the screen twenty miles ahead. The skipper recognized the cluster, not yet the low undulating coast, but ships lying at sea anchor awaiting cargoes, their owners saving money by not having them tied up in expensive berths. And the single blip of a small ship was still there, tagging behind, closer if anything.

"What are you staring at?" said Motsom, looking over his shoulder.

"Just checking we're going in the right direction," he replied with controlled nonchalance. And, turning back to the controls, did a song and dance routine with the wheel, spinning it first one way then the other with exaggerated gusto. The little ship corkscrewed through the water for a few minutes before resuming its previous course.

Motsom was none the wiser. "Can't we go any faster?"

"Not if you want to get there. The faster we go the more fuel we use. It's up to you."

Motsom tried to look at his watch in the darkness but couldn't make out the figures, so held it over the radar screen. "You've got an hour and a half left or the boy will die," he said, making it clear he had every intention of carrying out the threat. "What's that?" he questioned, his eye drawn to the single dot behind them.

"Nothing," the skipper shrugged, without bothering to look. "Just a coastal freighter I expect, heading for port same as us."

"How far away?"

"Couple of miles."

The wheelhouse door slid open and the cool night air crept in ahead of Boyd. "The Fish Kisser's coming round," he said with a smirk.

"Keep an eye on him," replied Motsom, wagging his gun at the skipper. "I wanna have a word with the slug."

Roger LeClarc drowsed as Motsom descended the ladder into the cabin. A full bladder had driven him to consciousness but his mind was still adrift. "Where am I?" he asked vaguely, his painfully swollen eyelids refusing to open properly.

"Get the boy out of here," Motsom hissed to McCrae and, as the deck-hand was being dragged up the ladder. He affected a snooty accent. "So, my dear Mr. LeClarc. How are you feeling?"

"I need a piss," said LeClarc indelicately, putting first things first.

There was no toilet on the boat, few skippers saw little need when they were already floating on the world's biggest cesspool. Roger tried to stand, but his legs wouldn't carry his weight, and he crumpled to the floor and wet himself where he lay, the warm liquid dribbling into a puddle at Motsom's feet. Stepping carefully to avoid the steaming fluid, Motsom shoved him back onto the bench.

"I'm sorry," cried LeClarc now gaining control over his thoughts and faculties.

"It's perfectly alright, Mr. LeClarc," said Motsom, who could have been a doctor tending a distressed victim of rampant diarrhoea.

"Have you found Trudy yet?" enquired Roger.

Trudy? queried Motsom to himself, but decided to play along. "No. Where is she?"

Roger tried sitting up, his head swimming, and grasped Motsom's arm pleadingly, "You must save her. She hasn't got a key, she can't open the door." Suddenly alert, he scanned the little cabin suspiciously, fearing he'd been caught in some nightmarish time-warp: Curled-edged calendars of 1950s pin-ups; coffee stained enamel

mugs and battered tin plates sitting in a fiddle rack; a
faded pre-war watercolour of Delft Town Hall. "Where
am I? Who are you?" he enquired lamely, then slumped
back, exhausted, and was instantly asleep.

"How's the Fish Kisser?" Boyd asked as Motsom
returned to the wheelhouse.

"Sleeping like a baby—he won't give us any trouble." Then Motsom turned to the skipper's dark shadow, "Where are we now?"

The shadow shrugged. "Not too far."

Motsom glanced at the radar screen and noticed
the bright outline of the coast ahead, then his eye was
snagged by the single blip behind them, close behind
them. "That ship's getting closer," he said, clearly
expecting a response from the skipper.

"I said, that ship's getting closer," he repeated,
spelling it out.

The shadow shrugged again, but his eyes remained
fixed ahead, his mind focussed on the future.

"Come here when I'm talking to you," Motsom
ordered, and the shadow moved toward him. Motsom
stabbed an index finger at the dot on the screen, now less
than a quarter of inch away. "How far?" he demanded.

"Look outside and you'll see," said the skipper,
barely concealing a grin.

Motsom catapulted himself across the wheelhouse
and was on the deck in a second. "Christ, he's right
behind us," he shouted. "Sprat, get below and keep
everyone quiet. If either of them farts, plug 'em."

"O.K. Billy."

Before Boyd could move, the hollow "boom" of a
loudspeaker hit them, then it burst into life with an
unmistakably English voice. "This is British fishery vessel, *Gladstone* ... Vessel off the port bow, we are calling
you on channel 37. Please respond."

Boyd jumped down the hatch into the cabin and Motsom ducked back into the wheelhouse as a search-light seared the deck.

"Faster," Motsom shouted at the skipper.

"You're crazy," he said guardedly, as he rammed both throttles forward. A ripple of power ran through the little ship and she shivered as the stern settled deep-er and the propellers chewed at the water.

The deep "boom" hit them again, almost immedi-ately. "Heave to. Heave to. You cannot outrun us. Turn your radio to channel 37 and heave to."

The skipper caught Motsom's eye in the glare of the searchlight, his wide-eyed expression asking, "O.K. big-shot—what now?"

Motsom was thinking, planning, scheming. "Stop," he shouted, then turned viciously on the skipper, his gun wavering under the old man's nose. "You say one word out of place and the boy will be dead in a second ... Nod if you understand."

He nodded, and pulled sharply on the throttles. The bow sank back into the water and the British ves-sel came alongside, as Motsom left the wheelhouse to stand on deck in the full blaze of the searchlight.

"Who are you?" shouted a figure hidden in the dazzle of the light.

"John Smith," yelled Motsom, not realising the eti-quette of the sea demanded the name of the vessel.

"Where are you from?"

"London."

"Where are you bound?"

Motsom deliberated for a second. "Just fishing," he replied.

"Standby," said the voice, then a few seconds later, "We're coming aboard."

The sea boiled into foam, tossing the trawler like

cork, as the powerful vessel came alongside. Two young officers in brass-buttoned naval uniforms jumped the gap. Motsom glued his feet to the deck and struck a pose.

"Are you the skipper, Sir?" asked one of the officers professionally.

"Sort of," replied Motsom cagily. "Is there a problem?"

"Why didn't you answer the radio, Sir?"

"Broken."

The officer gave him a cynical look. "Perhaps I could check it for you, Sir." He took half a step toward the wheelhouse but Motsom replanted himself. "No problem, Officer. We'll get it fixed when we get back."

"I'd like to take a look in your hold," the officer said coldly, dropping the "Sir."

"It's empty."

"I'd still like to take a look." This wasn't a request.

"We haven't started fishing yet." This wasn't an acceptable answer and the other sailor was nosing behind Motsom, peering into the wheelhouse. "This is a Dutch vessel. Why did you say it was registered in London?" he asked sternly.

Motsom laughed nervously and scratched his chin, "I'm sorry, I thought you meant where did I come from."

"And just why would I ask that, Sir?" the same officer enquired, with more than a touch of sarcasm.

"Stupid of me. Anyway, thanks for stopping, but we're fine and we'll manage without the radio." Motsom's conversation was over. "Goodbye and get off my effin ship," were the only words missing, but the officers made no attempt to leave. "Was there something else?" he queried, then wished he had simply faced them down.

"Yes, Sir, I want to check your log book and your record of catches," said one, "Shall we go in?"

The second officer was already sliding the wheel-house door open forcing Motsom to enter ahead of them. The smashed radio stared accusingly at him as he walked through the door, and the two officers were looking straight at it.

"It'll take more than a new transistor to fix that," one of them said, eyeing the bullet hole.

"Bit of an accident," muttered Motsom, without any hint an explanation was forthcoming. "These gentlemen want to check our books," he continued quickly, addressing the skipper. "Show them please."

The skipper smiled nervously at the two officers, his leathery skin, sun-dried and pickled by a lifetime of salt spray, creasing into deep folds. "Yes, Sir," he replied, and drew the men toward him as he reached the books from a rack above his head.

For several minutes the two officers poured intently over the logs, while Motsom turned his back and engaged in nonchalant business, as he flipped switches, studied maps, scratched his ear and scanned the radar screen. Please don't ask me any questions, he implored inwardly, carefully avoiding eye contact.

"Everything appears in order," said one of the officers eventually. "Thank you for your co-operation, Sir. Sorry to trouble you."

"That's alright, Officer," replied Motsom, turning around, breathing easier, managing an imitation smile.

"If we could just check the rest of the vessel now, Sir?"

He dropped the smile and choked, "Of course ..." then froze. Ideas rocketed around his brain, but none made sense. Shoot them—and what about the rest of the sailors—they were bound to be armed; take them hostage—but the old trawler could never outrun the patrol boat, and the tiny cabin was already overflowing with LeClarc; pray—it had never worked before. Ten seconds of tense anticipation followed—ten seconds of heart stopping anxiety, as Motsom stood absolutely motionless, a glazed stare in his eyes.

"Just the fish hold, Sir," the officer continued, as if there had been no hiatus. "Perhaps you'd escort us."

Motsom took another breath and three minutes later, the empty hold checked, they were apparently satisfied as they thanked Motsom and apologized again for any inconvenience.

"No trouble, Officer," replied Motsom as he escorted them on deck and watched as they leaped back to their own ship. Remaining on deck, shivering slightly in the cool breeze, he waited as the other vessel crept stealthily ahead, then lifted its bow and roared off into the night. Motsom's lungs deflated with a huge sigh of relief, then he stepped back into the wheelhouse and nearly fainted. The smashed compass binnacle was staring him straight in the face. He had forgotten all about it.

"They must have seen it," he was explaining to McCrae and Boyd two minutes later in the wheelhouse. The skipper had been bundled below and trussed alongside his deck hand and, without a hand at the helm, the little trawler was wallowing in the lazy swell. "They couldn't have missed it," Motsom continued. "One of them was leaning right against it."

"So why didn't they say nothing?" asked Boyd.

"'Cos they knew something was up," replied Motsom his patience wearing thin. "That kid must have sent out a message before you got to him this morning," he added, giving McCrae a killing stare.

"It wasn't my fault," McCrae shot back angrily. "I stopped him as soon as you told me."

"'Course it was your bloody fault, you're always ballzing things up."

"Oh yeah. Well who lost the f'kin Fish Kisser in the first place. If you hadn't ..."

"Stop bloody arguing," interjected Boyd. "We've got to do something." He paused for thought then his face brightened, "Why don't we just do what you told them; fish for awhile and hope they didn't notice the compass. In any case they might think it was an accident."

"As well as the radio!" exclaimed Motsom.

"You never know," continued Boyd, "Anyway as soon as they are out of the way, we make a dash for the coast, grab a car, and get the fat freak to Istanbul."

It sounded simple and, as McCrae asked rhetorically, "You gotta better idea?"

"O.K.," said Motsom, his features softening slightly. "That sounds reasonable. I always fancied a spot of fishing."

"We might even catch something to eat," said McCrae. "I could kill a kipper, I'm starving."

Two hours later, they were still there, steaming slowly back and forth as the net dragged the seabed. Normality had apparently returned. The skipper was in his in wheelhouse, his smouldering pipe clogging the atmosphere. The young deck hand was on the aft deck controlling the winch that held the steel hawsers which snaked down into the water and dragged the trawl. But nothing else was normal. Below in the tiny cabin, LeClarc still slept fitfully. His exhausted body refused to let him wake, but his cold wet clothing irritated his skin, making him twitch and turn. McCrae and Boyd both shivered on deck, carefully watching the deck-hand, while Motsom stared at the radar screen. "Mac," he shouted to McCrae, "come here."

"What Billy?" he answered, entering the wheelhouse.

"They're still there," he said, his finger glued to a bright spot on the screen. "Every time we turn, they turn. The bastards are onto us. This ain't going to work."

"We're going to run out of fuel soon," mused the skipper, stoking the flames.

Motsom glanced at his watch in the light of the radar screen, then shot the skipper a look. "You said that eight hours ago," he muttered, then turned to McCrae. "Find the fuel tank and see if you can work out how much we've got left."

Ten minutes later McCrae was back. "We've got tons of fuel. The auld bugger was lying. The tank's still half full."

"Right. Get the net up," instructed Motsom. "Let's try something different."

McCrae gave him a curious look, "What?"

Motsom swept his finger across the radar screen to a busy area ten miles further east. "Look," he said, as if he'd worked it out for himself. "These are ships at anchor. If we get in amongst them they might lose us, or end up following something else. We can get out the other side. Here," he continued, pointing to the far side of the mooring ground. "Then we'll only have a few miles to go to the coast."

"What are we goin' to do with this?" McCrae asked, his eyes roaming around the wheelhouse.

"There's plenty of fuel," replied Motsom with a twisted smile.

McCrae's eyes lit up as he breathed, "It'd make a great bomb."

"Shhh!" hushed Motsom, pointing to the skipper.

McCrae's shrug inferred, "So what?" as he asked quietly, "And the fatso—what are we going to do with him?"

Motsom clasped his hands together, then exploded them apart as he discharged a mouthful of air with a

"Poof!" "We'll have to let him go," he said as if he were discussing the lay-off of a faithful servant. "Poor Trudy."

"Who the hell is Trudy?"

"His bird I guess," replied Motsom, chuckling. "He was rambling about her—reckons she's lost her door key. Big deal."


Trudy's door key, the one to her mother's apartment, was not lost. It was with the pathetic bundle the nurse had tried to give to Lisa McKenzie shortly after her arrival at Watford hospital.

"Perhaps you'd like these," the nurse had said, offering her Trudy's purse and smashed watch. Lisa erupted in a burst of grief at the sight of the familiar items and couldn't bring herself to take them. To do so would have meant acknowledging the finality of the situation: especially the wrecked remains of the watch, a poignant reminder of her sixteen- year- old daughter whose time on earth had all but ended when the hands stopped.

"I'll take them," said Peter McKenzie.

"It's her things the ambulance men brought in with her," the nurse explained. "Her clothes were a bit messy," she continued euphemistically, "and the police took them. I hope you don't mind."

"No, that's alright," he mumbled." Anything the nurse said would have been alright, all they cared about was Trudy, their little girl.

"Trudy is in very poor condition," the skinny young doctor had said as they surveyed the comatose figure at the centre of a spider's web of wires and tubes. "Physically she's not too bad, mainly cuts and bruises, they'll heal quite quickly." His voice became graver, "The problem lies with her mind—clinically speaking she was dead when the police found her."

"Dead," echoed Lisa, her eyes fixed on the monitor, gaily "beeping" in time to Trudy's heart, oblivious to the pain.

"Yes. Didn't the police tell you what happened?"

"Not really," replied Peter. "Although we understand she was in someone's cellar."

"Not exactly," replied the doctor, unhygienically picking and poking his nose while recounting how she had been found by the electrician called to trace the mysterious use of electricity, and the locksmith who had prised open the door at the bottom of the pit.

"The first policeman," he referred to his notes, "Detective Jackson, started mouth to mouth resuscitation and heart massage immediately, but the problem is that her brain had been starved of oxygen for a long time."

"What does that mean?" asked Peter.

"It means we won't know for a little while what is going to happen ..."

"She will live—won't she?" Lisa's frantic voice cut in.

The doctor allowed the silence to grow for a few seconds, letting the couple draw their own conclusions from his sad eyes. "It is too early to say," he eventually conceded, but his expression clearly said, "Don't bank on it."

"Was she ..." Lisa's voice trailed away, then she tried again, "Did he ..."

The doctor helped her out. "There was no sexual activity in the last day or so, but before that ..." he stopped and shrugged, letting Lisa's imagination loose.

"I just hope they find the bastard," she spat, with as much spite as she could muster.

"They," whoever "they" were, had not found LeClarc, although there was now no question "they" were trying hard and had a fairly good idea where he was. For more than three hours the trawler had been weaving in and out of moored ships, making erratic turns, speeding up, slowing down, and taking every conceivable evasive action. But, like a sleek shark patiently circling its prey, every time they emerged from behind a massive moored oil tanker or a giant freighter, the tenacious hunter would always be waiting. Almost invisible in the pale moonlight, just a blip on the radar screen, no matter how they twisted and turned, it was always there, stealing through the dark, stealthily sneaking up on them, then veering off to keep station a mile or so away. The predators had become the prey; the piranhas the prawns.

For the first couple of hours Motsom had been convinced the captain of the other vessel had some kind of sixth sense—a shark's sense—enabling him always to be in the right place at the right time. Slowly, reality dawned—there was more than one shark. There were in fact three.

How did they know? Motsom wondered, as he stood next to the skipper, ordering this way or that. What had given the game away? Then he shot the skipper a suspicious look and stretched above his head for the logbooks. Seconds later, without a word, Motsom smashed a fist into the old man's face and sent him sprawling across the floor into the chart table.

"Mac," bawled Motsom.

He came running.

"Look," He held up one of the books. The missing corner of a blank page told the tale.

"He must've slipped a message to one of those scum," he said. "That's why they kept quiet about the compass. He'd warned them."

"What shall I do with him?"

"Take him below and get Sprat. We're going to have to make plans."

Motsom jabbed at the dots on the screen a few minutes later, a definite note of concern in his voice. "I think it's this one and these two," he said.

"We could just give ourselves up," offered Boyd, but the chill of Motsom's glare had him backtracking immediately. "Just kidding."

"Why don't we bomb it and get away in the life-boat?" suggested McCrae, anxious to exercise his peculiar skills.

"How far do you think we'll get? The life-boat's a bloody rowing boat," shot back Motsom. "Plus, they probably know who we are—me anyway."

Billy Motsom was correct. The crews of the three patrol boats, two Dutch and one English, were well aware of their identities. Their location and activities had been monitored all day, ever since the skippers' failure to respond to the radio that morning and the brief mayday message from the deck hand. The discovery of the stolen Saab, in which they had jumped the canal bridge, added to the weight of evidence when it was found abandoned, not a mile from the home of the trawler.

The fishery officers, two British detectives in borrowed uniforms, had reported directly back to Superintendent Edwards aboard one of the Dutch vessels with the scrap of paper the old trawler skipper had pressed into his hand.

"3 Gunmen. 3 Hostages. Help," was all it said, nothing else was necessary.

"Look," cried McCrae with alarm, "They're getting closer."

The circling sharks were closing in. The three bright dots were definitely nearer the centre of the screen—and they were the bullseye. Dawn was only an hour or so away, the hunters had been stalking all night and were moving in for the kill.

"A dawn raid," Motsom mused, knowing the long-standing police practice of catching their quarry half-asleep, and leaped into action. "Mac. Start a fire," he shouted. "Sprat, launch that bloody rowing boat. We'll take a chance. With any luck they'll be so busy trying to put out the flames we can get away."

McCrae was halfway out the door when Sprat Boyd stopped him with a word. "Wait!"

Boyd hadn't moved from the radar screen, and he didn't look up for fear of catching a disapproving stare from Motsom. "I've got a better idea," he said. The others drifted back as he continued talking, sensing their faces over his shoulder. "These big ships," he pointed to the anchored vessels, "they've all got bloody great long ladders down to the water. I've seen them. Why don't we drive by one real close and jump. Leave this tub going flat out so they'll chase it for bloody miles 'til the fuel runs out."

"Or hits something and smashes to pieces," added McCrae, warming to the idea.

"And just how do we get ashore?" bitched Motsom.

Boyd had an answer. "We swim to the ship and pinch a proper speedboat. They must have them."

Motsom wasn't sure. "I can't swim very well ..." he admitted, then pride got the better of him. "O.K. we'll give it a try, I don't fancy rowing all bloody day."

Five minutes later the trawler disappeared off the patrol vessels' radar screens as its tiny blip blended with the large blob of a slab-sided freighter. But the 'patter' of its engine still reverberated across the water, sending out a homing signal to the watchmen on the decks of the patrol boats. Then the little boat slipped behind the monster and the "patter" deepened to a dull echo. Thirty seconds later it turned into a deep-throated roar as Boyd slammed the throttles wide open, leaped out of the wheelhouse and dived over the side into the inky water. The trawler picked itself up and, freed of its malignant cargo, danced across the waves, its powerful engines designed to drag tons of fish from the sea-bed, now light-heartedly making a dash for the open sea.

The sharks were quick to respond as the trawler bounded from behind the freighter, attacking it with a salvo of searchlights and the blare of a loudspeaker. "Heave to. Heave to or we'll shoot." But the driverless vessel turned a deaf ear, raced drunkenly toward another moored ship, then veered easterly—Holland and home.

# *chapter fifteen*

"Why can you never find a policeman when you want one?" D.I. Bliss muttered angrily, as he drove the stolen black Mercedes through central Turkey.

"It's the same in Holland," said Yolanda, through a yawn, catching him by surprise as she woke.

"No wonder people steal things," he grumbled, shuffling through the car owner's cassette collection, seeking something soothing—Brahms or a Bach adagio perhaps. "We've been driving for hours and haven't been stopped."

"Nearly three hours," she noted, glancing at her watch. Then she stretched extravagantly and ended by combing the fingers of her left hand through his hair.

"I haven't even seen a police car," he continued despondently, a soft warm feeling running through him as her fingers played with the hairs on the back of his neck; he slipped a likely looking tape into the player.

"I don't know if we'd be able to get them to believe us anyway," she added, then clamped her hands over her ears at the raucous blare of a Turkish version of "Jailhouse Rock."

The road, which earlier had been as peaceful as could be expected anywhere on a early Saturday morning, was now buzzing with carloads of families, busloads of tourists, and truck-loads of everything imaginable, and unimaginable. A ribbon of humanity, and all their worldly possessions, streaming across the Steppes of Anatolia, according to the map they had bought at a gas station, several hours, and a few hundred miles, earlier.

She yawned again as the parched mountainscape slid by, as it had for hour upon hour. The grandly named Steppes of Anatolia, turned out to be nothing more than a barren rocky desert. Occasionally, they would pass a green tree , cannily growing spindly and sickly in the hope of avoiding the woodchopper's axe or a voracious goat. Some even more enterprising trees lodged themselves precariously into fissures up on the side of escarpments but, otherwise, the scorched landscape appeared almost devoid of life. "I think the Valley of Death is somewhere around here," muttered Bliss, his geography slightly askew as he scoured the dusty landscape, disappointed at the absence of Cossacks and a regiment of plumed Hussars. "Nothing but bloody goats," he moaned, with a venom speaking of previous injurious experience. It's a bit like life, he thought, bored by the never-ending undulating landscape, though the odd rocky outcrop and a small craggy mountain added occasional interest. A few romantic precipices and a failed marriage went through his mind, then he caught himself: his marriage hadn't failed—failure suggested catastrophic collapse—his union with

Sarah had gradually dissolved until it became two tenants with shared facilities and memories, and a grown-up daughter, who, like her mother, had flown the coop. "I should call Samantha; she might be worried," he told himself, remembering that he'd half promised to meet her for Sunday brunch. Then he had an unsettling thought. "Yolanda?" he said nervously.

"Ah, ah," she hummed sleepily.

"You remember what we did in the airplane yesterday?"

"Yeah," she replied, her eyes closing, the start of a dreamy smile sprouting around her mouth, and she left her lips parted a fraction, in preparation for a wider smile, which she knew, was coming. He blushed and stuttered, "We didn't, um, we didn't, um, take any precautions."

The smile bloomed. "I know," she said. "Isn't it wonderful." Then the blossom faded. "What do you want? Boy or girl?" Without giving him an opportunity to speak, she prattled on. "I would prefer a boy myself, we could call him Peter or Caas ... although I've often thought Dave was a nice name." Her resolve started to crack, seeing the mounting look of concern on his face. "We could have a girl next ..." was all she managed before the smile burst back into bloom and turned to laughter. "Don't worry Dave, I take a pill."

Relieved, he laughed with her. Then he glanced into her deep blue laughing eyes and, looking ahead, saw that the sky had picked up the colour and spread it to the horizon.

"Where's the truck, Dave?" she asked, forcing herself awake.

"There," he replied, aiming a finger at a point about two miles ahead. On cue, the truck rose from a slight depression into full view, crested a hill and disappeared again. "According to the map there are no more intersections until we get to Ankara, and we should be there in about an hour."

"We must get to a telephone in Ankara," she said. "If I can call the captain he will know how to get the Turkish cops to help."

"I could always call Edwards ..." he began, then changed his mind. Samantha, his daughter, would be first—he needed sympathy not screaming.

"I hope he stops somewhere soon," she said, the truck cresting another hill. "I need a bathroom and some food."

"I need a shower," mused Bliss, recalling his sweat-soaked minutes frantically digging into the warehouse compound during the night.

Yolanda sniffed. "We both need showers—and new clothes."

"We're not going to steal them," he jumped in firmly, thinking she might have that in mind.

The lunar-like landscape dragged by unendingly. The only evidence of human habitation was an occasional cluster of peasants' houses, providing shelter from the sun for a skinny donkey or a flea-ridden goat. Sometimes the remnants of a dry stone wall would rise in the middle of a scrubby dry pasture, meander across the landscape for half a mile or more, then sink slowly back into the dusty soil; marking out some long-forgotten boundary, when the land still had a semblance of fertility—before the Angora goats, a zillion mohair suits still on hoof, had scoured every last blade of vegetation.

Two hours later Ankara was a distant red smear of rooftops in Bliss' rear view mirror. The truck had not even slowed and Yolanda crossed her legs, fearing it might never stop. Spreading the map that was, for the most part, as barren as the landscape, she stuck her finger on the next town: Kirpehir, at least an hour away. "Can we stop somewhere Dave? I really have to go. We'll have plenty of time to catch up."

"We'll never catch up if we don't find another gas station," he muttered as he scanned the deserted roadsides ahead, and a desultory idea took hold and shocked him with its simple logic: I don't have to go back. I could set up a truck stop and stay right here—forever.

"What is it Dave?" said Yolanda, seeing him smile.

"Just a silly thought," he replied, but was buoyed by the feeling of liberty. Realizing that, if he chose, he could be free—free from Edwards; and past relationships. That's not freedom—that's escape. You're just running away—running from difficult situations. Anyway, look at the place—who'd want to live here? One glance at Yolanda with her expensively unruly hair, Cartier watch, and bank of credit cards told him to forget it.

A few scrawny bushes, clumping together for protection against the goats, lay off the road several hundred yards ahead. Bliss aimed for them, laughing. "If kissing your wife in a taxi is a crime, having a pee by the roadside probably carries the death penalty. But at least it will get the attention of the police."

They bounced off the road and disappeared in a storm of dust, and Yolanda was out, fleeing through the gritty grey cloud. Two trucks and a handful of cars flew by, then Bliss noticed an ominous break in the traffic. Where's the next car, he wondered, peering deeply into the rear view mirror, drumming his fingers on the steering wheel.

"Hurry up," he muttered, his right leg joining in the restless rhythm of his fingers.

Still no traffic. His anxiety rose. "Come on, come on." Then he saw it; in the mirror, rising over the top of the last hill, a huge lumbering low-loader carrying half a power station on its back, and behind it a mile or more of solid traffic. Leaning on the horn, he screamed, "Yolanda."

"Just coming," she shouted testily, unaware of the urgency of the situation, then ran from behind the bushes still tugging at her dress.

He slammed the car into gear and was already inching forward when she leaped aboard, then he jumped the throttle and sent the wheels spinning across the rock-strewn desert.

Too late. The low-loader was already passed, together with several trucks, a dozen cars and a bus. Bliss kept to the desert trying to outpace the vehicles, throwing up a whirlwind of dust and debris for hundreds of yards. Then a sharp scar of a deep ravine loomed ahead, forcing him to re-join the road before it ran over an iron girder bridge. Swerving aggressively, he intimidated the driver of a new Volkswagen into letting him into the line, but there were still six cars and a bus behind the oversized load, and the red and white articulated truck, with its human hostage, was getting further away by the minute.

Twice, he nearly killed them, recklessly overtaking in the face of oncoming traffic. At the third attempt, Yolanda laid a hand on his arm, "Dave, be careful." Then her words, "Think of the baby," relaxed the strain and spread a smile across his face.

Twenty minutes later they were still trying to catch the kidnappers. Bliss unkindly implying it was all her fault for taking so long—even suggesting she should pee for Holland in the next Olympics. Finally, he scraped by the giant truck ascending a steep hill, the transformer on its back weighing it to a crawl. Then he looked in his mirror and saw again the dreaded inscription "Trust in Allah" plastered across the top of the cab.

"Kirpehir," proclaimed the dusty signboard at the entrance to the dusty town, and the detectives' uneasiness was rising to a panic. According to the map there was only one main road through the town, but they worried the truck might stop and transfer its hostage to another vehicle, or drive surreptitiously into a warehouse and vanish altogether.

Houses seemingly grew out of the desert as they entered the town—the rocky desert outcrops merely taking on a more geometric shape—as rough conical stone mounds transmuted into cubes, with tiny windows and bleached wooden doors. As the Mercedes bumped and rattled along the steeply inclined cobbled road, they scanned side streets for the articulated red and white trailer, and were occasionally startled by a vibrant splash of colour: Tex-Mex red or guacamole green; the entrepreneurial householder having taken advantage of a few cans of paint destined for a more avant-garde city, which had fallen off the back of a passing truck.

"There it is," she screeched, suddenly jabbing her finger at a parking lot at the end of the main street—a truckers' oasis. Dozens of huge rigs jammed every available space and some had even overflowed onto the high street itself. A strategically placed row of black and yellow booths, marked "Telefon," seethed with truck drivers checking in with their bosses or wives; others, no doubt, making arrangements for a clandestine adventure in some city well away from their bosses or wives. All around the parking lot enterprising merchants had set up stalls, turning the entire area into a vast colourful bazaar, and one side of the square, where Bliss flagrantly parked the Mercedes under a "No parking" sign, was taken up with the facade of a Mosque, its single Minaret pointing to the sky like a space-rocket ready for launch.

"I'll phone the captain if you find some clothes and look for a police station," said Yolanda, then nodded toward the parked truck on the other side of the square. "How long do you think they'll stop?"

Bliss shrugged. "Not long. There's two drivers so they can take turns. But there's only one road out of town, if they're stopping now it means they still have some way to go. As long as we check every ten minutes or so we'll be able to catch them."

Yolanda nodded her agreement, "What's the time now?"

Brushing the dust off his watch, he remembered to add two hours before replying, "Nearly twelve o'clock."

"Okey dokey. Let's be back here in fifteen minutes."

Leaving the car, they had managed to take only a couple of paces before they were almost knocked to the ground. A powerful blast of white noise from a trio of metal horned megaphones shrieked at them from the Minaret. Yolanda clamped her ears again as the dreadful noise was superseded by the discordant singsong voice of the Muezzin calling his flock to the Mosque. Religious fervour instantly seized the entire town. Everything stopped; cars were abandoned in the streets; stores suddenly deserted; young girls whisked out of sight. The truck drivers melted from the phone booths and men scurried into the mosque from all directions.

"Great," she said, noticing the vacant phone booths. "I'll call the Captain."

"I could try Edwards ..." he began, then changed his mind. "I think I'll call my daughter."

"She'll be worried."

He shook his head. "No. She's so busy with her career she probably doesn't know I'm away—that's the advantage of living on your own; no one misses you."

"Is that an advantage?" queried Yolanda quietly.

Yolanda was bubbling with excitement when Bliss returned to the car with a suit, shirt, and underwear neatly tied in a brown paper parcel.

"What is it?" he said, noticing her grin from a distance.

"I spoke to Captain Jahnssen. They've found LeClarc," she said breathlessly.

His voice jumped, "Alive?"

"Yeah," she said, quickly, "But I'll tell you in a minute, we've got to keep going. The truck's still there; the drivers are in a café. I need clothes. Grab some food and lots of drink."

Returning ten minutes later, arms overflowing with packets, bags and bottles, Bliss didn't immediately recognize the veiled woman standing next to the Mercedes, even wondering if he was in the right square but, turning around, spotted the truck. Then Yolanda saucily lifted the veil and gave him her most lascivious wink. Not now, he thought, his mind racing with the memory of what lay under the shapeless black dress. The heavy black shawl, draped over her golden hair and drawn across her face, certainly made a mockery of the old Turkish saying Abdul had taught them in Istanbul. "The thicker the veil the less it is worth lifting," he had claimed.

Yolanda rummaged through a paper bag as soon as she got in the car. "I've got some black hair dye, soap, deodorant, a toothbrush and some toothpaste ..." she paused, giving the tube a quizzical look, "I think it's toothpaste."

"I'd rather have a wash," he said, grabbing the deodorant and plastering it under his arms. "Where's LeClarc?" he continued, excitement in his tone.

She turned up her nose. "Phew. I think you smelled better before ... Dave — quick, they're going," she said, brushing it aside.

The truck was edging slowly out of the square and heading back to the main road.

"Damn!" mused Bliss. "I was going to try calling Samantha again."

"My turn to drive," she said, shoving him out and sliding into the driver's seat. "You can get changed on the way."

A few seconds later, the truck turned onto the main road and set off, ever eastward, and, with the burning sun high overhead, the Mercedes fell into line.

"What did the captain say about LeClarc?" he tried again, as they swung onto the main road.

"Wait a minute," she said, noticing the red warning light. "No gas."

He buried his face in his hands, "Oh shit!, I forgot."

"Gas station," she said, as if trying to summons one magically. And there it was, conveniently placed, two hundred yards ahead.

"How did you do that?" he laughed.

She beamed and took the credit.

With a full tank, new clothes, and a chancy selection of food and drink, they raced eastward and caught up to the truck.

"What did the captain say about LeClarc?" he tried again, as they relaxed with the truck back in their sights.

"Something about a trawler—apparently they had to chase it with a helicopter and drop someone on board at high speed."

"Why would they have to chase a trawler?"

She shrugged. "The crew had been tied up—anyway LeClarc is safe. The captain's calling the Turkish police to tell them where we are. Someone should be with us in about an hour so you should get some sleep."

"Just be careful. The last time I went to sleep you crashed the car."

"That wasn't my fault."

"Yes it was," he said firmly, gave her a contradictory smile and fell asleep, exhausted.

Five hours later Bliss was jerked awake by the bumpiness of the road. "Where's the cavalry?" he asked, his eyes taking in the lush surroundings of a tree lined river gorge where he had expected to see a posse of Turkish police. "And where's the truck?"

Yolanda was manoeuvring the car onto a grassy knoll under some Eucalyptus trees. "I saw the police about an hour ago, six carloads all going the other way, I thought they'd turn around and catch us, but they didn't. I think they had set up a road block but left before we got there."

"Brilliant," replied Bliss.

"The truck's over there," she added pointing through the trees. "They have stopped at another café. We have time to stop and eat."

"And wash," he said, noticing the sound of running water as he climbed out of the car and headed to a convenient tree.

"Yolanda," he called a few seconds later, "come and look."

"What?" she said, leaving the car., She caught up to him under the trees and they stood in amazement, looking down at a fairy-tale scene. Rays from the hot afternoon sun, heading westward again, were filtering through the Eucalyptus trees and dancing in dozens of tumbling waterfalls at their feet.

"It's beautiful," said Bliss, totally lost for a more appropriate description. A cataract of polished rock basins formed a giant's staircase with water cascading gently from one pool to the next, then overflowing into the next, down and down again, sometimes falling six feet or more while other times trickling sideways, only a few inches, into another pool before plummeting into yet another. The crystal clear spring water gurgled and laughed as it plunged over and over again in the tree-lined gorge.

Two minutes later they were showering naked under a six feet high waterfall. They washed themselves, and each other, in the soft smooth water and stood for minutes just letting it pour over them. Then they washed each other again, their soapy fingers playing and exploring as their wet lips met and locked. Finally they broke apart as Yolanda considered dying her hair black to match the locals, but then decided not to bother.

"You only bought one toothbrush," he complained as she cleaned her teeth.

"We'll share," she said, taking it out of her mouth and jabbing it into his.

Then they laid together in a perfectly sized pool, staring at the blue sky through the waving fronds of Eucalyptus, the water swirling gently round them on its way from one waterfall to the next.

"In England a place like this would be filled with screaming kids and people with rubber tires and inflatable things," said Bliss.

"The same in Holland," she agreed, "and you would have to pay to get in."

"Can we stay here forever?" she asked, as her hand swam under the water and gently played between his legs. He closed his eyes and his mind drifted. "Um. Yes please," he replied.

"The truck's moving," she said lazily a minute later.

"Damn," he replied and kissed her quickly as they climbed out of the pool. "No towels," they exclaimed together, and stood dripping wet, laughing, on the edge of paradise.

"We'll use my shawl," she said.

A minute later they were bouncing back along the track toward the road, clean, happy, and refreshed—Bliss driving as Yolanda gave directions.

The dying rays of yet another day slanted across the landscape as they drove. Mile after mile of barren brown mountains were broken only by the occasional green stripe of a verdant valley. Goats and sheep outnumbered the peasants a thousand to one, and Yolanda had swerved a few times to avoid a wild camel as she drove and Bliss slept.

"I think the next town is called Dlyabakir," Yolanda said, slowly reading the name, then a note of concern crept into her voice. "Edge of the map, Dave."

"I know," he replied. "How's your geography?"

"Syria—I think, but it might be Lebanon, Jordan, even Israel ... Shit!" she exclaimed. "I might have bought the wrong costume."

"Don't worry. Immigration and customs will stop the truck at the border and it'll be easy to rescue the guy." The he squirreled an audiocassette out of his pocket. "Nearly forgot," he announced, "I picked it up at one of the market stalls—only cost a few lira."

"What is it?"

"Handel's 'The Arrival of the Queen of Sheba,'" he announced, triumphantly, slipping the obscure aria into the player. Three triumphal bars sang out then it snapped with a twang and the machine vomited out a stream of tape. "Damn."

The mountainous landscape gave way to scrubby desert by the time the sunset. They had eaten well and Yolanda congratulated him on his excellent choice of food. Claiming, truthfully, to have no idea what they were eating, he admitted it tasted better than raw herring.

"So would goat poop," laughed Yolanda, adding, "We'll go back to Istanbul and have bluefish when this is over," her eyes glazing at the prospect.

"Can we still stay in that Hotel?"

"The Yesil Ev," she reminded him.

"Yeah. I'd like to try out that bed properly."

"So would I, Dave," she replied sweetly.

The start of a smile was wiped out with a sudden concern. "I hope they haven't thrown our suitcases into the street," said Bliss.

"No. I gave them my credit card. They'll just charge us until we get back."

His sharp intake of breath alerted her to his thoughts. "Don't worry Dave. I can afford it. Anyway, we are staying for at least another week; I want to show you all the sights."

"Now you're talking ..." he started, but was cut short by the sudden blinding lights of an oncoming vehicle, the first for many miles, and the Mercedes' tires dug into the dusty desert as he swerved. In a flash the car was past and the lights went out.

"He's driving without lights," he complained bitterly, the policeman in him wanting to tear after the offender with a ticket.

Another unlit car flew out of the darkness and briefly flashed its lights, catching Bliss unawares again, although he managed to stick to the road this time.

"What the ..." he started, then checked in his rear view mirror and spotted the shadow of a dark car.

"Yolanda, we've got company."

"Police?" she said hopefully, swivelling to look.

"I don't think so," he replied nervously.

"Bandits?" she enquired, with an excellent Southern drawl.

Bliss checked the mirror again. "Possibly. Let's see what happens if we slow down." They slowed and the following car matched their speed, making no attempt to pass. He sped up again and two miles later the sinister car was still there. At every turn his heart began to jump; expecting to find a roadblock just around the corner, expecting the occupants of the following car to leap out wearing bandannas and carrying machine guns.

"Hold tight," he said, ramming his foot to the floor. The Mercedes nearly took off. "Keep looking," he shouted and she spun round in her seat.

"We're losing him," she said after a few moments.

"As soon as we've rounded the next bend," he warned, "I'm going to turn off my lights and do a one-eighty."

They shot round the corner at nearly a hundred miles-an-hour and Bliss jumped on the brakes, then pirouetted the car around. Without stopping he drove straight at the following vehicle and stabbed on his high beams. Blinded, the driver lost control and careened off the road, bouncing out of their view into the desert and crunching into a rock.

Bliss spun the car back around, gripping the wheel hard to stop his hands shaking, and his lights picked up the occupants clambering out.

"I wonder who they are?" Yolanda breathed rhetorically.

"Do they look like bandits?" he asked as he stood on the accelerator.

"It's difficult to tell," she replied, still straining her neck.

Bliss agreed with a nod. With their swarthy skin, deep-set dark eyes, black greasy hair, and villainous smiles, all the locals looked candidates for the "most wanted" page of the *Police Gazette*.

Three more cars passed without lights, the drivers relying on the moonlight and Allah. After the third, Bliss turned off his lights and drove without difficulty. "If you can't beat them, join them," he said to Yolanda who translated the saying into Dutch for his amusement.

Five hours, three towns, and a hundred unlit cars later the red warning light came on again.

"Low on gas," said Yolanda who had taken over the driving.

"Town up ahead," he said lazily, as he noticed a radiant glow on the horizon.

"Which town?"

His eyes searched in the dim light. "It must be off the map," he concluded. "Syria maybe," he added, sitting up attentively. "We'll get help from the border police wherever it is."

She consulted the dashboard clock. "It's three o'clock Sunday morning. We'll be lucky if anyone's awake."

"Fingers crossed," he replied, as they rounded the next bend, and were suddenly confronted by the "town": nothing more than a border crossing besieged by a bunch of squatter's huts. A half dozen trucks were pulled off to the side and the drivers stood around, enthusiastically shaking hands, jabbering excitedly, and gesticulating wildly as if they had just conquered Antarctica or climbed Everest.

Yolanda eased the unlit car onto the desert and killed the engine. "I'll take a look," she said, throwing the shawl over her head and slipping out of the car as he tried to protest.

"Damn woman,"

Ten minutes later she slunk back. "Dave it's not Syria. It's Kurdistan," she said, forlornly slumping in the seat.

"Kurdistan," he repeated," Isn't that part of Iraq?"

"Uh, uh."

They sat in silent deliberation for several minutes; thoughts of home and family interwoven with frightening images of the Gulf war: bloated bodies of gassed Kurds, and fanatical Iraqis chanting, "Death to westerners," tortured hostages, and terribly mutilated prisoners of war.

"Dave," she enquired slowly, "Do you think we should carry on?"

"Yolanda!" he scowled.

For once she agreed. "Okey dokey, Dave. Well that's it then."

# chapter sixteen

"Well ... Where the bloody hell is Bliss?" shouted Superintendent Edwards, forcing his staff sergeant to clamp his hand over the mouthpiece of the phone.

"They don't know Sir."

Edwards, adopting a silly, child-like voice threw the sergeant's words back at him, "*They don't know, Sir.*" Then he spat, "Well bloody well find him. He was supposed be on that ship Friday. He should have been back here yesterday."

The sergeant, hand over the mouthpiece, kept his voice down. "According to the Dutch he was in Turkey yesterday, with one of their detectives, chasing a truck."

"What?"

"Sir ...?" There was more.

Edwards rose in unison with his tone. "What?"

"Perhaps you should speak to Captain Jahnssen, Sir."

"Why?"

"Well, apparently they've stolen a car and the Turkish police are chasing them."

"Serves 'em bloody right," said Edwards, snatching the phone. "Jost. What's all this crap about Bliss and one of your men in Turkey?"

The sergeant watched, fascinated, as Edwards' face reddened to a boil. Then he exploded, "A woman. I bloody well knew it." Clapping his hand over the phone he snorted loudly into the air, "Umph! The randy bastard. Chasing a truck my ass! He's chasing a fanny."

Taking his hand off the mouthpiece he started on the captain again. "Well where the bloody hell are they?"

He listened intently for half a minute, sticking an occasional "When?" "How?" and, "Why?" into the conversation, before adding, "I'll call you back in ten minutes." Then he slowly lowered the phone as he sat, the colour draining from his cheeks.

"Something wrong, Sir?" enquired the sergeant.

Edwards' face clouded. "The Dutch are pretty worried. Apparently Bliss and his bit of skirt were headed into a hostile area—fundamentalist rebels—even the Turkish cops won't go there. Jost has been trying Interpol and the Turks all day but nobody knows what to do."

"Anything we can do?"

"I suppose we'd better inform the duty officer at the Foreign Office. According to Jost all western governments have been warning people not to go to that part of Turkey since the Gulf war."

"The F.O. will be ticked off to hear we've got a man there then," replied the sergeant, reaching for the phone.

"Wait," snapped Edwards, slapping it back to the cradle. "Let's think about this." Pausing, he doodled a skull and crossbones on a scratch pad as he ran through various scenarios in his mind, then shook his head seriously. "We haven't got a man there—officially I mean."

He let the words sink in for a few seconds, then, satisfied by the expression on his junior's face, continued, "If some off-duty bobby takes his bird somewhere against Foreign Office advice that's not our problem."

"I agree, Sir?"

"In fact," Edwards continued, ducking under a canopy of authority, "I specifically ordered Bliss back to England on that ship on Friday, didn't I?"

"That's correct, Sir, you did."

Edwards reached into a drawer. "Well, Sergeant, I think it's time I wrote out some discipline charges for our Mr. Bliss. Starting with disobeying an order ... Chasing a fucking truck, eh!"

Edwards was wrong. Bliss and Yolanda were no longer chasing the truck. Neither were they in Turkey. They were in Iraq, hiding inside the container amidst the pallets.

"This is stupid, Yolanda," whispered Bliss, his voice echoing out of the darkness as the driver waited for the Iraqi border guards to wave him through. "They'll kill us if they find us, and Edwards will kill me if they don't."

"I think you are right, Dave. I'm sorry. It's my fault."

It *was* her fault. They'd sat in the Mercedes at the border watching the truck with resigned detachment as the border guards checked the contents.

"At least we can tell them we followed it this far," said Bliss with some satisfaction.

Yolanda stared at the truck in thought, then asked softly. "Are you married, Dave?"

"I thought you didn't want to know."

"I don't really. But I was thinking about the man they've got in there: wondering if he has a wife and children."

"Divorced," he admitted, his neutral tone giving nothing away—no bitterness, no regret; Gone, but not forgotten.

There was some relief in her sigh. "Any children?"

"One—Samantha; I told you, she's a lawyer." A dozen memories of his daughter immediately flooded his mind as he realized he still hadn't called her, then he shook it off, thinking: there's little point; what could she do? Anyway, she's too wrapped up in her job and London's gritty nightlife to worry about me. "Alright," he said, getting the message and caving in, "You're right. If I was in that truck would I want someone to risk their life to save me?"

"Well?"

"Let's do it for his kids then," he said, as they abandoned the car and made off toward the truck, then he pulled her up. "What about you? Why would you do it?"

"I have a child as well," she said, hiding behind the softness of the words and the darkness of the desert.

"I expect many of those kidnapped people have children," he continued, skirting an obviously tender spot while adding further justification.


The guards had moved onto another rig by the time they arrived at the red and white eighteen-wheeler. They clambered into the container without difficulty, hid among the pallets, and, as they waited for the doors to slam, Bliss had second thoughts and started backing out. "This is crazy ... even if we find out where they're taking him, there's no guarantee the others will be there. And how the hell are we going to get out?"

"I don't know," she said quietly, holding his hand, "but we have to try."

He relented; life had become so surreal nothing mattered anymore. "As soon as we get there we'll raise the alarm and get out."

"And straight back to Istanbul for that holiday I promised."

"Are you serious?"

"Of course."

He smiled in the blackness, and they leaned on each other, huddling warmly in the numbing cold of the desert night.

For the first twenty minutes the road was straight and flat, then the paved surface gave way to rock strewn mountain passes. They cuddled, spoon-like, and snoozed as the truck bumped and jolted its way along the rugged roads; struggling sluggishly uphill, or straining against the squealing brakes downhill. They tried sleeping in turns but the constant shaking and jarring instantly awoke them whenever they dropped off even for a minute.

"Sun's up," said Bliss several hours later.

"How do you know?

Finding her hand in the darkness he pressed it against the container's warm skin. Then the smell of hot metal gradually enveloped them as the pleasant warmth of the morning simmered into the searing heat of mid-day. Their thoughts dragged with the hours, and Yolanda's pensive silence concerned him. It wasn't like her—a few hours earlier she'd been flying through life with panache—had she crash landed? It couldn't be their predicament; she'd led the flight all the way from Holland and could have bailed at any time, if she'd wanted. Sifting through his memory banks Bliss found a red flag. "It must be her child," he said to himself. "She kept that quiet," and realized he knew nothing of her offspring despite the three—or was it four?—days they'd shared everything—absolutely everything, tooth-brush included. What should he have asked? Age, sex, colour—there's a thought! Blonde with blue eyes he might have guessed but knowing Yolanda's reckless dis-regard for convention, anything was possible. Was it too late to ask?

At every stop during the day they begged the doors to open and let in a cool mountain breeze but were dispirited time and time again.

"There's no more water," Bliss said by late afternoon. Then coolness returned and they swayed and jolted from evening into the numbing cold of the desert night, shiver-ing uncontrollably in their sweat soaked clothes.

The final stop was different, around midnight they guessed. The truck lurched to a standstill on a smooth section of flat road when a shouted com-mand was followed by the whine of a gate. Then they were through, and a minute later the engine's drone turned into a hollow rumble as they drove inside a building. An electric door buzzed to a close behind them.

"We've arrived," he said, his chattering teeth hav-ing difficulty with the words and a clamour of activity followed as the cab was detached from the truck.

"I think they're taking him out," Bliss whispered a few seconds later as he heard voices behind the false wall.

Yolanda was gripped by a sudden panic. "What if they don't open the back doors? Maybe these boxes are only for show."

The thought had occurred to him. "Let's wait," he replied, thinking fate had brought them this far—surely not for nought.

Slowly the voices moved away, absolute stillness tensed the air and they clung to each other like guinea pigs in a sensory deprivation experiment.

"We can't get out," she whispered worriedly after awhile, her muted voice sounding like a shout in the black metal tunnel.

"Shhhh."

"I knew I shouldn't have drunk all that water," she moaned as she squirmed to a corner. Then the back doors flew open. "Get down," he hissed and she flattened herself behind one of the stacks. The brilliant flood of fluorescent light stung after twenty hours of blackout, and they squinted madly, trying to see what was happening.

Two burly men with baseball caps and jeans— truck drivers anywhere—clambered into the truck, and were heaving the heavy pallets around as if they were Styrofoam. Yolanda sidled back to Bliss and made him jump as she stuck her mouth to his ear. "Any ideas?"

He shook his head as another pallet was disappearing, and found himself fighting the almost overwhelming temptation to walk smartly to the back of the container, warrant card in hand, announcing, "Metropolitan Police—you're all under arrest."

"What if we creep off behind one ..." he began

She stopped him with a shake of her head and whispered, "They'll see us."

"There's plenty of time," he said quietly, the sound of his voice masked by the men rumbling the pallet along the steel floor.

Six pallets later, they still had no plan.

"We could do a runner," he breathed, as another pallet was pushed off the back onto the tines of a forklift. She didn't bother to reply.

Only four pallets remained, the men chose the one straight in front of them.

Yolanda found Bliss' ear, "Could we push one of these on top of them?"

Bliss considered for a second, then found her ear again, "I don't think so."

Another stack was being grabbed by the men, and manhandled toward the back of the truck. Just two left.

"I know," whispered Yolanda, digging into her purse for her gun. "You divert them and I'll shoot."

"You're armed?" he mouthed, and could have kissed her.

"Where's yours?"

"The sergeant's got it."

Giving him a funny look, she mouthed, "Ready?"

The men were returning, jabbering to each other as they walked the thirty feet through the almost empty trailer, their heavy boots clanking on the metal floor. Bliss stood poised, his legs vibrating with tension, then a shout shook him rigid. They've seen me, he thought, and desperately tried to get his legs to move, but the footsteps stopped, the shouter called again and the men retreated.

"They've gone," said Yolanda a few seconds later as she heard a door close. "Quick."

Jumping off the back of the trailer, their eyes searched the warehouse for a hiding place or a way out. Bliss saw the giant door through which they had come. "We could just drive it out," he suggested.

"Then what?"

"Go to the local police and tell them what we know," he tried lamely.

"Dave this is Iraq. This place is probably run by the police. Anyway we've been through this before."

Without warning he grabbed her and pulled her under the truck. "Camera," he explained, pointing at the high ceiling. She saw it and ducked. "We've got to get out before they come back to finish unloading. It must be their meal break."

Then Bliss' eyes picked out an ordinary looking door at the back of the warehouse. "I wonder what's in there?"

"We can't stay here," said Yolanda, "so we'll have to find out."

They slithered together across the floor, praying the camera watcher was asleep.

The sleeping guard hadn't stood a chance. Stripped, bound and gagged in under a minute, they took a risk with the security camera and bundled him into the back of the trailer. The scrawny man was little more than an undernourished teenager, and his uniform was such a tight fit on Bliss that Yolanda gave him a screwy smile. Poking out his tongue in retaliation, he pointed the way with the guard's gun and they headed for the elevator.

They pressed themselves into the corner as the enamelled elevator rattled downwards and hissed to a halt. The doors opened with a tired sigh and the silent emptiness laughed at them.

It was two hours before they breathed freely again. Two hours of mind sharpening anxiety as they eased open door after door, expecting every time to hear sirens or feel the sting of a bullet. Two hours of constant apprehension; two hours of concentrated tension; two hours of sweat-soaking, nerve racking, mouth-drying, diarrhoea-inducing fear. Fear that every camera was eyeing them; every step might break an invisible beam; every door would be alarmed; every movement picked up by a sensor; and every sound heard by a hidden microphone. Room after room had shown them it's empty face. Desks, chairs, filing cabinets, and all the detritus of a modern office complex filled each room. And at least a hundred computers idled in neutral, their engines ticking over with a constant buzz—all that was missing were the drivers.

"Nobody here," said Bliss checking his wrist before realizing he'd left his broken watch in his suit pocket.

"It's half past four in the morning," said Yolanda as they stood back at the lift. "What shall we do now?"

He was looking very thoughtful. "What day is it?"

"Sunday," she replied confidently, then corrected herself, "No, I think it's Monday."

"It must be Monday," he said, quickly working it out for himself. "Do you realize we haven't slept in a bed since last Thursday."

"Well there's no beds here, Dave."

He nodded, "They must work here and sleep in another building. We'll have to wait 'til they arrive."

"What about the guard?" she cried in alarm.

Both had tried to forget the nearly-naked youth tied in the truck and the trace of a grin broke through Bliss' serious expression. "We could brush him down, give him his gun back and say sorry."

Yolanda shot him a look, then smiled. "You're joking?"

"Come on," he laughed, "I've got an idea."

An hour later they snuggled together in a wide ventilation duct above the computer room. The guard, still bound and gagged, was lying in the bottom of the elevator shaft. "He's quite safe," insisted Bliss. "Although God knows what will happen when the day shift arrive and find him missing."

"Let's get some sleep," suggested Yolanda with a yawn and she nuzzled into his shoulder and instantly nodded off.

The scream of a jet engine shook them awake a few hours later as the air conditioner revved up for the day.

"Stay here," he whispered, then inched his way along the duct above the computer rooms to peer down through each of the gratings into the offices below. Hundreds of fingers were flying across keyboards, and technicians in white coats were fiddling with bits of machinery as they constructed and de-constructed computers. In one of the small rooms Bliss found what he was looking for—a familiar face—a face so typically British that it had to belong to one of the snatched men.

"Psst, psst," hissed Bliss.

"What the ..."

"Shhh," he whispered, "I'm up here in the air duct. Don't say anything. Just nod."

The head nodded.

"Can you talk?"

The head swayed slowly from side to side. Then the man picked up a pen and wrote on a large scratch pad. "Wait a minute."

"Peter," he shouted across the room with a distinctly Welsh accent.

"Yeah."

"I'm going for a crap boy'o. Back in ten minutes."

Peter's tone rose in confusion. "Why are you telling me? I hope you don't want me to come and wipe your bum?"

The man was still writing. "Toilet—second room on left."

"Won't be long, Peter," he continued, for the benefit of the guards, as he got up to leave.

Bliss slithered through the duct and sniffed out the toilet, the rustling of his clothes swallowed in the gush of forced air. The man was already sitting, the top of his bald head pixilated by the grid of the register. "We've come to rescue you," Bliss whispered.

"Who the hell are you?" he asked, head down, eyes boring at the door.

"Detective Inspector Bliss, Metropolitan Police.

The man was on his way out—set-up on his mind. "Yeah right—you expect me to believe that?"

"I am ..." started Bliss, then paused, realizing that nothing he could say would persuade a determined disbeliever. "Tell me what I would need to do to convince you," he continued, recalling his hostage negotiation training seminars.

The man re-sat, stumped, then took a chance. "O.K., say I believe you. How do we get out?"

That's a good point, thought Bliss, realizing he had no idea. "How many of you?"

"That depends."

Bliss didn't understand and said so.

"There's eight," the voice continued, the owner quickly glancing up at him, "But they might not want to escape."

Bliss' voice rose incredulously, "Why?"

His eyes returned fearfully to the door. "Because of the Americans."

Six had escaped, five men and a woman, world experts in their field. People who could coherently discuss data encryption, system analysis, and advanced programming in their sleep.

"What happened?" asked Bliss, then wished he hadn't.

"Do you remember that downed pilot they tortured during the war. They showed him on T.V.?"

"Yes," Bliss mumbled, wincing at the memory of the beaten pilot who'd been propped in front of the world's T.V. cameras wearing a face more mangled than a horrifically mutilated horror mask.

"He looked good compared to what they'd done to the Americans," he continued, adding, "Not the woman; they left her face alone, but she couldn't stand up."

From his perch in the ventilation shaft Bliss couldn't see the terror in the man's face as he recalled the occasion. The six Americans had been caught the same day they had escaped. Three days later the Welshman and his English colleagues were ushered into a room, "Come and say goodbye to your friends," the Iraqi officer had said.

The Americans were propped upright in armchairs, their pulped faces staring blankly through slits in puffy eyelids; smashed hands and arms flopped at crazy angles in their laps. Few could speak and none had anything to say. One tried a smile of recognition but managed a toothless bloody grin.

"Say goodbye," the officer ordered and the sorry group mumbled obediently, "Goodbye." Then the guards entered and carried the shattered bodies outside.

The officer prodded them forward. "Come and wave," he said.

"They shot them one at a time," continued the fragmented face peering up at Bliss, pleading for some kind of help, "and they made us watch until the only the woman was left." His eyes closed, trying to shut out the images but he kept talking. "They stoned her to death," he said, as tears squeezed from between his tightly closed lids. "An' that bloody bastard of an officer said, 'We always stone whores to death.' And Mary, the Englishwoman, said 'Doris wasn't a whore.'" He opened his eyes and stared at Bliss through the grating. "Do you know what that bastard said? He said that any woman who screwed forty soldiers in one night was a whore. Then he picked up a rock and hit her right in the face." The tears were streaming down his face. "Sorry," he mumbled.

Bliss found himself choking back tears. "You've got to get out. They know we're onto them."

The man wasn't listening, the horrendous images torturing his mind were too powerful to let go. "Mary killed herself the next day," he rambled, as if Bliss had not spoken. "Wired herself up to the power supply and switched it on. Blew every fuse in the place."

Bliss tried again. "You must escape."

"Ripped her eye out," continued the man, his brain still struggling with Doris' nightmare. "Then they all picked up stones—like a coconut shy at the fair—but the coconut was Doris' head."

"Sir," tried Bliss, more forcefully. "They will kill us all if we don't get out."

"I know," he replied, as if part of his brain had been listening all along. "We should try to get out. I'll talk to the others tonight and give you a decision tomorrow."

"Tomorrow!" exclaimed Bliss in a strangled shout.

"It's the best I can do. We get an hour together each evening in our sleeping quarters. I can't talk to the others during the day."

Bliss was panicking. "What about lunchtime?"

"No go. They bring it round to us."

Bliss suddenly realised he and Yolanda had no food and little water. Neither did he have any idea how they were going to escape. "Can you get any food and drink for us?" he asked. "We didn't expect to spend another night here."

"I'll leave some in my filing cabinet," he replied, pulling up his pants, then he pointedly flushed the toilet and was gone.

# *chapter seventeen*

 

"It's the Home Secretary's Principal Private Secretary." The sergeant enunciated carefully as he handed the phone to Superintendent Edwards.

"Shit!" breathed Edwards.

"Edwards?" the manicured voice queried as he put the phone to his ear.

"Yes, Sir."

"Glad we caught you so early," the P.P.S. continued chattily, as if he were an old friend. "Thought you might be in late this morning after such a busy week-end. The minister would like to have a quick word with you, if that's alright—is this a secure line?"

"Yes, Sir," he replied, flushing the sergeant out with a wave.

"Hold on, I'll transfer you."

The phone hummed hollowly for fifteen seconds and Edwards began to wonder if he'd been disconnected. Then a click heralded the minister's bouncy voice. "Well done Edwards, I understand your men did a good job with that LeClarc fellow. What happened by the way?"

"Well, we had a bit of a chase, Sir. The air-sea rescue people dropped one of our chaps onto a trawler off the Dutch coast. We'd tried getting a man aboard from a high speed launch, but the trawler was all over the place with no one at the helm."

"Sounds like quite a caper old chap."

Edwards chuckled as demanded. "Anyway, we got LeClarc back, but, unfortunately, the kidnappers had already got away."

"So you didn't actually catch anyone then?"

"No, Sir, the kidnappers ..."

"Superintendent Edwards," the voice broke in coolly.

"Yes, Sir,"

"Look, we think it might be in everybody's interest to forget all this nonsense about kidnappers."

"I'm not with you, Sir, there was definitely ..."

The minister cut him short, "Superintendent, I'm probably not making myself clear. Let me explain ..." he paused, "no I've a better idea, why not meet me in my club for a spot of lunch. Twelve o'clock at Queens'. Is that alright with you?"

"Fine, Sir ..." But the phone had already clicked, chopping off his reply.


"Glad you could make it," said the minister, pretending Edwards had a choice. The table, recessed into an obscure nook, had been specifically requested, and the minister guided him to a chair. "Had a bit of a bump, have we?" he continued, noticing the swelling around Edwards' lip where King had thumped him.

"Walked into a thick plank," he replied, keeping very close to the truth, as he saw it.

"You order exactly what you'd like," said the minister, looking over the top of his spectacles. "Personally I shall start with a spot of the Paté Maison, they do it awfully well with just enough truffle to make it interesting—know what I mean?"

Edwards had absolutely no idea. "Of course, Sir, sounds good to me."

"Then," he said, scanning the beautiful calligraphy of the menu in its gilt frame, "I think the lobster." He looked up with a smile, "Although you might not want more fish if you've been in Holland for a few days."

"No, Sir, the lobster would be fine."

The headwaiter, hovering obsequiously, swooped in to take the order the moment the decision had been made.

The wine came almost immediately, pre-ordered to give it an opportunity to breathe; a vintage Chateau bottled Burgundy. "Nothing special," according to the minister, obviously relying on his department's entertainment budget.

"So," the minister leaned forward conspiratorially, "down to business." His deeply shadowed eyes roamed the surroundings. "This is completely off the record," he began, then paused, waiting for an acknowledgement.

Edwards nodded, "Naturally."

"Good," he said, beckoning him closer across the table with an almost imperceptible crook of his index finger. "Strictly between you and I," he paused, ratchetting up Bliss' discomfort. "And if I discover you've repeated any of it, I'll deny every word and cause you an awful lot of problems. Do you understand?"

A tic twitched Edwards' left temple causing a blink. "Yes, Sir," he gulped.

"Good, good. Well you'll understand our situation better when I've filled you in. More wine?" he enquired, downing most of his first glass in one gulp.

Edwards felt like saying, "For God's sake get on with it man," but settled for the wine.

With a final check to ensure they were not being overheard, the Minister started. "We've known about these ..." he paused, searching for a suitable euphemism for kidnap victims, then started again, "We've known about these chappies for sometime. The Yanks cottoned onto it after they'd lost several of their top people. The trouble was we weren't sure what was happening at first. There was always some plausible explanation; a body would turn up, or they'd be blown to bits in front of witnesses. A couple of them were in that plane that blew up over the Atlantic, one of ours and a Yank. Eventually we put two and two together and realised it was just too much of a coincidence."

What was too much of a coincidence, wondered Edwards, completely in the dark, and who are, "We:" Special Branch, MI5, MI6 or some other government spy service too secret to even have a designation. "I'm not really with you ..." he started but the minister silenced him with a twitch of the head and a warning look. The hors-d'oeuvres had arrived.

Once the waiter had moved away the minister busied himself picking out the bits of truffle. "Why do they insist on overdoing the fungus?" he complained rhetorically. Suddenly aware of Edwards' presence he looked up from his task and started talking again, still dissecting the paté, still hunting truffle. "We're pretty certain that the other side have got them," he said in a doom-laden tone. Then, concentrating furiously, he scraped de-truffled paté onto a sliver of toast, took a bite, and closed his eyes. A rapturous expression worked its way over his face as the aroma flooded his mouth and he relaxed with a long, satisfied, "Mmmm."

Edwards' impatience got the better of him, "Sir."

The minister pulled himself sharply back. "The point is we need to keep the whole thing under our hats. We can't afford to let word leak out that these ..." he paused and looked up, "that these chappies are still around."

Edwards was no wiser and his puzzled frown clearly gave him away.

"I can see you're not quite with me, Superintendent. Let me put it another way. If word got out that any of these chappies were actually working for the other side, it would cause chaos. Every system they've ever worked on would be vulnerable."

Edwards was catching on. "But surely, all we have to do is change passwords and alter the systems."

"I know that Superintendent, and so do you, but Joe Public doesn't know that. If the man-in-the-street got wind their bloody piggy banks might not be safe, or the other side might be listening to their phones or reading their e-mails, all hell would break loose. God knows what would happen to the stock markets and oil prices."

"I see," said Edwards. "You believe public confidence would be jeopardized if they knew top people were missing, even if they weren't in a position to do anything."

The minister gave a smile that said, "Good boy," then replied, "Actually we think that's precisely what the other side's playing at. You see, it might be difficult for these chappies to break into our systems, even though they are top people. But once we admit that the other side even have them, the damage is done."

The waiter interrupted, "Everything to your liking, Sirs?"

"Too much truffle in the paté again, Phillips," whinged the minister. Phillips was waiting; he got the same complaint every week. "I shall have a word with the chef, Sir."

"Thank you, Phillips."

The lobster, smothered in a thick cream sauce with a crust of Stilton cheese was, according to the smiling minister, pure cholesterol. "It's alright as long as you eat plenty of veggies," he said, sliding the broccoli off to one side, pulling a face.

"Sir," enquired Edwards, leaning forward, "Can I ask how many they have?"

"No idea," he replied succinctly. "But between you and me we believe they've got at least twenty—maybe more. The Yanks have lost quite a few, but they've managed to keep it quiet. The widows have all been happy— as happy as widows can be I suppose. We've smoothed things over with the odd awkward coroner. If that King fellow hadn't tipped us off about LeClarc, he would have been grabbed and it would have just been put down as someone missing at sea." He stopped long enough for a couple of mouthfuls of lobster, then carefully scrutinized the august room before canting across the table with a serious eye. "Tell me Superintendent: Does LeClarc have any idea he was going to be kidnapped?"

"No, Sir ..." started Edwards, but the minister silenced him with a finger.

"Think carefully before answering, Superintendent. Lives hang in the balance."

Edwards obligingly put on a thoughtful face for a second before confirming, "I'm certain he knows nothing, Sir. He did ask about the strange men on the trawler, but we didn't let on who they were."

"Perfect, perfect. And what about King? Can you keep him quiet about all of this—national interest, that sort of thing? Maybe we could give him some sort of award."

"Um ... um," Edwards tried to butt in.

The minister warmed to his idea. "I like it. I'll get someone to work on that right away. Nothing too fancy, give him an O.B.E. or something for unspecified services. Anybody asks, just lower your tone and tell 'em it's all hush hush."

Edwards swallowed hard, keeping his mouth shut.

"You could probably find him a job somewhere, if he wants it. Sounds a bright sort of chap. Got a police background, hasn't he?"

"I believe so, Sir, " said Edwards giving nothing away, thinking: Fat chance.

"Good, good. Well, like I say, I'll get someone working on it. The main thing is to keep it all under our hats."

"Sir, can I ask a question, Sir?"

"'Course you can old chap."

"Who is the other side, Sir. Do we know?"

"No idea. Thought it was the Ruskies at first, but they couldn't afford it. Christ, did you see their last rocket launch? They all sat around in their woolly coats 'cos they couldn't afford to put the heating on. It could be the Chinks, they're years behind us. Could even be some crazy African country that fancies itself. The Yanks reckon it could be the Iraqis, but they're paranoid about the Iraqis—if Saddam Hussein breaks wind they say he's developing toxic gas—and they freaked out about the Iraqis getting their hands on a ton of those computer game things."

Edwards choked. "Iraq, Sir?"

"Precisely, Superintendent. That's what I said. Apparently they bought a few thousand kiddie computer toys for Christmas, but the Yanks reckon they could turn 'em into guided missiles ... Humph!" he snorted his disdain, though Bliss was unsure of the target of the minister's disapproval—Iraqis, Americans, or guided missiles, he wondered.

"The Yanks reckoned they were onto something when the Iraqis booted out the U.N. Inspectors. You know, the chaps looking for Bubonic Plague and chemical weapons after the Kuwait affair."

Edwards nodded, not trusting himself to speak, but he remembered.

"But keeping a load of foreign computer boffins under wraps is much more difficult. I don't reckon they're up to it myself. What do you say?"

"Well, Sir ..."

"Quite, Superintendent, my views exactly." Then he sat back, relaxed and changed the topic. "So, you got all men back safe and sound?"

"A sergeant broke his wrist on the ship."

"Clumsy—that all?"

Edwards poised, a large piece of lobster hovering in front of his face, kept his face blank in thought. "That's all, Sir."

"Well done, Superintendent, I'll even have a word with someone at the Home Office. See what we can do about your promotion—must be due."

Edwards swallowed hard, saying nothing, changing his expression to one of modest gratitude.

"Excellent, excellent," said the minister. "Now for dessert I can recommend the crème bruleè." Then he leaned across the table, glanced suspiciously left and right, and whispered, "Steer clear of the fruit salad, half of it comes out of a bloody can."

# chapter eighteen

"Roger Francis LeClarc." The court usher's voice boomed around the packed courtroom. An expectant hush fell over the crowd. Experienced specta- tors swivelled into position for a clearer view of Roger. First-timers, lured by the media—"*Internet sex-slave chained in dungeon,*"—craned like kids at a monkey house, hoping to glimpse something bestial. Out of the public's view, a door, at the bottom of the stairs leading to the prisoner's dock, clicked open. A large white fig- ure was prodded into motion by a smartly uniformed officer. "Wait," he commanded as he turned and locked the door behind him, then he nudged the listless figure up the stairs. Roger, wearing a one-piece, white paper coverall, rose like a voluminous spectre into the dock.

The hospital had been unable to supply anything more suitable than the disposable paper suit because of his bulk; the police didn't care—the appearance of weird- ness only strengthened their case. His parents, on the downhill slope of an emotional roller-coaster, would have brought him some decent clothes had they thought, but their elation at his rescue had swung from despair to disgust, and their concern had sunk in confusion.

"Stand up please, Mr. LeClarc," the court clerk instructed.

Roger was already standing, doubled over with heart-rending sobs, and the crisp suit rustled alarmingly as he pulled himself upright, his head still deeply buried in his hands. Then the guard roughly pulled the hands away, leaving the tears to dribble down the bloated face.

The clerk raised his eyebrows and put the inflection of a question into his voice. "Roger Francis LeClarc?"

Roger dumbly looked across the courtroom to his mother, head down, face in her handbag, and sought guidance and comfort.— *"Never mind our Roger. Here's a bar of chocolate, you'll soon be better."*

She didn't look up—*How could you do this to me you little bugger?*

"Are you Roger Francis LeClarc?" the clerk tried again, knowing very well the man in the prisoner's box could be no other.

A dozen journalist's pens doodled as he considered his reply, but Roger's full name, address, and date of birth had already been circulated to the twenty reporters crammed into the press box, the twenty or so others in the public gallery, and the tail-end-charlies barred to the street with their cameras and camera crews.

The "whirr" of the electric clock high on the wall above the magistrate pierced the air for five long seconds before Roger admitted he was indeed the man whose name had been called. Even then his sniffled "Yes" was heard only by those closest.

The spark of a courtroom buzz was quickly stamped out by the clerk, "What is your address?"

Roger tried, several times, but his head swam, and the information sank in a whirlpool of unfamiliar images. The clerk helped him out. "Do you live at 34 Junction Road, Watford?"

Forty reporter's pens scribbled unnecessarily. His little terraced house in Junction Road had been besieged by cameramen, reporters, and rubber-neckers ever since the call for a doctor had rung through the airwaves late on Friday evening.

Roger wiped his eyes. "Yes."

The legal rigmarole of reading out the charges took the clerk several minutes. Kidnap, unlawful detention, sexual assault, assault occasioning grievous bodily harm, and attempted murder were high on the list, and a few minor offences were thrown in for good measure.

"Do you understand the charges?"

"I didn't mean to ..."

The clerk stopped him mid-statement. "This is not a trial, Mr. LeClarc, all his Worship wants to know is: Do you understand the charges. Yes or no?"

Roger's lawyer helped him out with a deep nod. "Yes," mumbled Roger, though in truth his mind was still at sea.

The Crown prosecutor, a weedy man with comically-large glasses, overly-flamboyant teeth seeking to escape, and strands of lank brown hair flopping over his face, leaned forward to examine his notes, then rose to his feet and waited while the audience settled. Satisfied, finally, he breathed deeply and let his eyes dart between the clerk and the Magistrate, ensuring they too were ready, pens poised. His squeaky voice matched his shrew-like appearance. "The defendant has been charged with a number of serious crimes and, at this time particular moment in time ..." he paused, eyes everywhere as if looking for a way out, then finished with, "the Crown is applying for a remand in custody for seven days."

Then he sat. That was it. An entire performance in one sentence.

Roger's defence lawyer was even more succinct. Rising to his lofty six feet six inches, he stilled the whole room with his weighty presence and boomed, "No objection," with such confidence that half the people present would have sworn he'd declared his client. "Not guilty."

The lay magistrate, a butcher in real life, looked down the barrel of his nose and put a bead on Roger. "Do you wish to say anything at this time, Mr. LeClarc?"

Roger sniffed very noisily, causing a few grimaces, then muttered something unintelligible through sobs.

"I can't hear you," said the Magistrate turning an ear.

Roger wiped his nose with his hand and mingled snot with tears. He tried again, blubbering uncontrollably.

"What did he say?" asked the Magistrate of the clerk.

"He said, 'I love her,' Sir."

"He's got a bloody funny way of showing it," muttered the Magistrate, much louder than intended, and shot an angered look at the press gallery that said, *"If any of you scum print that I'll have you for contempt of court."*

"Take him down," ordered the clerk, and Roger's ghostlike figure drifted back down the prisoner's staircase.

Roger's parents, clinging tightly together, were pounced on by half a dozen cameramen as they tried to slip out the back door a few minutes later. A seemingly sympathetic policeman had assured them they would go unnoticed if they took that route. But the same policeman, with a sly grin, had tipped off one of the reporters just a few seconds later. He had a daughter Trudy's age.

Camera's clicked and several cassette recorders were shoved in Mrs. LeClarc's face.

"Your comments, Mrs. LeClarc?" was one of the many demands flung at her.

"Our Roger's innocent," she screeched, with a scowl nasty enough to guarantee a spot on the front page of several tabloids, captioned: *"Internet fiend's mother say's innocent."* The power headline *"Netted"* would be reserved for Roger's photo, as soon as a friendly cop could be induced to cough up a copy and, should Trudy die, some assistant editor would torture the language yet again.

Trudy's mortality was problematic; her fractured body hesitating somewhere between life and death. Less than a mile from the courthouse, Peter and Lisa sat next to each other by the side of her bed, hanging onto every faint breath the scrawny pale body took. The array of machines, monitors, and tubes had become no less frightening as Sunday had dissolved seamlessly into Monday. They had slept little, woke guiltily after the briefest cat-nap, and spoke only of Trudy. Even the staples of small talk—movies seen, books read, holidays taken or planned, the state of the weather—were deemed inappropriate.

Margery had flitted in and out all day Sunday, toting food, messages of sympathy and support, and more flowers, before getting the train back to Leyton in the evening so she could feed Trudy's cat. Peter had given her the train fair, and a handful of money to buy food and anything else she needed. "Be very careful," he had said earnestly, as if she faced some terrifyingly perilous journey.

Just after they had politely refused an offer of breakfast from a trainee nurse —*"How can we eat?"*—a policeman they'd not met before interrupted their vigil to tell them about Roger's up-coming court appearance.

"It's only a remand hearing," he'd said, trying not to sound enthusiastic. "It'll just take a few minutes."

There was no argument, neither of them would leave Trudy's bedside. Although, they agreed, they would at some time want to confront the person who had done this to their daughter, now was not the time. The young officer's shoulders slumped in relief. The prospect of having to deal with a distraught mother in the face of a determined press corps was not one he relished.

Doctors came and went, nurses fiddled and fussed. But, apart from an encouraging smile and an occasional sympathetic word, nobody gave any indication as to what they thought about Trudy's chances of recovery. One doctor had lingered long enough to make a few sweeping generalizations. "These things sometimes take weeks or even months to sort themselves out," he had said, then added, "A coma is the way a body deals with severe trauma. It is just like a long sleep."

"Why won't she wake up then?" asked Lisa, with a certain naïvety.

"She's still tired," replied the doctor as if addressing a child.

"I won't be a minute Luv," said Peter, giving his exwife's hand a tender squeeze, before slipping out of the intensive care cubicle after the doctor left.

Two minutes later he was back.

"Have you called Joy?" Lisa enquired solemnly, managing to name Peter's second wife without contempt.

He nodded. "Uh, um."

"Is she coming to visit?"

Peter's concerned face turned away, then he looked back and came out with the truth. "She said she won't come if you're here. She's never forgiven you for the curry." Then his face warmed in ironic memory as he recalled the incident in the Indian restaurant.

"I'm staying, Peter," she said, without rancour.

"I don't expect you to leave," he replied, squeezing her hand again.

Lisa sank back into the chair and found no comfort in its padded seat. It lacked the viciousness of the old wooden kitchen chair. Although she still got cramps from continual sitting, she felt no great attachment to it. Peter made her get up and walk around the room whenever her saw pain on her face, and she had even willed herself out of the chair from time to time, when she had felt herself drifting off to sleep.

"I'll wake you if anything happens," Peter had promised on numerous occasions, but the mere thought of sleep was repugnant. Only by remaining awake could she be certain to keep Trudy's spirit alive. Succumbing to sleep was tantamount to abandoning her to God-knows-where.


Yolanda and Bliss were having no difficulty sleeping, in fact they slept most of Monday as they lay side by side in the ventilation duct somewhere under the Iraqi mountains. Shafts of light filtering up through vents from the rooms below illuminated the maze of tunnels with a metallic glow that was both soothing and comforting. The low-pitched hum of the fan and the constant flow of warm moist air lulled them through hours of restful slumber.

"What's the time, Yolanda?" Bliss whispered in her ear as he awoke. She stretched noisily and Bliss cupped his hand over her mouth to stifle her wakening yawn.

"What time is it?" she asked through his fingers.

"I asked first," he muttered, found her wrist and brought it to his face. "Seven forty-five."

"Have they gone yet? I'm hungry," she breathed into his ear.

"I'll look," he mouthed silently.

He was back in a minute, the tinny scratching noises sounding like a herd of mice as he scrabbled through the ducts. "They're just getting ready to leave," he whispered. "I want to see what happens at the elevator when they go," he added, scuttling off in the other direction.

"One guard gets all the prisoners together in the elevator," he said, on his return. "There are still a few people around, cleaners I think, but we should be able to get out soon."

It was nine-thirty before the dimming lights and the dying fan told them the staff were leaving, and another half an hour before they took the plunge and dropped down through a vent inside a store cupboard. The Welshman had left enough food for an army in the battered metal filing cabinet, but they had to drink the water from a tap in the washroom. As they sat in a couple of cheap plastic chairs, munching a pile of goat meat sandwiches, there was only one question on their minds and Yolanda asked first, "How are we going to get out Dave?"

Bliss had the germ of an idea but was still developing it when a sudden noise caught their attention and jerked them upright in their seats.

He winced. "What was that?"

They listened.

"The elevator?" she suggested.

"Footsteps," breathed Bliss, "Quick."

The rustling of wrapping paper seemed deafening as he grabbed the sandwiches and threw them back into the filing cabinet. "Get under the desk," he whispered, his eyes desperately scouring the nearly naked room for a hiding place.

Orders were being bellowed, doors flung open, men shouted.

He ducked behind the filing cabinet, she scrunched herself into a ball under one of the kneehole desks.

"I can see you," she hissed, peeking out.

He sized the other desk—too small.

Flicking off his gun's safety catch he heard Yolanda do the same.

Gruff foreign voices were getting closer. They're searching for the missing guard, he realized, as he eyed the panelled ceiling—too high. He wasted seconds trying the other desk.

"I can still see you," she hissed as his knees protruded.

Doors were banging open all around. Get behind the door, he thought, and rushed toward it. Two seconds later he changed his mind—they were bound to check. His brain was swirling with the white noise of indecision—there was nowhere to hide; there was no solution.

The door to a nearby office flew open with a crash and a flurry of words. "We're next, he thought, standing in the middle of the room, turning one way then the other, stunned to inactivity by overwhelming fear. Then he pulled himself together. "Stay still," he barked at Yolanda, and, gun at the ready, marched smartly into the corridor, slammed the door behind him and stepped across to the room opposite. His ill-fitting guard's uniform attracted no attention as he strode swiftly through the room and out into another corridor opposite the toilets where he'd talked to the prisoner. His shaking gun couldn't have hit a barn let alone a door as he slipped unseen into the toilet, dashed into a cubicle and vomited until his stomach was empty.

Ten minutes later he was still there, standing on the lavatory seat, his eyes and gun focussed over the top of the stall door. The voices had drifted away. The footsteps had wandered off. Fighting back the sickly bile taste in his mouth, he kept his statuesque pose on the pedestal for a further five minutes, forcing himself to count every second, fully cognisant of the old hide-and-seek trick of pretending to go while leaving a fifth-columnist in hiding who pops out and shouts, "Fooled yah," just when you were convinced it was safe to emerge.

Cautiously, silently, Bliss crept back to the office, the blood deafeningly pulsing in his ears; then he saw the office door—wide open. His heart sagged—maybe I've got the wrong office—willing it to be the case. He raced inside: Right office, right filing cabinet, right desk. But everything was wrong—she was gone. His mind swam, his legs buckled and he steadied himself against the desk. That's why they left so quickly— they've taken her for questioning. He retched at the thought. "Do something you idiot," the voice in his mind insisted, but what?

I should have warned her, he thought, recalling he had not told her what they had done to the American woman. He hadn't seen the point in both of them being scared to death.

"Move," said the voice. "Shoot your way out. Take some of the bastards with you; don't just stand there."

He moved. Striding offensively down the corridor, he checked the gun again and headed for the elevator. His hand reached out for the call button. Here goes, he thought, then a noise snapped his finger away. Diving for cover behind a totally inadequate chair, he curled into a ball and did his best stop the gun shaking. Nothing happened; the empty corridor hummed quietly with the electric purr of lights and computers, but whatever made him jump was silent. The only thing jumping was his pulse. He pulled himself together, uncoiled slowly, and warily moved back toward the elevator, then a call froze his tracks.

"Dave ... Over here?" Yolanda sang out from her hiding place behind a cupboard. Then she burst into a torrent of tears.

"I thought you were a guard," she sobbed into his chest as they hugged. "I was just going to get the elevator to ..."

"I was sure they'd got you," he mumbled, clinging tightly to her as he blinked back the tears.

"I thought they'd got you too."

Their tears mingled with laughter as they clutched each other and made their way back to the office.

They finished most of the sandwiches in the relative safety of the air duct and Bliss told her the full story of the Americans.

"We have to get them out, Dave," she said, very subdued.

"I know," he replied. "But how?"

The night passed slowly, ideas came and went. Fear flowed through their veins at the realization that every conceivable plan had serious flaws and horrendous risks. There were so many unanswerable questions: "Where are we? Where are the guards? How many guards? Would they shoot on sight? How can we get out?"

"There was a gatehouse," offered Bliss, "We stopped on our way in."

"I remember."

"But we've no idea where we are, we might come up in the middle of Baghdad."

"No," she shot back. "We would have heard traffic noise before we stopped."

"I don't remember hearing any city noises since we left the border."

"We're probably still in the northern mountains."

"That's why there was only one guard last night."

"My God!" cried Yolanda, "I'd forgotten all about him. He's still under the elevator."

After hearing of the treatment meted out to the Americans, Bliss had closed his mind to the soldier. "Might be dead or escaped," he replied with unconcerned casualness.

"We could find out," she suggested.

Worming their way along the air ducts they eventually reached the elevator shaft and Bliss peered into the semi-darkness. "I think he's still there," he said, clambering down the maintenance ladder.

"Yolanda," he called in a whispered shout. "Get some water and the rest of the sandwiches."

She was back in a minute and Bliss held the guard's own gun to his head as he removed the gag. The young man hungrily scoffed the food, fearful Bliss would snatch it away. Then, with his shirt tied back into a gag, they tested the ropes on his wrists and legs and clambered back up the shaft, looking high above them at the underside of the elevator cabin.

"I've got it," Bliss whispered excitedly and his voice echoed eerily around the shaft.

"What?"

"I know how to get us out."

With fearful expectancy, the Welsh computer expert checked the filing cabinet on his return to the office the following morning. "The food's gone," he whispered to Peter, his colleague, but found no satisfaction in acknowledging the fact that he hadn't imagined the voice in the air duct.

"What are you going to tell him?"

"The truth," he replied, "Everyone's too bloody scared to escape."

"He'll be pissed off."

"His problem."

"My wife will be pissed off as well."

"Bollocks, she thinks she buried you six months ago. Who's going to tell her any different?"

Peter had a far away look in his eye and a wistful edge to his voice, "I wish I could get back. I really miss her, and the kids."

"We all do. But the chance of getting us out of here is ..." He turned to his keyboard, "Let me work it out."

Reaching over he clicked on the screen, then almost fell out of his chair.

*"Hi. This is your friendly neighbourhood cop. We're taking you home tonight. Bring a picnic and be ready to run."*

His finger jabbed the delete key not a moment too soon as one of the Iraqi technicians entered the room.

"Everything is alright, I think, Gentlemen?" enquired the Iraqi, attempting to perfect his English.

They nodded silently and started work.


The elevator doors opened for them on time as usual at eight o'clock that evening. The regular guard, moustachioed, with a ferocious overhanging brow, stood with his arms folded as they lined up: Eight men in an assortment of ill-fitting clothes, unshaven, tired and pallid from months of working in artificial light without exercise. A day on tender-hooks fruitlessly awaiting Bliss' hushed voice to filter down through the grating in the ceiling had taken a further toll on the Welshman and his face was drawn with the strain. The guard counted them one by one as they entered the elevator. Satisfied with his flock he stepped after them and pressed the "up" button. Three seconds later, the elevator jerked to a halt and hung suspended. Exasperation showed on his face as he picked up the red telephone and pushed the emergency button. Nothing happened. He stabbed the button again. Nothing. Then he started fighting with it, banging and jabbing it over and over again. Fully absorbed, he neither heard nor saw the emergency escape panel in the roof sliding open.

Bliss dropped on top of the guard with such ferocity that he ripped the emergency phone out of the wall and the cleanly snipped wires showed why he had received no reply.

"Quick," Bliss shouted to the stunned audience. "Who wants to be a guard?"

Nobody moved.

"Come on, help me get his clothes off."

The men were petrified, fearing it was an elaborate trap. Yolanda's voice called from above, "Quick, help him or we'll all be killed."

Two men leapt to action, stripping the guard in seconds and manhandling his body up through the hatch to Yolanda. The Welshman slipped on the jacket and grabbed the gun, then Yolanda released the brake and jumped down to join them. Bliss prodded the "up" button and the elevator started ascending again. "How many guards at the top?" he asked, his eyes seeking contact with any of the prisoners.

"One usually," replied one of the men, then he stared accusingly at the Welshman, "I thought we agreed not to escape."

The Welshman shrugged, the matter was out of his hands.

Bliss quickly gave them instructions. "Walk out normally and one of you fall over in front of the guard."

It worked like a charm. The guard spontaneously bent to steady the falling man and Bliss smashed him hard on the back of the head. Now they had another uniform and, with the guard's nearly naked body in the elevator, Bliss stabbed the "down" button.

"Come on," called Yolanda, throwing her shawl over her head, leading the charge toward the garage.

The Welshman grabbed Bliss' arm. "Wait a minute boy's, we decided we wouldn't risk escaping."

Bliss felt a little exaggeration would not go amiss "It's too late for that—we've already killed three guards."

"Oh my God! Have you any idea what they'll do to us?"

"Only if we get caught," shouted Yolanda still running.

"This place is a fortress," continued the Welshman, then his face brightened in optimism. "You've got helicopters, right?"

Bliss shook his head.

"Well you'd better have half the British army at the gates or we may as well give up now."

"Leave it to us, Sir," Bliss replied, with a confidence implying, "I have all the answers, I am a policeman."

"Will there be anyone in the garage?" he asked as they rushed down the corridor"

"Not usually," replied a Liverpudlian, his singsong accent instantly recognisable by any Beatles fan.

The garage was deserted and a different truck had

replaced the one in which they had arrived; another secret compartment speaking of another victim.

What could have been a dignified retreat turned into a disorganised rout as men were coerced into the truck by Bliss, Yolanda, and Owain, the Welshman. One petrified man had to be manhandled aboard—his arm twisted painfully behind him as he fought against freedom.

"Everybody in," shouted Bliss, slapping the button to raise the giant steel shutter, then he slammed the door on the trailer's secret compartment, leaped into the cab, fired up the engine, and fought with the gear lever to get it into reverse.

"Driven one of these before have you?" asked Owain sceptically.

"Of course I have," he lied.

"Try pressing that red button there then," he pointed. Bliss pressed and the gear slipped neatly into place.

"Now for the tricky bit," said Bliss, once the truck was outside. Running back into the garage he attacked the electrical control box which powered the big door, looping wires around the steel rail on which the door ran. "Here goes," he muttered, hitting the "door close" button, running as it started its descent. Banging the truck into gear, he jerked the rig crazily along the road as he tried to get the hang of the clutch.

"What are you going to do now?" asked the Welshman.

"That depends," said Bliss.

"Depends on what?"

Behind them an immense blue fireball ignited the garage with a loud "crack" and every light in the complex went out.

"On that," said Bliss triumphantly.

"Blimey, what happened."

"I think they've blown a fuse," he said, grinning for the first time in two days.

The main gatehouse was closer than Bliss had anticipated and the giant truck was still kangarooing wildly as they approached the tubular barriers. An emergency light illuminated the box itself and a guard jabbered frantically into a mute phone. Two more guards were struggling with a huge steel gate, desperately trying to manhandle it shut behind the barriers.

"Look out," yelled Bliss, as the flash of a pistol spurted from the hand of one of the men. "We'll have to crash the barrier. Get down; cover your head."

The giant truck lurched toward the barrier in a series of violent hops as Bliss fought with the controls. He was in the wrong gear but couldn't find the right one. The guard who'd fired was frantically yanking the gate and already had it halfway across the road. Bliss jammed his foot on the accelerator and aimed straight at the steel barrier. The truck leaped ahead and wrenched the barrier out of its socket as easily as if it were a doll's arm, then it flung the heavy steel pole at the guard with such ferocity it nearly cut him in half.

"He's dead," shouted Bliss, without a second glance. The moment the huge steel barrier smacked into the body and crushed it against the gate, all life drained out of the bundle of flesh and bones and it flopped into a ragged heap. Bliss had never killed anyone before and drove pensively for a few seconds wondering why he felt no remorse.

"Where are we going then?" enquired the Welshman above the roar of the engine as Bliss found another gear and they sped away from the compound. There was only one road out of the place and Bliss was fighting to keep the truck on it. He had no idea where they were going but longed to be able to say, "Home."

"What are they doing at that place?" he yelled, ignoring the man's question.

"They're going to take over the world," Owain shouted, as if he were talking about some corporate merger plan. "Or at least that's what they're planning."

Bliss felt like saying, "Nonsense," but asked anyway, "How?"

The Welshman looked at him for a few seconds, balancing the pros and cons of telling or keeping his revelations for some more senior authority. He started with a question. "What's happens when there is a *coup d'etat*?"

Bliss turned to him blankly and the Welshman carried on, "What's the first thing the ringleaders do when some tin-pot dictator tries to overthrow some other tin-pot dictator?"

"Shoot them," shouted Bliss.

"No," then he paused, "Well they might do ... but first they seize the radio and TV stations."

The road started to climb, Bliss searched for a lower gear and the Welshman waited until the engine had stopped screaming. "They always take over the communication systems first," he continued, "You see, whoever controls information controls the country. Propaganda is everything. Look at the Gulf War when the Yanks made all that fuss about their bloody Patriot missiles knocking out the Scuds. It was a pack of lies; they didn't shoot down a single missile, but as long as the world, and the Iraqis, believed it, that was all that mattered."

Bliss hadn't heard about the missiles. "I thought the Patriots ..."

"Yeah, so did everyone else, Dave, apart from all the people who were blown to bits by the Scuds."

"I still don't understand what they're doing now," said Bliss, cresting a hill and ramming the gear stick into a different hole.

"They're planning revenge against the western world," he replied darkly.

"How?"

"They've got this grand scheme and if they pull it off, it'll be a real doozey."

"There's lights behind us," shouted Bliss anxiously.

"Well you didn't think they'd just let us go did you?"

"I thought we might get a good start. We'll never get away in this."

"What else have you got," snapped the Welshman angrily. "A bloody Ferrari?"

"There's another one," shrieked Bliss, noticing a second pair of headlights, and the truck started bouncing on the verge as his concentration drifted.

Owain shouted, "Look where you're going. I'll watch behind."

One set of headlights was quickly closing the gap as they climbed higher and slower. Bliss fought with yet another gear change to quell the engine's complaint, but as soon as he'd found the right gear, they crested the top of a rise and were barrelling downhill again.

"They're gaining on us," yelled the Welshman.

Bliss risked a look in the mirror. "At least they're not shooting."

"They might blast us with a bloody missile. They're crazy enough."

"They won't want to kill you. It cost them a lot of money to have you brought here and now they haven't got the Americans ... what's their plan of anyway?"

Owain pondered for a moment, trying to decide where to begin, then he started at the end. "They've got their hands on a super virus."

"Like AIDS?" queried Bliss.

The Welshman gave a look of astonishment, then realized it was just a lucky guess. "Yes," he replied, "It's exactly like AIDS to a computer."

"Wow!" exclaimed Bliss, impressed as much by his insight as the significance of the malaise.

Owain sneaked a quick look in the mirror. "They're right behind us," he said with panic in his voice.

Bliss was confident. "They won't shoot."

"I wouldn't bet on that, they've already got most of what they need." Then he stuck his head out of the window and quickly pulled it back. Fear strained his voice. "Dave, we're on the side of a bloody cliff. Keep away from the edge for God's sake."

Bliss could see it. They were on a narrow ledge cut into the mountain. On one side, the headlights lit a vertical wall of rock, on the other, a black void that could have been ten, a hundred or a thousand feet deep. He shot another look in the mirror and was horrified to see a set of lights right behind them. "Hold tight," he screamed and stood on the brake. The air brakes locked, the tires protested with a deafening screech, and the truck snaked and crashed sideways into the cliff face. Ragged boulders clawed at the side of the trailer, ripping out chunks of metal in a huge shower of sparks, lighting up the terrified face of the following driver.

The pursuing car couldn't stop. Despite the driver's frantic efforts he fishtailed wildly and was forced to start passing the trailer, only inches from the brink.

"Wait, wait," muttered Bliss to himself as he watched the car in the mirror. "Softly, softly catchee monkee," he continued as every nerve in his body strained.

"Now!" he yelled, as he thrust his foot back on the accelerator and wrenched at the wheel. The huge truck lunged forward, bounding back off the solid wall, heading toward the cliff edge, leaving the car nowhere to go. The Welshman screamed in terror as he saw the abyss approaching. Bliss reacted by spinning the wheel back again. The trailer's whiplash took a sideways kick at the car and sent it spinning off the edge in a spectacular dive, and a blaze of headlights lit a crazy path across the sky as the car somersaulted, flipping like a falling autumn leaf. Finally, it flattened itself, and its passengers, against the rocks two hundred feet below.

Bliss rammed his foot back on the brake and the truck slid to a stop as it rounded a bend. The screams of the four guards in the car had died with them—all Bliss heard were screams from the truck's trailer, its occupants now exposed by a gaping hole where it scraped the rock wall.

The second car was still flying toward them and Bliss grabbed his gun, ran to the rear of the trailer, dropped to his knees, took a deep breath and aimed. As the car rounded the bend he fired, pumping round after round. In three seconds he fired six shots and extinguished one headlight. The car kept coming, weaving, speeding, dangerously out of control. Stunned by the unexpected attack the driver reacted too late, then the brakes bit and the skidding car kissed off the rock face and buried itself under the back of the trailer.

Night returned instantly without the car's lights, and voices at the front of the trailer were calling, shouting, demanding. He ran back. Two bodies had been pulled from the wreckage of the truck and laid on the ground. The unnatural shape of one was enough to confirm to Bliss that the man was dead. The other figure, slender with a mop of golden hair glinting in the starlight, caused Bliss a heart tremor.

"Dave, I've been shot," Yolanda said calmly as soon as he bent over her.

"How?" he managed to force his taught throat to say.

"Just as we were leaving."

Bliss remembered—the single flash from the man he'd killed with the barrier.

Men stood around, stunned. "Don't just stand there," Bliss shouted angrily, "Two of you get to the back and keep watch. "You," he said, pointing to a shadow, "see if there's any guns in the car, we're going to need them. Owain, help me with Yolanda."

She let out a cry and bit her lip as they lifted, and Bliss felt the sticky warmth of blood on his fingers as he carried her. "We've got to get you to a hospital," he said as if it were a matter of calling 911. "What happened to the other guy," he asked. "Was he shot?"

"No. Hit by a rock when we crashed."

Bliss felt himself going pale. How many more would die? How many more would *he* kill?

Shadowy figures crowded Bliss as he knelt over Yolanda. His racing mind offered no solutions. Feeling his hands starting to shake, he clasped hers more tightly, trying to squeeze warmth and comfort into them, hoping to draw inspiration from them.

Owain broke the silence." Are you O.K., boy'o?"

"Yes ... No ... We've got to get away quickly."

"We'll never get home," wailed one of the others. "Why didn't you leave us alone?"

"I wish I had."

The Welshman's nasty tone stung. "You should've had a proper plan."

"Stop bloody whining you ungrateful bastards. We didn't have to rescue you ..."

Another voice cut in. "You haven't rescued us. You're goin' to get us all killed."

Hearing mutters of agreement, Bliss rounded on them. "You would've been killed anyway you stupid bastards. Do you think they would ever have let you go?"

"What about your people. Why can't they help?" persisted the complainer.

"No one knows we're here," he was forced to confess.

"Dave?" Yolanda's thin voice drifted up from the ground. Bliss bent to her. "We can't go over the mountains. It'll take forever."

He knew.

They desperately needed a lifeline and Owain threw it. "There were planes back at the place," he said nonchalantly.

"Why didn't you say so before?" shouted Bliss.

"I thought you knew what you were doing," he sneered. "Thought you had a plan."

Bliss ignored the obvious contempt, "How do you know about the planes?"

"We used to hear them taking off. Why, can you fly?"

Bliss looked down at Yolanda. He didn't need to ask.

"I could try," she said.

Ten minutes later they had dumped the body of the dead man back into the trailer and unhitched it from the cab. Shouting, "Keep clear," Bliss used the powerful motor to push the mangled trailer toward the cliff edge. The car, containing the bodies of two guards, still jammed under the rear of the trailer was dragged along with it.

The trailer's final journey was something of an anti-climax. No fireball; no ear splitting explosion; no screams. Just a dull thud echoing up the side of the escarpment as the huge container crumpled onto a ledge five hundred feet below. The secret compartment had become a flying sarcophagus for the man killed when the trailer crashed into the rock wall; an ironic internment for someone whose life had apparently ended a year earlier in a fiery head-on collision with a train.

The drive back toward the compound was nerve-wracking as they anticipated an attack at every turn. Several of the men clung to the outside of the unlit cab with guns at the ready and spoken words were few. Each man prayed silently to his own god. Those without gods prayed there was one. A few flickering lights showed up in the distance. Candles or oil lamps thought Bliss. "They haven't fixed the fuses," he said, more to himself than anyone else.

"It took two days to get the power on after Mary killed herself ..." Owain's voice faded at the bitter memory.

"Everybody out," said Bliss as he eased the truck to a stop a few hundred feet off the road. "We'll walk the rest of the way."

Using the flickering lights as a beacon they stumbled toward the compound in the dark, well away from the road. The man with the smashed arm screeched in pain at every jolt from the rocky ground and the others took it in turns to shush him. Yolanda had tried walking, but her knees collapsed the moment her feet touched the ground. Bliss had scooped her up, carefully laid her over his shoulder, and struggled manfully for several hundred yards before accepting Owain's offer of help.

The rising moon gradually warmed the sky with a soft yellow glow, and their surroundings slowly took shape. The mountains became visible as spiky grey splodges against a starry, deep blue canvas, and the camp buildings showed up as black boxes in the foreground.

"The airfield must be on the other side," said Bliss scanning the huddle of buildings through the perimeter fence. "I can't see any planes here."

"There might not be any," cautioned the Welshman. "They might just fly in supplies and guards, then fly out again."

"Why didn't they fly you in then?" asked Bliss. "Why use a truck?"

"They brought us in from Turkey," he replied, expecting Bliss to realize the significance. He did not.

"So?" he said

"The United Nations no-fly zone," explained Owain in an exasperated tone. "They're not allowed to fly in Northern Iraq.

An hour later they had skirted the compound to approach from the south and found their path blocked by a river. The sluggish water glistened with moonlight and ran like a ribbon of thick dark molasses along the valley floor. Bliss knelt on the bank and peered intently, trying to gauge depth and current, then he reached forward. Imagining the water to be warm, even sticky, he flinched as the coldness bit into his questing fingers.

"It's bloody freezing!" he exclaimed with a note of surprise. "It must come from the mountains."

"That's a fairly safe bet," sneered Owain, "considering we're surrounded by them."

Spurred by the Welshman's sarcasm, Bliss ripped off his socks and shoes and slipped knee deep into the water. "Stay there," he commanded, but could have saved his breath. No one was following.

Primal fear caused him to hesitate, just for a second, then he gingerly stepped forward. Apart from the numbing cold, the river posed no threat. It was barely waist deep and he was soon guiding the little group across.

The moonlight painted everything with a grey wash that distorted perspective, erasing clues as to size and distance. The four aircraft shaped objects at the end of the runway could have been jumbo jets or two-seat

Cessnas. Bliss pointed to the assortment of planes and asked Yolanda. "Could you fly one of those?"

"Dave, I don't know," she answered honestly. "I don't even recognize them."

"Isn't flying one plane the same as any other?"

"The basic controls are the same, but you have to learn each type."

"I hope you're a fast learner—I just learned to drive a truck."

She gave him a look of astonishment, then buried her head in her hands, and burst into laughter. The laughter quickly turned to a bout of violent coughing and ended when she brought up a handful of blood. As she wiped her hands on her skirt Bliss saw the dark stain smeared across her palm in the moonlight.

"Take it easy. We'll soon get you to a hospital."

"Okey dokey, Dave."

# *chapter nineteen*

The ridged metal flooring of the old Russian freight plane, an Illushyn according to Yolanda, bit into Bliss' backside. The figure lying by his side stirred with a groan. "What's the time Dave?" she enquired.

"It's still very dark," he replied without bothering to find his watch. "How are you feeling?"

"It hurts a bit."

He found her hand and soothed it. "Try to sleep as much as you can. You'll need all your strength to fly this in the morning."

"Dave ..." she started, then stopped herself, wondering how best to disillusion him with the news that she was certain she'd be unable to fly such a large plane. "We'll be alright," she sighed, and drifted back to sleep.

The choice of the Illushyn had been a matter of chance. Two of the four aircraft were jets. "I've never flown a jet," she explained, "I wouldn't even know how to start it." The third appeared to be undergoing repairs, or demolition, with several important looking chunks laying on the ground. That only left the twin-prop Russian freighter, and the stench had taken their breath away as they clambered in through the cargo hatch.

"Kidneys," said Owain, retching as he tasted the distinctly metallic flavour of stale urine.

"Reminds me of my wife's steak and kidney pie," said one of the others, his voice cracking with nostalgia.

"Smells like a bloody shit-house to me," said another, with a handle on reality. "Animals, I'd say."

"Yeah, and we know what sort," shot back another, recalling the behaviour of the Iraqi guards.

Yolanda had been gently lifted aboard and carried forward toward the cockpit. "Put me down," she requested between gasps.

Bliss struggled to contain his impatience. "We should take off as soon as possible."

"In the morning."

Impatience got the better of him. "Yolanda ... We have to go now. They'll be searching everywhere. If they've got dogs they'll trace us from the truck."

"They'll lose the scent in the river."

"Damn!" swore Bliss, immediately realizing his mistake. "We shouldn't have gone straight across, we should have walked downstream. They'll pick up our tracks. We must leave now."

"No dice," she continued, "I've got to see what I'm doing and where I'm going. We wouldn't get off the ground and, if we did, we'd hit the first mountain ..." Her speech slowed and faded as she drifted to sleep.

"Yolanda!" he called in a panic, shaking her arm in the darkness.

She woke with a start. "What?"

"It's O.K.," he said, glad he'd been wrong—glad it was only sleep. "Get some rest. Maybe they won't start looking 'til the morning."

Owain sidled up, drawn by Bliss' concern. "Is she going to be alright?"

"I hope so. We can't get out without her."

"It'll be your fault if we all get killed," Owain complained.

"So! Sue me ..." started Bliss then stopped—this was no time for a fight. "Sorry ..." he began, then idled in thought: Sorry for what? Risking my life for a freak like LeClarc; for chasing a kidnapped stranger across two continents; for trying to rescue you and your ungrateful mates; for getting Yolanda shot ... This is all way over my head. I'm a cop—not James Bond. "Sorry," he said, leaving Owain to fill in the blanks, then moved on, "Tell me about this computer virus."

"We call it C.I.D."

Bliss, still pre-occupied with concern for Yolanda, unthinkingly blurted out, "Criminal Investigation Department?"

"No you idiot. Computer Immune Deficiency."

"Sorry," he said, for a third time, determined to concentrate.

"It works by making the computer blind to viruses."

"How?"

"We don't know. That's what they needed us for. They've got it working now they want to find a way to stop it."

"I still don't get it."

"Computer viruses behave the same as human viruses," he explained. "It's like getting the flu. The computer gets sick, makes mistakes, slows down, and gradually deteriorates. Without treatment the virus eventually kills it, and every time we find a cure, there's a slightly different strain waiting to take its place."

"So what's different about C.I.D.?"

"It isn't really a virus. It doesn't make the computer sick, it masks the presence of other viruses. When a computer has C.I.D it rejects any attempt at a cure because it won't accept it's sick. Then it passes it to every other computer it connects with."

Bliss was catching on. "So the Internet will spread the virus, or whatever it is, from computer to computer."

"Not just the Internet. Defence systems, banks, communication and navigation satellites all operate on relays of computers—it's called convergence. If it gets into the system anywhere it will infest the whole lot. The Iraqis reckon ninety percent of the world's computers will be infected within six months of 'D' day."

" 'D' day?"

"Yeah. The beginning of the end—the invasion. They're calling C.I.D. the Millennium Vengeance, so we reckon it'll be soon."

Bliss slowly repeated, "The Millennium Vengeance," and tried to grasp its significance. "Do unto others as they have done unto you, I suppose."

Owain nodded. "As far as they're concerned, we filthy western imperialists crushed their economy and turned them into a backward third world country. Now they're bent on revenge."

Bliss thought for a moment, then asked, "If it isn't stopped?"

Owain sucked in a deep, noisy breath. "Chaos," he declared simply. "Absolute, complete bloody chaos ... Oh, it'll seem funny at first. You might even find an extra million or two in your bank account. But it won't be so bloody funny when planes start crashing; ships get lost and run aground; satellites fall out of orbit; defence systems start declaring war on each other ..."

"Surely the experts will realize there's something wrong and shut the computers off."

"Experts," he snorted, his opinion showing. "They'll be the bloody problem. They're convinced their systems are foolproof—protected with passwords, firewalls, virus scans and even 128-bit encryption."

"What's that?"

"128-bit encryption ..." he started, teacher-like, then changed his mind and offered a simplified explanation. "It's just an unbreakable code to stop unauthorized access. But C.I.D. doesn't break into the system: it's part of the system. That's the clever thing; it disguises itself so well even the guy who designed it wouldn't find it."

Yolanda groaned as she sought a more comfortable position, but Owain's passion demanded Bliss' attention. "Do you have any idea how crucial computers are to the way we live, Dave?" he whispered. "Imagine what it will be like without faxes, phones, radios, television. Even the power stations will shut down. Commodity markets will go haywire; stock prices plummet. Then the whole trading system will collapse as the computers get C.I.D. It'll throw the western world into a tailspin. We'll be back to buying local produce at the corner store."

"That's not such a bad idea," suggested Bliss, completely sidestepping the potential hazards of global dysfunction.

Owain ignored him and forged ahead with his catalogue of catastrophe. "Look at the fuss they made about the Y2K—remember—when all the computer clocks had to be switched from 1999 to 2000?"

Bliss nodded. "So?"

"That bug was a gnat's bite compared to what the Iraqis have got their hands on." He paused, shaking his head in dismay, contemplating a disintegration of modern society. "There'll be worldwide shortages of manufactured goods," he continued, "Most factories can't operate without robots ..."

Bliss interrupted, "I hadn't thought of that."

"Everything's run by computers, Dave, and they're networked like a billion-headed hydra: Bite off one head and the whole thing dies. One infected machine will destroy them all. It would take years to rebuild the systems and you'd only need to miss one infected one to screw the whole thing up again. There'll be civil wars as communities fight over dwindling resources. It could take us back to the bloody stone age. Survival of the fittest; most ruthless; best armed."

"Christ, that's going a bit far isn't it. You're making it sound like the third world war."

"Well?"

Bliss' voice jumped an octave. "You're serious."

Owain nodded gravely. "Worldwide anarchy. Control the Internet and you control the world—that's what they're after—total world domination without firing a shot. A megalomaniac's dream. We've created a bloody monster, and all monsters turn on their masters eventually—all it needs is for some crackpot in the Middle East to tweak the hydra's tail and one of the heads will take a chunk out of the Dow Jones."

"But they aren't going to control it, they're going to destroy it," said Bliss, punching a huge hole through the Welshman's theory.

Owain's voice rose in frustration. "That's the whole idea you bonehead; that's why they needed us. We were supposed to be finding a program to control the C.I.D. If they have the antidote, the rest of the world will be forced to pay their price, whatever it is ..."

His tirade was interrupted by a loud, "crack," that rang through the hollow interior of the freight plane. Sleeping men woke with a start. Bliss jumped, then held his breath as his ears strained. Nothing happened. He tried to recreate the sound in his mind. What was it ? Gunshot or metal cooling from the day's heat.

"What was that?" questioned Owain, his staccato shout startling everybody again.

Bliss felt a tug on his arm. Yolanda had woken, her voice was weak. "I'm going to throw up she said, and did. As the vomiting ended the coughing began: violent spasms full of pain. "Sorry, Dave," she said when she finally stopped.

He cradled her head in his hands. "You'll be fine. We'll be back in Turkey in no time."

"Dave listen." Her voice, distressed by the bout of coughing was barely a whisper, "I can't fly this."

A tone of annoyance crept into his voice. "Why not?"

"It's not a bloody car," she began angrily; angry at herself; angry for getting them into the situation; angry for letting him down. But then she picked on him, hoarsely shouting. "I'm not superman. I can't just turn a key and drive away." The exertion started her coughing again.

Stroking her forehead he waited until the convulsions stopped. "Look I know it's not easy but we don't have any choice. Remember what you said to me at the border?" She shook her head slowly—he sensed the movement and felt the vibes—she didn't want to remember.

"You told me to do it for my daughter," he reminded her. "Won't you at least try for your kid's sake."

His words found their mark and for a few seconds there was utter silence—the world waited. Then a searchlight's beam splashed across the tarmac, breaking the spell as it struck the windshield and spilled inside.

"They're looking for us," said Bliss as he held her tightly, feeling her frail body jerking and twitching as she sobbed. "I'm sorry," he added, regretting he had added to her suffering with mention of her child.

"Who'll look after him, Dave?" she asked, revealing she had a son.

The searchlight persisted, sweeping back and forth, probing, seeking, pursuing.

A voice full of fear cracked the tense air. "They're going to find us."

"They will if you don't belt up," Bliss whispered harshly. "Who's got the guns?"

Voices murmured their acknowledgement.

"Right," he continued. "Those with the guns get near the hatch—at least we can take some of the bastards with us."

He started to rise but she held him back. "Do something for me."

"What? Anything," he said, thinking: It's her child—she's going to ask to me to take care of him if she doesn't make it. Now what?

"Shoot me," she said.

His gasp of surprise could be heard throughout the plane. "What?"

"Don't wait 'til they find us. You might run out of bullets. Shoot me now."

He tried to pull away—she held on. "Promise you'll shoot me before they find us."

"But we might get away."

"How? I can't run. I can't even walk. Please promise you'll shoot me."

A splash of light picked out her features as her head lay on Bliss' rolled up jacket. He could almost feel the pain dragging down the corners of her mouth and furrowing her brow. The sparkle in her eyes had evaporated in sadness. "Shoot me now," she implored earnestly, "before it's too late."

He swallowed hard, and his right hand trembled, rattling his gun's muzzle against the metal floor. The fingers of his left hand delicately traced the lines in her brow. "I can't," he said so softly she didn't hear.

"Please, Dave. Kill me."

"I can't," he insisted. "Not yet anyway."

"You won't do it will you." Her sad eyes looked away and stared into the future. "You know what they did to the American woman. Do you think it will be different for me?"

"But you're hurt," he protested.

The searchlight had passed, he could no longer see her face but felt the shake of her head. The calmness in her voice belied her fear. "They won't care. They'll rape and torture me, then they'll stone me to death, won't they?"

She's right, he said to himself, but would not dignify it by an admission.

"If I'm going to die ..." she carried on.

He interrupted, "You're not going to die ... think of your son. He needs you."

Tears he couldn't see dribbled down her cheeks. Hurt he couldn't feel gnawed into her mind. "He doesn't even know me," she whimpered, then catalogued her nightmare. A teenaged girl's rebellious relationship—rejecting her father's business wasn't enough. A migrant Turkish worker—one of a million drawn to northern Europe in search of golden pavements: Darkly mysterious, dangerous, irresponsible, and irrational, reckless even—of course, but wasn't that the point?

The pregnancy had struck like a tornado and she'd taken cover until it was too late to do anything—other than run or brazen it out. She ran—to him. Cut off from her father's largesse she lost some of her glitz, and Mr. Mysterious quickly tired of supporting a snivelling teenager and her child, so he shoved off in search of a more glittering pasture. But with him went their infant son, destined for a traditional Muslim upbringing with a distant relative in Turkey. "What did you expect?" her father had scolded when she'd slunk home distraught. And he was right. Mr. Mysterious had always made it clear that marriage was out of the question, citing all the impediments of a mixed-race relationship she'd given Bliss. "You're a foreigner," he'd summed up, leaving her thinking: Aren't we all?

Bliss listened, his mood darkening as she recounted the horror of losing a child—not by death. "I could have got over that," she said. "It's the not knowing that kills you inside."

"And you never found him?" enquired Bliss, stifling a tear.

"No," she admitted simply, "I never found him." though the simplicity of her words discredited the years she'd devoted to her quest.

That explains her knowledge of Istanbul, thought Bliss, realizing immediately how little he knew and how wrong he'd been: Exotic luxury getaways, he'd assumed, and had imagined her being pampered and mollycoddled at the Yesil Ev—manicures, mud-baths and mountains of Bosphorus bluefish. Whereas, in truth, she'd been ferreting out clues, greasing greasy palms for snippets of information, and scouring the seedy back-streets and smelly bazaars of Istanbul for a spotty teen with strikingly blue eyes. No wonder she jumped at the prospect of a trip to Istanbul, and no wonder she was reluctant to get involved with another foreigner. She was still dealing with the aftermath of the last.

"I could help you ..." Bliss started.

She stopped him with the force of her voice. "Dave, listen. I'm just trying to be sensible. If I'm going to die I would like to remember you were the last man who made love to me, not some ..."

He tried again, more forcefully, "You are not going to die."

"We're in the middle of Iraq. No one knows we're here. We've killed a load of their guards. Half the army's probably looking for us and I can't fly this stupid plane." She gasped several deep breaths, winding herself up to a finale, then concluded, "We are going to die, and I'm trying to tell you I love you. I love you more than I've loved any other man."

He was stunned into silence. This wasn't happening, this wasn't real. Then a line of lyrics from an old song flooded his mind. "If you love me, let me go." Over and over the words repeated themselves as he sat in the darkness. "If you love me, let me go."

"Dave, please say something."

The words of the song raced round and around while he fought to find the accompanying tune. He wanted to say something, to give her an answer, but his mind was stuck in a loop. "If you love me, let me go," it repeated again and again. Finally, he broke free. "If you love me, kill me." he said softly. "Is that what you're asking?"

"Yes," she replied firmly.

He went cold at the thought. "I do love you, Yolanda but ..." he paused, his brain trapped in a deadly embrace. Knowing he could neither kill her, nor live with the guilt of not doing so, his senses withdrew and his mind clouded with a deep purple haze shrouding all conscious thought. He closed his eyes and found the words, "Kill me," stamped on the inside of his eyelids. He looked inward and the same words leaped out of the haze. "Kill me," he read. Everywhere he looked the words were there. "Kill me. Kill me. Kill me."

A few seconds later,—that felt like a week—Owain returned. "I think they've gone." Then he prattled on, picking up the remnants of his previous conversation as if nothing had happened. "They could sell the antidote to the highest bidders. They could hold the rest of the world ransom."

Bliss, lost in his own mind, heard only the voice in his head. And Yolanda's shapely mouth had now appeared through the haze, repeatedly imploring, "Kill me." His entire body was trembling, he knew it and could feel it, yet it was a body belonging to someone else—he was miles away: in London rowing across the Serpentine in Hyde Park, with Samantha, his daughter, a carefree little six-year-old laughing and splashing the mucky water.

"They'll have industry and governments begging them for the antidote. 'Kuwait,' they'll say. 'You want Kuwait? Take it.' Israel," Owain paused. "That'll be the real test, when they ask for Israel so they can turn it into a fundamentalist Islamic state. What the hell will the Yanks do then?"

Images of Samantha grew in Bliss' mind as his thoughts of Yolanda and her lost child swirled. What did his little daughter know of suffering compared to Yolanda or her son? Not that she was little anymore. Had she suffered? Had there been a Mr. Mysterious in her life—or even a child—that he didn't know about?

Owain's questions had become rhetorical. "The Yanks will posture and bluff, I s'pose, they're good at that, but they'll have to give in eventually. Try fighting the Gulf War again without computers and you'd get an entirely different result."

Bliss finally managed to get his mind working again, forcing himself to come up with the title matching words, "If you love me, let me go."

"Can you imagine what will happen if we escape and try to tell everyone what is going on?" Owain was questioning, oblivious to Bliss' inner turmoil.

Bliss thought for a second, his mind still wrestling with the lyrics. "They'll isolate all the computers and try to find a way of stopping it," he said eventually.

"Don't be so naïve, Dave," scoffed Owain. "Just the knowledge of its existence would destroy the economies, and jeopardize the security, of half the world. They're not going to admit it's even possible. The slightest hint it could be happening would send the stock markets into a nose dive."

"What do you think they'll do?"

Owain and his fellow captives had obviously given the subject considerable thought. He knew the answers: "The Government will deny it; claim we've been brainwashed; make out we're lying; try to buy us off. They might even try to liquidate us. It wouldn't be difficult, after all, we are officially dead anyway."

"I don't believe you," snorted Bliss in disbelief.

"Get an education, Dave. The press and our families might have swallowed the stories of our deaths, but I bet the people at the top had their suspicions—how many inexplicable train and plane crashes can you put down to pilot error?"

"But what will they do when computers start crashing?"

"Probably blame some fifteen-year-old hacker from a flea-ridden backwater in south east Asia; hold a show trial just to make everyone happy, and pray it doesn't keep happening."

"We'll sort something out," Bliss replied dismissively, more concerned with Yolanda. Her words wouldn't leave him. He didn't want to think about anything else. He couldn't think about anything else. "If you love me, let me go," swam around in his mind and finally met up with the right tune as he remembered the correct lyrics. "If you love me, let me know. If you don't, let me go."

"I love you," he said, no intention of letting her go, then he lay down beside her and protectively rested his arm across her chest, feeling the soft swell of her breasts as they rose and fell in time with her breathing. "You'll be O.K., Love," he whispered softly, but she was asleep.

The stars evaporated at the first hint of the rising sun. The moon's golden face, still visible above the western mountains, faded to a fuzzy white. Those who had managed to snatch some sleep were stirring and now they crept, one after another, to a far corner of the plane to relieve themselves. Someone farted. No one laughed.

Bliss woke Yolanda with a gentle shake. "It's Wednesday. Time to go home."

"Is it morning?"

"Almost," he replied, desperately urging the day to dawn.

Her face screwed up at the foul taste of dried blood in the back of her throat and she turned her head away to spit. "Dave, I need a drink."

"We haven't anything."

She coughed and retched again. "Water," she whispered.

He frantically searched his surroundings in the dim light but found nothing. Owain had heard Yolanda's plea. "What about the river, Dave?"

A few minutes later Bliss was running, crouching, and weaving across the tarmac, constantly expecting a bullet to rip into his body. He tore across the flat landscape, heading for the perimeter fence, and the riverbank beyond. Suddenly, not a hundred yards away, a platoon of guards swept out of the early morning haze. He threw himself headlong to the ground and cursed as his gun went spinning out of his hand to clatter noisily across the stony soil.

They must have seen me, he reasoned, as he lay in the scrubby grass awaiting a burst of machine gun fire. Anticipation of pain was almost as painful as pain itself; it wasn't courage that urged him to raise his head and invite the zap of a bullet—his mind had chosen instant death over tortured life. He looked up, the guards hadn't moved. Instinctively he ducked again, then froze. There was something odd about some of the guards: Too skinny, too straight, too rigid. Opening his eyes wide he stared. At any other time, in any other situation, he may have laughed out loud at the realization he had tried to surrender his life to a regiment of spindly trees.

Daylight came long before the sun had climbed above the surrounding mountains. Yolanda, refreshed by the cool river water, resurfaced and allowed Owain and Bliss to prop her into the pilot's seat. Then she sat, immobile, staring at the unfamiliar instruments with a puzzled expression. The delicately etched indentations at either side of her mouth, the one's Bliss had found so enthralling at their first meeting, pulled into deep grooves by her pallid, sunken cheeks. Worry lines scarred her brow.

Ten minutes later the spluttering cough of the starboard engine ripped into the milky atmosphere of the early morning. The engine barked to life with a throaty howl, and injected a wad of oily black smoke into the clean, misty air. Then Yolanda turned her attention to the port engine and teased it to life.

"Let's go," shouted Bliss above the roar, but she shook her head and pointed to the dials with a sweep of her hand that explained nothing.

Two figures, ghost-like in the hazy dawn, emerged hastily from the control tower, seeking to confirm their suspicions. Bliss, still edgy from his encounter with the phantom patrol, furiously waved at Yolanda, urging her to take off. She looked at him with a pleading expression, trying to tell him something. Her mouth was moving but the weak sounds were lost in the maelstrom of noise and vibration. Realising it was important, he leaned over and stuck an ear to her mouth. "Chocks," she breathed.

"Shit!' he exclaimed, then shouted to Owain, above the noise, "The wheels are still chocked, I'll have to clear them."

The distant figures were approaching haltingly, unsure of the wisdom of their actions.

Without a moment's hesitation Bliss slipped out of the cargo hatch and made for the massive wheels. As he kicked away the second chock the plane started to roll, threatening to leave him behind. Running wildly he lunged for the hatchway and narrowly missed a bullet which ricochet off the underbelly with a high pitched "zing." The next bullet came even closer, burying itself into the flapping hatch cover as he fought to drag it shut against the increasing wind pressure.

The plane slewed down the runway, gathering speed as Yolanda fought with the controls. A couple of bullets, silenced by the engine's noise, went unnoticed as they perforated the fuselage. The heavy plane lumbered into the air with less enthusiasm than a 30lb turkey at a Thanksgiving shoot.

Bliss, breathless from his run, slid into the co-pilot's seat and watched, awe-struck, as Yolanda deftly handled the controls—swinging the plane to follow the river valley. Pain, severe pain, had drained all colour from her face, her clothes were ragged and filthy, yet he found himself totally entranced by her features. "I love you," he said not realizing she was paying him any attention.

Her reply was reproachful. "But you wouldn't shoot me."

"I don't believe you ..." his response came quickly, angrily, then he checked himself as he detected the shadow of a grin on her lips. She could still tease. He looked at her for a moment and deliberately held his reply, allowing her grin to subside. "Maybe I'll kill you when we get to Istanbul," he said sternly.

"How?"

He laughed, "Screw you to death."

"Dave!" she exploded with mock offence, and the exertion took its toll, doubling her in another bout of coughing.

"Take over," she yelled in alarm as her convulsing limbs snatched at the controls and started the plane bucking and twisting. Bliss overcame a moment's indecision and grabbed at the control column in front of him.

"Gently," she cried, as she let go of the controls and was immediately slapped back into her seat by a spasm.

Bliss' brain was on fire. Sweat leaked freely from every pore. Muscles, paralysed by fear, locked his limbs. His fingers clamped so tightly around the controls that his deathly white knuckles appeared ready to burst. Paranoia seized him. "We're going down!" he called, convinced the fast moving ground was rushing up to meet him.

Owain's high-pitched Welsh accent twanged in the taught atmosphere, "You can do it, Dave."

Bliss found himself mesmerized by the speeding landscape and the ground's magnetic pull seemed to be enticing him earthwards. Then survival instinct overcame the almost irrepressible urge and he was relieved to see the plane's nose rising as he hauled back on the stick.

Yolanda, clutching her heaving chest and fighting for breath, flapped her free hand at him. "Not too fast. Take it slow." He relaxed a touch and eased back on the stick, dipping the nose until it was pointing at the horizon, then he patted himself on the back: "I did that."

Owain was surveying the bewildering array of dials and was fairly satisfied he had located the altimeter and gyroscopic compass. "We're going to need more height," he said and Yolanda sleepily nodded her agreement. Bliss over-reacted and hauled back on the stick too quickly, risking a stall. She leaped forward with a painful cry and squeezed the control column. "You must be gentle," she instructed. Exhausted by the exertion she slumped back into the seat, closed her eyes, and began drifting off. "Wake me if anything happens," she sighed.

"No!" he screamed.

"Flying's easy," she whispered reassuringly.

"It's coming down that worries me," he replied, attempting a tired joke.

She yawned deeply and let sleep overtake her.

The atmosphere was as tense as an over-inflated balloon, perspiration trickled from Bliss' brow to form a dewdrop on the end of his nose. He tried unsuccessfully to lick the globule away and felt the plane twitch as he momentarily diverted his attention from the control column. Concentrating furiously, he got the plane straight, then cleared his nose with a loud snort that made Owain look up. "Do you know where we're going?"

"Not really," admitted Bliss with masterly understatement. Then he added, "North," with a degree of confidence. "We think Turkey is somewhere north."

"You're doing O.K., boy'o," encouraged Owain.

"I just wonder why they're not chasing us," said Bliss, his eyes fixed firmly ahead, not daring to look behind.

Owain leaned over Yolanda's slumped body to peer out of the side window at the empty sky. "No power," he said. "You knocked out their power so they've got no radar, no radio, no phones. That's what I was trying to tell you," he continued, his earlier pessimism clearly vindicated. "That's exactly what will happen all over the world if the C.I.D. isn't stopped." He went back to staring at the dials. "Are you sure you haven't flown before?"

A nervous twitch was infuriating Bliss' right eye but he couldn't take his hand off the stick to rub it. "I'm ...I'm just keeping everything in the same place as Yolanda left it," he stuttered. "I've ... I've no idea what I'm doing."

Owain checked the altimeter. "We're still climbing. I think we're at 8,000 metres." Then he corrected himself, "No, that must be feet."

"Do you think we're high enough?"

Owain scratched his chin contemplatively. "Maybe."

Bliss thought hard, trying to recall his school geography lessons. "Everest is twenty-seven thousand feet," he said.

"We're nowhere near the Himalayas."

"I know, I was just trying to get some idea of how high to fly. I think I'll try to stay at about ten thousand feet. What do you think?"

It was the Welshman's turn to panic "How will we know when we're over Turkey? How will we find an airport?"

Bliss reassured him, "Yolanda will know. She'll be alright when she's had a rest. She's got to wake up to land us."

Owain's mumbled tone was ominous, "What if she doesn't wake up?"

Bliss risked a quick glance toward the pilot's seat. She had formed herself into a self-comforting ball and seemed to be sleeping. "She'll be alright," he said with a silent prayer.

"People have managed before," said Owain finishing his thoughts aloud. "I've read about it in *Reader's Digest*."

"I've no intention of trying to land this, if that's what you're thinking," said Bliss, as a distant range of mountains caught his eye. Craning forward he squinted for a better view. The starboard wing immediately drooped as he relaxed his grip. "Damn!" he shouted and struggled for control. Overcompensating, he dropped the other wing. "Gently," said her voice in his mind, and he carefully brought the craft under control again.

A head poked into the cockpit. "Is there any heating? We're freezing to death back there."

Bliss kept his eyes fixed ahead. The distant jagged mountains had grown into a castellated fortress and were approaching at an alarming speed. "Not now," he shouted.

The voice in his ear persisted. "It'll be your fault if ..."

"Go away," he yelled, frantically. "Owain. Wake Yolanda. We've got a problem."

She woke, screaming in pain as she uncurled and huskily demanded a cigarette.

"Is that a good idea ..." started Bliss, but one look at the approaching mountains told him not to argue. "Take the controls and I'll light one for you," he continued, as she forced her limbs into position to fly.

"I've got it," she said, and Bliss cautiously slackened his hold until she was in full command.

The plane banked sharply away from the mountains under her expert control, then she forced the throttles as far back in their sockets as they would go. The warm engines picked up and thrust the plane forward with a kick. Bliss delved into her purse, found cigarettes and a lighter, and was pleasantly surprised by the taste of his first puff in ten years.

Rising out of the dusky blue shadow of the mountains, the circling plane emerged into the full glare of the sun; Yolanda spotted a saddle between two peaks and headed straight for it. They were at least five hundred feet above the ridge but Bliss' was trying hard not to look as he took another puff and watched Yolanda expertly handling the controls. Every breath was a fight, but her hands and feet were rock steady and her eyes pierced the sky ahead. She didn't ask for the cigarette again and he smoked it, inhaling deeply, feeling the calming effect as his body relished the thought of him renewing his old habit.

"Are you alright?" he asked, checking she was still concentrating.

"I'm Okey dokey Dave," she replied, in a light-headed tone that concerned him; he took a final drag on the cigarette, determined it would be his last whatever happened, then closed his eyes and tried picturing Samantha, but came up with an image of her mother, his ex-wife, Sarah. With a shudder he quickly replaced her with a memory of Yolanda—naked, gambolling in the waterfalls in southern Turkey—then opened his eyes to find the rocks skimming by just below. He held his breath, then exhaled with a puff of relief as the plane safely hopped over the ridge and slid into the valley beyond.

Her lungs were straining in the thin atmosphere and she felt herself slipping back to sleep. "Dave ... You'd better practice landing ... I might not be able to help."

Bliss was in the midst of a nightmare. "How the hell do I land?" he wailed, feeling as if someone had scrunched his testicles in a garlic press.

Yolanda's explanation was punctuated by bouts of coughing and Bliss found himself dealing with information overload. Air speed, brakes, flaps, rudder, and a dozen other factors appeared critical and he tried to memorize each. "It's better to be too fast than too slow," she said as fatigue finally drained her. "You can always go round again," she breathed as her voice faded.

"D'ya think you can do it, Dave?" enquired Owain as Yolanda drifted off.

"I can try. Unless you've got a better idea. Anyway she'll probably be feeling better by then."

The complainer was back. "It's still bloody freezing."

Owain was rude. "This ain't fuckin' British Airways."

Bliss was kinder. "Find the heater switch and we'll put it on." He turned to Owain, "The problem isn't how to land, it's where to land. Is that Iraq down there or Turkey?"

Owain surveyed the scorched brown plateau. "It could even be Iran," he suggested unhelpfully. "I've no idea without a map."

Bliss was getting the hang of flying and allowed himself the luxury of taking his eyes off the sky for a second as he searched the cabin. "Try up there," he said, with a meaningful nod toward a document pouch. Owain reached in, rifled through a bundle of papers and selected some maps. "Great," he cried as he began unfolding them. Five minutes later he'd changed his tune. "Bloody useless," he said, screwing them up and stuffing them back in the pouch. "I've no idea where we started. What's that old saying. You've got to know where you've come from ... How bloody true."

A speck, just above the horizon, glinted in the steeply slanting rays of the early morning sun. The tiny flash of reflected light triggered an alarm in Bliss' mind and set his nerves jangling. He gave a warning shout to Owain. "There's a plane."

Owain swept the horizon but saw nothing until the sunlight struck it again. It was now bigger; much bigger.

"Shit," cried Bliss as he lost control. "Wake her up," he screamed as he tried to stop the plane from staggering across the sky.

Yolanda moaned but wouldn't wake.

Silver flashes marked the approach of the sleek jet fighter as it swept toward them out of the deep blue sky. Like a raptor attracted by the writhing of wounded prey this killer sensed the agony of its larger quarry. But the raptor held off, seemingly stopping mid-air, as if suspended by an invisible thread, gauging the distance, testing the air, watching for its quarry's death throes. Bliss jinked the plane. The fighter responded instantly, blocking their path one way, then the other. The gap was closing, the fighter hadn't stopped, merely slowed.

Bliss' fearful eyes were glued to the approaching plane as his faltering voice cut the air. "You'd better warn the others."

Owain didn't move, couldn't move. "Why?"

An answer would have been fruitless as the gap narrowed in seconds to a mile or less. Suddenly the fighter rocketed into the stratosphere and disappeared, leaving a thread of vapour hanging in the still morning air.

"Where is it?" Bliss screamed.

Owain slammed his face against Yolanda's window and strained skyward. "I can't see it."

"Mind the controls," yelled Bliss, then risked a quick look, craning forward to squint at the empty sky, fully expecting to see the fighter, or a missile, hurtling toward them. Nothing, and looking down he was just in time to catch the nose of their plane slice neatly through the fighter's vapour trail, then he glanced out of his side window and had the fright of his life.

"Oh my God!" he shrieked.

"What?"

"Look," he croaked.

Owain looked. The fighter was there, right alongside, wing-tip to wing-tip, no more than a hundred feet away. The pilot, clearly visible in his cockpit, slowly turned his head toward them and flicked up his visor. Bliss felt the anger in the man's piercing cold glare.

"If looks could kill," whimpered Owain, shaking at the intensity of the stare. "What are we going to do?"

For five seconds the other pilot kept up the hazing, then stabbed a finger rearward, over his shoulder; three quick meaningful jabs.

"He's telling us to go back."

"Bollocks to him," said Bliss with chutzpah, "I don't know about you but I'd rather die quickly in an air crash than go back and let those bastards get me on the ground."

"I'm with you, Dave."

The pilot insistently stabbed the air three more

times, re-enforcing his instruction, and even turned his head over his shoulder pointedly.

"Not bloody likely," mouthed Bliss as he shook his head at the pilot.

A crinkle of a smile creased the pilot's eyes and, with a malicious jerk of his leather-clad fist, he gave the thumbs-down.

"Bugger you," mumbled Bliss, holding the man's gaze and, a split second later, he viciously flicked the freighter's controls, flinging the old crate sideways, directly into the path of the fighter.

"What the fuck ..." shouted Owain in alarm.

The highly alert fighter pilot twitched his controls and slipped effortlessly out of reach. A few seconds later he was back.

"I think they want us alive," said Owain.

"I bet they do," replied Bliss. "But they'll be disappointed." He returned the fighter pilot's malevolent stare, holding his attention, awaiting another opportunity to smash him out of the sky. Without breaking his gaze, the pilot made an angry performance of tapping the side of his helmet.

"Radio, Dave," said Owain, getting the message. "He wants to talk."

Snatching a pair of headphones off the back of Yolanda's seat, Owain rammed them onto Bliss' head and twiddled with the controls. They burst into life with such ferocity he almost jumped out of his seat. "D'ya speak English?" the voice demanded.

"Yes," responded Bliss guardedly, as his confused brain wrestled with the American accent.

"Boy! Are ya crazy or what?" the voice continued.

Bliss still wasn't comprehending. "Are you American?" he quizzed timidly.

"Sure thing, Buddy. Why—who're you expecting?"

The tension melted from Bliss, leaving him soaked from head to toe. He tried to reply, but his mouth wasn't cooperating.

"Hey Bud. Are ya still there?"

Bliss responded finally, "Yes. Sorry ... I'm a British police officer ..."

The American cut in, "Yeah, and my ass is an alligator."

He tried again. "I'm a police officer ..."

"Listen, Bud. This is your one and only chance. You're in the UN no-fly zone. Now do yourself a favour and ..." he paused, doubt crossed his mind and was reflected in his voice. "Say again."

Bliss spoke every syllable with authority. "I am a British police officer escaping from Iraq. The pilot's been shot and I need help."

"Oh, brother!" exclaimed the American. "Are ya expecting company?"

"Why?"

"Something's coming up mighty fast behind you."

"Help," he yelled in a panic. "I've got a load of escaped prisoners."

"O.K. Bud," the pilot was saying in his ear. "Leave it to me."

Two minutes later the American was back. "All clear," he said without explanation, then he flung a flurry of questions at Bliss. "Who are ya? Where've ya come from? Where are ya going? What's your fuel status?"

After giving his name and rank to the first question he was forced to admit he had no idea about any of the others.

"Boy, you sure as hell don't know much. Maybe I should send ya back and let the Eye-Raks deal with you."

Anger and frustration simmered through Bliss' veins and he tore into the American, "Listen you effin smart-ass ..." then he calmed, "I'm sorry, but I've got a seriously injured pilot and a group of freed hostages. I can't fly. I've never flown before. I don't know what the hell I'm doing, and I certainly can't land."

The American mocked him with a reasonable attempt at a British accent. "Cor blimey a red hot limey." Then added, "O.K., Bud. I get the message, but who's flying the plane now."

"I am," he admitted. "But I don't know where I'm going or how to land."

The American seemed to ignore the response, suddenly concerned at how close he'd come to downing an aircraft full of fleeing Brits. "Boy is it your lucky day," he said. "We're supposed to shoot first and ask questions later. Well, let's get ya out of here."

Changing course as instructed, Bliss headed the plane northwest and tried unsuccessfully to relax. After a few seconds he risked taking his eyes off the controls to cast a quick look at Yolanda. She'd slumped lower in the seat and the life had drained from her cheeks and lips so they melded.

"She's alright," said Owain, sensing Bliss' concern. "Just asleep."

"He's checking with H.Q.," said Bliss, nodding toward the pilot off his right wing. Owain looked, and wryly smiled in agreement.

Bliss pictured the frantic activity in London as sleep-starved, night duty officers scurried to phones, asking questions, demanding answers.

Fumbling in his pocket, he was amazed to discover he had not lost his watch. "5 a.m.," he muttered, as the strap parted with the old battered Timex; still set on London time. He smiled, thinking of Superintendent Edwards' explosive reaction to a 5 a.m. call telling him his officer had been found in Iraq with Yolanda. "I'll bloody have him," Bliss pictured him hollering as he stormed the office, spouting disciplinary charges: "Absent without leave. Disobeying an order. Fraternizing with the opposite sex on duty."

Superintendent Edwards wasn't shouting, neither had it been necessary for anyone to call him. Since the stolen Mercedes had surfaced at the Iraq border on Monday afternoon, diplomatic wheels had been in full spin, and he'd hitched a ride to south eastern Turkey aboard an RAF plane with a few Foreign Office personnel and several hard-faced men who seemingly conversed only in code—secret service, he assumed, but didn't risk asking.

Bliss' mind turned to home as he peered at the bright blue sky over Turkey. "It's probably raining in London," he thought out loud.

"It's bound to be raining in Cardiff," complained the Welshman. "It always bloody rains in Cardiff."

"Will you go back?"

Owain gave a little shake of his head. "There's nothing for me there. In fact, I'd be surprised if anyone missed me."

"I don't think they did," replied Bliss with a degree of insensitivity.

Owain shot him a curious look. "You knew about me?"

"Vaguely," Bliss admitted. But he avoided being drawn further, adding, "I just knew there was a possibility you were missing, that's all. No one was sure."

The Welshman shrugged. "I've got no family, none that cares anyway. What about you, what will you do when you get back?

"I'm not going back, not for awhile anyway. I'll stay with Yolanda until she's better, then we've got a week planned at a posh hotel in Istanbul."

"Then what?"

Bliss was silent for a moment, contemplating deeply. He threw another glance at Yolanda and smiled fully for the first time in several days. "I'd ask her to marry me, but she's got this thing about foreigners," adding laughingly, "And it wouldn't work—I can't stand raw herrings."

Owain returned to thoughts of his own future and had obviously given up on the possibility of life after Iraq. "Like I said, they won't let us go. They'll be too scared we'll blab to the press."

"Maybe you should call the press as soon as we land, before they have a chance to stop you."

Owain gave him a sidelong glance. "I thought you were supposed to be part of the Establishment."

"Not me," said Bliss. "Never have been. Always a rebel. But freedom of speech and equality are dirty words in the police and The Establishment doesn't like smut." He snorted his disdain. "Hm! The Establishment: the old-boys club of politicians and senior officers who'll cover-up anything inconvenient with a pack of lies and a veiled reference to the *Official Secrets Act*."

The Yank was back on the radio. "O.K., Davey. Everything checks out, we'll be landing in about ten minutes. Just follow me."

"I think we're going to make it, Owain," he said confidently. "Maybe we will be able to stop them."

Owain had a confused look. "How?"

"Isolate Iraq and cut off communications until you've discovered the antidote," he answered with child-like simplicity.

Owain shook his head. "It's too late. Some of the infected computers have already gone out."

"What do you mean?"

"The multi-national trade embargo's a joke—it's got more leaks than a Russian submarine. Computers and equipment pour in from Turkey, Jordan, and Allah knows where else. They've been shipping in computers from everywhere—new ones, latest models, even video games. They've got more variety than Radio Shack and they've built the C.I.D. program right into the hardware ..."

Bliss interrupted, thinking back to his nightmarish truck ride across the mountains with Yolanda, "Is that what was in the crates—computers?"

"Yeah. They're bringing them from Istanbul in crates marked 'plastic body bags.'"

"But they can only doctor a few hundred at a time."

Owain sounded exasperated. "I told you. They only need one infected computer to do the damage. Obviously the more that get into the system the faster the C.I.D. will spread after 'D' day."

Feeling slightly foolish, Bliss changed the subject. "Wake Yolanda. She'll need a few minutes to get used to the controls."

Yolanda opened her eyes as Owain gently prodded her arm.

"Where are we?" she asked sleepily.

"We'll be landing soon. Can you take over?"

"I'm very tired," she said in a slurred voice. "I don't think I can ..." She made an effort to move then slipped back. "You do it, Dave."

The radio buzzed. "How'a' we doing, Bud?"

"The name's Dave,"

"O.K., Bud ... sorry, Dave. So, have ya got the pilot awake yet?"

Bliss looked to his left, Owain was gently shaking Yolanda but she obviously wasn't able to fly. "It's O.K., leave her," he said. "I can do it."

The American was getting impatient. "Davey, old Bud, are ya there? We're approaching the glide path."

"I'll have to land," he said.

Yolanda heard and mumbled "Just be gentle Dave. Slow and gentle."

"O.K., Bud. I'll be right alongside ya. Just try to keep level with me. Start by throttling back.

There were a few moments silence as the planes flew in tandem, the other pilot gave him an encouraging look. "O.K., Bud. We've got clearance to land."

Bliss felt a surge of adrenalin.

"Are ya sure you understand the controls?" the American was saying as the blood started pounding in his temples. He recalled Yolanda's instructions as his eyes scanned the instruments. "I think I'll be alright," he replied.

"We've still gotta few more miles. Ask if you ain't sure."

His anxiety level rose another notch and put a tremor in his voice, "No. No, I'm O.K.".

"Right. Just follow me. Let's go."

The pilot's face sank slowly out of sight as he called, "C'm on down, Bud." Bliss eased the control column forward, dipping the nose until the ground appeared to be rushing up at him. Instinctively he pulled back.

"No, keep the nose down."

"I can't ..." he started.

"Sure ya can, Bud. It's just like parking a car."

"At a hundred miles an hour?"

His pulse was racing off the scale, his voice almost a scream.

Owain tried to calm him. "Dave, you can do it," he said with as much control as he could muster. "And I think you're right. We will stop

them. Get us out of this alive and we'll come up with the antidote."

The headphones were singing in his ears. "Slow down, Dave, slow down, slow down."

"Airport," shouted Owain, straining to look out the front window and seeing the control tower in the distance.

Yolanda stirred. Bliss caught the movement in the corner of his eye, but his inner relief was masked by a veneer of terror.

"You're still too high," the other pilot was saying in his ear.

He edged the stick forward in response and eased the throttles. "Get down. Get down," a voice in his head was saying.

"Lower, lower," the American insisted.

"Runway," shrieked Owain, seeing the end of the tarmac strip rush beneath them.

"Still too high," shouted the American. "Abort! Abort! Abort! Power up."

Yolanda's words came back to him. "Go around again, Dave."

Bliss resisted. He couldn't do it again. His nerves wouldn't stand it. With his teeth clamped together he hit the flaps. The plane dropped fifty feet and he felt the seat slam into his backside as they plunged onto the runway with a crunch that should have ripped off the undercarriage. The control column came alive, leaping and bucking in his hands, threatening to wrench itself free.

"Throttle back, throttle back," someone was shouting, but he couldn't risk losing his grip on the stick.

"Brake! Brake! Brake!"

Yolanda's words calmed him, "Gently, Dave. Take it easy."

A clump of buildings shot past in a blur.

"Slow down you bastard," he screamed as he fought with the brakes.

"Gently, gently," her voice urged, and he felt her feet taking some of the strain.

"Throttle back!" the American screamed, his composure lost.

"End of the runway," yelled Owain.

Yolanda's voice pierced his overburdened mind. "Push the throttles back."

He pushed: Fast and hard. The engines roared in pain as the propeller blades were flung into reverse. A convoy of emergency vehicles poured into the plane's slipstream as it screamed toward the end of the runway, careening from side to side, wings tilting dangerously, first one way then the other. Unread warning signs flashed past. Owain braced himself as a huge wooden crash barrier raced toward them. Bliss tried to force the brake pedal through the floor. Too late. The heavy plane shot off the end of the runway, smashed through the barrier and tried to shake itself to pieces as the wheels ploughed through a patch of gravel before being ripped off. Wheelless, the plane belly flopped, and skidded to a standstill in a spectacular shower of sparks.

"Out! Out! Out!," he cried, grabbing Yolanda and physically dragging her through the fuselage to the cargo hatch.

A blanket of foam showered them as they tumbled out. Bliss was blinded, and he stumbled with Yolanda in his arms until someone grabbed him and guided him away.

He laid her down gently and caught hold of the airport fireman's arm. "Doctor," he yelled. "Quick, get a doctor."

Several men came running, one of them was Owain, his face and hands brushed with streaks of blood.

"I am medic," said a man wearing a facemask, as he knelt beside Yolanda and sought her pulse, then he gently pried open an eyelid and looked deep into her eye. His face was genuinely sad as he turned to Bliss and slowly shook his head. "I am sorry, Sir."